P9-DEZ-413

Gregg

SURRENDER

"Why doesn't it matter to you that none of the things you accused me of are true?" Rolling Thunder asked huskily, his heart pounding in anticipation of her answer.

Tanzey lifted her eyes to his. "Because I love you," she murmured. "I have fought this love with every fiber of my being, but I cannot fight it any longer."

His insides warm and glowing from her words of love, Rolling Thunder could not hold back any longer. He drew her close and covered her with kisses.

And soon he heard her gasp with pleasure, and felt her arms twine around his neck, as she returned kiss for kiss with passion. And Rolling Thunder, oh so very gently, lowered her to the pallet of furs beside the fire. . . .

ROLLING THUNDER

Cassie Edwards

A TOPAZ BOOK

TOPAZ
Published by the Penguin Group
Penguin Books USA Inc., 375 Hudson Street,
New York, New York 10014, U.S.A.
Penguin Books Ltd, 27 Wrights Lane,
London W8 5TZ, England
Penguin Books Australia Ltd, Ringwood,
Victoria, Australia
Penguin Books Canada Ltd, 10 Alcorn Avenue,
Toronto, Ontario, Canada M4V 3B2
Penguin Books (N.Z.) Ltd, 182–190 Wairau Road,
Auckland 10, New Zealand

Penguin Books Ltd, Registered Offices:
Harmondsworth, Middlesex, England

First published by Topaz, an imprint of Dutton Signet,
a division of Penguin Books USA Inc.

First Printing, November, 1996
10 9 8 7 6 5 4

 REGISTERED TRADEMARK—MARCA REGISTRADA

Printed in the United States of America

Chapter Three

Sitting comfortably in her leather saddle on her strawberry roan, a horse as feisty as herself, Tanzey rode along the trail, several ranch hands trailing along behind her. She had risen with the sun and had dressed in her usual comfortable attire of buckskins.

Anxious to be on her way to find a fresh new herd of wild mustangs, she had gobbled down her breakfast of eggs, milk gravy, and biscuits, with hot coffee, under the constant protests of her mother, who was against Tanzey's plans for the day.

It was Tanzey's stepfather who had interceded. He had calmed her mother by telling her that he would send several ranch hands with Tanzey Nicole. She would be safe enough.

Tanzey had left it at that, smiling slyly at her stepfather, who had learned long ago that if she had her mind set on something, no one could change it.

Yes, he would send the men with Tanzey, knowing damn well that more than likely she would send

Affectionately I dedicate *Rolling Thunder* to my dear, longtime friends, Vincent and Suzan Campo of New York. Also Romaine Hash, Mary Graham, Mildred Guillet, Aurora Fattah, Debbie Frazier, Gennie Marie Feehan, Rosa Ewing, Joyce Evans, Lois Ecklund, and Theresa Hill.

One shade the more, one ray the less,
Had half impaired the nameless grace
Which waves in every raven tress
Or softly lightens o'er her face,
When thoughts serenely sweet express
How pure, how dear, their dwelling place.
And on the cheek and o'er that brow,
So soft, so calm, yet eloquent
The smiles that win, the tints that glow,
But tell of days in goodness spent,
A mind at peace with all below,
A heart whose love is innocent.

—GEORGE GORDON, LORD BYRON

Chapter One

Oh, memories that bless ... & burn!
Oh, barren gain—and bitter loss!
—ROBERT CAMERON ROGERS

TEXAS ... 1855

It was another Comanche dawn. Morning having chased the night from the sky, the sun was brilliant along the eastern horizon.

On her sorrel, and holding her steed steady with her reins, Feather Moon, a ravishingly beautiful Comanche princess, watched a white man on a horse in pursuit of a herd of boars.

Feather Moon's Comanche warriors sat stiffly in their saddles, awaiting her orders.

Ooetah, Big Bow, sidled his horse closer to her. "*Mah-tao-yo*, little one, are you certain you want that white man as your personal captive?" he asked as he glanced over at Feather Moon.

Big Bow then watched the white man again as he, unaware of being observed, slowly circled on his horse around a boar that he had managed to separate from the others.

"*Hakai*, what? You ask such a question as that of

Feather Moon?" she said, giving Big Bow a scolding
look. "You have been with me as I have watched
this man from afar enough times to know that he is
what I want in my lodge as I grow old. I want him
for my husband, no matter that first he will be captive, *then* husband."

"*Huh,* yes, I know that is your plan and has been for
many Comanche dawns, but I still ask you, Feather
Moon, if what you plan is wise?" Big Bow persisted.
"Must I remind you that our band of *Ner-mer-nuh,*
Comanche, are friendly with the white eyes? Some,
even our war chief, who is your cousin, have ridden
with the Texas Rangers, to help rid the land of white
man outlaws and Indians who have turned renegade."

"You do not have to give me a history lesson of
who I am," Feather Moon spat, stiffening her spine.
She shook her black hair back from her shoulders. It
lay in long, lustrous waves against the buckskin fabric of her dress, along the slender line of her back.
"We, the Penateka band of Comanche, known as
Honey Eaters by some, Timber People by others, are
known to align ourselves with the white man. Some
of our people *have* worked with the Texas Rangers!
But that does not alter my decision to have this particular white man as my own personal property!"

Feather Moon's heart pounded as she watched the
white man aim at the trapped boar, having backed
the wild-eyed animal with its nine-inch-long tusks
up against a wall of rock. It was not the excitement
of seeing the man be a success on the hunt, but instead, it was his handsomeness that stirred her very
soul into wanting him.

That very first time she had seen him riding giant-
like on a lovely pinto horse, she had become instantly
intrigued with his shoulder-length, flaming red hair,
and his genuine, rugged handsomeness. She had

known then that he would never belong to anyone else; that he would be hers!

"Big Bow, surely just one white man will not be missed so badly that a whole war would break out between the white eyes and our Penateka band of Comanche," Feather Moon softly argued. "No one will ever think to come to our village to look for the missing white man, since we are not known to take white captives. In our village, not even one white eyes' scalp waves from scalp poles."

"Perhaps soon, because of your selfish, spoiled needs, our Comanche scalps will fly from the white man's scalp poles," Big Bow said in a low snarl.

"Big Bow, you push your luck far this Comanche dawn by speaking out so vehemently against this which I have decided to do," Feather Moon said, her jaw tight as she glared at him. "Do you forget that I am a Comanche princess? It is for you to follow my orders, not for me to follow yours."

When gunfire splintered the cool morning air with its sharp sound, Feather Moon turned again toward the white man. She smiled when she saw him slip his smoking rifle into the gun boot at the side of his horse, then quickly dismount, his whole attention on the boar instead of being wary of who might come up on him while he had so carelessly separated himself from his firearm.

"*Mah-tao-yo*, little one, you have time to change your mind," Big Bow said, reaching to place a gentle hand on Feather Moon's arm.

She slapped his hand away. "I will not change my mind," she said, her eyes not leaving the white man as he knelt beside the downed boar, to study it. "And to give you some peace of mind, please know that I will keep this man hidden in my lodge until enough time has passed for his family to give him up as dead."

"If his family is like the family of the Comanche, never will they give him up for dead," Big Bow said, but slid his rifle from his gun boot, anyhow, knowing that talking was useless this morning with the stubborn, beautiful princess.

"*Mea-dro*, come, let us go!"Feather Moon shouted, grabbing her own rifle from its gun boot. She sank her moccasin heels into the flanks of her sorrel and rode off in a hard gallop toward the white man, the warriors following her.

The skirt of her fringed dress lifted above her knees. Her hair whipped high into the wind.

Her eyes were anxious as she drew a tight rein along with the others around the white man, giving him no chance to even think about trying to escape.

Brant Hunter was stunned by the suddenness of the appearance of the Comanche. They had come upon him so quickly, he knew they must have been hidden close by, watching him, waiting for him to become careless.

Slowly he rose to his feet, his hands held away from his belt on which was sheathed a sharp bowie knife, for he did not want to give the Comanche cause to think that he would be foolish enough to try and use the knife on so many of them.

"You are Comanche. What do you want of me?" he asked, knowing they were Comanche because he had trespassed today on their land. He hoped that these were a faction of Comanche who knew English well enough to converse with him. "I have only barely trespassed on land that is yours by treaty. I would not think that is enough to warrant you drawing your weapons on me." He nodded down at the boar. "If it is the boar that you want, take it. I'm not that attached to my early-morning kill. I give it up willingly."

Brant looked slowly around the circle of Indians, who had not budged their rifles' aim on him.

When his eyes came to the woman, his breath caught in his throat. He had never seen anyone as beautiful. Not even his twin sister, Tanzey Nicole, could match such loveliness as this. This Indian maiden's long hair was blacker than the feathers of a crow, falling down over her shoulders in luxuriant profusion, halfway to the ground.

Around her forehead was a tiny band, scalloped on the upper edge, after the fashion of a crown.

Attired in a fringed, fancily beaded dress that fit her snugly, he saw just how tiny and shapely she was.

Her copper face shone with a quiet radiance. Her facial features were that of perfection, her slightly slanted coal-black eyes pulling him into the mystic of the power she seemed to have over her Comanche warrior companions.

Weak-kneed by being finally so close to this white man that she could see the color of his eyes—so green they seemed to be the mirroring of spring grass—Feather Moon for a moment was speechless.

"Feather Moon," Big Bow said, bringing her out of her reverie. "We must leave now. To stay is to tempt being caught."

Feather Moon sidled her horse closer to Brant. "Mount your steed," she said, her voice more soft than threatening. "Now, white man. You go with us."

"I am to be a captive?" Brant asked, his voice rising in pitch with each word spoken.

"*Huh*, yes," Feather Moon said, lifting his horse's reins, then handing them to him.

"I have not mastered your Comanche language as it seems you have mastered mine," Brant said, placing his foot into a stirrup, swinging himself into the saddle. He stared into the deep dark eyes of the woman. "So how am I to know yet whether or not I am captive?"

"In time you will learn all Comanche words," Feather Moon said, smiling softly over at him. "*Huh*? It means, yes. It means that you are captive. White man, you are now *mine*."

She laughed when she heard his sharp intake of breath.

Her laughter faded into another soft smile. "And you do not need to tell me your white man name," she said flatly. "From now on you will be called Fire In The Sky."

Her gaze shifted upward. She watched the wind flutter his flaming red hair across his broad shoulders. "It is because of your hair that you have been given Fire In The Sky name."

Brant stared at her in disbelief. He was stunned speechless to know that she had an Indian name chosen for him. For her to have already picked out a name for him meant that she had planned this capture before acting on her desire to have him!

He swallowed hard as one of the warriors slapped the rump of his pinto, causing it to ride off in a hard gallop, the lovely maiden soon catching up with him. When their eyes met and held, Brant felt something strangely sensual pass between them. He could feel himself being drawn into the mystique of this lovely Indian maiden, and knew that this was a threat in itself, for under any other circumstances, he would pursue her as a man pursues a woman!

But now?

He was not sure how to feel, or to act in her presence.

For the first time in his life, a woman was making him feel awkward, perhaps . . . even . . . shy!

Chapter Two

Let thy loveliness fade as it will,
And around the dear ruin each wish of my heart
Would entwine itself verdantly still.

—THOMAS MOORE

SIX MONTHS LATER

The sounds from the courtyard at Fort Phantom Hill near Abilene rumbled in through the open window at Tanzey Nicole Hunter's left side. She stood over a wide oak desk beside her stepfather, Ronald Davis.

Tanzey could hear the squeaking of wheels as wagons came and went from the fort. At the sudden, loud noise of horses' hooves clopping on the stamped-down earth outside the window, she had to believe that soldiers had returned from one mission or another.

Tanzey cringed when she heard their laughter, resenting their happiness when her own was presently on hold.

She stared down at Colonel Franks, the top man of authority at this fort. Although he was dressed neatly in his blue uniform with its gold tassels and buttons, he was no less swarthy and unseemly in appearance. It was hard for Tanzey to control her anger as she had listened to him make excuse after excuse, for six long months, because he could not find her brother Brant.

During Tanzey's other jaunts to the fort, she had described more than once her brother's appearance so that the resident artist at the fort could sketch posters of him to pass out among the settlers. If someone found Brant along the trail, be ... he .. dead or alive, they could notify her.

Tanzey had stressed to the colonel that her twin brother had her same flaming red hair. He had the same large green eyes. Like Tanzey, he was tall and willowy.

She had been told more than once that her lips were sensually wide. Her brother's were wide, but she had never thought to wonder whether or not the women saw them as sensual.

But she did know that his lashes were the same as hers ... thick and full.

Her same age of twenty, Brant was way more mature than most young men his age. Hard work had given him his wide shoulders, his muscles, and had taken away the more childish, youthful look about his face. Even though he was her brother, Tanzey saw him nothing less than handsome.

"Sir, I haven't heard yet what I came to hear," Tanzey blurted.

When the colonel's only response was to glare up at her, her body stiffened amid her buckskin attire, the breeches and fringed shirt a disguise she wore each day as she rode alone or with her stepfather's cowhands.

When there was such a land as this Texas, where men outnumbered women two to one, it was safer for a woman to take on the appearance of a man whenever possible. Especially if the woman was not prone to womanly duties in the house, and instead preferred riding free on a horse from dawn to dusk.

Tanzey's wide-brimmed hat, soiled with her own sweat, and its tall crown, under which she most times hid her long red hair, lay now on a chair just inside the door of this colonel's quarters.

Tanzey leaned over the paper-cluttered desk and placed her hands, palm-side down, on the desk. "Sir, you have given no hint whatsoever of whether or not you are still daily sending out sentries to look for my brother. Are you? Are there soldiers even now out scouring the land for signs of Brant, or ... or ... his possible abductors?"

"Ma'am, it's been six months now," Colonel Franks said, lifting a half-smoked cigar from an ashtray. "I'd say if your brother was alive, he'd have showed up by now." He lit the cigar. The smoke billowed up in Tanzey's face.

She coughed and gagged, but did not budge. She was determined to get answers or to make the colonel uneasy over her persistence. She was tired of his lame excuses, of his utter incompetence!

She flinched when she felt a heavy hand fall upon her right shoulder, yet she knew whose, and did not resent it. The hand belonged to someone she loved, and whose pain was deep also over her brother's disappearance.

Knowing what to expect next and not wanting to hear it, she turned a guarded expression toward her stepfather. He was gaunt and empty-eyed, for these past weeks he had spent many long hours on horseback while searching for Brant himself.

Since her brother's disappearance, Tanzey had not seen her stepfather eat one decent meal. His own buckskins hung like loose sacks from his body. He

scarcely lifted a razor to shave. He blamed himself
for Brant's disappearance. Ronald had not allowed
anyone to go boar hunting with Brant the day Brant
had rode out alone. Ronald had said enough time
had been spent in searching for the murdering beasts
that had downed many of their cattle.

Having a deep-seated grudge against one boar in
particular, which was responsible for killing several
of his father's cattle and for having threatened his
own life. Brant had stubbornly not listened to his
stepfather's advice. He had left early in the morning,
even before Tanzey knew that he was gone, or she,
too, would have left with him!

Brant had not been seen since.

"Tanzey, we've got our answer, now let's go
home," Ronald said, his voice drawn. "Hon, the colonel is right. It's time to—"

"No, I won't give up that easily," Tanzey said,
shrugging his hand away from her shoulder. "I'll
never accept that Brant is dead. Not until I . . . see
. . . his body."

She gazed down at the colonel again. "Did you
send someone out today, sir, to look for my brother,
or am I to assume that you perhaps never even did
at all, *ever*?" Tanzey said, her green eyes flashing
into his.

"If you assume that, you are wrong," Colonel
Franks said, sighing heavily. He slid the cigar to the
corner of his mouth and clenched it between his
teeth.

Frowning, he paused, then removed the cigar and
smashed it out in the ashtray.

He cleared his throat and squirmed uneasily in his
chair. "Now, let me explain a few things to you,
ma'am," he said. He slid a look over at her father,
then focused his attention on her again. "I just can't

send the cavalry out, over and over again. It risks too much with the Comanche. I don't want to arouse them into distrusting me. At this moment in time, we are at peace with the 'Honey Eater' tribe of Comanche. In the not-so-long-ago past, their war chief, Rolling Thunder, rode with the Texas Rangers. Time and again, he and his warriors have helped in our attempt to rid the land of other marauding bands of Comanche and white outlaws. Even *Mexicans*, who from time to time cross the border with their own sorts of havoc-spreading."

"I've heard this all before," Tanzey said, frustratingly raking her long, lean fingers through her hair. She turned to her stepfather. "I knew we were wasting our time coming here today. This man, he . . . he . . . cares nothing about Brant."

"Tanzey, no one could ever care for Brant as much as you," Ronald said softly. "You are his twin." He glanced down at the colonel, then looked pleadingly at Tanzey again. "The colonel has surely done all that he can. Let's go home and not bother him any further."

"I promise you that I will send for you if I am brought news of your brother," Colonel Franks said, rising slowly from his chair behind his desk. He placed his thumbs down the front of his neatly ironed breeches, grabbed the waist, and shifted them up higher past his bulbous stomach. "But it would be better for the both of you if you will just accept that Brant is dead. Surely the very wild boars that he was hunting turned on him and killed him. Time and again that has been known to happen."

Too spirited and too stubborn to take what he said as a possible truth, even though she knew that one boar in particular had almost taken Brant's life not that long ago, Tanzey glared at the short, squatty colonel. She placed her hands on her hips, just above her holstered pistols.

"Sir, I have you to know that my brother was too skilled at hunting to allow that to happen," she challenged angrily, forcing the memory of the sow that had cornered her brother from her mind. She knew that Brant would never forget that one experience and would have never let it happen again.

"If he *is* dead, heaven forbid," Tanzey further said. "It has to be at the hands of two-legged walking animals, not four! Perhaps at the hand of the very Indian you only moments ago mentioned. Who can say whether or not Rolling Thunder has been truthful and a true friend to you, after all? What if he captured my brother and took him as a captive?"

"Hogwash," Colonel Franks said, folding his arms across his chest. "Never. The white people in this area have *way* less to fear from Rolling Thunder's band of Comanche than the recently dishonorably discharged Lieutenant Dan Adams. I suspect him being behind many of the raids and murders in the recent weeks, cleverly disguising so many of them as though they were done by Indians."

"Lieutenant Dan Adams?" Tanzey said, raising an eyebrow. "Yes, I have heard of him. It is rumored that he is a heartless man who kills for the plain enjoyment of killing."

"Yes, that fits his description well enough," Colonel Franks growled. "Right now he is a man without a country. He's a damn rapist. A killer. A *traitor*. If ever I get my hands on that son of a bitch, you will see what I do with such men as that!"

"I have also heard of Rolling Thunder," Tanzey said, softly kneading her chin as she recalled the one time she had seen him riding in the distance. He had been too far away for her to see his facial features.

The one thing she recalled about him was his beautiful white mustang and how tall he had sat in his Indian saddle, and how wide his bare copper shoulders looked beneath the glaring sun that day.

There had been something about him, in how he wore only a breech clout, so savage-like, and by the way his long raven-black hair fluttered in the wild breeze, that had kept her eyes on him far longer than normal.

Since then, when she had wondered about him, she had reminded herself that he was not just any man.

He was an Indian.

He *was* . . . a . . . savage!

"So why not do as I suggest?" Colonel Franks said, stepping from behind the desk. He placed a thick hand on Tanzey's elbow, which she brushed aside. "Go home. Go about your business. You have done all that is humanly possible for your brother."

Tanzey grabbed her hat from the chair and plopped it on her head. As she walked between the colonel and her father out of the room, to the porch that circled three sides of the colonel's cabin, she slid her hair up inside the crown of her hat.

"My family moved to Texas from Kansas for mustanging," she said, sliding the last swirl of hair beneath her hat. She turned and stared at the colonel. "We are into horse breeding and trading. We expected more protection from the fort than what you have thus far offered. As I see it, this fort, you, and all the men who are housed here are a waste of taxpayers' money!"

She stormed down the steps in her high-heeled leather boots and swung herself up on the seat of her buggy. She grabbed the horse's reins and waited for her stepfather, who was offering apologies to the colonel for his outspoken stepdaughter.

"Colonel, Tanzey Nicole speaks her mind often without thinking," Ronald said, slipping his own hat on his head as he took it from the back of the buggy. "Believe me, Colonel, beneath my daughter's stubborn exterior lies a sweet and caring soul."

As Tanzey's father chatted further with the colonel, she looked around at the activity of the fort. Her eyes caught something that made her throat grow dry. On the far side of the courtyard was a stack of buffalo hides as long as a city block, and as high as a man could reach throwing hides out of a wagon. It was so wide that it must have been made by driving wagons down both sides of the pile.

She was abhorred by this . . . by the buffalo slaughter it had to have taken to gather up so many pelts.

She turned and glared at the colonel. She quickly drew his and her father's attention by the coldness of her voice and by the accusation it carried. "Just perhaps, *sir*, you are no longer looked to as a friend by Rolling Thunder," she said bitterly. "What Indian could befriend such a man who condones such a buffalo slaughter that supplies you with the piles of pelts that are inside the walls of your fort?"

She ignored the ashen color of her stepfather's face as he stood there listening to her actually shame the powerful Colonel Franks.

"No wonder Indians hate white people so much," she said venomously. "The white people have come and taken what once belonged solely to the Indians. Especially the buffalo! Soon there will be no buffalo for the Indians, *or* the white eyes!"

Seething, and now truly believing that her brother might have been a victim of an act of vengeance against white men for taking what once belonged solely to the Indians, Tanzey could not find any more words to match the tumultuous emotions inside her.

She turned her eyes away from the colonel and waited for her father to board the buggy.

When he was finally beside her, she snapped the reins and sent the horse and buggy quickly away from the gawking, silent colonel.

"Tanzey Nicole, it's not wise to make enemies with men as powerful as Colonel Franks," Ronald said. He took a handkerchief from his rear pocket and dabbed beads of nervous perspiration from his brow.

"I most certainly do not see the colonel as my *friend*," Tanzey said, laughing sarcastically.

They rode from the fort and turned right, into the wind and blazing sun.

Tanzey became quiet, as she, for the first time ever, truly felt now that her brother might be dead. The odds were stacked too much against him.

She fought back tears.

She swallowed lump after lump in her throat.

She didn't want to do anything further to upset her stepfather.

She had said enough today to last a lifetime of regrets on her part as far as her father was concerned!

And besides the worry about Brant, her stepfather had enough worries to deal with. He had only a few hired hands. He couldn't afford to hire any more. Brant had worked as hard as a dozen men!

And now that he was gone and Tanzey felt that he might not return, she knew that she must take up where Brant had left off.

She loved her stepfather dearly.

She adored her mother.

Yes, she must do what she could to help ease the load that now lay heavy on her father's shoulders. She would go out tomorrow and do some mustanging. She would find where they grazed. She would then lead her father's cowhands to them.

A thought sprang to her mind that caused a coldness to circle her heart. If she was responsible for so many of the wild mustangs being rounded up, wouldn't she be as guilty as those men at the fort who took the buffalo's pelts? Did not the Indians depend on the mustangs for their existence, as well as they did the buffalo?

And wasn't she riding right into the face of danger if she went out on her own to find the wild horses?

Yet her loyalty to her stepfather made her know that she must put the Indians from her mind.

However, she could not help fear the Comanche finding her alone on the trail as she searched for the mustangs.

Brant had been alone.

Brant had disappeared.

them back when they had rode out of eye range of the ranch.

Tanzey never enjoyed going against her mother's wishes. But her mother, LaDena, had never known the freedom that Tanzey had learned to love while riding a horse and doing things usually only done by men.

Her mother was from Boston, a woman used to frills and lace, a woman who was as timid as a bird when it came to doing anything beyond the walls of her house.

When LaDena had gone to Kansas that one summer long ago to visit an aunt, Tanzey's father had swept the beautiful, petite thing right off her feet with his charm and handsomeness, and she had never since seen the likes of Boston again.

While living with her first husband, she had hated Kansas.

Now, while living with her second husband, she liked Texas no better!

But Tanzey's mother had forced herself to adapt to such horrible places in order to please first one husband, and then her next.

Tears sparkled in her eyes when Tanzey thought of her true father. He had been dead now for ten years. But before he had died, he had taught both Tanzey and her brother the skills of shooting firearms and taming and breeding horses.

When he had died and her mother had remarried out of sheer desperation for her and her children, LaDena had been lucky to have married such a good man.

Tanzey's stepfather had a heart of gold, *and* he had been as adamant as her true father at making sure that she and her brother knew the art of defending themselves.

After their move to Texas, Tanzey's stepfather had even tried to get her mother involved in such teachings.

But LaDena still shied away from such horrors as guns and horses, retreating quickly back inside her warm cocoon of safety ... her house.

Tanzey drew a sudden tight rein. "Whoa!" she shouted, her roan coming to a shimmying halt.

She wheeled the horse around and faced the ranch hands as they also drew tight reins and stopped. "You've come with me far enough," she said, reaching up to tuck some fallen locks of her hair back inside the tall crown of her hat. "I'll go the rest of the way by myself."

"Now, Tanzey, that's not what your pa said," Terry McKee said. "There ain't no way in hell that I'll return to the ranch if you ain't with me."

Tanzey gazed at Terry, who was perhaps the oldest of the crew, and the most dependable. His face bronzed tan by the sun looked like leather stretched across bone. His steely gray eyes shone through the bronze, kind and caring.

"Terry, I don't need a baby-sitter," Tanzey said, sighing heavily. She rested a hand on the pistol holstered at her right waist. "Now, get along. All of you. Or by damn I might be forced to draw my firearm on you."

"Hell's fire, Tanzey," Terry said, slowly shaking his head back and forth. "You ain't got a lick of sense. Do you know that?"

"I've got enough sense to know how to take care of myself," Tanzey argued. "And you know that Father never expected me to allow you to ride with me much farther than this. Get on home. There's plenty of chores for you to do there." She tipped her hat back with a finger and smiled smugly from man to man. "And *I'm* sure as hell not one of them."

"What in hell do you think you can succeed at doing out here all alone 'cept probably get shot by outlaws or captured by renegades?" Terry further worried aloud, his jaw tight. "Tanzey, I insist that you let us go with you. We'll work together on this. We'll all find that herd of mustang you've got your heart set on findin'."

Tanzey thought for a moment about outlaws and renegades. She swallowed hard when her thoughts then slid to her beloved brother, who had set out on his own six months ago because he was as stubborn as his twin sister.

But she pushed the worry aside quickly.

Without a second thought, she whipped her pistol out of its holster and aimed it at Terry.

Terry flinched. "Tanzey Nicole, good God," he said, edging his horse away from her.

"Go home, Terry," Tanzey said, her eyes wavering into his. "This is something I've got to do. I've got to do it for Father. Brant is no longer here to do his part. I'm going to take up the slack and do it *for* him."

"That's downright stupid," Terry spat. "Damn it, Tanzey, put the gun away. Come on home with us. If anything should happen to you—"

"It won't," she said, quickly interrupting him. She motioned with her firearm. "Now, git. Leave me be. Do you hear? All of you! Leave ... me ... be!"

"Tanzey ..." Terry said, trying one last protest.

"Go on, Terry," Tanzey said softly. She shifted her gaze and looked from man to man. "And don't return to the ranch all at once. Scatter. Enter one by one, or Mother will know that she's been duped."

"She's not the only one," Terry uttered beneath his

breath, then swung his horse around and rode off
with the rest of the ranch hands.

Tanzey sighed with relief.

She slung her pistol back inside its holster, then
turned her horse around.

She had a set destination . . . where she had seen
many hoofprints of horses another time when she
was out searching for signs of her brother. She realized that she would soon enter the land of the Comanches, known as "Comancheria," but rode on
anyhow.

And when she rode farther and farther on land
that she knew was forbidden to her by treaty with
the Indians, she still didn't let that concern her. She
had only one thing on her mind. Her determination
to find those horses again that were so beautiful, so
healthy, so *wild*!

She would follow them and discover their true
grazing grounds.

She would then return to the ranch and tomorrow
lead the ranch hands to them.

The glory would be hers, though, for having found
them *today!*

Although she knew she had to be on guard now
on Comancheria, she could not help but relax enough
to enjoy the scenery.

It was a land of sheer beauty.

It was a land of not only seas of nutritious grass,
but also where rocky hills and canyons were covered
with scrubby cedar.

A number of rivers cut southeastward across Comancheria, low-banked and sand-filled.

Growing in the sandy soil along the larger streams
were extensive thickets of plum bushes and
grapevines.

Rivers that had cleared streams were lined with

cottonwood, elm, walnut, pecan, and persimmon trees.

The mesquite trees were the most commonly found, providing wood for fires; its beans valuable food for people and horses.

This land was a place of wild horses, buffalo, and deer.

Tanzey rode into the welcome shade of many cottonwood trees, their rustle overhead as the wind blew through them having the sound of falling rain. It was so peaceful, Tanzey could not help but lean her head back and close her eyes.

In her thoughts she was thrown back in time. While living in Kansas, when she and her brother were just children, she and Brant had often taken picnic baskets down by the river. They had eaten their mother's wonderfully fried, crisp chicken until they felt as though they might burst.

One time they had fallen asleep beneath the cottonwoods after a long day of swimming and splashing in the river. A thunderstorm came quickly from the west and awakened them with a sudden, drenching rain.

"Never did we ever scamper back home as fast as that day," Tanzey whispered to herself, laughing softly.

The lightning had been like bolts of silver streaking vividly from the heavens all around them.

The thunder had sounded like huge explosions in their ears!

Her thoughts were brought back to the present, and her eyes flew open when she heard the soft neighing of a horse coming from somewhere close by, and then an answering neigh.

"The mustangs," she whispered to herself.

Ever since her family's move to Texas, Tanzey had

been intrigued by the wild mustangs. They were small, agile, and tough, capable of surprising speed.

They possessed great endurance.

Most had small, pointed, alert ears, with quick, wicked eyes.

And once tamed, they served well their owner, for they often were aware of danger way before a rider.

Mustangs were also good at foraging. They were known to live on the bark and twigs of trees for days.

Yes, Tanzey thought to herself. The mustangs were frugal, wiry creatures; lovely in their wildness.

Once tamed, though, they brought much money at the railhead at Fort Worth!

Tanzey slowed her horse's pace and rode in a slow lope toward a clearing that she saw a short distance away.

She drew a tight rein and stopped with alarm when she not only saw many mustangs through the break in the trees, where they were circled around a large water hole, drinking.

She saw something else that made her heart skip a beat.

It was an Indian on a beautiful white mustang!

Tanzey was well hidden from the Indian's view, but from this angle, *she* could see him well enough. She had to believe that he was Comanche, for she was on Comanche land.

She studied his attire, confirming her belief about what tribe of Indian he was from. She had learned some pointers about how to distinguish the local Indian tribes from each other. The Comanche moccasins had buckskin uppers with a seam down the heel, with the lower border of the upper sewed to a stiff sole of tanned buffalo hide.

Like this Indian's leggings today, so thickly fringed, his moccasins could be distinguished by their long fringes. Fringes ran from the lace to the toe and along the seam at the heel.

And she knew that the Comanche men parted their hair from the center of the forehead back to the crown, forming a braid on each side. They were known to paint a streak of yellow along the part.

Yes, she concluded, this Indian was Comanche. And she had to believe that he was from the peaceful band of Comanche known as the Penateka, who were also called Honey Eaters because of their love of honey.

It was this band of Comanche whose village was not that far from this watering hole.

The name Rolling Thunder came to mind, for Tanzey knew that he was from the Penateka tribe. In the eyes of those who were stationed at Fort Phantom Hill, Rolling Thunder was an admired, trusted man.

In Tanzey's eyes, no Indian could be trusted, especially now, when her brother was missing so close to Comanche soil!

Her eyebrows quirked as she further wondered about this Indian, whether or not he might be Rolling Thunder . . . ?

But something else grabbed her undivided attention. She stared at the rifle in the Indian's right hand. As he held his reins in his left hand, he edged his steed slowly forward toward the browsing wild mustangs.

She gazed quickly at the horses. Thus far the mustangs had not caught the Indian's scent, nor heard his approach. They still stood calmly beside the water hole. Some were still quenching their thirst, while others were grazing on the thick grass along the embankment.

A movement seen out of the corner of Tanzey's eyes drew her attention back to the Indian. Her breath caught in her throat when she saw the Indian drop his reins, then lift his rifle and take aim on one mustang in particular.

"No!" Tanzey whispered to herself.

Her insides froze inside at the thought of the Indian shooting the beautiful horse! She had heard that the Comanches ate horses when there was nothing else to eat.

But today she had seen many buffalo!

Many deer!

She had seen, oh, so many things that the Indian could have eaten without killing a beautiful, innocent mustang stallion!

But she was helpless. If she rode up and defended the mustang, she would put herself in jeopardy. Thus far, as she sat among the thick shadows of the cottonwoods, she had not been detected. If she moved even one inch now, while the Indian was so intently concentrating, he might hear her.

His aim could quickly shift from the mustang to *her*. What if he was the sort to shoot first and ask questions later?

Her heart pounded as she waited for the Indian to pull the trigger that would snuff the life from the beautiful animal.

Yet he seemed in no hurry to take what he had so obviously come after. There seemed something calculated by how he was still taking such careful, slow, and cautious aim.

Tanzey glanced toward the mustang, knowing that it still did not know that it was being stalked, then turned slow eyes to the Indian again.

She then studied the position of the Indian's rifle and exactly what he was so carefully aiming at. He seemed intent at shooting the horse through the muscular part of the neck above its vertebrae.

Tanzey knew enough about horses to know that if the Indian's aim was exact, he would not fracture the horse's spine.

He . . . would . . . not kill it!

Was that his intention?

To just disable the horse for a moment, instead of killing it?

Tanzey jumped with alarm when the Indian suddenly pulled the trigger.

The shot rang out loud and clear, reverberating its hollow echoing sound through the trees, high into the canyons, and across the body of water where the horses suddenly began a frenzied stampede.

All fled but the one that had dropped to the ground, obviously momentarily paralyzed, but thankfully not dead, as it had seemed was the Indian's first intentions.

"What he has done seems to have only momentarily paralyzed the horse," Tanzey whispered to herself. She was stunned to know this new way of capturing a wild mustang.

Edging her horse farther back somewhat, so that the Indian was sure not to see her, now that he was dismounted and leaning over the downed, stunned animal, Tanzey watched him carefully slip a hackamore, a loop of rope, about the under jaw of the horse. He brought this up and tied it about the neck with a knot that would not slip when the animal once again moved to its feet.

In only a matter of minutes the horse snorted and rose back to its feet.

The mustang's nostrils flared.

It yanked at the rope and bucked for a moment or two, then settled down and seemed resigned to the fact that it now belonged to the Indian.

Tanzey could not believe what she had seen. And

being a marksman with a rifle herself, she decided that she would return to this same spot tomorrow and hope that the mustangs would have returned to the watering hole. She wanted to select her own horse from this herd and use the same tactic the Indian had used to capture one of them.

She had watched the Indian closely enough to know exactly where he had aimed.

She could hardly wait to try her hand at this new way of taming a beautiful, wild mustang.

Tanzey panicked when she realized that the Indian was wheeling his horse around to head her way.

Her pulse racing, fear grabbing her at the pit of the stomach, Tanzey looked desperately around her for a better hiding place.

When she saw a low shelter of rock, she quickly dismounted and led her horse beneath it.

Scarcely breathing and holding onto her horse's reins for dear life, Tanzey watched the Indian drawing closer and closer, the tamed mustang dutifully following behind him.

Tanzey glanced quickly at her roan, praying that it would not neigh and disclose their presence there.

Remembering two small lumps of sugar in her rear pocket that she had placed there before leaving her house, Tanzey slipped them from her pocket and held them out for her steed.

As the horse nuzzled her hand and took his time eating the sugar, Tanzey turned and again watched the Indian's approach. Up this close now, she could see his full facial features.

Her face grew hot with a strange sort of heat when she saw just how handsome he was. He was of a medium stature with a bright copper-colored complexion, and an intelligent countenance.

He had an aquiline nose, thin lips, and a firm chin.

He wore no shirt.

His chest was bare.

His shoulders rippled with muscles.

His beautiful, midnight-black eyes were slightly slanted.

Tied with beaver fur and decorated with feathers, silver ornaments and beads, the Indian's raven-black, thick, coarse braids fell below his waist.

He wore close-fitting fringed buckskin breeches and buckskin leggings that extended from the upper portion of the thighs to the foot.

After moving to Texas, Tanzey had seen many Indians, but never had any of them given her cause to stare in wonder at them.

But this Indian was different.

He stood out from all the others that she had ever seen.

She could not help but wonder if this truly *might* be Chief Rolling Thunder. When he had been pointed out to her before, he had been on a beautiful white mustang, exactly like the one this Indian rode today! That Indian had sat as tall and straight in his saddle!

She had only half paid attention when she had heard women at the trading posts talking about Rolling Thunder's handsomeness.

She had thought that they were only intrigued by him being an Indian, not by how he *truly* looked.

Now she knew that she had been wrong. If this *was* Chief Rolling Thunder, he *was* worth marveling over.

She watched him until he was out of sight.

A thought suddenly came to her. Never had she had the chance to follow a Comanche as now, to find their village, to spy on them, to see if her brother might be held captive there.

But the lowering sun in the sky didn't allow her this chance today. She knew that she had no choice but to return to the safety of her home. She knew the dangers of being out on the range after dark.

When she felt that the Indian was well on his way back to his village, Tanzey mounted her strawberry roan and headed for home.

When she saw her stepfather's spread of land through a break in the trees, she sighed with relief. She truly felt lucky to have returned home safe today.

And she knew the risk of heading out again tomorrow to try her luck at downing a mustang in the same manner she had witnessed today.

But she had to.

She would never rest until she at least tried!

Her horse unsaddled, brushed down, and fed, Tanzey walked from the barn toward the ranch house.

She got only halfway from the barn to the rambling two-storied log cabin, when her mother came in a flurry out on the porch.

"Tanzey Nicole, where have you been?" LaDena asked. She placed her hands on her hips angrily and nodded toward the sun that was dipping low and orange along the horizon. "It's almost dark. What did you find to do today to keep you gone so long from the house? Pray do not tell me that you left our property and rode alone on land that does not belong to us. Pray do not tell me that you went alone looking for your brother again!"

"Mother, don't you see?" Tanzey said as she reached the porch and gave her mother a warm hug. The familiar scent of her mother's perfume curled up Tanzey's nose. The crisp starched fabric of her dress and the lace that lay along the top of the bodice scratched her cheeks.

"Don't you see that I'm all right?" Tanzey contin-

ued. "Why work yourself into hysterics over me
every day of your life? Mother, I'm twenty. Don't
you think I'm old enough now to know my own
mind?"

"You might be twenty, but you are still my little
girl," LaDena murmured. She stepped away from
Tanzey. She curled her nose at her daughter's out-
doorsy, sweaty smell. "How can you stand wearing
those dreadful men's clothes? And how can you
stand smelling like a man?"

She grabbed Tanzey gently by an arm. "Come with
me, young lady," she said, her chin lifted haughtily.
"You are going to sit in a bubble bath for hours if
that is what it takes to get that stench off you and
make you smell like a lady."

Her mother reached for Tanzey's hat. She cringed
when she lifted it from her daughter's head, the
sweat still wet along the inside of the crown.

She tossed the hat aside, then led Tanzey on into
the house.

Tanzey was hardly aware of her mother's continued fussing.

Nor was she even aware of being undressed in the
privacy of her bedroom and led into a steaming hot
copper tub of water.

Her mother's words were only a faint sort of hum
as she bent low over the tub, scrubbing Tanzey's
back, then under her arms, all the while scolding her
for being so reckless for being gone for so long.

Tanzey's thoughts were elsewhere, on the Indian
and his handsomeness.

Then her thoughts would drift to how the Indian
had shot the mustang.

She went over and over again in her mind exactly
where the Indian had aimed to make sure he only
momentarily paralyzed the animal.

She must take as careful aim tomorrow and shoot a mustang through the muscular part of the neck above the vertebrae!

Missing by even a fraction would be fatal to the horse, *and* Tanzey's confidence and ego.

No, nothing would keep her from leaving the ranch again tomorrow. Not even her sweet mother, whose nerves were frazzled.

Tanzey again thought of the Indian. One day soon she would run across him again, and this time she would follow him!

Just perhaps he *could* lead her not only to his village, but also to her brother!

She would never give up on finding Brant!

She must check out all possibilities!

She could search for him until all possibilities of finding him were *exhausted*!

She smiled to herself, knowing that just perhaps, by following the Indian, by observing him for longer than a brief moment, she might discover why she was so strangely infatuated with him.

She even expected him to visit her *tonight* ... in her *dreams*!

Chapter Four

What so false as truth is,
False to thee?

—ROBERT BROWNING

Early the next morning, before anyone else had stirred from their beds, Tanzey rode from the ranch, a sturdy coil of rope hanging from her saddle.

Her heart beat with the excitement of what she hoped lay before her. She so badly wanted to capture a wild mustang in the exact manner the Comanche Indian had captured the beautiful, wild steed yesterday. She had hardly slept a wink all night while going over and over again in her mind how it must be done.

And when she hadn't been thinking of that the long night through, the Indian had entered her thoughts.

She frowned now at how his image in her mind's eye had caused such strange, surely forbidden, stirrings within her.

Even now, as she thought of how handsome and strongly muscled he was, a warm gnawing began at the very pit of her stomach.

For certain, having become this intrigued with the

Comanche warrior, things had awakened within her that she had never felt before!

"This is downright asinine," she whispered to herself. She absolutely must forget about that Indian. She mustn't *want* to see him again. They were from different cultures—different *worlds*. Surely he would look at her with contempt, for she was just another white person who had invaded the land that once solely belonged only to Indians.

And she kept reminding herself that just perhaps this very Indian might be responsible for her brother's disappearance!

If she *must* think about the Indian, she must do it with a loathing!

But even that thought could not convince her to stop thinking about him in a positive way. She did not want to think that a man who was held in such high esteem by those at the fort could be so two-faced, so hungry for vengeance.

Even while Rolling Thunder had rode with the Texas Rangers, the buffalo had suffered no less carnage by the white men!

The Comanche warrior had obviously turned his head then and looked the other way! Why would it be different now?

So torn with her thoughts, doubts, and hopes, Tanzey slapped her reins and led her horse into a harder gallop, which took more concentration than loping along the trail.

Yet still, the Indian that she had seen yesterday would not leave her mind. *Could* he have been Chief Rolling Thunder? She had heard that he was a war chief.

"War chief," she whispered, shivering at the thought of what that title represented. This Indian

probably took to warring as his chosen way to settle arguments.

She hoped that his title of war chief was just that,
a title, a way to separate himself from those of his
people who were not as strong, as powerful, or as
intelligent.

"Intelligent," she thought, smiling wryly. If he saw
her in her buckskin attire today, and her sweat-
stained wide-brimmed hat, where her hair was
tucked in a tight swirl beneath it, would he be smart
enough to detect that she was a woman instead of
the man she tried to portray on the trail?

Or would he be able to define the swell of her
breasts beneath the loose-fitting shirt?

Would he be able to see the shape of her legs
where the breeches had shrunk to be just a mite too
tight than that which she preferred?

She smiled while thinking about all of the men she
had fooled since she had arrived at Texas. She had
without question been accepted among the rowdy
cowhands from all of the neighboring ranches during
the long trail ride to the railhead at Fort Worth.

She did not think that *any* Indian would be any
wiser than those wisecracking men who would kill
to have a woman in their bedroll on those long and
lonely nights beneath the moonlight at their various
campsites.

No, she did not worry about being detected as a
woman. Now, while just crossing onto Comancheria
land, surely even a *man* might not be safe. To trespass on Comanche land could be an open invitation
to get an arrow in one's chest . . . or *back.*

Seeing the familiar scope of land that she remembered from yesterday just prior to coming up on the
Indian and the herd of mustangs, Tanzey tightened
her reins somewhat.

She rode in a slower lope beneath the cottonwoods, the leaves rustling again overhead like sweet, falling rain.

She did not allow her thoughts to stray today on those many times shared with her brother beneath the Kansas cottonwoods.

Today she must keep alert.

Not only was she near the spot she had seen the mustangs yesterday, she knew that the Indian had also been up ahead just a short distance. Now she could even see the water hole where the mustangs had been browsing and where the Indian had been stalking.

Yes, a part of her wanted to see the Indian again, but not under these circumstances. She would rather come upon him on land that belonged to the whites instead of Comanche.

Tanzey much preferred being closer to her home, so that if she had cause to flee from Indians, she would not have that far to ride.

Today, neither was the case.

She was far from home.

She was on land forbidden to her!

Her pulse racing, her eyes darting cautiously around her, Tanzey now only inched her roan along.

She scarcely breathed.

Her shoulders ached from holding them so stiff.

Her fingers trembled as she slid her right hand to the pistol belted at her waist.

She eyed the rifle in the gun boot at the horse's right side. Slowly her hand slid there, where she kept it until she came to the overhang of rock that she had found yesterday. She would go the rest of the way by foot. If she did not come upon the mustangs soon, she would make a quick retreat. The longer she was there, the more she felt a strange sort of presence. It was as though someone was there, watching her every move.

Yes, she thought, fear causing her throat to constrict, she ... no ... longer felt alone.

Yet there were no sounds, no movements, *nothing*.

Surely she was just imagining someone was there out of guilt of being on property that was not hers.

She must get this done and over with quickly!

Once she fired the rifle, she would certainly be in danger.

But she had already calculated how long it would take the Indians who heard the gunfire from their village to search and find her.

She would have enough time to return to land beyond Comancheria.

She would hightail it for home with her mustang ...

"*If* I get one this morning," she whispered as she tied her horse's reins to a low tree limb.

After slipping the heavy coil of rope from her horse, then slinging it over her left shoulder, she grabbed her rifle and moved stealthily beneath the cottonwoods.

She kept her eyes on the shine of the water through the break in the trees a short distance away.

She was probably foolish to think the mustangs would be there again today. There were many watering holes in the area. There were many cottonwoods under which to rest while browsing at the water's edge.

Her heart flip-flopped with excitement at seeing a lone mustang dip its nose into the water as she stepped out into the open.

She stopped, motionless, her gaze glued on the beautiful, wild thing, its color a deep velvet-black. She was afraid that it would detect her presence at any moment now, if not by smell, but sheer instinct.

But it never caught her scent.

It never sensed her presence.

It blew bubbles into the water, raised its head, and shook its heavy mane, then turned and wandered to a thick stand of grass and began idly nibbling it.

A movement beyond the mustang caught Tanzey's quick attention. She gasped with pleasure as several other mustangs came into view at the crest of a high hill, their shadows cast down on the ground below them.

She swallowed hard when one of the mustang's eyes locked with hers. She waited for it to alert the lone mustang.

She was surprised when it wheeled around and, instead, led the others away to safety, leaving the one to fend for itself.

Not wanting to lose this opportunity, feeling that she had already taken too much time, Tanzey slowly knelt down onto one knee.

She slipped the rope off her shoulders.

She raised the rifle and took careful aim, then lowered the rifle and inhaled a deep, shaky breath.

What if she missed? she worried to herself.

What if she killed the mustang instead of only rendering it helpless for the amount of time it would take for her to rope it?

"I know how to do this," she whispered determinedly to herself as she tried to build her confidence. "I watched the Indian. I went over it again and again in my mind last night. I . . . can . . . do it!"

When the mustang lifted its head and neighed and shook its mane, Tanzey's heart skipped a beat. If it wheeled around and rode off, she would never have the same opportunity again!

And she so badly wanted this beautiful steed!

Not only to prove to herself that she *could* capture it, but to have it as hers, forever!

She ached to run her hands along its muscled legs, to have it nuzzle at her hand.

"I . . . can . . . do it," she whispered, slowly lifting the rifle again, aiming it.

She held a steady aim.

Her heart beat soundly within her chest.

Her mouth was dry.

Slowly her finger pulled the trigger.

With her first shot she downed the mustang.

Grabbing up her rope, she ran to the horse and went through all of the necessary movements to ensure that she would return home, the proud owner of the most hauntingly beautiful mustang that she had ever seen.

Rolling Thunder had seen the intruder on his land before he entered the hidden cover of the cotton-wood trees.

Curiosity over the white man coming alone on the land of the Comanche had kept Rolling Thunder from approaching him with questions. The white man had seemed intent on something. Rolling Thunder had decided to discover what, and then approach him.

He had stayed far enough away so that the white man would not be aware of being followed. He had even not interfered when he had seen the white man dismount and take a coil of rope from his saddle.

He had become apprehensive only when the white man had slipped the rifle from the gun boot.

But when Rolling Thunder had realized what the man was after, the *mustang*, he had decided to see the white man lose at trying to capture Lightning, the name that Rolling Thunder had given this particular mustang long ago after the mustang had, more than once, eluded him.

Still on his horse, Rolling Thunder was stunned and intrigued by the white man's skills at downing the mustang in the way practiced by himself. Never had Rolling Thunder seen a white eyes capture a mustang by "creasing," the name for the procedure that Rolling Thunder had used yesterday to down the mustang that now belonged solely to him.

As Tanzey roped the horse, Rolling Thunder still watched. He was in awe of a white man who had such skills at not only creasing, but also at roping the mustang so quickly, before it regained its full composure.

Suddenly Rolling Thunder's horse neighed, drawing a return neigh from Tanzey's tethered steed.

Hearing the horses and realizing that she was no longer alone, Tanzey rose to her feet in a start, her hat flying from her head in her haste to see who was there.

Tanzey's flaming red hair spilled down across her shoulders, then tumbled on down her back to rest at her waist.

Rolling Thunder gasped with surprise to see that what he had thought was a man was, in truth, a *mahocu-ah*, woman.

Tanzey gasped when she saw *him*. It was the same Indian that she had seen yesterday.

Again she was dazzled by his handsomeness, yet she knew that his appearance should be the last thing on her mind.

He had caught her taking a valued mustang from land that was his by treaty.

What would his punishment be?

Would he take her captive?

Or ... kill ... her on the spot?

She glanced at his weapons. Yesterday he carried a rifle. Today he carried a bow and quiver of arrows slung across his back.

And he had one of the largest knives she had ever seen sheathed at his right waist.

Her gaze shifted to his broad, bare chest, and then lower, blushing when she gaped openly at his brief breechclout. Why, he was barely clothed with that tiny thing covering his ... his ... private parts! she thought to herself, startled by his skimpy attire.

When the wind fluttered the breechclout somewhat away from his bronze, muscled legs, Tanzey gasped and looked quickly elsewhere.

In her moment of awkwardness, she dropped the rope that she had not yet fastened around the mustang's neck.

When she heard the mustang rush to its feet and ride away, her heart fell.

She turned glaring eyes at the Indian. "You are the cause!" she said, her voice tight with anger. "But, of course, you are glad that the mustang got away. It's on Comancheria land. Even though it is wild, you lay claim to it because it has not wandered as far as the land owned by whites."

So in awe of this person being a woman, with the shooting skills of a man and dressed like a man, Rolling Thunder did not pay attention to what she was saying to him.

And no matter what she wore, he saw her as nothing less than ravishingly beautiful.

He was stunned by her sheer loveliness.

Her eyes!

Her hair!

Her perfect facial features!

Then another thought came to him. This woman had the same hair and eye coloring of his cousin's white captive. Even the faces were similar! It was as though they might have been born from the same womb!

When Rolling Thunder paid no attention to what she said, Tanzey's words faded away. She was not sure how to feel as the Indian still stared at her. Why didn't he say something? Never had she been so unnerved as now!

Unsure of what he should do, now that the identity of the intruder on his land being a woman had thrown him off guard, Rolling Thunder gazed at her a moment longer, then wheeled his horse around and rode away.

Still, he could not believe what he had seen!

This person who had the skill to crease the mustang was a woman, and she was so absolutely, breathtakingly beautiful.

She would be hard to forget, that was for certain.

And he most certainly could not allow himself *to* forget her. He must always remember that she had been wrong to trespass on his land.

For sure, he would watch for her to do it again.

He did not want her to come near his village, where she might discover a white man there who had her same features and hair coloring.

He wanted no troubles with the white pony soldiers over his cousin having taken the white man, who was now her husband.

If this flaming-haired white woman made it a habit, though, of coming this close to his village, she might herself be taken captive, her silence ensuring the safety of his people!

Tanzey stared blankly after the Indian as he rode away from her in a slow, casual trot. She had mixed emotions: surprise for having been left untouched by the Indian and regret over her having spoken so angrily to him.

Up to that point he had not shown any resentment or moves toward harming her. Just perhaps if she had stayed quiet, he might have offered some conversation. If this Indian *was* Rolling Thunder, he should be able to speak English because of his association with the Texas Rangers.

She watched him.

He sat so tall in his saddle!

How right he looked on the beautiful white mustang!

He *did*, oh, so resemble the Indian that she had seen that day when he had been pointed out to her to be Rolling Thunder!

Surely it was *he*!

The same proud back . . . the same beautiful horse!

She watched him until he rode out of sight, then slid her gaze up at the high hill where she had earlier seen the mustangs, now seeing none.

Disappointment eating away at her insides over more than one thing, she grabbed up her rope and went to her horse, then headed back in the direction of her ranch.

Strange, she thought to herself, how she felt unlucky not to have been accosted by the Indian. She wished for more than his abrupt departure.

She wanted to see him again.

She wanted to know him better.

It was apparent that he had no harsh feelings toward her, and hopefully the whites in general.

He had gazed at her as though he was intrigued by her.

Then why had he left? she pondered over and over again in her mind.

She fought the need to see him again, even to think

of him as anything other than an Indian was forbidden.

She smiled, knowing that the word "forbidden" had not stopped her yet when she wished to do something.

Nor would it now.

Tomorrow she would retrace her steps.

Just possibly she would see the Indian again.

Just possibly she could follow him to his village, to see if her brother might be there.

While searching before for her brother, her father had only gone just so far. He would never ride onto land owned by the Comanches. He always turned and returned to their ranch. He feared all Indians, even those who were known to have aligned themselves with the Texas Rangers!

She, on the other hand, was truly afraid of no one, or anything.

Chapter Five

Ruddy and brown—careless and free—
A king in the saddle—he rides at will
O'er the measureless range.
—JOHN ANTROBUS

Although Tanzey realized the risks, she had left again early in the morning to ride out to the same watering hole that she had been at the past two days.

Anxiously she rode toward the thick stand of cottonwoods in the distance.

She squinted as she drew closer to them, unable to see much except for shadows. It was a hazy day, the temperatures already rising.

For the most part, the days were warm and pleasant, the nights cool and foggy.

Strange as it seemed to Tanzey, the weather in Texas was much more pleasant than Kansas.

In Kansas, a person scorched in the summer and froze in the winter.

In Texas, it was not hard to find something pleasant about each and every day, except for when the hurricane season came and frightened her to death.

And the storms that seemed to come out of nowhere, with the fierce, lurid lightning, were nothing to be envied, either.

Tanzey snapped her reins and rode in a harder gallop toward the cottonwoods. Today she was not certain what she might find at the watering hole. She rested a hand on her rifle in its gun boot, thinking that surely she would not be fortunate enough to get a second chance at getting herself a prized mustang. The one that she had downed yesterday had been exceptionally beautiful, but also as clever as it was beautiful.

It had escaped her rope at its first opportunity

"Damn the Indian for interfering," Tanzey uttered angrily to herself.

The mere thought of the Comanche brought more than anger into Tanzey's heart. Seeing his face and his muscled body in her mind's eye made her go warm and mellow at the pit of her stomach.

These were new feelings for her, and she could not deny enjoying them.

Even though she had a secret yearning, a desire for this Indian, it was impossible to cast them aside. This was the first man she had felt anything other than brotherly love, and that special bond that she felt for her stepfather as well as her real father.

"But this man who is no kin to me, who has stirred my heart so strangely, is an Indian," she whispered, running a hand along the lean, long neck of her horse. "Why ... did ... I have to become infatuated with ... an ... Indian?"

She could not see a future with this man, since there were so many things standing in their way of any kind of life together.

And she felt foolish for her thinking the Comanche might even feel the same way about her! Although she had seen something in his eyes as he had stared at her that had made her heart skip several beats, she surely had been imagining he found her attractive.

She glanced at her attire, then reached a slow hand to her hat. This morning, when she had looked in the tall, full-length mirror, she had cringed at the very sight of herself.

No washing would remove the stains on her buckskin breeches.

No scrubbing with lye soap would remove the sweat stains beneath the arms of her favorite fringed buckskin shirt.

And her hat!

For the first time in her life, something had made her dread placing her hat on her freshly washed hair today. Although the perspiration stain on her hat was dry, just knowing it was there, perhaps rubbing its ugly scent into her hair, made her cringe with distaste.

Yet she still did not feel safe enough to ride along the trail with her hair loose and flowing down her back. There were too many dangers in revealing to the wrong men that she was a woman.

Her knees grew strangely weak as she entered the shade of the cottonwoods. Her gaze swept around her for any signs of the Comanche, only now realizing that the true reason she was there was not at all for the mustang.

It was to see the Indian again!

No matter how much she tried to convince herself that she only wanted to see him and follow him to his village to search for her brother, she felt something more for this Comanche.

She had to see if he affected her the same today, as yesterday!

If so, she feared the worst might be true . . . that she might be falling in love with a man who was, in part, her enemy, who for certain . . . was forbidden to her!

Tanzey's heart sank when she arrived at the watering hole.

There was no handsome Comanche warrior.

There were no mustangs, only many hoofprints left along the embankment, which did not indicate they had been there today. The hoofprints could have been made yesterday, or the day prior.

Even as she gazed up at the butte, shading her eyes with a hand, she saw no signs of mustangs. Apparently two days of people shooting off their firearms had alerted them against coming here *again*.

Again she looked slowly around her, into the shadows that deepened where the trees were thicker, and again saw no one or anything. The Indian might have felt the same warnings as the mustangs and had decided not to reveal himself to her again.

But if he *was* there, she thought to herself, he was probably hiding, watching her, pondering his next move.

This thought caused a slow shiver to crawl up and down her spine. She was trespassing a third time in three days! The Indian might not let her get off so easily this time. If it was his habit of taking captives, to quench his hunger for vengeance against the whites, then she had opened herself up to this possibility.

And just perhaps that was the fate of her brother.

He had trespassed.

He had been taken captive.

But that was a much better thought than to allow herself to think that her brother was *dead*. If he was being held against his will at an Indian village, in time there would be ways to get him released to freedom again!

Sighing, knowing now that she should turn back and get back on land that was not Comanche, Tanzey slid out of her saddle to not only let her horse have a drink, but also herself. In her haste to leave home this morning, she had forgotten to bring a canteen of water.

She had not eaten breakfast. Her stomach ached even now from hunger.

She led her strawberry roan to the water's edge and left him there to nuzzle the water. She sank to her knees and drank big gulps from her cupped hands.

Her thirst quenched, she rose back to her full height and turned to look around her. As she wiped her mouth dry with the sleeve of her fringed shirt, she spied a yucca plant. It was heavy with fruit, which tasted like bananas.

She started to go to the yucca plant but stopped when someone suddenly stepped from behind an overhang of rock, his horse at his side.

Tanzey's breath was stolen and her insides felt warm and melting when she found the Indian of her fascination there, his midnight dark eyes momentarily locked with hers.

Again she saw something in his eyes besides a loathing. It was a look of wonder; a look that revealed to Tanzey that he most surely was as intrigued with her as she was with him.

Strangely not at all afraid now, but instead feeling self-conscious in his presence, actually wishing that she had taken more time with her choice of clothes today, Tanzey quickly reached up and yanked the hat from her head.

She watched the Comanche's eyes follow the path of her hair as it tumbled from its swirl atop her head and fluttered down across her shoulders. With only a slight shake of her head to encourage it to go farther, it tumbled on down until it rested in luscious red curls at her waist.

Rolling Thunder gazed at her hair, wanting to touch it, to run his fingers through the ringlets that seemed to be the reflection of the sun.

Then he looked into Tanzey's grass-green eyes again. He did not see defiance in them as he had the day prior.

Instead he saw a softness about her features that proved to him there was more to her than met the eyes.

Yes, he was intrigued and fascinated by her beauty. She was as beautiful as the stars in the sky at night.

But he had to remind himself that he had come today to watch for her, to see if she was brazen enough to come on his land again.

After thinking about this possibility the long night through, having not slept a wink, he had decided that if she did trespass again, he would be forced to take her captive. Anyone who made it their habit to come this close to his village this often might one day wander closer.

He could not allow this to happen. His people's lives were private. They most certainly were not to be interfered with!

Even his white eye friends from the nearby fort came only a certain distance to his village, then stopped and waited for his sentries to ride out to see what they wanted.

Except for one white man, Rolling Thunder's village was off-limits to all white eyes. He, who was at first a captive, now fit into Rolling Thunder's band of Comanche as though he were one with them.

He was now the father of the child that Rolling

Thunder's cousin was carrying inside her womb. The
white man was his beautiful cousin's husband!

His plans seeming to go awry, moment by moment, since he felt too much for this white lady that
he did not want to feel, that which was the exact
opposite of what he *should* feel, Rolling Thunder
yanked his horse's reins and walked on past Tanzey.

When he got to the watering hole, he led his horse
to stand beside the white woman's.

Then he turned once again, discovering that she
had turned and had watched him.

As his horse nuzzled the water, Rolling Thunder
stepped up to Tanzey.

Slowly, again, his eyes traveled over her.

She felt awkward beneath his close scrutiny, yet
she felt something more than that. With him so close
that she could almost feel the heat of his breath on
her face, her heart went crazy in its erratic beats!

She stared at him, in awe of the smoothness of his
copper skin. It was so beautiful. *He* was so beautiful!
She so badly wanted to run her fingers over the sin-
ews of his *shoulders.*

"Why do you so carelessly travel alone?" Rolling
Thunder asked, his jaw tight. "Why do you come on
land of the *Ner-mer-nuh,* of the Comanche?"

Tanzey flinched with the suddenness of him saying
something to her, when only moments ago she wondered if he ever would, and if he even knew enough
English *to* carry on a conversation with her.

This had to prove that he *was* from the band of
Comanche who had aligned themselves with the
Texas Rangers. If he was from a band of Comanche
who were at constant odds with the whites, she could
have been killed that very first time he had seen her.

Again she wondered if this Comanche might be
Chief Rolling Thunder . . . ?

Again she stared at him, then past him, at his white mustang, then into his mesmerizing eyes once again.

"I speak your language fluently enough," Rolling Thunder said, his eyes locked in silent battle with hers. "So why do you not answer me? Tell me why you so blatantly cross treaty lines?"

His gaze swept over her again, then he smiled slowly at her. "Where are your women's clothes?" he asked. "Are you ashamed of being a *mah-ocu-ah* . . . a woman?"

That did it. The last sarcastic remark about her appearance made her lift her chin haughtily, while deep inside herself, where her desires were formed, she regretted with all of her might for having worn these dreaded clothes today!

"I wear what I damn please," Tanzey snapped angrily. She placed her hands on her hips. "And I have you know, I am *very* proud to be a woman."

Her gaze moved slowly over him, her face growing hot with a blush when again she found his breechclout too skimpy.

As the breeze quickened and became strong enough to mold the breechclout against him, she was aware of him having been blessed by the gods where it mattered for a man to be well-endowed.

Seeing his bulge made her throat grow dry.

Her pulse strangely raced.

She looked quickly away, smiling awkwardly up at him when she realized that he had caught her reaction to his anatomy.

Oh, Lord, she had never been as embarrassed, she thought dishearteningly to herself. She did not want to venture a guess of what he might be thinking about her being so obviously stunned by his . . . by his . . .

Rolling Thunder's heart pounded inside his chest to know that she had eyed his manhood with such interest. And he could tell that she was quite taken with what she had seen. If she could feel the heat that being so near her had aroused in him, she might want to make a quick retreat.

He wished to reach out for her and hold her.

He wished to strip those ugly clothes from her body and clothe her with kisses!

And it was for certain that their mutual feelings for one another had changed his plans for today. He was so moved by her beauty and by her bravery to speak her mind in his presence, he just could not force captivity upon her.

Anyone as free and courageous as she should be allowed to remain free!

And he did not dare take her to his lodge, for he would be unable to hold back his feelings or his need for her there.

He would send her away today, and he would keep a watch out for her in the future, to make sure she did not go too far in her ventures on his land.

He could not take any chance of her discovering the white man at his village, who ironically resembled her identically.

Rolling Thunder gave Tanzey one last lingering look, then went to his horse, mounted, and rode away.

Tanzey was stunned that he would leave so abruptly, allowing her to go on her way again, unharmed. She could tell that he did not like intruders on his land.

She watched him until he rode out of sight, so careless and free, a king in the saddle, then hurriedly mounted her roan and began following him. She couldn't let this chance to find his village slip away again. She wouldn't be satisfied until she saw if her brother was there, although doubting it. If this Indian *was* Rolling Thunder, surely he was too much of a friend with whites to imprison them.

No, she had to be wrong ever to think that her brother might be at this Indian village. Why would he have been abducted, and she left free to roam at her will?

It saddened her, and brought the sting of tears to her eyes, to know that she would, in time, have to accept that her brother was dead. She *truly* doubted she could find her brother at the Comanche village. She realized that just perhaps she was following the handsome Indian for another reason . . . to see where *he* lived, and to see if he . . . had . . . a wife!

Tanzey became uneasy when she lost track of the Indian.

She looked guardedly from side to side.

She strained her neck to look into the distance where the land was flat and green with a sea of grass.

She saw him nowhere!

It was as though he had vanished from the face of the earth!

She moved cautiously onward until she entered an enchanting valley. She found herself surrounded on all sides by steep cliffs covered with cedar. Here and there were little groves of mesquite and groves of oaks. Through the center of this lovely setting flowed the crystal clear waters of a narrow stream that was alive with innumerable speckled trout.

Her breath caught in her throat when, in the distance, she saw an Indian village. It sat peacefully amid a thickly timbered grove, which broke the force of the north wind in the winter season and in the hot time of the year offered the village shade from the sun.

Tanzey drew a tight rein and slowed her horse down to a slow lope. She edged her steed closer to the trees on the one side of her, hoping that she would be lost from view in their shadows as she rode onward toward the village.

From a distance the Indian village was attractive. There were numerous dwellings, including tepees, all of which were covered with tanned buffalo hides.

Tanzey saw great herds of horses in large pens and corrals near the wider stretch of the stream at the far edge of the village. As in the white world, it was obvious that to the Indians, horses constituted wealth, for never had she seen so many in one place.

Not even on her stepfather's ranch, which was vast in comparison to most in this area.

Beyond the village and the grazing horses, scattered over the luxuriant surface of the valley, were antelope, deer, buffalo, and wild horses. Some were grazing, others were standing lazily in the shadows of the oaks. It took on the appearance of a paradise on earth. . . .

Tanzey's horse suddenly bucked and neighed. She yanked the reins sharply and steadied herself in her saddle.

Her head jerked to one side, and her eyes widened when Rolling Thunder rode free of the shadowed trees and blocked her path.

"*Hein-eim-mu-see-itc,*" Rolling Thunder insisted in a low hiss.

Seeing his anger and hearing it in his voice caused a cold fear to enter Tanzey's heart. She tried to pretend that she wasn't afraid of him. She forced courage into her voice.

"I can't understand you," she said, patting her horse, calming it. "You know English. Use it when you speak to me."

"Rolling Thunder asks what do you want here?" he said, his eyes flashing into hers. "I gave you the chance to leave our land. You still are here. And you even brazenly followed War Chief Rolling Thunder! You have forfeited your right to freedom!"

He motioned toward his village with the wave of a hand. "You wish to see how we 'savages' live?" he said sarcastically. "Well, now, *tosi-mah-ocu-ah*, white woman, you have the opportunity, for you will be there, my *captive*."

"Your . . . what . . . ?" she gasped, paling.

"I spoke English well enough, so why do you act as though you did not understand?" Rolling Thunder said mockingly. "*Mea-dro*, let us go now to my lodge."

He grabbed Tanzey's reins from her and looped them around one of his wrists.

He then, in a flash, grabbed her rifle from the gun boot at the side of her horse.

Before she could stop him, he yanked her pistol from its holster.

He gave her one last lingering stare, then wheeled his steed around. He yanked on her reins and rode away, her horse having no choice but to trail along behind his.

Tanzey no longer felt such an attraction, such an infatuation toward the Indian. In what seemed a blink of an eye, everything had changed. She could not deny being afraid.

Another thing that she knew for certain was his name! He was Rolling Thunder! He had referred to himself by that name!

Knowing this confused her. When people spoke of him, they had never said that he had *ever* taken white captives!

Why then did he now?

How could he see her as a threat to his people?

Her eyes wavered when something else came to her. If Rolling Thunder saw no harm in taking *her* captive, would he not also as easily have captured ... her ... brother?

Were this war chief's actions being guided by his thirst for vengeance?

If he had taken Brant captive, was he dead or alive?

A tremor coursed through her at the wonder of what her own final fate was to be.

Chapter Six

All that's best of dark and bright
Meets in her aspect and her eyes.

—LORD BYRON

Rolling Thunder led Tanzey's horse farther into the village.

Tanzey's spine stiffened as she became surrounded by Comanche men, women, and children as they pushed forward to get a glimpse of her. Some even touched her, as though in awe of her.

Afraid of being there, she could not help but shiver at their touch, flinching as though an electrical shock raced from their fingertips into her body.

She eluded their dark, questioning eyes, by focusing on anything but them.

She looked slowly around the village. Her heart raced at the thought of possibly seeing her brother in the shadows.

Of course, until *now* she had never truly been given reason to believe he was there.

It was just that she would not accept him being dead.

If he was an Indian captive, at least . . . he would be alive!

Not seeing anyone vaguely similar to her brother, Tanzey temporarily pushed the concern of his welfare from her mind. She had her own welfare to think about. She had to find a way to get through whatever was planned for her! She had no idea why she was *here*.

Swallowing hard and trying to get a different mind set, she looked farther than the village.

She watched the hundreds of browsing horses.

She gazed at the beautiful, waving seas of green grass.

She looked farther still at the distant mountains. The sun was slowly wiping the mountains clean of their bluish-purplish haze as it crept up from behind them.

Tanzey's attention was drawn back to what was happening around her. She looked guardedly from side to side when the crowd gave way and formed a passage through which she was taken.

She shifted her gaze again. At the end of the human passageway stood a lodge that Rolling Thunder seemed headed for. She surmised that was his lodge.

Her eyebrows forked when she noticed how a smaller tepee was erected so close to the larger one, as though it might be part *of* the lodge. She had to wonder to whom it belonged?

A wife . . . ?

A . . . child . . . ?

Before she moved to Texas, she had read enough books on various Indian tribes to know some of their customs. It was a known fact that it was the custom of the Comanche to have more than one wife if they wished, and that some wives did not share the husband's lodge.

Those who didn't, lived separately in smaller dwellings close to their husband's.

The children lived in these smaller lodges with their mother.

Those particular wives only entered the husband's lodge when they were summoned, or when they went there to clean or to cook.

It was strange, Tanzey thought to herself, how jealous she felt over thinking this smaller tepee snuggled close to the larger one might be Rolling Thunder's wife's lodge! She wanted to feel nothing but a loathing for this powerful war chief! He had *given* her cause to hate him! Why then couldn't she?

As though he knew she was thinking about him, Rolling Thunder glanced over his shoulder at Tanzey. His eyes wavered when he saw her uneasiness and how her fear had paled her color.

His heart sank at the thought of her being this afraid, when always before she had seemed so strong-willed, so *brave*.

Yet a part of him was glad to know that she had a vulnerable side. If she were thoroughly hard, he could never love her. He wanted a woman to have a soft, sweet side to her nature. When he held her, he wished for her to melt into his embrace, to cuddle close to him, to cling.

A woman who had no soft feelings was no woman at all.

Yes, he had to believe that this white woman was a lot of pretense! Her clothes were pretense, so why not her outward self?

He smiled while thinking about this woman's softer side. She would yield soon to his kisses. He would bring out all of the softness and sweetness that lay hidden beneath that stark, ugly exterior of man's clothes!

For certain he had not wanted to bring such fear into her life.

He had not wanted to be forced to bring her to his village as a *captive*.

Through his reign as war chief, and even earlier, when he was a young warrior and held a deep grudge toward the white eyes because of their intrusion on land that once only belonged to the red man, he had never brought a captive to his village, much less his private *lodge*.

But this woman had forced his hand.

And, yes, she would be a part of his lodge. He would have it no other way.

She would not be taken by another man from his lodge.

He, himself, wished to unlock the mysteries about her . . . why she wore men's clothing, why she stubbornly returned to the land of the Comanche more than once, and why she looked so much like the white man captive of his cousin!

It did not seem possible that two white eyes could have the same flaming hair and not be related.

Yet the man who was now called Brant Fire In The Sky had not spoken of a sister.

But surely he had eluded the subject for fear of her being taken captive herself.

Still, though, he knew that Brant Fire In The Sky's reason for having been taken was a unique one, in that he had been sought out by a Comanche princess, not by warriors who were antagonistic toward whites.

But even then the white man had not spoken of a sister, not even his family. It was as though he had been an island in himself, alone in the world, until he had married Feather Moon.

The true test would come soon when he realized

that a woman fitting his description was now a captive.

He smiled at the thought of how interesting it would be to see Brant Fire In The Sky's reaction to the flaming-haired woman!

Brant Fire In The Sky's heart beat like claps of thunder as he gazed from the entranceway of his tepee at his sister being escorted through the village by Rolling Thunder.

Angry to see that his sister had no choice and was surely a captive, Brant started to stamp from the lodge. He would demand her release.

But a soft hand on his wrist stopped him.

He dropped the buffalo hide flap, and turned to face his wife.

He saw a soft pleading in her midnight-black eyes.

He felt the trembling of her fingers as she lifted a hand and slowly traced his facial features.

"Do not go and interfere in what Rolling Thunder has done this morning," Feather Moon softly pleaded. "*Toquet*, it is all right. Rolling Thunder would never harm the woman."

"The woman is my *sister*," Brant Fire In The Sky said, gently taking her hand from his face. "*Ob-be-mah-e-wah*, get out of the way, my wife. I cannot stand by and watch my sister mistreated."

"She . . . is . . . your sister?" Feather Moon gasped.

"My twin," Brant Fire In The Sky said, turning again to look from the lodge. "We are part of each other's lives as though we are one heartbeat. I must go and see why she has been brought here. Your people should have allowed me to send word long ago that I was all right."

He started to leave, but Feather Moon stepped around him and blocked his way. "*Nei-com-mar-pe-*

ein, I love you," she murmured. She placed a hand over the small swell of her stomach. "I love *peta*, my child . . . *our* child. Do not do anything foolish that you will regret later."

Brant Fire In The Sky sighed heavily as he thought of their child and how proud he was to be Feather Moon's husband. Never had he seen anything as beautiful as Feather Moon, or as delicately sweet.

Today she was dressed in a bright calico short gown, beautifully embroidered. Her knee-high moccasins were dyed red, a blue broadcloth skirt reaching out beneath the gown.

Her copper face was angelic in expression.

Her hair flowed almost to the ground.

He drew Feather Moon into his arms. "You know how much I love you, and how happy I am that we will soon be parents of a child," he said thickly. "But, my sweet, pregnant *mah-tao-yo*, little one, you must understand that I also love my sister. I must see why she has been brought here."

"You now know Rolling Thunder well, do you not?" Feather Moon murmured, clinging to him to still block the entranceway.

"*Huh*, yes, until *today* I thought I had grown to know him well," Brant Fire In The Sky said, easing her from his arms. He framed her face between his hands, feeling the silken texture of her skin against the calloused palms of his hands. "But now? I think not. My sister should not be here unless she was allowed to ride in on her own, of her own free will. But did you not see? Your cousin held her reins. She was being led into the village as only a captive would be brought here!"

"Rolling Thunder must have been given cause to take her captive," Feather Moon said softly. "Somehow she must have become a threat. I beg you to

trust Rolling Thunder's decision as to why he
brought your sister here. His reasons must be valid.
He never does anything without first thinking
through his options. Trust him, Brant Fire In The
Sky."

"My sister Tanzey couldn't have done anything
bad enough to warrant being brought here as a captive," Brant Fire In The Sky grumbled. "Sure, she's a
feisty, daring young lady. But she would do nothing
foolish enough to get herself taken captive."

"She must have, or she would not have been
brought here," Feather Moon said. "Be patient, Brant
Fire In The Sky. Let us see what happens now. *Please*
do nothing to threaten your stability among my people who are now yours. You are trusted by my people. Are you not now allowed to use your white man
name Brant along with your Indian name? Are you
not allowed to wander through the village? Do you
not now own and carry a knife? Have you not been
promised that soon you would even be trusted
enough to go hunting with the warriors? Are you
not happy with me, your *wife*? Have you not been
christened by my people as *Chemakachos*, the good
white man?"

Loving Feather Moon so deeply, Brant Fire In The
Sky listened to her, yet his mind wandered back to
the day that he was captured while boar hunting.
Princess Feather Moon had led the capture. She had
told him that she had been watching him for days,
falling more in love with him each time she saw him.
Her chieftain cousin had given her his blessing to
take what she wanted in life, even a white man captive for a husband.

Brant Fire In The Sky had at first hated Feather
Moon. He had seen her as calculating and nothing
less than spoiled.

But it had not taken long for him to see her true side.

She was gentle and sweet.

She was an armful of softness when she had come to him that first night, unclothed!

He had not been able to turn her away when she had given herself to him sexually.

He had that quickly become lost, heart and soul, to the Comanche maiden.

That had been six months ago.

Because of loving her so much, he had not fought his captivity.

Because of loving Feather Moon so much, he had turned his back on his past life!

He wanted her and would do anything to keep her as his own!

And he had adapted well to the Comanche life.

His only regret was not being able to tell his family that he was alive, and well.

But he had made his choice and was living with it.

He had another family now.

He had a wife.

He would soon have a child.

They came first in his life now.

And as long as he knew his other family was all right, he did not feel guilty for having placed them second in his life.

"Brant Fire In The Sky, you look at me strangely and you do not answer things that I asked you," Feather Moon blurted, hurt heavy in her voice. "Do you regret being here with me? Do you not truly love me after all? Has it always been too much for me to hope for?"

"Aw, Feather Moon," Brant Fire In The Sky said, drawing her gently into his arms. "I could never regret being with you. My heart. *Ein-mah-heepicut*, it is yours. *Nei-com-mar-pe-ein*, I love you."

"You make me so happy," Feather Moon whispered as she lay her cheek against his chest. "And, my husband, I promise not to let harm come to your sister. In time, when the time is right, when my chieftain cousin will allow it, you will be with your sister and talk with her."

That was enough for Brant Fire In The Sky to accept what was happening. So taken by this woman who was now his wife, he knew that he would do anything to stay with her, to have those moments at night with her that were privately theirs.

And the child!

He was so eager to have the child as a part of their lives.

Tanzey tried to pull away when Rolling Thunder placed his hands to her waist, to lift her from her saddle. "Don't touch me," she hissed, her eyes flashing into his. "I can dismount without your help."

Rolling Thunder ignored her. He could not look little in front of his people by allowing her to speak to him in such a disrespectful fashion. He sank his fingers into her flesh, and as she struggled and pounded his chest with her fists, he yanked her from the horse.

He did not bother placing her to her feet. As though she were no heavier than a sack of flour, he threw her over his shoulder and carried her into his lodge.

Her face flushed hot with anger, Tanzey gave Rolling Thunder one last blow on his shoulder, then gasped when he released her suddenly, causing her to fall awkwardly to the floor.

The stuffed bulrush mats cushioned her fall, yet

she still could not help but wince as she leaned up on an elbow, her free hand rubbing her sore backside.

"And so now you have proved you are not only an abductor, but also stronger than me," Tanzey said. She gazed angrily up at him as he stood glaring over her. "What can I expect from you next?"

When he didn't respond, she rose slowly to her feet. "I have always been told that your band of Comanche don't bother white eyes if they are not bothering you," she said guardedly. "I did no wrong except cross the treaty line and ... and ... down a wild mustang. Nothing more. Surely you will not keep me imprisoned for such a small mistake on my part."

Still he did not respond to her.

He was not ready to converse with her about anything.

He still had much to think over, mainly—what was he going to do with her now that he had her?

"Do you have other captives in your village?" she asked, giving the entrance flap a quick glance.

Then she turned to him. "Do you possibly have a male captive in your village, a man whose hair coloring matches mine?" she said.

Her heart skipped a beat when she thought she saw movement in the back of his eyes at the mention of the man whose hair was her same color.

Did that mean that he knew who she was talking about?

Could Brant truly be here, only footsteps away ... ?

Rolling Thunder gazed at Tanzey a moment longer, then turned and walked toward the entranceway.

Tanzey watched him leave in his easy, elastic gait. It was as though he were shod with velvet springs.

He had such grace and dignity!

Yet to her he was now nothing less than a heartless savage, someone who surely would take more captives than one.

Oh, just perhaps her brother *was* here!

But would she even be given the chance to find out?

She had no idea what this Indian's plans were for her.

She eyed the entrance flap. Her heart beat erratically with the thought of possibly slipping out long enough to take a quick look through the village for her brother.

And she also recalled the smaller lodge just outside of this one. She was curious to see whose. Did he have a wife who had no choice but to sit by and watch him take another woman into his lodge, a white woman at that . . . ?

"I so badly want to see . . ." she whispered to herself. "Dare . . . I . . . ?"

Chapter Seven

Just as tho' the ordinary
Daily things I do,
Wait with me, expectant,
For a word from you.

—DAVID CORY

Tanzey chose not to try and leave the tepee, not yet anyhow. Rolling Thunder would not be careless enough to leave her there, unguarded.

Her shoulders tense, and scarcely breathing, Tanzey looked guardedly around her.

Her knees somewhat trembling, she edged closer to the fire pit in which lay cold gray ashes.

She glanced down at the bulrush mats that covered the floor, then at a larger, plush cushion and inched her way toward it.

Watching the entrance flap, she eased down on the cushion.

Her pulse seemed scarcely to beat as she waited for Rolling Thunder's return.

She could hardly believe that he had brought her to his lodge and then left so abruptly.

But she did not expect him to be gone for long.

And when he returned, what then?

What did he have planned for her?

She could hardly believe that she was a captive!

How could she have let this happen?

Why had she been so foolhardy and careless in her behavior?

She had never truly believed that she was in danger. She was now twenty, and she had done as she pleased whenever she pleased since she was old enough to ride a horse and to shoot a firearm.

While in Kansas, there weren't many Indians to put fear into her heart.

But there had been plenty of black-hearted outlaws roaming the land, wreaking their havoc in one way or another.

Even *they* had never given her cause to fear them!

"So now, how has it happened that I have allowed myself to become a captive of an *Indian*?" she whispered to herself.

She folded her arms stubbornly and glared at the entrance flap.

She would escape at her first opportunity.

She would ride straight to Fort Phantom Hill and let them know that they wrongly trusted the Comanche war chief who had aligned himself with the Texas Rangers! He had probably only done so as a ploy, so that from then on they would see him as a friend, an ally, someone they could trust, while all along, he wreaked havoc along the countryside as others got blamed.

Once she was at Fort Phantom Hill, Tanzey would chide Colonel Franks for being wrong to trust *any* redskin savage!

Sighing, realizing that thinking such angry things and being so overwhelmed with feelings of anger was not going to get her anywhere. It only exhausted her. And she needed her full strength to stand up against Rolling Thunder when he arrived back at his lodge.

She could not allow him to best her again!

She waited and watched for what seemed forever.

She lay a hand over her stomach when it growled.

She wished now that she had taken the time to eat before leaving her house. If Rolling Thunder truly wanted to find a way to punish her, starving her to death would work.

She loved food.

Again her stomach growled. She tried not to think of what she *could* have had for breakfast had she not been so foolish to leave before the cook had started preparing the morning meal in the kitchen.

But how could she forget how wonderful bacon, sausage, eggs, and milk gravy, spread in thick gobs over biscuits, would taste when the hunger pangs in her stomach were almost unbearable?

"I . . . must . . . stop thinking of food!" she whispered to herself. "There are more important things to worry about besides *food*!"

She squirmed on the cushion.

She heaved a deep sigh.

And still she waited.

To pass the time, Tanzey looked around her, at the way the Indian lived.

A shield hung on a rack by the entrance way.

The inside of the tepee was painted with stripes of geometric designs.

A bed, made crudely from wood, was at the far back of the large tepee, directly opposite the entrance, in the place of honor. It was raised off the ground about four to six inches.

Robes made from bear pelts were spread over the bed, to form the cover and bedding.

Beneath the bed was a space used for storage.

Several pillows lay on the west side of the bed, made from the skins of smaller animals. Tanzey surmised they were surely stuffed with grass or straw.

Parfleche bags hung from the rafters. Tanzey had to believe that food was stored in them.

Elsewhere, along the floor and next to the sides of the tent, were ornaments, bowls, dishes, and Rolling Thunder's personal belongings.

A green pouch of water hung from a pole on the opposite side of the entrance flap from where the shield hung. The entrance flap was made from a pelt, fastened at the top.

There were no visible firearms. Tanzey assumed Rolling Thunder kept them hidden.

Her gaze fell on a chest that was partially hidden beneath a blanket. She eyed it for a moment, then crawled over and scooted the blanket aside.

Having seen these types of wicker chests in the open-air markets in Mexico, she studied it. There was no lock on it. All she had to do was raise the lid and see what was inside it.

Thus far, she saw nothing out of the ordinary about this tepee. It was like the ones she had seen in books about Indians. But this *chest* seemed misplaced, as though it didn't belong.

Slowly she reached a hand to the lid of the trunk, then drew it back again when she heard someone just outside the tent, talking.

When the conversation was over and silence ensued, again Tanzey focused on the chest.

Her heart beat soundly as she placed a hand on the lid and slowly opened it.

"Books?" she said aloud.

Her eyebrows raised in surprise as she stared down at the many volumes of books that filled the chest to the top. "Can . . . he . . . read? Or . . . did . . . he steal these?"

She sat down beside the trunk.

She lifted one of the books and spread it open on her lap.

When she found a signature at the top of the inside cover, which most certainly wasn't the Indian's, she could not help but assume that these books were a part of this war chief's plunder while raiding the white settlements.

"He *is* a savage!" Tanzey said, bitterness thick in her voice. "He had to have killed someone to have these in his possession."

When she heard someone entering the tepee behind her, Tanzey jumped to her feet with a start.

She quickly closed the book, placed it back inside the chest, and closed the lid.

She then turned slowly around, expecting Rolling Thunder to be there, glowering at her for snooping and discovering ugly things about him.

She gasped with surprise when she didn't find Rolling Thunder there, but, instead a lovely white woman. The woman was dressed in a floor-length, fringed buckskin dress. Her blond hair was drawn back from her face and lay in a long braid down her back.

More than one beautiful, long, thin shell earring hung from each ear, her ears having been pierced in three or four places.

She was a shapely lady, her large breasts straining against the inside bodice of the dress.

And she had the loveliest eyes the deepest color of violet.

As the woman stood there, staring back at Tanzey, she held out a large wooden tray of food.

Tanzey's heart skipped a beat when she recalled

the smaller tent outside. She paled when she thought of whose it might be.

This white woman's!

Surely she had been brought to this village as a captive!

Surely she now belonged to Rolling Thunder!

Had he even taken her as . . . his . . . wife?

Her violet eyes never leaving Tanzey, the woman stepped farther into the lodge, then eased the platter of food down onto the floor beside the fire pit.

"Who are you?" Tanzey asked, inching her way toward the woman. She tried not to focus on the abundance of food piled high on the platter, her hunger so bad now, she felt dizzy. "Why . . . are . . . you in the Indian village?"

Her gaze swept over the woman again; then she again looked into her luscious violet eyes. "What is your name?" she prodded.

When the woman didn't respond and just stood there staring back at her, Tanzey lost her patience. She went to her and grabbed her by a wrist. "Tell me who you are?" she demanded. "Why are you in the village? Are you . . . ?"

Before she asked the woman if the was Rolling Thunder's wife, she realized she was squeezing the woman's wrist too hard, for the woman flinched and tried to get it free.

"Oh, I'm sorry," Tanzey said, dropping her hand to her side. "I didn't mean to . . ."

Before Tanzey could say anything else, the woman turned and ran from the tepee.

Tanzey stared blankly at the closed flap, puzzled, stunned, and knowing no more now than she did before. She had to assume that either the woman was a deaf mute, or she couldn't speak because she had been traumatized.

Tanzey's heart sank when she could not help but think the latter. Surely the woman had been traumatized speechless when she had been taken captive by Rolling Thunder!

A child cried from somewhere close by. Then she realized that the baby's crying came from the small tepee just outside.

"No," she gasped at the thought of the child being the white woman's and Rolling Thunder's!

No matter how much Tanzey tried to hate the Comanche war chief, there was no denying that she was still infatuated with him. Discovering the white woman, who was definitely a part of his life, and now also a *baby*, sent splashes of jealousy through her heart.

She pressed her lips stubbornly together. She had to see for herself if the child was the white woman's. She ran to the entrance flap and smoothed it aside just in time to see the woman step from the small lodge next door.

Pains of regret shot through Tanzey when she discovered a child in the arms of the woman. The child was bundled in a blanket, making it impossible for her to see if it was a boy or girl, or whether its skin was white or copper.

But it was for certain that the child belonged to the woman. The way she held the baby so close, rocking it in her arms as she slowly paced back and forth to comfort the baby, made Tanzey know that she had to be the child's mother.

She watched the woman pace back and forth until the baby stopped crying.

She watched the woman tiptoe back inside the smaller lodge with the baby.

So badly wanting to try and talk with the woman again, Tanzey started to leave the tepee.

She gasped with alarm when a powerful arm was suddenly there, blocking her way.

Eyes wide, she gazed up at a huge Comanche warrior as he glared down at her.

Knowing that the warrior had been ordered to guard her, Tanzey went back inside the tepee and sat down beside the large platter of food.

Hungrily, she grabbed a piece of meat and quickly ate it.

She ate various cooked vegetables, and then enjoyed some fruit of the yucca plant, finding it sweet and satisfying. It helped wash the greasy taste of the other food down her throat.

After she was comfortably full, Tanzey turned and gazed at the trunk again, remembering the books and the signature she had found.

Could they be the white woman's?

Was her lodge too small to keep the trunk there?

Or did they belong to someone else, a prize taken after a raid on a white settlement?

All of these things that Rolling Thunder was possibly guilty of made Tanzey ache. She so badly wanted to believe that Rolling Thunder could not be guilty of any wrongdoing, yet he had taken her captive, hadn't he?

Rolling Thunder came into the lodge. He stopped and stared down at Tanzey, glanced over at the platter of food, then looked at her again.

"And so you have eaten?" he said.

He knelt down beside her and picked up a piece of meat on a small roasting stick. He bit into the meat, yanked it from the stick, then chewed it as he lay the stick aside.

"Why do you care whether or not I eat?" Tanzey said, frowning at him. "I'm surprised that you even had food brought to me. Why did you? So I would be strong for whatever else you have in store for me?"

"And what do you think that might be?" Rolling Thunder asked, his eyes twinkling into hers.

"I have no idea what to expect next," Tanzey said, sighing. "When I woke up this morning, I did not expect that would be my last time in my own bed, in my own room. I would have never expected to be harmed by you, an Indian who is trusted by the whites."

"When you chose to go against treaties, you should have then known the chances you were taking," Rolling Thunder said, his voice low and measured. "Treaties are made for a purpose. They are to keep white people off Indian land, and Indians within their own boundaries. I see to it that my people stay where they belong. It is expected of you also to stay on land that is *yours*."

He leaned his face closer to hers. "Why did you travel onto land of the *Ner-mer-nuh*, Comanche?" he asked dryly. "Surely it was not only to get yourself a wild mustang. They ride on your land as wild, and as plentiful. So what else brought you here?"

"You know why," Tanzey said, her heart pounding. "I am not the only captive. I know of the white woman. So surely there is also a white man being help captive. My *brother*. My *twin*."

Rolling Thunder's eyes narrowed. He ignored her reference to her brother. Now that he knew that Brant Fire In The Sky *was* her brother, he would avoid talk of him now, at all cost. In time she would understand why her brother was there. Not so much because he had been brought there as a captive, but now, because he did not want to leave and be a part of that other world that he had known before having met his Comanche princess wife.

It was her mention of a white woman that puzzled Rolling Thunder. "Did you say something about a woman captive?" he asked, arching an eyebrow. "What woman? What captive?"

"Please spare me your acting skills at playing dumb over the woman being here," Tanzey said, laughing sarcastically.

She nodded toward the trunk of books. "And where did you get your collection of books?" she chided. "From some poor suspecting soul you murdered in order to have them?"

She leaned her face closer to his. "Which person did you kill to get the books?" she hissed. "Which cabin did you burn?"

She leaned away from him when she saw how his eyes were suddenly sparked with anger, yet she spoke relentlessly onward. "Do you make it a game to steal white women, rape them, then keep their children to raise as savage warriors?" she challenged. "The white woman who brought me the food? The woman has been traumatized speechless! Don't you feel ashamed for having caused this? Don't you feel ashamed to be using her as a slave? And the poor child! Pity the child if it *is* yours. The child will be branded a 'breed' for the rest of its life. It will be laughed at . . . scorned . . ."

"*Suvate*, enough!" Rolling Thunder suddenly bellowed in a voice more powerful than Tanzey had ever heard before.

She swallowed hard.

Her insides recoiled with a sudden, renewed fear. She took a slow step away from him.

"You not only ride like a foolish person onto land that is not yours," Rolling Thunder hissed, "but you are foolish enough to speak in such a way to Rolling Thunder, and even more foolish to wrongly accuse him of such things. Stay quiet, *tosi-mah-ocu-ah,* white woman, or be sorry for having such a loose tongue in the presence of this powerful Comanche war chief!"

Tanzey sucked nervously on her lower lip as she watched what his next move might be.

She took another slow step away from him when he stood his ground, glaring at her.

Rolling Thunder could hardly contain his anger. It was intense for having been accused of such horrendous acts—the books, the white woman, the *child,* especially since he had always worked *with* the white pony soldiers instead of being a marauding renegade.

And the only reason he had brought this flaming-haired, spiteful-tongued woman to his lodge today was because he feared that she would bring trouble to his people!

Thus far, the only person he had brought trouble to was himself!

But, *ka,* no, he reminded himself—he had not only brought her there in an effort to protect his people, but to have her for himself. Because she had trespassed on Comanche soil and because she was following him as he rode toward his village, she had given him a valid excuse *to* abduct her.

Now she was his, and he would not allow her bitter words to change things. In time she would discover just how wrong she was about so many things.

Then she would stop fighting her feelings for him.

She would accept what fate had brought into their lives.

She would cherish it.

And when there were babies born to him, they would be *hers,* no one else's!

Emitting a low growl from the depths of his throat,

Rolling Thunder took a quick, bold step toward Tanzey. Angrily, he grabbed her and kissed her.

Then he released her and stormed away, leaving her head reeling with a passion she did not want to feel.

"Lord, what is happening to me?" she whispered, her heart pounding so hard she felt the pulse beat in her ears.

She touched her lips delicately with the tips of her fingers. Her lips still throbbed from his kiss.

She ran her tongue over the bottom lip. She still tasted him there.

Trembling from the newness of such passion, and troubled over who had aroused these wonderfully blissful feelings inside her, Tanzey crumpled down onto a sleeping pallet of soft rabbit and elk skins.

Amid the fragrance of sage and cedar, she coiled up into a fetal position. She stared up through the smoke hole in the ceiling.

The sky was darkening.

She could hear the distant sound of drums.

She could feel the soft breeze of evening blowing across her face as the unsecured entrance flap fluttered in the wind.

She felt a strange mellowness come over her.

And as she recalled the kiss *and* its passion . . . she could not help but sigh and close her eyes to relive it.

And then she heard the baby from the close-by tepee begin to cry again.

Tanzey was that quickly catapulted back to reality.

She sat up and glared around her. How had she, only because of the wonders of a kiss, forgotten where she was, and *why*?

"It won't happen again," she whispered harshly to herself. "He'd best not even try!"

Chapter Eight

Love me for love's sake, that evermore
Thou may'st love on,
Through love's eternity.
                    —ELIZABETH BARRETT BROWNING

A full night had passed, and it was well into the next day. Outside, in front of the door of the smaller tepee, two logs lay side by side. Between them fire had been kindled. Long sides of venison had been attached to the end of a thick stick, by which the meat was held over the fire.

Tanzey dreaded having to eat it. She would never forget how it had looked when it had been placed there earlier by the white woman. She had peeked outside as the woman had fit the meat on the spit for cooking. Raw, red, and fresh from a kill, the meat resembled a drooping bloodred flag as it hung over the blaze of the fire.

Her boots and socks removed, Tanzey sat beside the cold ashes of the fire pit. Staring into space, her thoughts were deep and troubled. She was frustrated from having been totally ignored by the Comanche chief. Since her abduction, he had only been in the tepee with her for a short time.

He had not even slept in the lodge.

Yet when he had carried his bedroll outside, she had felt relieved that he had chosen to sleep elsewhere. After the heat of his kiss, the passion of it, she had feared what night might bring.

Although she could not deny how his kiss had affected her, that she now felt more alive than ever before in her life, she had feared going farther with her feelings.

How could she forget the white woman and child?

What could he have done to render the woman speechless?

He had surely forced himself on her sexually.

Had he at knifepoint?

Had he ravaged her with hopes of purposely hurting her as he took what he lusted after?

Had he raped her more than once, over and over again?

Had he enjoyed her fear? Her pain? Her humiliation?

Had . . . he . . . abducted her dear brother?

Tanzey forced such thoughts from her mind. They were too unbearable to think about. Surely her imagination was running wild because of her inability to get out of this situation.

Nervously she ran her fingers through her hair, trying to untangle the witch's knots that had been created through her night of restless sleep.

She stiffened when she gazed down at her soiled, wrinkled buckskin attire.

She could even smell the perspiration that had dried on it.

Oh, surely she was not only a sight, but a stinking mess, as well.

Not wanting to even think about how she looked or smelled, hungering so for one of those wonderful,

warm baths filled with fragranced bubbles that her
mother had introduced her to, she could not stop her
thoughts from straying back to the white woman and
how she must have reacted to Rolling Thunder's
lovemaking.

Tanzey found it hard to understand how anyone
could find being with him so distasteful as to lose
one's speech.

No matter how hard Tanzey tried, she couldn't
imagine being appalled by Rolling Thunder's lovemaking, hating it so much *she* would become unable
to speak.

The man did not seem capable of rape. If so, surely
he would have not left the lodge last night.

Surely he would have forced himself on her if it
was his habit to do such things with women.

Even the thought of being held within his powerful
arms made her knees grow weak with desire.

Closing her eyes and recalling his kiss made her
shoulders sway in a soft swoon!

No! Surely the woman had not been afflicted in a
terrible way by this Indian war chief. Surely . . . it . . .
had to be something else that had taken her ability to
speak away.

She rose quickly to her feet when she heard a noise
behind her.

Stiff and not knowing what to expect next, Tanzey
turned on a heel and emitted a soft sigh of relief
when she found it was only the woman.

The meat that the woman had placed on the spit
over the fire earlier had cooked, for it now lay in
large heaps on a tray.

The woman sat the tray on the floor and turned to
walk away, but Tanzey was too quick for her. She
rushed to her and grabbed her by a wrist.

When the woman spun around and gazed at Tanzey with a soft, quiet pleading in her eyes, Tanzey recalled the other time she had hurt the woman's wrist.

Tanzey dropped her hand to her side, yet walked to the entranceway and blocked it so that the woman could not leave just yet.

"Please help me," Tanzey murmured. "Isn't there something you can do to help me escape?"

The woman's response was only to stare at Tanzey.

"Can't you understand what I'm saying?" Tanzey asked. "Or do you just not want to respond to what I say?"

Still, the woman did not respond.

"Where is Rolling Thunder?" Tanzey persisted, hoping that if she continued plying the woman with questions, she would be forced to react in some way.

"Are there other captives in this village?" Tanzey asked, watching the woman closely for her reaction to *this* particular question.

There was no more response with that question than with the others. The woman just stood there, a blank look on her face.

"I want to take a bath," Tanzey said. "When will I be allowed to take a bath? Do you think you might loan me one of your dresses? I smell like a skunk, don't you think?"

The woman finally reacted to something, to Tanzey's reference of smelling like a "skunk." She smiled.

That gave Tanzey hope.

That meant that the woman could hear.

She just couldn't speak.

The woman's smile faded. She looked sympathetically at Tanzey, gently touched her face, then slipped on past her and left the tepee.

Tanzey turned and stared at the entrance flap that

was still swaying from the woman's passage through it. She was puzzled even more now about the woman, in that she could hear but not *speak*.

Then she suddenly paled when a thought came to her that caused a spiral of fear to sweep through her. She clasped a hand over her mouth to stifle a gasp when she recalled reading in books how some Indian captives' tongues were removed.

She shuddered to think that this was why this woman couldn't speak!

"But surely not," Tanzey whispered, lowering her hand to her side. She truly didn't think that Rolling Thunder seemed the sort to resort to such inhumane behavior!

Yet just how much *did* she know about him?

Sighing heavily, Tanzey started to sit down to eat, but the very sight of the food made her feel sick to her stomach. She couldn't get the white woman off her mind!

Again an uncontrollable shiver raced across her flesh. If Rolling Thunder was capable of such devious acts against *that* white woman, then might he be as devious to her?

If so, then she had best try and not give him anymore reason to treat her as viciously. From here on she must be more careful with what she said to him, and *how* she said it.

For certain it was best for her not to speak so hatefully to the Indian captor again, or else he might rid her of *her* vindictive tongue, to quiet *her*.

Tanzey jumped with alarm when she heard someone shouting her name just outside the entrance flap.

Rolling Thunder!

He was calling for her to come outside!

Wild-eyed, Tanzey stared at the entrance flap. For the first time since her abduction, she was so afraid of Rolling Thunder and what he might have planned for her that she felt ill. Just now, the way he shouted her name, so angrily, his voice filled with such venom, was enough to turn her insides to stone!

When he shouted her name again, Tanzey knew that she had no choice but to go outside and see what he wanted with her. For certain the guard would not stop her exit this time. Yet she was no less a captive than before, perhaps even more so!

Her heart pounded erratically as she moved in slow steps toward the entrance flap. Her fingers trembled as she shoved the flap aside and peered outside.

She found herself staring into the face of the sun, its brilliance causing a sort of ragged halo around Rolling Thunder as he sat on his horse, staring down at her.

Shielding her eyes, Tanzey was able to see Rolling Thunder more clearly. But just as she focused on him, he dismounted from his horse and grabbed a deer carcass from a travois that was attached behind his horse and threw it at her feet, leaving one more carcass on the travois.

She took a quick step away from the deer that lay at her feet. She eyed it questionably, and then Rolling Thunder.

"Do you see the deer carcass?" Rolling Thunder said sourly. "It is the woman's place to dress and cook the meat for her man. You are mine. You share my lodge. You must prepare this meat *for* our lodge."

He smiled slyly down at her. His anger at her, over her thinking that he was heartless rapist savage, and her accusation of him having stolen the chest of books from settlers he had slain, had made him decide to show her how a true captive was treated.

Beginning today, for several days, he would be relentless in making her do labor *of* a captive!

Then she would have true cause to complain!

Only when she apologized for having accused him of things he had never been guilty of would he show her the other side of how it would be to share a lodge with him.

He looked forward to the day when he could hold her and cherish her.

He looked forward to the day when she would want him to!

Forgetting how only moments ago she had decided to tame her tongue while in his presence, Tanzey stubbornly placed her hands on her hips and defied him with a glare. "I'll have you know I am not your woman, and I will *not* clean *or* cook the deer for you," she said in a low, measured hiss.

Rolling Thunder's midnight dark eyes narrowed. "You refuse?" he said, his jaw tight. He smiled smugly down at her. "Then, you will go without food!"

"There is food already waiting for me in the tepee," Tanzey said, laughing beneath her breath.

Then she paled when he slid quickly from the saddle, grabbed her by the wrist, and half dragged her inside the lodge.

He released her wrist and bent low over the tray of food. He lifted it, smiled devilishly at her, then went to the entranceway and tossed the food outside onto the ground.

He turned to her. "Now you have no food, do you?" he said. He reached a hand out and ran a finger along the curve of her jaw.

She slapped his hand away.

"Now I know why the word Comanche means 'snake' to so many!" she said angrily. "You are a snake. Do you hear me? A low-down, slithering, spineless snake!"

Rolling Thunder's eyes gleamed as he slipped both of his muscled arms around her waist and yanked her close to him. "A snake, you say?" he said in a harsh whisper.

His eyes were in a silent battle with hers as she glared up at him.

Tanzey tried to pull free of his grip, but his fingers were like steel bands around her waist.

Her breath was stolen away when he slipped one of his hands up and twined his fingers through her hair, then shoved her lips against his in a fiery, frenzied kiss.

The power of the kiss, the rapture it evoked within Tanzey, made her forget everything but the thrill of being in his powerful arms again.

But it was too short-lived.

He jerked himself away from her.

He stared down at her, his expression no less angry, then left the lodge without another word.

Tanzey was too stunned to move. Again his kiss and embrace had overwhelmed all of her other feelings that she knew she *should* feel for him, for he was her enemy! Her captor!

But she was slowly becoming powerless. Her needs, her desires, were taking over her mind, her very *soul*. While she should be hating and dreading Rolling Thunder, she instead wanted him!

She hungered for his arms. For his *kiss*!

Even though she tried to feel hate for him, each kiss, each embrace, taught her more and more how it felt to be a woman in love with a man!

"I am so confused!" she cried, frustratingly raking her fingers through her hair. "Oh, what am I to do?"

Only moments later, a lovely, pregnant Indian

maiden came into the lodge. Rolling Thunder came in after her and stood at her side. "Feather Moon will teach you how to prepare the deer for food and clothing," Rolling Thunder said, his gaze locked with Tanzey's. He frowned down at her. "You are in my lodge, yet you have not spoken your name to me."

"You never asked what it was," Tanzey said, focusing her attention on Feather Moon. She raked her eyes slowly over Feather Moon. Her gaze fell on the tiny ball of her abdomen that revealed her pregnancy. She could not deny how seeing this pregnant woman affected her! She was so jealous she wanted to scream at the woman! Tell her to get out of her sight!

Instead she forced herself to stay calm, to keep her tumultuous feelings at bay.

She forced a mischievous smile up at Rolling Thunder. "But why should you ask my name?" she chided. "Why do you even bother with me? You have enough women at your beck and call. One woman has given birth to your child, while this other one is, would you say, five months into her pregnancy with another one of your children? You keep busy, Rolling Thunder. I don't see why you needed to add *me* to your harem."

Feather Moon stepped closer to Tanzey. "You speak out of turn to my chief," she said, lifting her chin haughtily. She did not feel it was her place to clear up the misconception that she was Rolling Thunder's wife. He would tell the white woman when he felt it was important for her to know. "You should not show such disrespect to the war chief of our people! It is not wise, *tosi-mah-ocu-ah*, white woman, especially when you are his captive!"

Tanzey gave Feather Moon a silent stare filled with loathing. But she kept her silence. She had already said too much.

Feather Moon slid a hand over the slight mound of her abdomen. She smiled smugly at Tanzey, thinking how shocked, perhaps even abhorred she would be, if she knew exactly *whose* child she was carrying. Tanzey's very own brother's!

"I think it best that you just do as Rolling Thunder says and forget battling verbally with him, *or* me," Feather Moon softly advised. "Your name. He ... asks ... your *name*." Of course Feather Moon knew Tanzey's name. Brant Fire In The Sky had spoken it often enough in her presence!

But Feather Moon could not let on that she knew, or she would give away the secret that this woman's brother was only a few footsteps away. Tanzey's knowledge about Brant Fire In The Sky had to come later ... after she proved that she would be civil to Rolling Thunder and would willingly become his wife!

"*Mah-tao-yo*, little one, I can speak for myself," Rolling Thunder said, giving Feather Moon a gentle hug. "But I thank you for caring enough to do so."

"My cousin," Feather Moon whispered, so that Tanzey could not hear. "You know that I would do anything, anytime for you." She returned his embrace, then left the lodge.

"Go after her," Rolling Thunder said, gesturing with a hand toward the entranceway. "Follow her teachings today, for this is the beginning of your knowledge of how the Comanche live. If I were you, I would listen and do as you are told. The winter with its cold, drafty nights is not that far away. What you make from the deer's skin will be what you will wear. The food taken from the carcass will be what you will eat."

Tanzey knew from all that he was saying that he did not plan to ever let her go. If he was already thinking ahead to winter, then she knew that her captivity was not to be a short-lived one.

She was there, forever, unless ... unless ... she found a way to escape.

That was where her *true* ambition lay—in escaping!

But having to play this by ear, one thing at a time, Tanzey stepped outside. She looked for the pregnant woman and found her sitting beneath the shade of a cottonwood tree beside the stream. Two young braves were carrying the carcass of the deer to her.

After dropping it next to Feather Moon, they followed Rolling Thunder as he led his horse and travois away from his lodge to another smaller tepee, and stopped before it.

When an Indian maiden stepped from the tepee, and Rolling Thunder nodded to the young braves to lay this other deer at her feet, Tanzey gasped. It seemed impossible that one man could have so many women dangling from strings for him, as though they were all puppets, following him like he was a puppet master.

Surely he had feelings for this woman also!

If so, she had to wonder just how many more he cared about?

First there was the white woman with the tiny baby, and then there was the pretty pregnant lady, and now this other woman?

She firmed her jaw, not wanting to be just another plaything for him, yet knowing that she had no control over why he did what he did, or when.

Seeing the woman thank him with a big hug as he leaned down to accept it made Tanzey's insides swim with renewed jealousy, and made her more determined to get free of him. Although she had strong feelings for him, she wanted a man to love her and nobody else. She would never, ever share a man!

"Kee-mah, white woman, *tosi-mah-tao-yo namasi-koh-too,* quick, quick!" Feather Moon shouted. "Come and watch and listen to my teachings."

Tanzey noticed how quickly and easily Feather Moon had already split the carcass in half and had begun stacking the meat in large slabs on one side of her.

She gazed down at her bare feet and studied the stamped-down earth that led to the stream, then decided that she could get by without her boots, at least for now. She was not going anywhere just yet—she was trapped.

She begrudgingly went and sat down beside Feather Moon and paid attention to what she said and did.

"When the hide is new, it is placed upon a log like this," Feather Moon said, spreading the cleaned hide along a log, so hewed that it presented a flat surface, one foot in width.

"With this instrument," Feather Moon said, showing Tanzey an adze, "I will cut away all of the flesh and a part of the bulkiest portion of the hide, until the whole hide presents a uniform thickness."

Feather Moon nodded toward a frame that leaned against the trunk of the cottonwood tree. "The hide then will be stretched upon that frame and rubbed with a pumice stone. I will then use a preparation compound of basswood bark pounded very fine and mixed with the brains of the deer, which is applied day after day until the skin is thoroughly saturated, making it soft and flexible."

Feather Moon went into detail as to how the meat would be cured and kept for future use.

And by the time the afternoon was over, Tanzey felt as though she could clean a deer and prepare its hide, blindfolded.

Tanzey had watched the woman that had gotten the other deer leave her lodge and prepare it farther down the stream from where she and Feather Moon sat.

When Tanzey had questioned Feather Moon about the lady, Tanzey had been surprised to discover that this woman was not a love interest of Rolling Thunder's, after all. She was recently widowed.

Feather Moon said that Rolling Thunder, whose heart was big toward those who were less fortunate than he, had provided this woman with deer kills that her husband would have brought to her, had he not died while defending his village from marauding renegades.

Feather Moon's words about Rolling Thunder stayed all afternoon in Tanzey's mind. Feather Moon had said that Rolling Thunder was feared, as well as admired. His word was law among his weaker brethren, and none of all his tribe could stand before him in single contest.

The afternoon had ebbed into evening.

A cold front had passed through, leaving the night air filled with a chill.

Tanzey was chilled to the bone. When she entered Rolling Thunder's lodge and noticed that he had started a fire, one that had already died down somewhat, she lifted a piece of wood and placed it on the fire.

Feather Moon hurried to the fire pit and knocked the wood aside. She turned glaring at Tanzey. "Never lay wood across a fire," she said. "Move it up *to* the fire, end *first*. That is the Comanche way!"

Tanzey sighed heavily. "I am not Comanche," she murmured. "So what does it matter how I do anything?"

"Never forget that you are with the Comanche and you must do as the Comanche do, or forever displease our chief," Feather Moon said in an icy tone.

Tanzey watched Feather Moon leave in a huff. She felt so alone, so downhearted. All day, while she had been with Feather Moon, she had tried to pry answers out of her about the white woman with the child and about herself being pregnant.

Were both children Rolling Thunder's?

She had asked more than once about a white male captive, especially after having asked the first time and receiving a guarded reaction from Feather Moon. It was as though Feather Moon knew answers about her brother Brant that she just would not confess to knowing!

Tanzey's curiosity about Feather Moon had now been piqued too much not to investigate her, and with whom she shared her lodge. She would find her answers at her first opportunity!

Sick at heart, somewhat listless, and feeling dirty with the blood spatters on her clothes, face, and hands, Tanzey sat before the fire and waited for Rolling Thunder's return. Surely he would give her permission to take a bath! Surely he would have some clean clothes to offer her!

"Or is he enjoying shaming me by making me look and smell like something inhuman?" she whispered harshly to herself.

When Rolling Thunder finally returned to the lodge, Tanzey gave him a hard glare.

When he ignored the glare, sat down beside the fire, and began methodically cutting long strips of buffalo hide into strong ropes, twisting braided buffalo wool hair from the manes and tails of horses into them, Tanzey could no longer hold her tongue.

"All right, so you still want to play your games with me, do you?" she said, standing up. She stared down at him as she placed her fists on her hips. "I have done my chores, *sir*. Now, what else have you planned for me?"

He said nothing in return.

Tanzey turned with a start and stepped aside when the white woman brought a tray of food into the lodge and left it on the floor between Tanzey and Rolling Thunder.

Tanzey stared down at the delicious-looking morsels. She had had nothing to eat all day. She had worked up an appetite, that was for sure! As the aroma of the food wafted up and into her nose, she could hardly stand not grabbing up the platter and eating everything in one fast gulp!

Seeing the hunger leap into Tanzey's eyes at the sight of the food, Rolling Thunder nodded toward the tray. "Eat," he said softly.

"But I am so dirty," she blurted before thinking of how pitiful her voice sounded in its soft pleading sound.

"Eat," he said softly. *"Ein-mah-heepicut*, it is yours as well as mine."

When Rolling Thunder laid his roping materials aside, reached for a piece of meat, and jerked off a big bite with his teeth, Tanzey could not hold herself back any longer. She fell to her knees beside the fire and grabbed first one piece of meat and then another, matching Rolling Thunder, piece by piece, until it was all gone.

Rolling Thunder went to the water pouch and poured two cups of water, offering Tanzey one.

She could not help but be thankful for this offering. She nodded a silent thank you, drank the water in large, deep gulps, then handed the empty cup back to him.

Her stomach comfortably full, her thirst quenched, Tanzey sat down on a bulrush mat and waited for Rolling Thunder's next instruction.

For certain, no matter how she hated to admit it, she was at his total mercy.

Chapter Nine

Leave me a little love,
A voice to speak to me in the day end,
A hand to touch me in the dark room,
Breaking the long loneliness.

—CARL SANDBURG

Tanzey guardedly watched Rolling Thunder get a willow backrest from behind some blankets at the back of the tepee.

She watched him as he placed it beside the slow-burning embers of the fire in the fire pit, then casually sat down, resting his back against it.

Her eyes widened in surprise when he took a cigarette from a small pouch at his waist and placed it to his lips and lit it, the cigarette looking as though it was made from cottonwood leaves.

Never had she envisioned Indians smoking cigarettes! That seemed so much like a white man's pastime.

She would have thought that he would have smoked a long-stemmed pipe instead!

"Why do you smoke a cigarette instead of a pipe?" she asked without thinking. "I always thought Indi-

ans smoked pipes. Who introduced you to cigarettes?
The Texas Rangers?"

Rolling Thunder gave her a slow gaze, took another drag from the cigarette, then stared into the
flames of the fire.

"All right, *don't* answer me," Tanzey said, sighing
heavily. "You can stay silent forever and see if I care!
All I want is to be released. You are wrong to keep
me captive!"

Still he ignored her.

Tanzey gazed up at the smoke hole in the ceiling
and noticed that it was dark. She dreaded the
thought of having another full night ahead of her,
having to face then another long day of being ordered around by this bossy Comanche!

She turned to Rolling Thunder again. Yes, he was
bossy. But she could not help but be intrigued with
him the longer she was with him. When she let her
guard down, and allowed herself not to be so damn
mad at him, she found herself fantasizing about him.
The remembrance of his kisses set her insides aflame
with renewed passion.

Should he approach her tonight, what was she to
do?

She hungered for his arms and kisses, yet on the
other hand she could not help but hate him. Love
and hate blended into one emotion.

How could she ever be free of him now that she
had known him, even if she did find a way to escape? He would be with her forever, if not physi-
cally, mentally. Her heart would carry memories of
him and the passion he had introduced into her life,
as though they were a picture in a locket, trapped
there forever.

She smiled wryly when she thought of the one
thing that would keep him at a distance tonight.

Her filth!

Her stench!

If he approached her, all she would have to do was lift her arms and let him get a long whiff of her armpits! He would surely make a quick retreat.

Yes, never had she smelled this bad, not even after several long days of rounding up horses at her stepfather's ranch. Each evening, while out on the roundup, she had at least managed a quick bath in a river.

Her thoughts ended as Rolling Thunder came to her and stood over her. She stared up at him, flinching when he flicked his half-smoked cigarette into the flames of the fire pit.

Her eyes widened when he so visibly took long whiffs of her, then folded his arms across his chest. "You were right to want to bathe earlier," he said dryly. "You smell like a wet dog on a hot summer day."

Insulted, even though she knew that what he said was true, Tanzey rose quickly to her feet.

Their eyes met in silent battle.

"How else can I smell after being forced to go so long without a bath, and after having been forced to work all day without washing up afterward?" Tanzey then said, leaning her face up into his. "I'm glad my scent has made your lodge an unpleasant place for you to relax tonight." She leaned her face even closer. "I'm glad I smell like a damn dog."

To witness her spirited nature again, to know that she was filled with fire, intrigued Rolling Thunder more.

And although her stench was unpleasant, he knew that once she had bathed, she would smell like a flower.

Her skin would be as soft as a flower's petal.

Her taste would be as sweet, for he had already become familiar with all of these things about her.

He did not let down his guard so that Tanzey would know that he was enjoying toying with her. He forced a frown and grabbed her by a wrist.

"What are you doing?" Tanzey asked, trying to jerk away from him.

He forced her outside.

She looked past the small, nearby stream, toward the river, where the moon was reflecting into the water like a large white saucer.

Then she gazed up at Rolling Thunder.

Her heart skipped a beat at the thought of him taking her to the river and either watching her bathe, or perhaps entering the water with her to bathe her!

Either way, she would be unnerved by his presence. Her feelings for him, knowing she could love him under different circumstances, were a threat to her.

While unclothed and bathing, what if he touched her, caressed her, *kissed* her?

Even if he went further than that, she knew that it would not be rape. The possibility of being made love to by this handsome man made her weak in the knees, and strangely dizzy.

She wanted him.

She wanted his *heat*.

While waiting for him to make his next move, Tanzey was only half aware of what was happening outside. In the center of the village, a huge, outdoor fire was burning. There was dancing, storytelling, and games.

She had grown to know that most evenings in the village were devoted to singing and storytelling, both for entertainment and education.

Presently everyone gathered around the fire. Men

and women were standing a short distance from each other. When the music from the drums and rattles started, the men selected dancing partners by placing their hands around the women's waists, while the women did the same.

The huge fire reflected its dancing shadows against the yellow lodge skins as the men and women danced and chanted songs to the accompaniment of the rhythmic beat of the drums. They danced with freedom, every movement vivid and natural.

"You are to go to the river and bathe," Rolling Thunder said, releasing his hold on Tanzey. He gazed up at the full moon. "Bathe by the light of the Comanche moon!"

Hope rose within Tanzey.

Was he actually going to allow her to go to the river alone?

Was he foolish enough not to know that she would escape at her first opportunity?

If no one was with her, watching her, she most certainly would flee to the other side of the river and escape under the cover of darkness!

But one thing spoiled that plan as far as she was concerned. She had not yet had the opportunity to sneak around and see if her brother was at this village.

Yes, she would have to take a chance of being caught again.

She *must* take the time to look for her brother.

While the Comanche people were dancing and singing, they would not be the wiser as she crept from tepee to tepee, snooping!

Her hopes of being allowed to bathe alone, to then be free to snoop, were dashed when Rolling Thunder took one step that led him to the smaller tepee next to his. His eyes never left Tanzey as he shouted inside at the white woman, telling her that she would be taking Tanzey to the river. He instructed her to bring soap and clean clothes.

Tanzey was stunned by Rolling Thunder's trust in the white woman when she came from the lodge with the soap and dress, and he filled her free hand with a rifle.

Surely the woman was frightened into doing as she was ordered, Tanzey quickly decided.

She probably believed that she would die if she went against his orders!

"Use the rifle to guard my captive," Rolling Thunder told the woman. "Use the firearm on her if she tries to escape, but only wound her. Do not kill her. My time with her has only just begun."

Tanzey's face flooded with color as her eyes locked with Rolling Thunder's.

Then wondering at the woman's reaction to the meaning behind Rolling Thunder's words, Tanzey gazed over at her and saw that she had not been affected by them. Her golden hair hanging in one long braid down her back, her violet eyes not revealing any hate, fear, *or* resentment toward the Comanche chief for having taken another woman as his private property, puzzled Tanzey.

"*Mea*, go," Rolling Thunder said, motioning with the wave of a hand toward the river. "*Kee-mah namiso*, hurry. Do not waste much time at the river. It is nearing *nei-mah-tao-yo*, sleep time, for us all."

The white woman nodded. She motioned with the barrel of the rifle for Tanzey to walk ahead of her.

Tanzey gave Rolling Thunder a bemoaned look, then hurried on ahead of the woman. The merriment of the Comanche people were left behind—the laughter, the dancing, the singing.

When Tanzey reached the river, the drum music

was muted by the tall, towering cottonwoods that hung like umbrellas over the water.

As Tanzey slowly undressed, she became more self-conscious of her nudity than ever before in her life. It was not because of the presence of the lady.

Tanzey had the strange, foreboding feeling that other eyes were on her: perhaps some of Rolling Thunder's warriors who had seen her dressed like a man and now going to the river.

Her eyes flashing around her, looking up one avenue of the riverbank to the other, Tanzey saw no one.

Quickly she removed the last of her clothes and ran into the river. The air was cool enough to cause her to shiver as she walked shoulder-high into the water.

Then she remembered having forgotten to get the soap from the violet-eyed woman. And as though the woman read her thoughts, she raised the soap for Tanzey to see.

"Yes, throw it to me," Tanzey shouted at her, glad at least that the woman could hear.

Tanzey still pondered over why the woman could not speak, yet was afraid to know the cause. It might be too horrible to think about or to accept.

She only hoped that Rolling Thunder was not the cause. She did not want to think that she could love a man who might be capable of doing unspoken things to women!

Tanzey caught the soap and enjoyed rubbing it over her body, the scent like a French perfume she had smelled one day on her mother's dressing table. She had to wonder where this woman got this expensive soap. Was it a gift from Rolling Thunder after perhaps raiding a white settler's cabin? Or had he stopped a caravan of wagons and taken his plunder after killing and maiming the people: men, women, and children alike?

She shuddered as those sorts of thoughts kept invading her senses. She so badly wanted to stop them, but they kept tumbling into her consciousness, as though a way to warn her about what was to come tonight after she smelled better.

The white woman had brought a beautiful buckskin dress ornamented with beads for Tanzey. She would be wise not to accept the dress and wear her stinking buckskin shirt and breeches! To wear the lovely Indian dress might invite Rolling Thunder's advances, instead of repelling them.

After washing her hair and ready to leave the water, she gasped to see a young brave run down to the riverbank and sweep up her soiled clothes into his arms, then run away with them.

"Stop, you little thief!" she cried, waving her arms. She gazed at the white woman. "Go after him! Stop him! Those are my clothes. He has no right . . . ."

She glared at the woman when she ignored her.

Standing on tiptoe gave Tanzey just enough height to see what the child did with her clothes. She gasped and swallowed hard when he threw them into the fire, Rolling Thunder standing beside him, watching them burn.

"Why that scheming, ornery polecat savage," Tanzey fumed as she left the river and yanked the dress from the lady's arms.

With no towel, the dress would have to suffice at soaking up the water from her flesh.

And her hair!

It was one mess of tangles!

Tanzey's eyes widened when the woman slipped a small hairbrush from the pocket of her dress and handed it toward her.

The woman smiled and nodded, as though telling her to take it.

Tanzey hesitated, then grabbed the brush.

She closed her eyes and winced as she drew the brush through her tangled hair.

Then after many of the knots were smoothed out and she could brush her hair more easily, she gazed over at the white woman, who still stood waiting to escort her back to Rolling Thunder's lodge.

"Why are you so cooperative with Rolling Thunder?" Tanzey asked softly. "Are you afraid not to do as he asks? Has he ever harmed you in any way?" She placed the brush to her side and paused before asking the next question. "You cannot speak. Lord, woman, has . . . your . . . tongue been removed? Did Rolling Thunder order . . . it . . . removed?"

The woman laughed softly, slid her tongue from between her lips, and pointed at it to prove that it was there, then bent low and picked a wild yellow daisy and handed it to Tanzey.

Tanzey took the daisy, forking her eyebrows as the woman pointed first to the daisy and then to herself.

"Oh, I know what you are doing," Tanzey said, her eyes brightening. "You are trying to tell me your name. Is it Daisy?"

The woman's eyes beamed. She nodded anxiously. She again pointed at the flower and then at herself.

"Daisy," Tanzey said, smiling at her. "What a beautiful name."

Daisy nodded and pointed at Rolling Thunder.

Tanzey gazed at Rolling Thunder, then looked at Daisy again. "*He* gave you the name?" she murmured.

Daisy nodded anxiously.

"That means that he doesn't know your true name, doesn't it?" Tanzey said, putting two and two together as they continued relating things back and forth to one another without Daisy's benefit of speech If he named you, that means that you had no power of telling him your name. *That* has to mean that you had lost your voice *before* knowing him."

Daisy nodded anxiously.

"He found you?" Tanzey asked, her heart pounding at the thought of being wrong about Rolling Thunder. "He never harmed you? He is your friend?"

Daisy nodded and placed a fist over her heart.

"Did he ever . . . make . . . love with you?" Tanzey asked guardedly, closely watching Daisy for her reaction.

She gloried inside when Daisy shook her head back and forth. The fact that Rolling Thunder had not touched Daisy sexually meant the world to Tanzey! That also meant that the child was not Rolling Thunder's!

"If you aren't here as Rolling Thunder's love interest, then .. why . . . are you?" Tanzey asked, her pulse racing as she waited for Daisy to find a way to communicate an answer to this important question.

But Daisy's reaction to her question was alarming to Tanzey.

Daisy lowered her eyes.

She stood stone still.

It was apparent that she did not wish to communicate anything else about her reasons for being there.

But it was enough for Tanzey to know that she had been wrong about Rolling Thunder's relationship with Daisy. He had not forced her to be here. It seemed as though she had been brought here because she could not tell Rolling Thunder where she belonged! Perhaps Daisy's memory was lost by the same horrid experience that had robbed her speech.

Or it was just too horrible to *explain*!

At least Tanzey knew not to think the worst about Rolling Thunder any longer. She knew that she did not have to fear him taking advantage of her sexually, for if he was prone to such actions, he would have bedded Daisy long ago!

She was beautiful.

She was innocent.

She was at his total mercy!

Now feeling more comfortable with Daisy, Tanzey moved closer to her and cradled one of Daisy's shell earrings in the palm of a hand. "Your earrings are so pretty," she murmured.

Daisy's eyes brightened. She gently touched the lobe of one of Tanzey's ears, then nodded toward it.

Tanzey thought for a moment, trying to figure out what Daisy was trying to communicate to her.

Then it came to her! Daisy had noticed that Tanzey had no earrings, nor had her ears been pierced.

"No, I've never had my ears pierced," Tanzey said, laughing softly. "I'm brave to a point, Daisy. But I must admit, the thought of having my ears pierced frightens me to death."

Daisy motioned toward herself, then again toward Tanzey's ear.

"You are telling me that *you* know how to pierce ears?" Tanzey said softly.

Daisy smiled and nodded. She gestured toward herself with a hand, and then toward Tanzey's ear.

"You want to pierce my ears?" Tanzey said, shuddering at the thought.

Daisy removed one of her earrings and held it up to Tanzey's ear. She smiled and silently mouthed the word "pretty."

Tanzey laughed nervously and gently eased

Daisy's hand away. "Yes, it's pretty, but it's not for *me*."

Daisy placed the earring back on her ear, then smiling, walked back to the village with Tanzey.

Tanzey felt better about things now. She felt as though she had found a friend. And as though a heavy burden had been lifted from her shoulders, she knew that she would be able to go back inside Rolling Thunder's lodge with a changed attitude.

She did not even want to scold him for having destroyed her clothes. She knew how vile they were. They deserved burning!

And she could not deny how ladylike she felt in this clinging, beautiful dress, with its flared skirt and wide, long sleeves. The dress was trimmed with fringe along the sleeves and hem. The beads shone like miniature moonbeams in the night.

She even wished that she *did* have on a pair of the lovely earrings. They were so pretty, so feminine. Now that her attention had been drawn to them, she recalled having seen most of the Comanche wearing earrings. Surely that was one of their customs.

But even so, even without her own pair of bead earrings, she walked more demurely. She went back to the tepee and entered it under the scrutiny of Rolling Thunder as he stood with the other men close to the outdoor fire.

Daisy did not follow Tanzey into the lodge. Tanzey's pulse raced as she waited for Rolling Thunder to return. She knew that he had surely liked what he saw as he had watched her come from the river. His eyes had never left her.

Rolling Thunder stepped into the tepee.

He went and stood over Tanzey.

As she scarcely breathed and gazed up at him, he

gently wove his fingers through the wet tendrils of
her hair.

Their eyes met for a moment in a silent wonder,
and then he turned away from her.

He took several blankets from storage and made
himself a thick pallet on the opposite side of the
lodge from the bed.

After he was stretched out on the pallet, his back
to her, Tanzey crept to the bed and crawled onto the
soft pelts, her eyes never leaving Rolling Thunder.
She did not know what to expect next from him, for
this was the very first time he had slept in the tepee
with her.

Her heart pounded as she watched him, then realized that he was asleep by the slow and even way
he was breathing.

Thinking that she was safe from Rolling Thunder,
Tanzey gave into her need of sleep. It had been a
long, busy, tiring day. And according to what Rolling
Thunder had said to her, it was only the beginning
of her labors in this Comanche camp.

But being outdoors, doing her daily chores, at least
gave her the opportunity to look around, to watch
for any signs of other captives ... any signs of her
beloved brother!

Tanzey fell into a soft sleep.

She smiled in her sleep as she dreamed of her
brother being with her while on horseback in Kansas.

She dreamed of their picnics, of their devotion to
one another.

And then her dreams changed.

She felt warmth blossoming inside her as Rolling
Thunder's hands traveled over her body, her breasts
straining against his palms, her nipples hardening
against the heat of his flesh.

Her lips were pulsing beneath his as he kissed her with passion.

Her legs were slowly parting as his hands aroused feelings within her that she never knew she was capable of.

Tanzey awakened with a start when she realized that the fingers she was feeling were not in a dream. They were there, warm and real, as they ran through her hair.

Her heart throbbing, she looked up at Rolling Thunder as he continued to caress her hair.

His eyes were soft, yet pooled with desire.

His smile was gentle.

She, oh, so hungered for his kiss, but stubbornly slapped his hand away and turned her back on him.

When he left the tepee, jealousy claimed Tanzey's very soul to think that he would go elsewhere to quench his desires.

Perhaps he had gone to the beautiful pregnant maiden?

Would she give to him what Tanzey was not willing to?

Tanzey fought the jealousy that plagued her pounding heart!

How could the first man she wanted be an Indian?

"Oh, Lord, I do love him," she cried, watching the entranceway for his return.

She was not sure how much longer she could deny him anything!

Chapter Ten

No shade of reproach shall touch you.
Dread no more a claim from me—
But I will not have you fancy
That I count myself as free.

—ADELAIDE ANNE PROCTER

As the evening sun splashed bloodred across the western sky, Tanzey walked achingly into Rolling Thunder's tepee after having a refreshing bath in the river.

Not even caring that Rolling Thunder was there, sitting against his willow backrest, leisurely smoking a cigarette and watching her enter, Tanzey could not help but groan when a sharp pain shot through her back.

Ignoring Rolling Thunder who still watched her, she placed a hand at the small of her back and limped toward the fire pit.

Even the sight of huge platters of food did not lift her spirits. Several days had now passed, and on each of those days Tanzey had been hardly allowed to let up on the hard, steady labor that had been forced upon her.

She had risen with the sun and had been shoved

outside to work, and she had not entered again until the sun began setting in the west.

Every day, all day, she had carried water to and from the river.

She had prepared huge stacks of wood for the fire pit.

She had worked endless hours in the Comanche communal garden.

And she did not even want to think about the many animals that she had skinned, their hides hanging outside even now, waiting for her to cut them into moccasins, or sew them into clothes for herself, Rolling Thunder, and only Lord knew who else.

Tanzey had worked hard all of her life outside, always welcoming the wonderful fresh air, willingly choosing it over the stifling smells of the house, first at her true father's ranch in Kansas and then at her stepfather's ranch here in Texas.

But nothing compared with the work she had done these past several days.

For certain Rolling Thunder was a slave driver! If he saw her hesitate for a moment while doing her chores, he chided her about being lazy.

She had been stupid enough to let that chiding cause her to work too hard for a woman her size.

And it had gained her nothing but an aching body, a down mood, and anger at Rolling Thunder.

For certain it had not seemed to gain his respect or admiration.

"Unless he is a great actor," she thought to herself.

The way he had looked at her as he had watched her work was a look of sheer amusement. He had gotten his jollies from seeing her suffer.

She had gotten to know damn quick how the slaves must feel in the large cotton fields of the

Southern states, laboring day and night for their masters.

And although Tanzey did not like to admit it, she felt as though Rolling Thunder was . . . *her* . . . master.

This deeply saddened her, for even though she had been taken as his captive, his kisses had told her that he wanted something different from her.

She had even begun to think that he might love her just a mite, and that he had kept her at his village not so much as a captive, but as something more.

As someone to cherish.

As someone to love.

She did not like to think that he was keeping her only for her hard labor.

She was not sure how much longer she could go on.

She was not even sure if she wished to.

She sank down onto a thick cushion of pelts beside the slow-burning embers in the fire pit.

Making sure her legs were well hidden beneath the skirt of the clean buckskin dress, she drew her knees up to her chest and hugged them.

Laying her brow on her knees, she breathed heavily. Today she was more exhausted than ever before in her life. Oh, Lord, she was so tired, so bone-weary, so unhappy.

She could not fight back the tears that had wanted to come for many days now. The hard work, knowing that Rolling Thunder enjoyed seeing her work this hard, and the fact that she had never seen one sign of her brother in the village, were all just too much for her to bear any longer.

She could count the times she had ever cried on the fingers of one hand, but this evening she could not hold the tears back.

She sobbed, giving her some release from her pent-up emotions.

She frustratingly wove her fingers through her damp tendrils of hair.

She felt empty, oh, so empty and alone.

She could not understand how Rolling Thunder could be this heartless to her, to make her reach this point where she embarrassed herself by crying in his presence.

"I just don't care any longer," she whispered to herself. "What . . . is . . . there to care about? It's useless. Totally useless."

His eyebrows arched, Rolling Thunder leaned forward and stared at Tanzey.

He could not believe his eyes!

That she was actually crying!

He did not want to think that he had tamed her *this* much, as he would tame a wild mustang into total obedience!

When he had forced the hard labor on her, it had been for only one purpose.

To make her pay for having accused him of so many things that were not true.

He never raped women.

He never stole from white people, except for perhaps a few horses that strayed from their ranches.

And until she came along, he had never taken a captive back to his village.

Yes, he was guilty for having allowed Feather Moon to have *her* captive. But that had worked out more positively than negatively. Brant Fire In The Sky had fallen in love with her almost the same day she had taken him into her lodge! They were even awaiting the arrival of their first child!

But Rolling Thunder had never even considered taking captives. He had grown too close to the white eyes when he had ridden with the Texas Rangers. Never would he have done anything that might rile them into going against him and his people.

Until now.

Until this woman, whose name he still did not know, came into his life!

He flicked the cigarette into the fire pit.

He gazed at Tanzey.

The longer she hung her head and cried, the more Rolling Thunder did not know what to do. Holding and kissing her, and ah, caressing her, was all that he could think about for so long! It had been sheer torture watching her at hard labor in his village.

When he had looked at her with amusement in his eyes, that had been an emotion he had forced upon himself, in order to make her think that he cared nothing for her but to use her!

He had wanted to teach her a lesson, then later make it all up to her by giving her a loving she would never ever want to turn her back on again.

But he had only succeeded in wounding her spirited nature, since he had played his little game for too long.

He should have realized that she had reached her limit, but she had masked her tiredness well.

And now? If he went to her and drew her into his arms, would she shove him away and tell him that she would forever hate him?

Or would she welcome comforting arms?

Would she believe him if he told her that he was sorry?

Would she even allow him to make it up to her?

He watched her for a moment longer, liking the brave, strong side of her better. That was what had at first attracted him to her. He had to see that her spirit was revived ... that her tears were stopped!

Without further thought Rolling Thunder went to Tanzey. He knelt down on his haunches beside her. "A woman with the spirit of an eagle never cries," he said in a scolding fashion, in hopes of quickly bringing out the fiery side of her nature again.

He placed a hand to her cheek when she ignored him. "Some say that *tosa-amah*, tears, are silver rain," he said softly. "Lift your eyes to me. Let me see if you have silver rain spilling from your beautiful eyes."

His nearness, his touch, the caring in his voice, caused Tanzey's breath to catch. She scarcely breathed as she thought of how he had only moments ago compared her to an eagle. The way he had said it was so beautiful!

She swallowed hard as his hand moved beneath her chin and he gently lifted it, so that her eyes were level with his.

His eyes wavered into hers. "Have I been *mo-cho-rook*?" he asked, his voice drawn.

She wanted to be stubborn and not answer him. Yet hearing his caring voice as he looked at her made Tanzey not pull away from him. "I don't know what you just said to me," she murmured.

Her pulse raced when he placed his hands gently to her waist as he rose and drew her to her feet before him.

"In my Comanche tongue I asked you if I have been a cruel one to you?" he repeated. "If so, I am sorry. I did not mean for my punishment to you to go this far. You accused me wrongly of deeds I have never done."

Touched by his sincere apology renewed Tanzey's tears. These past days, when she had tried to hate him, she had not been able to brush aside those warm feelings he had awakened in her.

Even as she slowly wore herself out each day, whenever she would watch him go about his daily functions—his muscles cording, his beautiful hair fluttering across his powerful shoulders—she had not been able to hate him.

And now, as she thought of all of the things that she had accused him of, she could see that what he had done to her was his way of punishing her into believing him.

Oh, how badly she wanted to!

But there was still the white woman and child. If they were not his, why did not someone just tell her so?

"*Mi-pe mah-tao-yo*, poor little one," Rolling Thunder murmured as he watched the tears splash from her eyes. "*Kataikay*, do not cry. All will be well again. I will make it so."

When he drew her within his powerful arms, Tanzey melted inside. As one of his large hands stroked her hair and then her back, she shivered sensually.

Knowing that she could never hate him and that she loved him with all her might, she closed her eyes and enjoyed the ecstasy of the moment.

"I have so much to say to you. I should not have waited so long," Rolling Thunder said, bending low to whisper into her ear. "Will you listen? Will you believe?"

"Yes, yes," Tanzey whispered back, finding it so natural to stand there with him, embraced by him, her arms snaking around him, to hold him near and dear to her heart.

So quickly all of the anger and pent-up emotions within her were gone.

She closed her eyes and snuggled closer to him as he began telling her things she very much welcomed.

She had been right to allow herself to have feelings

for him, for he was a man of honor, a man who had much love to offer.

"The work forced on you these past days was to serve as punishment because you accused me of false deeds, and because you defied me from the moment I first saw you," he said softly. "And the white woman and child? Daisy and little Patrick? Why they are here? And why do I treat them so gently?"

Tanzey finally would hear about Daisy and if she was Rolling Thunder's wife!

She prayed that she would hear what she wanted to hear, not something that would tear her heart into shreds!

"Many moons ago I was on my way to Fort Phantom Hill," he said, his voice filled with melancholy, as though he were reliving that day. "I came upon a scene that I could not ignore. From a distance, I saw a white man chasing a white woman away from a cabin. The man tackled the woman, and before Rolling Thunder could get to them to rescue the woman, the evil man's seed had already been planted inside her."

Tanzey gasped. She knew that the color must be drained from her face, for in her mind's eye she was seeing what Rolling Thunder was explaining, and it made a sick feeling fill her very soul to know that Daisy . . . *had* . . . been raped.

But thank God, Rolling Thunder was not the one who was guilty of ravaging Daisy's body!

Trembling, Tanzey eased from Rolling Thunder's arms. He held her hands and gazed into her eyes as he continued the morbid tale. "When I reached the man and woman, the man was already on his horse and riding away," he said thickly. "He had seen me coming. He left in a panic. I only allowed his departure because I was too concerned about the woman.

She lay like a limp rag doll on the ground. Blood was all over the skirt of her dress. The man almost ripped her apart in the viciousness of his attack.''

A bitterness rose into Tanzey's throat.

She yanked one of her hands free and covered her mouth with it.

She turned her eyes from Rolling Thunder as she fought back the urge to retch.

''Are you all right?'' Rolling Thunder asked, not at all stunned by her reaction. He knew that she would be abhorred by the tale. That was another reason he had held back telling her for so long. It was never a pleasant thing to replay in one's mind, and heart, much less say it aloud as though it only happened moments ago.

Tanzey slipped her hand from her mouth. She turned her gaze to his again. ''It's so horrible,'' she said, her voice breaking. ''Poor Daisy. Now I understand so much. Why she can't speak. Why she adores *you*.''

''*Huh*, yes, she has warm feelings for me now, but then?'' he said, his voice drawn. ''She was in a state of shock by what had happened and did not notice who had come to her rescue. She was in a dazed stupor as I helped her to her feet. Her eyes were blank. When I went inside her cabin, I found a slaughter. The man had slain her parents and two sisters. He had let her live only for one thing. But he would have killed her had I not arrived on the scene. He had planned to rape her, then kill her.''

''The child is the child from the rape?'' Tanzey said, visibly shaken.

''*Huh*, yes,'' Rolling Thunder said.

He took her by the hands and led her down on a pallet of furs beside the fire. He drew her next to him and held her as he continued the tale, knowing

that she should know it all now, for never did he
wish to speak of it again. It always took something
from him. He would never forget the massacre, the
rape of such a beautiful, delicate woman.

"But I don't understand why she is here, instead
of with people of her own kind," Tanzey said, giving
him a questionable gaze. "And has she never spoken
since that day?"

"She needed immediate attention," Rolling Thunder said. "My village was closer than Fort Phantom
Hill. I brought her here. She was medicated. For
many days she lay in a bed, trembling. And her voice
would not speak the words she tried to say! She, in
time, came to trust me so much, that when I offered
to take her to the fort, she clung to me, her eyes
wide with fear, which I interpreted to mean that she
wished to stay with my people, instead of going to
be among her own kind. It was apparent that, because of the rape, she feared all white men."

"She seems to fit in so well with your people,"
Tanzey said softly. "And everyone seems to care so
much for her *and* her child. I have seen it in how
your people treat her like a delicate flower."

Rolling Thunder chuckled. "Yes, like a *sapannah*,
prairie flower," he said, nodding. "And that is why
I saw to it that a lodge was erected for her close to
mine, so that my innocent prairie flower would feel
safe at all times. I told her that it was hers *and* the
child's for as long as she wished to stay with the
Comanche. I have since supplied her with food,
clothing, and after the child was born, the means
with which to raise her son. I do not love her as a
man loves a woman. I love her as one loves an *E-
hait-sma*, which in my language means close friend."

Tanzey was touched deeply by how he felt about
Daisy, and by how he had shown such compassion

for her. She flung herself into his arms. "I am so glad that Daisy isn't your captive, and . . . and . . . that the child is not yours," she said, her voice breaking.

He held her to his powerful chest. "Why does it matter so much to you that none of those things you accused me of are true?" he asked huskily, his heart pounding in anticipation of her answer.

Tanzey lifted her eyes to his. "Because I love you," she murmured. "I have fought this love with every fiber of my being, but I cannot fight it any longer. I have no true *reason* to."

His insides warm and glowing from the words that she had just said to him, by her declaration of love *for* him, Rolling Thunder could not hold back any longer. He yanked her close and kissed her.

When he heard her gasp of pleasure and felt her arms twine around his neck as she returned the kiss with passion, Rolling Thunder held her gently as he lowered her to the pallet of furs beside the fire.

Tanzey's head spun with rapture when Rolling Thunder slid his hand up inside the skirt of her dress.

As his hand ventured farther up her leg, stirring even more new, wonderful sensations, Tanzey felt as though she were floating.

"Your name," Rolling Thunder whispered against her lips. "You have not yet told me your name."

"Tanzey," she whispered, her face hot with the heat of awakened passion. "My . . . name . . . is Tanzey Nicole."

His free hand swept several locks of her hair back from her brow. "*Nei-com-mar-pe-ein*, I love you, Tanzey Nicole," he whispered as he gazed at her passionately, devouring her loveliness. He smiled when he saw a puzzled look on her face. "In Comanche, Tanzey Nicole, I just said that I love you."

Her heart pounding, Tanzey wove her fingers through his thick, raven-black hair and drew his lips closer to hers again. "Please say it again," she whispered, her smiling eyes reaching clean into his soul. "Teach *me* how to say 'I love you' in Comanche?"

"*Nei-com-mar-pe-ein,*" he whispered huskily, then grabbed her closely to him as once again he kissed her.

Tanzey sucked in a wild breath of bliss when his searching fingers found that place between her legs that, until that moment, had been so secret—had been untouched by a man's hands.

She moaned with pleasure as he began his slow strokes on the swollen bud of her womanhood.

She closed her eyes and felt faint, the pleasure was so intense, so deeply felt.

"Do you want me to continue?" Rolling Thunder whispered, his eyes searching hers for answers. "Or is it something you wish to think about? It is not wise to rush a woman into lovemaking."

"If you stop, I shall hate you forever," Tanzey said, laughing softly.

She was absolutely stunned by her brazenness. She did not know the first thing about lovemaking, except that this felt good.

"You do not need rest first from your hard day of labor?" he asked, brushing soft, teasing kisses across her lips. "Do you first need food?"

"Please quit trying to talk me out of it," Tanzey whispered, gasping huskily when his hand cupped that mound of flesh between her legs that felt on fire.

When Rolling Thunder reached for one of her hands and placed it over the bulge at the juncture of his thighs, and she felt just how large and ready he was, she gazed up at him with a soft questioning.

Chapter Eleven

Above, the stars in cloudless beauty shine,
Around, the streams their flowery margins kiss,
And if there's heaven on earth,
That heaven is surely this.

—CHARLES SWAIN

"Love me," Tanzey whispered, her fingers touching his lips, marveling over how they could turn her insides to warm jelly. "Love me now."

Rolling Thunder sucked her finger between his lips, while his one hand stroked her woman's center until she felt mindless with the pleasure.

Then he knelt next to her.

Her heart pounding, she watched him unclothe himself.

When his final garment was tossed aside and his need of her was fully revealed, she now understood why touching him there through his buckskin breeches had so strangely stirred her insides.

As she had discovered from the feel of him then, she saw just how large his manhood was!

Intriguingly so!

Now, in his building need of her, aching with desire, his manhood had grown tight, smooth, its rounded tip velvet-appearing in its texture.

Blushing, her pulse racing, Tanzey slid her eyes upward and locked with his. Only out of the corner of her eyes did she see him take one of her hands and lead it to his throbbing member.

She sucked in a wild breath when he placed her hand on him, her fingers seeming to have a mind of their own as they slowly circled around him, clasping his need.

The heat of his flesh bled into the flesh of her hand.

Breathless, she still gazed into his eyes as he led her hand into an upward and downward motion on him.

As she watched his eyes while her fingers pleasured him, she could see in their depths how his passion flared with hungry intent.

And when he emitted a thick, husky groan, she knew that what she was doing was reaching clean inside his heart, his very *soul*, with sensual feeling.

The touch of him, his moans of pleasure, heightened Tanzey's own fiery needs, the flames fanned by a desire that was awash throughout her. It was so overwhelming and sweet, she was weakened by it.

His fingers trembling, he guided her hand away from his aching manhood. "It is too soon for such pleasure," he said huskily. "There is much I want to share with you before I am lost to everything but the ecstasy."

Smiling bashfully, her whole body feeling as though it was one large heartbeat, Tanzey allowed him to slowly undress her.

It was as though his eyes were his fingers, caressing, touching, setting her flesh afire with pleasure.

She drew a ragged breath when the last of her clothes were tossed aside.

She closed her eyes and threw her head back in a deep, guttural sigh when Rolling Thunder leaned close to her and flicked a tongue over the taut tip of one of her nipples.

And when his mouth covered the nipple, sucking, licking, while his hands moved slowly over her body, touching and exploring, bringing to life the secret places she never knew had feelings, she felt as though she were floating above herself.

She was being changed into someone else, a raging hunger filling her for things she never knew even existed before she had known Rolling Thunder.

She writhed in response as his lips and tongue followed the path of his hands.

She stretched out beside him, allowing him better access to her body so that he could freely feed her pleasure.

When his lips found that hot, moist place at the juncture of her thighs, and he flicked his tongue across her woman's center, Tanzey gasped with surprise.

Stunned that what he had done had felt so wonderful, yet seemed so wrong, so forbidden, her eyes flew open.

"Please, don't," she said, reaching a trembling hand out to him. "I . . . I . . ."

He placed a finger to her lips. "My beautiful Tanzey, do not deny me or yourself anything," he said huskily. "*Toquet, mah-tao-yo, toquet.* Let it happen. Enjoy. Let me show you paradise today to make up for the hell that I have put you through these past days."

She slid his finger away from her mouth. "What did you say in Comanche?" she murmured, trying to delay what she found so wonderful it was frightening to her.

"I said to you in Comanche to close your eyes," Rolling Thunder said. "Close them. Let me love you. And let me love you not in only one way, but many. What we do together is right, for we do not do it just for the pleasure, but because we love one another. When you love, you wish to give pleasure. Do not feel selfish for wanting also to receive it."

Before she could say anything else back to him, he stretched out over her and kissed her with a lazy warmth that left her weak.

Sweet currents of rapture swam through her as his mouth slid from her lips and again he paid homage to her body.

She gasped with rapture when he rolled her nipples with his tongue.

Her stomach rippled sensually when his tongue left a wet trail as it made its descent along her body.

When he again knelt over her, at the juncture of her thighs, and his tongue flicked against her throbbing mound of pleasure, she felt as though she was soaring, the pleasure was so intense, so wonderful.

And when something new seemed so near, the ultimate of passion seeming to be so close, he seemed to have sensed it and drew his mouth away from her and blanketed her with his body.

He twined his fingers through hers and held her hands above her head, his eyes dark and stormy with passion. "The pain will be brief, then you will know the full wonders of why the Wise One Above in the heavens saw that men and women were made for one another at the beginning of time," he whispered.

"Pain . . . ?" Tanzey whispered, an eyebrow arching. "How could anything you are doing cause pain?"

"When one is virginal, there is pain," he said, his

eyes searching hers, now knowing for certain that he was the first with her.

That made her his, forever.

And soon he would take her with him through the ceremony that would make their being together in a sexual way right for her in the eyes of her God, for he knew that much about the white people's world . . . that a woman wanted vows with a man who loved her.

Having never before associated pain with lovemaking, her mother too timid to prepare her for moments alone with the man she loved, Tanzey's body stiffened and she swallowed hard.

"Do not stiffen," Rolling Thunder said, brushing soft kisses across her lips. "Relax. Let me come to you with my heat. Let me fill you with it. Relax. Let your body become acquainted with how mine can pleasure you. You will then, forever, want these moments with me."

He gazed into her eyes. He kissed them closed. "Now is the moment," he whispered huskily. "Open your legs widely to me. Let me fill you with my heat. Take from me that which I offer you. Remember, sweet Tanzey, *nei-com-mar-pe-ein*, I love you. You love me."

"Yes, *nei-com-mar-pe-ein*," she whispered, feeling the heat of his manhood softly probing where she was tender and hot herself.

She spread her legs.

She lifted them over his waist.

She clung around his neck and cried out with pain as, with one insistent thrust, he was inside her.

And they he lay quietly above her, his manhood still within her. "Do you feel how I fill you?" he whispered into her ear. "Tell me how it feels to you. Is the pain gone? Are you feeling something more

now? Do you like how my body connects with
yours? Do you see how we now will unlock the mys-
tery of bliss as we rock and sway together?"

"Yes, I felt pain, but it is changing to . . . to . . .
something more," Tanzey whispered, her face hot
with a blush of building pleasure as he began slowly
moving within her. She was in awe of just how
quickly the pain had changed to something warm
and beautiful.

"I love the way you fill me," she whispered against
his mouth as he feathered soft kisses across her lips.
"I love the way you are moving within me. Oh, how
wonderful it is, how the pleasure seems to be spreading throughout my whole body. Love me. Oh, yes,
love me, Rolling Thunder."

"My love, *ein-mah-heepicut*, it is yours. *Huh*, yes,
my beautiful woman with hair of flame, give yourself
up to the rapture," he whispered huskily, then
plunged more deeply into her. He withdrew and
plunged again as he kissed her, his hands molding
her breasts.

His lips were in her hair, murmuring, whispering.

She ran her hands down the muscled length of
his back, whispering back to him, her mouth against
his cheek.

She tremored. Her senses were reeling as his hands
moved over her, finding that sweet, throbbing place
between her legs.

His fingers swirled on her as he moved rhythmically within her.

Engulfed in rushes of pleasure, she moaned.

He silenced her moans as he kissed her long and
hard.

She clung to his rock hardness, her body rocking
with his, swaying, rocking back and forth, swaying,

so overcome with pleasures so intense she felt as though she might faint.

Having never before felt such pleasure with a woman, Rolling Thunder touched her lips wonderingly with featherlike kisses.

His whole body seemed aflame with a silver, liquid fire.

His lean, sinewy buttocks moved rhythmically, his body growing more feverish by the moment.

He had not been prepared for the intenseness of this passion her body evoked within him.

No smoldering memories of other times with other women matched the moment of *now*.

He found himself lost to her, body, heart, and soul.

He cradled her close, the euphoria that filled his entire being almost more than he could bear.

"I cannot hold back much longer," he whispered against her lips. He gazed at her tenderly, finding her awesome in her loveliness. "Tell me that you are as eager as I to share the ultimate of pleasure. Tell me that you are ready now for it. I do not want to be selfish in my lovemaking. I want to share it with you, equally."

"You are such an honorable man," Tanzey whispered, smiling up at him. She giggled. "I cannot believe this is me behaving so wantonly. I have never even dreamed of such moments as this, for how could I? I never knew it could be this wonderful."

"Are . . . you . . . ready?" Rolling Thunder asked, his voice deep and husky with the violence of his need. "Tell me." He wove his fingers through her hair and brought her lips close to his. "Tell me to fill you more deeply. Tell me to take you to the stars and heavens with me!"

"Oh, yes," she whispered, overcome with a feverish heat that felt deliriously beautiful. "Take me. I am ready. Love me, my wonderful Comanche war chief. Give your all to me, my darling."

His steel arms enfolded her.

She loved the feel of his hard, taut body against hers.

She felt the true depths of his hunger in the hard, seeking pressure of his lips as he once again kissed her.

Wild ripples of pleasure swam through her as he plunged over and over again inside her.

She clung to him.

She swayed with him.

Their moans mingled.

And then the explosion of ultimate ecstasy claimed them both.

The fires of their passion spread through them, as though they were one heartbeat, one soul.

And when it was over, and Rolling Thunder lay at Tanzey's side, breathing hard, she could not help but feel somewhat dazzled by the experience.

"If anyone had told me that making love with a man could be this wonderful, I would have never believed them," Tanzey said, snuggling close to his side.

She shimmered with renewed passion as he wrapped his arm around her and held her even closer. "All of my life I have never thought of girl things," she murmured. "I loved everything boys did. My brother and I shared so much. It was as though he had a brother . . . not a sister."

"You speak of this brother with much feeling," Rolling Thunder said as she eased from his arms to sit up. He rose up next to her. "Do you wish to tell me about your brother?"

Just the mention of Brant threw Tanzey back into that world of reality, where the remembrances of why she was at Rolling Thunder's village came to her like a slap in the face.

She shivered and grabbed a blanket around her shoulders.

She turned a slow, questioning look his way.

"Why did you see me as a threat?" she asked softly. "Why did you feel the need to hold me captive?" She swallowed hard. "Daisy is white-skinned, and she is no captive. So can you say that I am the first ever to be held in your village against my will?"

The blanket fell away from her shoulders as she moved to her knees to gaze directly into his eyes. "Can you say now that you will still hold me captive?" she asked softly. "After what we have shared, do you not feel guilty for having kept me here against my will? Do you plan to still not allow me to go free? To go and reveal to my parents that I am all right? Surely they are heartbroken, for not only have they lost a daughter, but also a son. Do you ever plan to allow my freedom so that I can continue my search for my missing brother?"

Rolling Thunder's head was spinning with her sudden onslaught of questions. He tried to sort through them all, in order to give her some semblance of answers.

But it was her last question that clung to him the longest . . . the mention of a missing brother.

He reached a hand to her hair and slowly wove his fingers through the thick red shine of it. "I know a white man whose hair is like yours," he said thickly. "Your features are the same."

So stunned by his words, Tanzey's shoulders swayed.

She paled as she stared incredulously into his eyes. "Where did you see this man?" she then blurted out. "How long ago . . . did . . . you see him?" She grabbed his hands. "Oh, Rolling Thunder, that had to be my brother. You saw such a resemblance because he and I are *twins*, born only moments apart!"

"Fire In The Sky . . . ." he whispered, not loud enough for her to hear.

"Get dressed," he said, standing, already drawing on his fringed buckskin breeches.

"Why?" she asked guardedly, looking up at him.

"I have someone that I would like for you to see," he said, slipping his shirt on.

"Who?" Tanzey asked, her heart thudding as she stood and pulled the dress over her head. Could he be taking her to her brother? Was her brother truly alive after all? Was . . . he . . . there?

"You will soon see," Rolling Thunder said, glancing down at her bare feet. "Do not take the time to put on moccasins. I am eager to share something with you, the woman I love."

Her knees weak with anxiousness, her pulse racing, Tanzey left the tepee with him.

When Rolling Thunder made a turn to the right and walked toward Feather Moon's lodge, Tanzey looked up at him questioningly.

Her gaze was quickly averted when Feather Moon stepped from her lodge.

Feather Moon's eyes were wide as she silently questioned Rolling Thunder.

Tanzey looked up at Rolling Thunder and caught him giving Feather Moon a silent nod.

Tanzey looked quickly at Feather Moon, who nodded and quickly slipped back inside her tepee.

When she came from the lodge again only a moment later and someone that Tanzey adored stood at her side, Tanzey stopped and gasped. She stared, wide-eyed, at her brother and how he was dressed.

He wore the clothes of an Indian warrior. Even his hair was worn in two long braids down his back!

But when Feather Moon slipped her hand in his so possessively and he gazed down at her so adoringly, Tanzey grabbed for Rolling Thunder's arm to stop herself from toppling to the ground in a dead faint. It was obvious to her that this child inside Feather Moon's belly must be Brant's!

"How . . . ?" Tanzey said, her voice faint from the alarm of it all. "Why . . . ?"

Brant's eyes wavered into hers.

Chapter Twelve

No other with but hers approve;—
Tell me, my heart, if this be love.

—GEORGE LYTTELTON

"Sis," Brant Fire In The Sky said, rushing to her and grabbing her up into his arms. He held her close. "Thank God, you finally know. I'm sorry, Tanzey. Oh, God, I'm so sorry."

Tears spilling from her eyes, Tanzey clung to him. "You've been here all along, and you . . . and you . . . didn't let me know?" she murmured, reveling in his embrace, the wonderful fact that he was alive and well.

The smell of the buckskin of his clothes made her stiffen.

He was with an Indian maiden.

It was apparent that she was pregnant with his child.

He even wore clothes that made him look more Indian than white!

Her head spinning with questions, she eased from his arms. Her gaze roamed slowly over him.

And then her eyes locked with his. "I don't understand any of this," she said, her voice sounding hollow and drawn in her confusion.

Brant Fire In The Sky took her hands. "We need to talk," he said in a deep voice. He gazed past her at Rolling Thunder, then turned and gave his wife a silent gaze.

Then he turned back to Rolling Thunder again. "I would like to have time alone with my sister," he stated.

Rolling Thunder gestured with his hand toward his private lodge. "Go," he said gently. "Sit in my lodge. Take whatever time you need to talk with your sister, who is now my woman."

Brant Fire In The Sky's lips parted in a slight gasp.

He turned a quick, questioning look Tanzey's way.

She smiled awkwardly, and the blush that rose to her cheeks said more to Brant Fire In The Sky than words ever could.

Brant Fire In The Sky closed his eyes to control his emotions. He swallowed hard, then nodded toward Rolling Thunder. "Thank you," he murmured. "My sister and I appreciate your kindness."

Feather Moon came to Brant Fire In The Sky's side and laid a gentle hand on his arm.

He turned to her.

"*Penende*, honey, can I come and sit with you as you talk with your sister?" she asked softly. Her eyes pleaded up at him. "Please, husband? Allow it?"

Hearing her brother called "husband" by the Indian maiden caused Tanzey to flinch.

Yet she should not be as alarmed with his marriage to the Comanche woman as she should be by him not having told his family that he was alive!

And she should not be alarmed over her brother loving a Comanche, dressed like one himself.

Did she not love a Comanche war chief?

Did she not even now wear a dress worn by Comanche women?

It was ironic to her how they, who were twins, had both fallen in love with Indians from the same tribe and village—and who were cousins, at that!

As always, being twins caused them to have the same thoughts and say the same things simultaneously.

And now that they both loved Indians, it did seem only right that their fate would have led them here, to be the same again, as always before.

Always touched by the way his wife called him "honey" in Comanche, a term she had learned from him, Brant Fire In The Sky could not refuse her anything.

He dropped his hands away from Tanzey's. "*Huh*, yes, my pretty *mah-tao-yo*, little one, you can sit with me and my sister," Brant Fire In The Sky said, bending to brush a soft kiss across his wife's perfectly shaped lips.

She twined an arm around his neck and softly returned his kiss, then gazed up at him with question. "Then, why do you not take her into *our* lodge for talking?" she asked softly. "Would it not be best that way, so that she can become acquainted with your new life, the way you *live*, and with whom?"

Tanzey was stunned speechless by the devotion exchanged between her brother and the Comanche woman. She had never seen her brother with women before, even though she knew that he had gone into town more than once to be with them, to quench the hungers of his flesh.

She should have known that he would be this gentle with women, for had he not always been as gentle with her?

Even when they had been out on the roundup and

she had become just another one of the "men," he had protected her with his life!

Still, it did not seem right, this devotion to an Indian woman—an Indian woman whose personality was not what Tanzey would have expected her brother to be attracted to. Tanzey had seen Feather Moon's stubborn, spiteful side. Had she kept that hidden from her husband?

Surely so, Tanzey thought to herself, sighing.

"*Huh*, yes, we will talk in our lodge," Brant Fire In The Sky said, smiling down at his wife.

Tanzey was not sure if she could ever get used to her brother speaking Comanche, yet she knew that she, too, would soon speak it on a regular basis. To be the best of wives to Rolling Thunder, she knew that she must learn everything Comanche!

She went suddenly cold inside. She turned quickly and stared up at Rolling Thunder. Not once had he said that he would marry her.

Yes, he said that she was his and that she could not live elsewhere.

But the word "wife" had not been spoken to her yet.

Then he smiled at her in that special way that meant the smile was only for her. She suddenly knew she had nothing to fear.

He loved her.

He *would* marry her.

He would welcome children born of their flesh!

"Your offer was a most generous one, Rolling Thunder," Brant Fire In The Sky said, smiling over at Rolling Thunder. "But if you don't mind, I would like to invite my sister into my own lodge. You are welcome, too, Rolling Thunder. Would you come and share a smoke as my sister and I speak of things brothers and sisters speak of?"

Rolling Thunder gave Tanzey a questioning look. She smiled softly up at him.

Then he nodded at Brant. "*Huh*, yes, I will share a smoke with you in your lodge," he said. He took Tanzey by the hand and walked her toward Brant Fire In The Sky and Feather Moon's lodge.

When Tanzey entered the tepee, she stopped and looked slowly around her. It was no surprise to her not to find anything of Brant's in the tepee, except . . .

Tanzey's gaze stopped, and she stared at the rifle that she recalled her stepfather having given Brant two Christmases ago. He had taken this rifle with him that day he had left to hunt for boars.

It was the only thing left of his white culture, except for now, since his sister was with him again.

The lodge fire was burning in slow leaps across the fire pit. The smell of something cooking in a large black pot hanging on a tripod over the flames, and the sight of a tousled bed along the far back wall of the lodge, made strange ripples flood Tanzey's insides. All of these things were things of her brother's new life.

Eating food his wife cooked.

Sharing so much with a wife in the bed of pelts and blankets.

Her insides stiffened when she spied the makings of a cradle board, the child even more a reality because of this symbol of babyhood.

"Come on, sis," Brant Fire In The Sky said, gently taking her by an arm, yanking her thoughts back to the present. "Sit beside me. I want to hold your hands while we talk. I've missed you so much, Tanzey. So damn much."

Hearing those words when he had been so close these past several days while she was at the village, and when every breath she took was filled with the fear that her brother was dead, made a quick anger grab at Tanzey's heart.

"I never thought my brother could be so thoughtless," she said, placing her hands on her hips. "How could you do this to me? How could you do this to our family? I have been held captive against my will. But you? You surely haven't been. You are married to one of the Comanches! Don't you know that Mother and Father's hearts are bleeding even now over thinking we both are dead?" She gestured with a hand toward Feather Moon. "And all along you are here, safe, happy, and . . . and . . . even married? Brant, I'm not sure if I will ever understand . . . or . . . will ever forgive you."

She ignored the quick intake of breaths her sudden anger caused through the lodge.

She ignored Rolling Thunder and Feather Moon's incredulous stares.

She was not even swayed by the sudden hurt that her anger caused her brother.

A gentle hand on her arm drew her eyes quickly around. She gazed up at Rolling Thunder, touched by the caring in his eyes.

"My woman, do not say any more to your brother until you have heard him explain how things were forced on him," he said. "Like you, he was taken captive. Like you, he fell in love with his *captor*. So do you see how easy it was for him to forget his other world? Do you not even expect to forget it also?"

"No matter how much I love you, I can never turn my back on my family," she said, swallowing hard. "I don't see how Brant has."

"Listen, beautiful Tanzey, and then tell me you do not understand," Rolling Thunder said. He gave her a soft, reassuring kiss, then placed his fingers to her shoulders and turned her to face her brother.

She was scarcely aware of Rolling Thunder and Feather Moon slipping from the lodge, leaving her alone with her brother. Now it *was* only herself and her brother. Their worlds had come together again. She knew that she had no choice but to accept how it had happened.

Neither of them were children any longer.

They had both lost their hearts to loved ones. They had both lost their hearts to someone out of their own culture—to someone who, in the white world, was forbidden to them.

She knew that they would never be a part of that other world again, except to tell their parents of their fate.

Brant Fire In The Sky took Tanzey's hands and led her down on a cushion of soft pelts beside the fire. He sat down and faced her, still holding her hands. He relished the feel of her warm flesh in his. He had missed her these past days, weeks, and months.

"I hope that once I have finished with my explanation, your heart will be at peace and will join mine once again, as one, as twins should feel about one another," Brant Fire In The Sky said, his voice drawn.

His eager eyes searched her face, and then he looked deeply into her eyes, which mirrored his own in their soft color of green. "Tanzey, oh, Tanzey," he said, almost choked with emotion. "Oh, how I have missed you."

Unable to hold back her emotion any longer, Tanzey yanked her hands free and flung herself into his arms. Cheek to cheek, their embrace was long and sweet, their tears mingling.

"I'm sorry if I was too harsh," Tanzey sobbed, so glad that she was able to be in her brother's arms again, sharing their devotion and love. "But, there is so much I just can't understand."

"I know," Brant Fire In The Sky said, his hands caressing her back in slow, loving strokes.

Tanzey clung to him for a moment longer, then eased away from him.

She sat down, crossed her legs beneath the skirt of her dress, then lay her hands primly in her lap. "So please go on and tell me everything," she murmured. "I won't interrupt. I promise."

"I'm sure your first question is how I was captured," Brant Fire In The Sky began. "And *why* might be the second question lying heavy on your heart."

Remembering her promise not to interrupt, Tanzey only nodded.

"Tanzey, on the day I went boar hunting, I was not even aware of being encircled by Comanches," he said while remembering the moment he became aware of their presence, and being enraptured with Feather Moon instantly. "Suddenly they were there. I had no chance to fight back."

He motioned with a hand and made a slow gesturing movement to encompass the whole inside of the lodge. "I was brought here, to this very lodge, and was not allowed to leave for many days. Even then, when I was allowed to wander out, to get a breath of fresh air, to soak up the rays of the sun, it was in the close proximity of this tepee. *And* I was guarded. Day and night I was guarded."

He reached for a cigarette that he had earlier rolled from his makings from the leaves of a cottonwood tree.

Tanzey's eyes widened when he lit the cigarette with a twig from the lodge fire. Never before had she seen her brother smoke. This had to have been a habit picked up from Rolling Thunder. He enjoyed a smoke every evening.

"Tanzey," Brant Fire In The Sky said, after taking a deep drag from the cigarette, letting the smoke slowly waft from between his lips. "There was a certain reason why I was captured."

Tanzey leaned forward, anxious to know. The reason she had been abducted made some logical sense. It was apparent now that Rolling Thunder had not liked her snooping so close to his village. He apparently did not want anyone to know that they had taken her brother captive!

"Why?" she said, unable to keep her silence. "Why on earth, Brant, did the Comanche have cause to capture you? Were you trespassing on their land? Is that the reason?"

"Sis, please just listen," Brant Fire In The Sky softly pleaded. He flicked ashes from his cigarette into the fire, took another long drag, then lay it down on the edge of a rock and took Tanzey's hands.

"Sis, the only reason I was abducted was because of Feather Moon," he blurted in a rush of words. "She had seen me often as I had hunted. She fell in love. And since she is a Comanche princess and always gets everything she asks for, no one denied her the husband of her choice. *Me*, Tanzey. She wanted *me*."

"Good Lord," Tanzey gasped, paling.

"I was brought to this lodge," Brant Fire In The Sky said, gazing into the fire, remembering the very moment Feather Moon had dropped her dress to the floor, revealing the wonders of her body to him.

He smiled awkwardly. "That first night?" he said, his voice revealing his embarrassment. "Tanzey, Feather Moon seduced me. I . . . allowed . . . it. Tanzey, I loved her the very moment I saw her. I was lost heart and soul *to* the lovely Comanche princess. I knew from that first kiss and embrace that I could never live without her. My captivity became a time of paradise. I never wanted to leave."

"Brant . . ." Tanzey said, her eyes wavering into his. "My sweet Brant. You loved as quickly as I. But . . . but . . . thank goodness Rolling Thunder was not as pushy as Feather Moon. He never forced himself on me. And he did not bring me to his lodge purposely *to* seduce me. I now know that he abducted me because he feared I would see you here and go to Fort Phantom Hill and tell them. A war would have that quickly erupted between the Comanche people and the cavalry."

Brant Fire In The Sky drew her into his arms. There was a long moment of silence when they only embraced.

Then Brant held her away from him at arm's length. "Although I willingly slept with Feather Moon each night, and even sometimes during the day, and she knew that I did not want to leave her, ever, I was still not allowed to return home to reassure you and our parents that I was all right," he said, his voice drawn. "And it was not because they did not trust me. They feared the reaction of our family and what *they* might do when they knew where I would be residing. Only recently, before your arrival, had I even been allowed the freedom of the entire village. Only recently I have been given a knife—*and* my rifle. So you see, Tanzey, I was not able to let anyone know that I was all right."

Tanzey's gaze moved slowly over him. "Just look at you," she murmured. "If not for the color of your hair and skin, you would be considered Comanche."

"Yes, I do wear clothes of the Comanche," he said.

He went to the back of the tepee and picked up a rawhide case, then took it and handed it to Tanzey.

"Open it," he said. "See what's inside."

Tanzey hesitated for a moment, questioned him with a quiet stare, then sighed and placed the case on her lap.

She gazed down at it. It was envelope-shaped and laced together at the edges, and had a tie-down, fold-over flap.

"The case is made of *natsakana*, which means raw-hide in Comanche," Brant Fire In The Sky said. "Tanzey, open it."

Tanzey slowly lifted the flap. Inside she saw a man's buckskin outfit, leggings, moccasins, blanket, and what appeared to her to be braid wrappers made of beaver fur. The clothes were new and finely fringed.

"All Comanche men have a wardrobe case," Brant Fire In The Sky quickly said. "This is *mine*. Everything inside the case was made by Feather Moon's hands, *for* me."

"Oh, Brant," Tanzey said, her voice breaking, feeling too strongly now that she had lost her brother.

"And the clothes, or the ownership of such a ward-robe case, are not all that makes me Comanche," Brant Fire In The Sky said, swallowing hard. "I now have an Indian name. I was called by that name the very day of my abduction. Feather Moon gave it to me."

"An ... Indian ... name ... ?" Tanzey gasped, paling.

"I am called Fire In The Sky," he said. "Brant Fire In The Sky."

He then laughed awkwardly as he reached a hand to his braid. "Because of the color of my hair," he said softly. "Feather Moon says it is the color of the sun—of fire in the sky."

Tanzey sighed and looked away. "Lord." She gulped hard, then turned to him again. "Are you happy?"

"More than ever before in my life," he said, the contentment like sweet sorghum in the way he admitted the truth to her. He reached a hand to her cheek. "And you, Tanzey? I see something in your eyes I have never seen before. Have you fallen this much in love with your captor, as I have with mine?"

"I do love him immensely," Tanzey said, her eyes twinkling at the very thought of only a short while ago and what she and Rolling Thunder had shared.

"Are you going to marry him?"

"If he asks me to."

"I have a child on the way," Brant Fire In The Sky said, pride thick in his voice.

"Yes, I noticed," Tanzey said, smiling softly at him.

"What will our parents say when they learn that we both have chosen to marry Indians over whites?" Brant Fire In The Sky said, a distant look suddenly in his eyes. "We do have to tell them, Tanzey. Soon."

"But will you ... will I ... be allowed to?"

"I think the time has come for the Comanche to allow it," Brant Fire In The Sky stated. "They cannot expect to keep us a secret forever. We will have to make sure that our parents understand our true feelings. Only then will we be assured that those at Fort Phantom Hill won't interfere."

He smiled at Tanzey. "Tomorrow I will be allowed to go on the hunt with the warriors," he said, proudly squaring his shoulders. "That is proof enough that trust has been earned."

Tanzey gave Brant another warm hug, then left the lodge.

Rolling Thunder was waiting for her.

He questioned her with his eyes.

She smiled reassuringly at him.

She turned and watched Feather Moon move into the arms of Brant Fire In The Sky.

She turned and silently watched the activity in the village. Some people gathered around for a hunting dance, while others were erecting scaffolding for drying the meat that would be brought from the hunt tomorrow.

There were several drummers and singers. It was an even number of men and women lined up facing one another.

Tanzey smiled to herself as her brother and Feather Moon joined the dancers, facing one another.

Strange, she thought, how it looked so much like her brother belonged there as part of the Comanche, dressed like Comanche, with a hunter's shirt made of buckskin, fringed at the bottom and at the cuffs and tied in front with strings.

His leggings rose only to the knee. His moccasins were intricately beaded in designs of the forest.

His long braids bounced as he danced.

As the music continued, the women crossed over and selected a partner.

"Each hunt has a hunt leader," Rolling Thunder said when he realized how closely she was observing the dance. "He is always a respected warrior and a man of good judgment. If your brother proves skilled at hunting, one day he will be the hunt leader."

Touched deeply by how her brother had adapted so easily to the Comanche culture, tears streamed from Tanzey's eyes.

Rolling Thunder took her by the hand. They left the merriment behind and went inside his lodge. "And is all well now between you and your brother?" he asked as he led her down onto a thick cushion of pelts beside the fire.

"Yes, and it is wonderful to know that he is alive and ... and ... so happy," Tanzey said, hearing her brother's familiar laughter rising above the laughter of the others.

She frowned over at Rolling Thunder. "But I don't understand why he was not allowed to reveal himself to me these past several days," she said. "You know that the burden inside my heart would have been lifted had I known that he was here and alive."

"*Huh*, yes, I was wrong," Rolling Thunder said softly. "I should have told you."

"Feather Moon knew," Tanzey said. "She could have told me. Surely Daisy knew."

"Neither woman interferes in my matters, as I do not interfere in theirs," Rolling Thunder said flatly. "It was for me to work out, not for them to lead the way."

"Now that you have feelings for me that are special," she said, then her words trailed off when she again thought of Rolling Thunder having not mentioned marriage. She lowered her eyes, now silent.

Rolling Thunder saw her hesitance. He placed a finger beneath her chin and lifted her eyes to his. "What stole your words away?" he murmured. "What is on your mind that makes your eyes take on a look of questioning?"

"We made love, and there has been no mention of marriage," Tanzey blurted out. "I don't want to feel shame, yet how can I not?"

"You are here with me, I call you my woman, and still you do not know that you will be my wife?" Rolling Thunder said. "How can you doubt that? How?"

A sweet warmth filled Tanzey's heart. "I never

ever thought I would find a man I would want to marry," she murmured. "But you, Rolling Thunder, have changed so much about me. I feel ... like ... a woman now, not like just one of the guys. I doubted you only because I doubted myself."

"Then doubt no more," he said, drawing her into his gentle embrace. "We will say vows soon."

"You make me so happy," she murmured, sighing.

"Tell me what you want out of life, and it will be yours," Rolling Thunder said, easing her from his arms, gazing intensely into her eyes.

"Really?" she said, her heart pounding at the thought of leaving soon to return to her parents, to tell them all of the wonderful news. "Go with me *now*, Rolling Thunder, to see my parents. Please? Let us take Brant with us, *and* his wife. It would mean so much to my parents. It would mean so much to *me*."

Rolling Thunder frowned.

He rose slowly to his feet.

He stood over the fire and stared down at the flames. "*Ka*, no," he mumbled. He turned and gazed at her, frowning. "It .. is ... too soon."

Tanzey's heart skipped a beat.

Had she been wrong to hope for too much too soon?

Had he not meant anything he said to her?

Had he ... only ... used her?"

Speechless, she stared up at him for a moment, then bolted to her feet and ran from the lodge, sobbing.

Chapter Thirteen

Pale hands, pink-tipped, like lotus buds that float
On those cool waters where we used to dwell,
I would have rather felt you 'round my throat,
Than waving me farewell.

—LAURENCE HOPE

Dispirited by Rolling Thunder's negative reaction to her request to visit her parents, Tanzey once again felt like his captive.

But she knew she should be glad that Brant had been allowed to leave today to go on his first hunt with the Comanche warriors.

He had returned, proud and victorious, with a great buck on a travois trailing behind his horse.

All of the warriors had brought home meat for their families ... some buffalo, some deer, and some rabbit.

Tanzey recalled something her brother had told her about a particular belief of the Comanche, something that he had learned at a trading post.

He had told her that the Comanche put much trust in the horned toad before the hunt for buffalo. The horned toad was believed to be a help in locating the buffalo, for when the Comanche asked the toad about the huge, hairy beasts, the toads always ran in the direction of the buffalo.

The Comanche called the toad *Kusetemini*, meaning "asking about the Buffalo."

Today it seemed that *some*thing had led the Comanche to a bountiful hunting ground. And this had given this band of Comanche, as a whole, a reason to celebrate.

The village had been celebrating for hours. After the women had sliced the meat into very thin filets and hung them over large racks for a quick sun-drying, and after the hides had been pegged out on the ground, flesh side up, so that they could be fleshed and scraped for later tanning, everyone had danced until they were too bone-weary to go on any longer.

Much food had been consumed.

Tanzey had planned to avoid Rolling Thunder today, to punish him for being so callous about her request to return home to her parents.

But Tanzey had soon discovered that Rolling Thunder was to be the one to do the ignoring. It seemed that he had decided to play her own game, especially after she had avoided him the entire night and had left the lodge at early dawn to take a bath in the river before he had even opened his eyes.

When she had returned to the lodge, he had been gone. She had not seen him all day, until now, and now he was ignoring her as though she did not exist.

She was quickly learning that the Comanche had a passion for gambling, for as the women sat together away from the warriors, resting and getting their breath after the many hours of dancing and feasting, the warriors sat close to the outdoor fire, gambling.

The sun was lowering in the sky, brushing the many lodges with a pinkish haze. Tanzey sat with

the women, her gaze following her brother's movements as he gambled along with the Comanche.
Brant was so serious it looked as though his face
might crack if he smiled.

Yes, she thought to herself, gambling was one of
her brother's weaknesses. He had often stayed over-
night in Abilene after gambling into the wee hours
of the morning with other rowdy cowboys at the
saloons.

If he had won, he had spent most of the winnings
on the pleasures of a woman in a whorehouse.

If he had lost, he had stayed another day until he
felt the weight of coins in his pockets.

Tanzey felt a soft hand on her arm, bringing her
thoughts back to the present.

She turned and smiled softly at Daisy, so wishing
the lovely woman could talk. Tanzey needed someone to talk with about her feelings, and especially
about Rolling Thunder's stubborn attitude about
her parents.

She shifted her gaze to Feather Moon, who still
distanced herself from Tanzey. Scarcely did the
lovely maiden even smile at Tanzey, much less talk
to her. Feather Moon resented Tanzey, and Tanzey
could not understand why. She had no power over
her brother's feelings about the pretty Comanche
princess.

And even if she did, after seeing him so happy
with Feather Moon, knowing the depths of his love
for her, Tanzey would never again try to encourage
him to return to the life that he had known before
having been abducted.

Tanzey could only surmise that Feather Moon's
bitterness toward her was merely because Tanzey
was Brant's twin, someone Brant had known and
loved longer than his wife.

Yes, Tanzey had heard about jealous sisters-in-law.

She had heard about brothers and sisters drawing apart because of such feelings.

She set her jaw and glared back at Feather Moon, deep inside her heart vowing that never would this Comanche princess drive Tanzey and Brant apart. Their bond had been formed while in their mother's womb. Such a bond was forever.

A loud "whoopee" shook the very air that Tanzey breathed.

Her gaze jerked to her brother.

Finally something had caused his expression to soften and his eyes to dance.

It was apparent that he had won big stakes while gambling.

Then she noticed how his smile faded as things changed as quick as a thunderclap . . . Brant's luck not being what he had thought it was! He had thought that he was close to winning, but one more toss of the rocks that had been painted with strange sorts of dots, making them something akin to dice in the white man's world, and it was apparent that Brant had lost everything, while Rolling Thunder had become the sole winner!

As the warriors rose from the circle, they each clasped Rolling Thunder's hand and smiled at him while congratulating him.

Brant rose sullenly from the group of men and gave Feather Moon a downcast, nervous look as she walked slowly toward him.

Tanzey moved to her feet and guardedly watched her brother with Feather Moon. She expected Feather Moon to pout and be nasty over Brant's loss, for it was not a simple loss to these lovebird newlyweds.

Brant had gambled his and Feather Moon's lodge away!

"My husband," Feather Moon said, easing into his arms. "*Nei-com-mar-pe-ein*, I love you. It is all right you gambled our lodge away. I am only glad that you did not gamble away your wife!"

Brant Fire In The Sky's eyes widened as he softly gripped his wife's shoulders. "What do you mean?" he asked as he gazed into her midnight dark eyes. "Why would you say such a thing? Gamble you away? How could you think that I could ever do that?"

Feather Moon lowered her eyes almost timidly. "Because it is a husband's right to do this while in the heated passion of gambling," she murmured.

"Thank you for loving me so much that you only gave away our lodge," she said, reveling in the feel of his arms as he slipped them around her, holding her close.

Tanzey took an unsteady step away from them, stunned by what she had heard. She paled at the thought of Rolling Thunder ever considering gambling *her* away!

Her heart skipped a beat at the thought of how she was treating him even now!

So callous!

So cold!

So uncaring!

But only to make him have cause to stop and think of how he was treating her! He should be more understanding of *her* feelings where her parents were concerned.

Yet she had to remind herself that she was the one who was in danger of losing something she had never thought of possessing.

The man she adored; the man she would die for!

Therefore, to be assured of a future with him and to be assured of not giving him further cause to gamble *her* away, Tanzey knew that she must show him that she still loved him, and that *she* would be more understanding of *his* feelings.

He was a great leader of his people.

He held her back from seeing her parents not to hurt her, but to protect his people.

While he was their war chief, they *had* to be first, always, in his plans.

Tanzey was stunned to see Feather Moon gathering together materials for another lodge. She watched her brother just stand there, watching, as Feather Moon began standing up the tall poles, the many buckskin pelts that Feather Moon had kept stored away until now, lying ready to cover them.

Tanzey watched Rolling Thunder remove everything from Feather Moon's lodge, placing everything together close to the site of the new lodge.

And still not only did Brant stand and watch his wife tie large poles together for the tepee, but so did all of the village.

Frustrated, and seeing the young, pregnant woman laboring so hard that sweat rolled from her brow, Tanzey could take it no longer. She stamped over to Brant Fire In The Sky. She placed her hands on her hips. "How could you just stand there and allow her to build a lodge while you are just watching?" she said, her eyes searching her brother's face as he looked past her, still watching his wife.

Brant Fire In The Sky swallowed hard. He gazed over at Rolling Thunder as he came and stood beside him. When Rolling Thunder shook his head back and forth, a silent command for Brant Fire In The Sky not to interfere in the lodge building, Tanzey stood for a moment, speechless.

Although she had no good feelings for Feather Moon, it was hard to stand there and see the young, pregnant woman being put through such grueling, hard labor alone.

Tanzey took an angry step closer to her brother. "How could you just stand there and watch your wife do that?" she persisted. "Lord, Brant, she's *pregnant*. What if doing that makes her lose the baby?"

Brant Fire In The Sky gently placed his hands on Tanzey's shoulders. "Sis, you are interfering in things that you don't understand," he said softly. "Tanzey, what has happened here is the way of the Comanche. When a lodge is gambled away, the wife builds another one. The man watches."

"You are not Comanche," Tanzey said, jerking herself free of his grip. "You are a white man! Act like one! Protect your wife. Protect your child!"

"Tanzey, I have the skin, eyes, and hair of a white man, but my heart is now Comanche," Brant said. "My *child* will be raised *Ner-mer-nuh*, Comanche."

"Good Lord," Tanzey said, eyes wide as she stepped away from him.

She stared from Brant, over to Rolling Thunder, and saw their same stoic expressions. Then she turned and went to Feather Moon's assistance.

When Tanzey lifted only one pole, Feather Moon stamped over to her and knocked it out of her hands.

"It is not your place to help Feather Moon," the Comanche princess said haughtily. "It is Feather Moon's duty to make the lodge for husband and child. If my husband gambles this new lodge away, then Feather Moon builds another, and another, and another."

Unnerved, so confused by so many things, Tanzey stared frustratingly into Feather Moon's defiant, cold eyes for a moment longer. Then she turned on a heel and ran toward Rolling Thunder's lodge.

Tanzey could feel everyone's eyes on her.

She could hear the utter silence all around her as those eyes followed her until she finally escaped into the solitude and privacy of Rolling Thunder's lodge.

Feeling so alone, so out of sync with everything and everyone around her, now even her *brother*, Tanzey sank to her knees before the low embers of the lodge fire. She gazed into the fire for a moment, then turned with a start when Rolling Thunder knelt down behind her and slipped his arms around her waist.

"My *mah-ocu-ah*, woman fights fights not needed," Rolling Thunder said softly. "When will you stop fighting what life is around you? When will you accept the good of what is offered here, and forget anything that seems bad or unacceptable to you? You are loved. Your brother is loved. What more should you want of life than that? Do you not know that I would go to the ends of the earth for you? Do you not know that your brother's wife loves him as much? How can you see any bad in that? How?"

His words touched her deeply. She closed her eyes and melted inside when his hands slid up and cupped her breasts. "I don't like feeling angry and confused," she murmured. "But I just can't understand, or accept, the many ways of the Comanche women. And Feather Moon confuses me so! First she is strong, and then she is meek. I can *never* be meek. Never would I want to build a lodge for a husband who gambled one away!"

"If you love the man enough, you would do anything," Rolling Thunder said softly. "And do not consider Feather Moon as meek, ever. She is known for being spoiled. Surely you have seen it."

"Yes, I have seen it," Tanzey said, laughing softly. "And in time, surely my brother will also understand this side of his wife's nature and will not be as happy with her. And not only do I see Feather Moon as stubborn, but also cold and unfriendly."

"Your brother has seen Feather Moon's stubbornness, and yes, also sometimes her coldness, and he has overlooked it, for Feather Moon's good qualities outweigh bad ones one hundred to one!" Rolling Thunder said. "As do yours, my woman. That is why I love you."

Tanzey moaned softly as Rolling Thunder's thumbs circled her nipples, her nipples straining for his touch through the buckskin fabric.

"I want to feel free to love," she whispered. "I do love you so much, Rolling Thunder."

When his hands slid away from her breasts and he placed them at her waist again, but this time to turn her around to face him, she found herself gazing into eyes that were smoke-black with passion.

The intensity of his look, the need that was etched across his sculpted face, made her forget why she had ever been angry at him.

She just wanted to be held.

She wanted to know again the wonders of his lovemaking.

Suddenly everything else came second to those wants, those needs.

Her parents would be told the wonderful news when Rolling Thunder saw it was safe.

Brant's wife was *his* concern, not Tanzey's.

And, to secure her future with Rolling Thunder, Tanzey *was* willing to learn and to practice the habits of the Comanche, the same as her brother.

Destiny had led Tanzey and her twin brother to a way of life that still were linked.

For that, Tanzey was thankful.

Rolling Thunder's burning hot lips claimed Tanzey's in a frenzied kiss. He gripped her shoulders and spread her out on a thick cushion of pelts.

As he kissed her with such passion, she was scarcely aware of his hands disrobing her.

And the next thing that she was aware of was his own warm flesh against hers, his clothes piled with hers beside them.

Stars shone through the smoke hole overhead as Rolling Thunder shoved his throbbing need inside Tanzey.

Her hips gyrated as his moved powerfully within her.

He kissed her long and deep.

She lifted her pelvis closer to the rhythm of his body.

She locked her legs around him and rode him.

Spasmodic gasps fell upon her lips as Rolling Thunder gently squeezed one of her breasts, rotating the stiff, resilient nipple against his warm palm.

And then his tongue slid down her long, tapered neck, to her breast. He licked and sucked one nipple, then went to the other. With an exquisite tenderness and devotion, he worshiped her sweet, warm flesh with his tongue and lips.

Tanzey's sensations soared. Her fingers trembled as she moved them down the tight muscles of his back.

When she came to his buttocks, she splayed her fingers across them and followed his rhythmic strokes within her.

Suddenly Rolling Thunder rolled away from her.

He reached for one of her hands and led it to his pulsing manhood.

Her eyes locked with his, she saw the passion flame at their depths as she circled his velvet sheath with her fingers and slowly stroked him.

"Do you feel the heat of my passion?" Rolling Thunder whispered huskily, his face a mask of total desire.

"Yes," Tanzey murmured, knowing that she would forever be mystified by this part of his anatomy. "I feel the heat. I feel so many things while touching it. It seems to have a life of its own. It's capable of making everything within me change into something mellow, sweet, and melting. Touching it sends a thrill throughout me that makes my senses reel. It makes me seem foreign to myself in how it affects me."

"Not foreign," Rolling Thunder whispered, closing his eyes in ecstasy as her fingers still played him like an instrument. "You are a woman experiencing things *of* a woman. It is good that it was I who was here to be the one to teach you the true meaning."

"I never want anyone but you," Tanzey murmured, trembling inside when one of his hands went to her woman's center and began caressing it. She sighed as a finger slid inside her, slipped free, then went inside again.

Then he eased her hand from his heat. He bent low over her and flicked his tongue where his fingers had just been. In slow, wet strokes he fueled her fires with his mouth and tongue.

Tanzey was almost mindless with desire.

She gasped and moaned as he continued pleasuring her in such a way.

Too soon she felt as though she was ready to explode with the ultimate of rapture. She placed gentle hands to his cheeks and eased his lips away from her throbbing center.

Twining her arms around his neck, she urged his lips to hers.

And again he plunged inside her with his sleek, tight manhood. The spiraling need was spinning throughout Rolling Thunder. His breathing was ragged as his tongue slipped through her parted lips and touched hers.

His mouth eager, he kissed her urgently.

His hands found the soft swells of her breasts.

His fingers kneaded.

His thumbs caressed the nipples.

The spinning sensation flooded Rolling Thunder's consciousness. He thrust hard into her, his hands now at her hips, lifting her closer.

Feeling the wonders of the released passion throughout her, Tanzey groaned and clung to him, her body lifting and falling as his rhythmic thrusts increased in a demanding speed.

Afterward they both lay quietly together, their breaths mingling.

Lying on his side, Rolling Thunder drew Tanzey close and cradled her in his arms. "Please do not *na-ba-dah-kah*, battle, with me anymore about anything," he whispered against her lips. "Let us be lover friends?"

Having heard him use that Comanche phrase one other time and having asked him the meaning, Tanzey knew exactly what he was asking of her.

She also knew how to say "yes" in Comanche!

"*Huh*, yes," she whispered, cuddling closer. "I would love to be your lover friend forever."

"That would make Rolling Thunder happy," he said in a low voice.

He lifted her chin with a finger and gave her a kiss that made her insides quiver anew with passion.

She hoped and prayed that she could be patient with Rolling Thunder and his beliefs, especially his fears of allowing her to go to her parents. If he made her wait much longer, she was not sure if she could help but argue with him again!

Chapter Fourteen

Afraid? Of whom am I afraid?
Not death, for who is he?

—EMILY DICKINSON

A loud roar awakened Tanzey with a start. Wild-eyed, her heart pounding, she leaned up on an elbow and looked beside her, discovering that Rolling Thunder was gone.

Another loud roar, sounding like a beast from hell, wafted close by and caused goose bumps to crawl along Tanzey's flesh. She held back a shiver as she hugged herself when she heard the roar again.

She jumped with alarm when Rolling Thunder rushed into the lodge, clothed and bathed, his hair dripping wet, his wet skin shining.

"*Kee-mah*, come with me," he said as he went to the back of the lodge and uncovered a rifle that lay hidden beneath a tall stack of pelts.

Tanzey watched him slip many bullets into the pocket of his breeches, then belt a sheathed knife at his left waist.

She winced when once again she heard the roar. This time it seemed closer as the threatening sound tumbled down from the mountains.

"What is that?" Tanzey asked, slipping from the bed, the cushioned mats soft to her bare feet.

"A bear," Rolling Thunder said, tying his hair back with a band. "It seems crazed. It must be killed or else it will eventually kill some innocent Comanche."

He grabbed Tanzey's dress and held it out for her. "Get dressed," he said flatly. "You are going with me."

"What?" Tanzey said, paling.

"The bear is too close," Rolling Thunder stated solemnly. "I will only be assured of your safety if you are with me."

"Rolling Thunder, you saw my skills with firearms," Tanzey said, only halfheartedly taking the dress. "I don't need to go. I can stay here. I can protect myself."

She loved the hunt, but never had she gone after a bear. She had seen too many bears in the mountains and knew their size. When standing upright on their hind legs, they towered like menacing giants over most men.

"*Huh*, that is so," Rolling Thunder mumbled as he waited for her to dress. "But still I feel more comfortable if you ride at my side today. *Namasi—kohtoo*, quick, quick, Tanzey."

"Rolling Thunder, why should I, when surely the other women of the village can't leave their duties to be with their husbands?" Tanzey said, slowly getting the idea that he did not want to take her there only to protect her.

He did not trust leaving her here alone!

He was worried about her leaving and going to her parents!

"You are not most women," Rolling Thunder said, his eyes narrowing as he gazed down at her.

"You don't trust me, do you?" Tanzey asked, now

slipping on soft moccasins. "You don't trust leaving me alone."

"Perhaps not," Rolling Thunder said, a slow glow entering his eyes.

"All right, *don't* trust me," Tanzey said. She squared her shoulders and placed her hands on her hips. "But if I am expected to ride with you on a bear hunt, I assume you will let me carry a firearm?"

Rolling Thunder's lips lifted into a slow smile.

Then he went back to his cache of weapons. All along firearms had been only inches away, and she had not known it.

If she *had* known they were there, would she have held off the Comanche warriors at gunpoint while fleeing the village?

Or would she have stayed in order to keep Rolling Thunder's trust and love forever?

"Will you ever truly trust me?" Tanzey said as she took the rifle, relieved to see that it was her own firearm. He had taken it from her on the day of her capture. She had thought to never see it again!

"When your belly is heavy with child, *our* child, only then will I be able to truly trust that you will not flee when my back is turned to you," Rolling Thunder said, his eyes wavering into hers.

"I'm sorry, Rolling Thunder," Tanzey murmured, fighting back the hurt that his words caused inside her heart. "I wish I could reassure you. It just doesn't seem right that you feel you must wait until . . . until . . . I am with child, to trust me. I love you. You *know* that I love you. That should be proof enough that I would do nothing to hurt you."

The sound of voices and horses neighing outside the lodge caused silence to fall between Tanzey and Rolling Thunder. They gazed into one another's eyes for a moment longer.

Then Rolling Thunder lay his rifle aside and drew Tanzey into his strong embrace.

"*Nei-com-mar-pe-ein*, I love you," he whispered, his mouth brushing soft kisses across her lips.

Tanzey twined an arm around his neck and kissed him.

His kiss deepened and his free hand crept down her back, then reached up inside her dress and caressed her woman's center.

Breathless, Tanzey managed to find a semblance of rational mind to slip away from him.

When the bear let out another loud roar, followed by another and another, Rolling Thunder grabbed up his rifle.

Together they hurried from the tepee.

Outside, many warriors waited on their saddled horses. Among them were Brant Fire In The Sky, his rifle held snugly in one hand. He smiled down at Tanzey, and she could not help but marvel at how right her brother seemed to look more and more like a Comanche, his hair drawn back into two braids, a necklace of colorful beads around his neck.

When a young brave brought Rolling Thunder and Tanzey a horse, Brant Fire In The Sky's smile faded. He gave Rolling Thunder a silent, questioning gaze, then watched, narrow-eyed, as his sister swung herself into the leather Indian saddle.

Tanzey's eyes locked with her brother's as she slipped her rifle into its gun boot. A young brave secured a lasso at the girth of her saddle. She knew that her brother questioned her going on the hunt, but he held his silence. To question Rolling Thunder's decision would be the same as doubting his intelligence and authority!

And Brant Fire In The Sky knew Tanzey's skills with firearms. He knew that she could probably outshoot any Comanche warrior who stared blankly at her. They also silently questioned her presence, while all of the other women were mulling around together, dutifully watching their men prepare to leave for the hunt.

Tanzey's gaze sorted through the women and found Feather Moon. She was standing among the others. Her hands were resting on the soft round mound of her belly, tears streaming from her eyes as she gazed raptly at her husband.

Again the bear gave off a great roar.

Again it sounded closer.

Again shivers raced along Tanzey's flesh!

"*Nah-ich-ka*? You hear? *Mea-dro*! Let us go!" Rolling Thunder shouted. He waved his rifle in the air as he looked over his shoulder at his warriors. "Let us claim the *pza-or-boisa*, crazed bear!"

Rolling Thunder slid his rifle into his gun boot, and before leaving for the campaign, he raised his arms toward the heavens, where the Wise One Above lived in the sun. He said a prayer out loud for all of his people to hear, asking that he and his people would receive the blessing of the Great Maker during this time of crisis.

When the final word of the prayer was said, the warriors let out several loud whooping sounds and rode off.

Tanzey rode beside Rolling Thunder, square-shouldered and straight-backed in the saddle.

She had not had the time to brush her hair before leaving. It fluttered loosely around her face and shoulders in the breeze of the hard, galloping ride. She enjoyed morning rides like this, but preferred them with less danger. Going on a hunt for deer, even an occasional antelope, had always been invigorating to Tanzey.

But never had she done anything as dangerous as going out to find a bear that seemed intent on killing.

She tried to hold down the fear that kept creeping more deeply into her heart at the thought of possibly coming face-to-face with the bear. By the sound of its bellowing cries, it had to be huge. It could be perhaps the most dangerous adversary that Tanzey had ever faced.

She flicked her reins and rode onward, never getting more than a foot or two away from the side of Rolling Thunder's white mustang. For the first time in her life that she could ever remember, she sought the protection of a man.

And it felt good, even sweet, to be this close to the man she loved in the eye of approaching danger.

Everything in her mellowed as she cast Rolling Thunder a lingering stare. She just did not see how any man could be so handsome that he stirred her to wanting him even now while growing closer and closer to the moment of the dreaded danger.

Her love for him was something wild, yet beautiful. She wanted him every second of her life now that she had found such paradise in their lovemaking. If he stopped now and took her from her horse and laid her down amid the rich grass and wildflowers, she would do nothing to stop him as he made love to her in the presence of his warriors.

A tingling between her legs, the warmth spreading as her body rocked and swayed in the saddle, made her feel as though Rolling Thunder's hands were there. They had been caressing her, bringing her to life in places that had been barren until he showed her what it meant to be aroused.

The rhythmic rocking of the saddle against her tender woman's center made a warm glow begin to spread. She closed her eyes as the pleasure over-whelmed her.

A loud burst of roars from the bear from some-where not that far away caused Tanzey's eyes to open wildly. Heat rushed to her cheeks when she realized what had just happened to her, how her sen-sual side had surfaced at such a strange time as this, how the pleasure had spread like wildfire through her as the saddle wiggled against that part of her that was still tender from the lovemaking of the night before.

She was aghast at the thought of having found the ultimate of pleasure by herself, away from the comforting, loving arms of Rolling Thunder.

She looked slowly around her, to see if anyone had noticed.

Mortified, she realized Rolling Thunder's eyes were on her, his lips tugged slowly into a knowing smile.

Tanzey swallowed hard and looked away from him. Her heart raced with humiliation. She could not help but wonder how he truly felt about what he had obviously witnessed.

Had she proven to be wanton in her behavior?

Surely not. What had happened had not been planned. It had just happened!

But what puzzled her the most was how she *could* feel such pleasure and not even be touched by the man she loved!

It frightened her to know that one could become so sensual, alone!

Tanzey could not help but forget her troubled thoughts when she became aware of traveling down a winding valley, a very rapid stream dissecting it. When she turned to the right alongside Rolling Thunder, she found herself rounding the point of a high bluff.

Thick, shadowed shrubs lined the path. Cottonwood trees loomed high overhead, their rustling leaves giving off their familiar sound of rain.

When they arrived at the extreme point of the narrow valley, Tanzey found it hard to keep her horse at bay.

He whinnied.

He yanked at the bit.

He trembled and snorted.

Rolling Thunder eased his own nervous horse closer to Tanzey's. "Hold him steady," he said, his hands tight on his reins. "Horses are smart, especially mustangs that once shared the wildness of the land with bears. The mustangs know the closeness of a bear. Their primal instinct gives them fear. Even a faint scent of the hunting bear makes a horse tremble in terror and become unmanageable."

"Then, we are near the bear?" Tanzey asked, her voice drawn with the building fear.

"*Huh*, yes," Rolling Thunder said, his hand slipping his rifle from its gun boot as his eyes looked cautiously from side to side, then ahead, where the path was darkened by thick brush. "A horse knows by the scent that this great beast, the bear, could kill him as a fox kills a rabbit, cracking his bones as easily."

He sidled his horse closer to Tanzey's. "All Comanche horses are trained to stand by as sentinels," he said. "It is all in the horse's ears. The Comanche horses have been taught to 'wave' his ears alternately if a coyote or bear is near. If it is a man he becomes aware of, he pitches both ears forward."

Tanzey stiffened as she stared at Rolling Thunder's

steed's ears. He ... was ... waving his ears alternately!

Her gaze then followed the path of Rolling Thunder's. Everything was so mutely quiet, whereas not that long ago they could continuously hear the bear's loud voice.

She feared that was a bad sign ... that the bear was somewhere out there now, watching, waiting, calculating when it should attack, already eyeing what it wanted for its morning meal.

Overwhelmed by fear, she gulped hard, whereas usually she faced it with determination and unfailing courage.

But she knew that her fears were warranted. She could even see the same fear in the eyes of all of those warriors who rode today on the hunt.

Suddenly there was a great crash of splintering wood. All of the horses went wild, quivering, tossing their heads, digging their hooves into the dirt.

Some horses even reared as the bear came into the open only a short distance away. The brown bear was at least ten feel tall as it walked erect on its hind legs.

The great, snarling mouth, filled with gleaming white teeth, emitted growls that sounded like low rumbles of thunder as the bear's dark little eyes peered from man to man.

The warriors fought hard at getting their horses calmed.

And when they finally managed to get them under control, two of the warriors broke away from the others and galloped after the bear.

Spellbound by the warriors' courage, Tanzey watched them throw their nooses over the bear's neck.

While one twitched the bear over on its back, the

other threw his lasso over the bear's hind legs, then subjected him to a most uncomfortable stretch as they pulled him in opposite directions.

The warriors leapt from their steeds and lunged toward the bear.

A knife killed the bear and as it lay in great pools of blood, a warrior scalped his hide.

Tanzey sighed deeply and smiled over at Rolling Thunder. "I'm glad it's over," she said, wiping pearl beads of sweat from her brow. "But why did only two men go after the bear?"

"They were the first to break loose from the others," Rolling Thunder said, at peace with himself over allowing someone else such a kill, a feast guaranteed many days in the warriors' lodges.

He gazed at Tanzey. "These two warriors have many children to feed," he uttered. "And even though bear meat is eaten, it is not regarded as equal to buffalo, beef, or venison."

He gazed at the men again, who still plunged into the bear carcass with their sharp carving knives. "Bears are hunted considerably by the Comanche for their oil," he said. "It is used primarily in preparation of various kinds of skins."

While everyone had been so absorbed in watching the warriors prepare the bear, no one had noticed the horses becoming edgy again, their hooves digging nervously in the ground beneath them, their nostrils flaring as they sniffed the air.

No one noticed the rustling of the tall grass at their right side, or how the branches of the trees parted as something made its way toward the men and the one woman on horseback.

And when they finally became aware of the new threat, it was too late. The huge brown bear suddenly appeared from what seemed out of nowhere, only a few feet from Rolling Thunder.

Rolling Thunder's horse emitted a loud shrieking sound, shook its mane, then bucked and threw Rolling Thunder from the saddle.

Stunned, Tanzey watched the bear fall to its four paws and nudge Rolling Thunder awkwardly from the path.

"Oh, God, *no!*" Tanzey shouted, paling when the huge bear's mouth opened wide.

Its sharp white teeth flashed in the sunlight.

Its small eyes narrowed on Rolling Thunder as it lifted a heavy paw above him, its sharp claws distended.

Before the bear could take a wide swipe of Rolling Thunder with its claws or its powerful jaws and sharp teeth, a shot rang out from somewhere close by.

The bear's body lurched with the blow from the bullet, not once, but twice, as the gunfire continued in quick, flashy spatters of red.

And then the bear collapsed onto its side—its eyes frozen in a death stare, its fur covered with blood.

Tanzey's throat was dry.

She stared disbelievingly at the bear, then stifled a sob of relief behind a hand when her gaze shifted to Rolling Thunder, who was rising from the ground, unharmed, brushing dirt and dead pine needles from his clothes.

Brant Fire In The Sky rode up next to Tanzey, his rifle still smoking from firing it.

He slid from the saddle and stood over the bear, then turned smiling eyes to Rolling Thunder.

"It was your firearm that downed the animal?" Rolling Thunder said, going to stand beside Brant Fire In The Sky over the downed bear.

Tanzey slipped from the saddle and went to Rolling Thunder. She hurried into his embrace. Pressing her cheek against his chest, she hugged him tightly.

Tears splashed from her eyes to think that she had come so close to losing him.

And she would never forget how she froze at the sight of the bear being such a threat to Rolling Thunder.

Would fear have stopped her from rescuing Rolling Thunder had they been alone on the trail?

She gazed over at Brant. She was glad for more than one reason that he had saved this powerful Comanche war chief's life! In the Comanche village, her brother would now be looked to as someone more special than just a white man married to a Comanche princess!

"*Huh*, yes, it was my rifle that downed the bear," Brant Fire In The Sky said, proudly squaring his shoulders.

"Thank you, courageous brother," Rolling Thunder said, lifting a warm hand of appreciation to Brant's shoulder.

Rolling Thunder gazed again at the bear, then at Brant Fire In The Sky. "My brother, touch the dead bear with your hand and yell, *Ahe*, I claim it, so that you can, alone, achieve the honor."

Brant Fire In The Sky gave Rolling Thunder a quizzical stare, glanced over at Tanzey, looked slowly around at the quiet warriors whose eyes were on him, then did as he was told. He fell to his knees beside the bear and placed both hands on the carcass.

"*Ahe*, I claim this bear as mine!" he shouted, his eyes showing the pride he felt.

Tanzey crept a hand over and twined her fingers through Rolling Thunder's. She stood proudly beside him as the Comanche warriors came, one by one, and gave her brother an affectionate hug.

Then Rolling Thunder stepped away from her and embraced Brant Fire In The Sky. "You are looked to as a warrior of great courage," he said. "There will soon be a celebration in your honor!"

Brant Fire In The Sky looked over Rolling Thunder's shoulder at Tanzey.

Their eyes locked.

Their smiles spoke so much that words could never say.

Chapter Fifteen

In the dusk of day-shapes,
Blurring the sunset,
One little wandering, western star
Thrust out from the changing shores of shadow.
—CARL SANDBURG

Tanzey glanced over at her brother. She could see him straining his neck as he gazed toward the village. She could see the anxiousness in his eyes. She knew that it was because he was eager to show off his bear kill to his wife.

More than that, her brother was eager to see his wife's expression when Rolling Thunder told everyone that it was Feather Moon's white husband who had come to Rolling Thunder's rescue.

The body of the brown bear was proof of that, as it lay, uncut, on the travois at the back of Brant Fire In The Sky's steed. He would prepare the animal later so that he could show off its size to his wife.

Everyone could also see the animal that had almost killed their war chief!

The bear, which had been a danger to their people, was dead.

None of their loved ones had been injured on the hunt.

And there was plenty of red bear meat for three of the lodges.!

Tanzey smiled to herself. It had been a good hunt, and Rolling Thunder was alive!

She looked over at him, her insides melting as he slid her a soft smile.

When she saw something enter his eyes and recognized the look that he got just prior to their lovemaking, she knew what he was thinking about. The celebration was something wonderful for his people. But it was a hindrance to what she and Rolling Thunder were both eager for.

To be alone.

To embrace.

To kiss.

To explore each other's bodies with their lips, tongues, and hands.

Rolling Thunder edged his steed closer to Tanzey's. "Tell me what is on your mind at this exact moment," he said, his eyes dancing into hers.

Tanzey laughed softly, blushed, then leaned closer to him. "I am sure the same that is on yours," she murmured.

"You know that the celebration of the hunt comes before the celebration of our bodies, do you not?" Rolling Thunder teased. "Do you think you can wait, my beautiful Tanzey Nicole?"

"Can you?" Tanzey said, her husky voice strange to her. "Or do you think we could be at the celebration in spirit only?"

"Perhaps," Rolling Thunder said, chuckling.

Then his smile changed abruptly when several warriors who had not been a part of the hunt came from the village in a hard gallop on their horses.

Tense, knowing that something must be wrong, Rolling Thunder nudged his heels into the flanks of his horse and rode away from Tanzey toward those who were approaching him.

Tanzey watched for a moment, then rode after him. She had seen the sudden change in his mood.

She knew that something was wrong, or why hadn't the warriors just waited for the hunting party to arrive at the village?

Curious and wary, Tanzey flicked her reins and rode in a harder gallop after Rolling Thunder.

She drew a tight rein beside him just as he came face-to-face with his warriors and stopped.

"Why do you ride from our village to meet me with faces of gloom?" Rolling Thunder asked.

He looked slowly from man to man.

"Colonel Franks from Fort Phantom Hill met with some of our warriors outside our village at our usual place of council," Big Bow said sullenly. "He asked to see you. I told him that you were on the hunt. He said to tell you, upon your return, that some white eye settlers' ranches close to Fort Phantom Hill have been raided by marauding Comanche renegades and their outlaw brothers. Colonel Franks has asked if you and our warriors will join in the search for those responsible for the raids. Colonel Franks said that your knowledge of the land and its hiding places is much greater than the white eye pony soldiers'."

Tanzey was frustrated from having not understood everything the warrior had relayed to Rolling Thunder. He had spoken some words in Comanche ... some in English.

And he had spoken so quickly and chopped, she had only been able to grasp onto the words "marauding Comanche renegades" and "ranches." The news about both could not be good, for the warrior who spoke of those things to Rolling Thunder was somber.

So was Rolling Thunder as he sat on his horse, receiving the news.

She could not hold back her silence any longer.

"Rolling Thunder, what did the warrior say?" she asked, reaching over to anxiously grab his arm.

He turned to her. "There is more trouble being spread along land that is occupied by white eyes," he answered. "Renegades and outlaws are raiding and killing not that far from Fort Phantom Hill. Colonel Franks of Fort Phantom Hill has sought our help. To keep a peaceful bond with the pony soldiers, I will go and do as he requests. I will lead him where the renegades and their outlaw brothers might be hiding."

Tanzey's pulse raced. She paled at the thought of her very own family living on a ranch not that far from Fort Phantom Hill. Her mother and stepfather and the ranch hands could never be powerful enough to stave off an attack by bloodthirsty, murdering, thieving renegades and outlaws.

"My parents," she gasped. "Lord, Rolling Thunder, what if they are one of those who ... were ... ?"

He placed a gentle finger to her lips, silencing her words. "Do not borrow trouble by seeing in your mind's eye that which might not be true," he said.

Tanzey shoved his hand aside. "But I must *know*," she blurted out. "You must allow me to go and *see*."

Rolling Thunder frowned at her. "This would be the worst of times for you to leave my village," he scolded. "Until the ones who are casting dark clouds over the land by their evil deeds are stopped, you will not be safe unless under my protection."

Tanzey sighed impatiently. "I don't mean to insult you by saying this, Rolling Thunder, but I have survived quite well up until now without your protection," she said, her jaw tightening. "Please do not cause a rift between us by ... by ... ordering me not to investigate my parents' welfare."

"The side of you who wishes to behave like a man makes you say things you should not say," Rolling Thunder said, his voice drawn. "The woman side of you should welcome a man's protection .. a man's concern."

"I am being myself by worrying about my parents," Tanzey said.

She looked sharply to her right side when her brother rode up beside her. She saw him as a welcome reprieve, for she was near to saying things to Rolling Thunder that he might never forgive.

"What's wrong?" Brant Fire In The Sky asked, forking an eyebrow. He looked from Tanzey to Rolling Thunder, then back at Tanzey again. "What's happened? Tell me."

Tanzey's words spilled hurriedly across her lips as she explained to her brother about the raids, and about Rolling Thunder's bad timing of being stubborn.

"Brant, tell him that we should go and see about our parents," Tanzey pleaded. "Brant, please tell him. I don't think I can stand not knowing much longer."

Brant Fire In The Sky's eyes locked with Rolling Thunder's. "And so you do not think it is wise for my sister to go and check on our parents?" he said guardedly.

"Do not ask, even yourself, to go, not to your ranch, or to ride with the Comanche," Rolling Thunder said, expecting Brant Fire In The Sky's next words. "It is too soon for you to be seen anywhere.

This is not a good time for the Comanche to be faced with questions about you."

"But you allowed me to go on the hunt with you," Brant Fire In The Sky said, feeling his sister's angry eyes on him, as though boring a hole through him. "Why would you not let me go elsewhere with you? It doesn't make sense, Rolling Thunder ... unless ... unless my sister and I both are still seen as captives in the eyes of your people."

"*Ka*, no, not *captives*," Rolling Thunder said, sliding a slow gaze to the woman he loved. "You both mean much to my people. For now, let that be enough. Stay behind. Stay safe. That is all I ask of you. Soon you, as well as I, will make our appearances at your parents' ranch. Soon."

He paused, his eyes locking with Tanzey's, hating to see the defiance in the depths of hers. He did not allow her defiance to sway his decision to see that she be kept out of harm's way.

He gave Brant Fire In The Sky a sharp glance. "But not now," he said flatly. "That is my final word. *Suvate*! It is finished!"

Angry, Tanzey emitted a huffy, frustrated sigh, then rode off from Rolling Thunder toward the village.

Rolling Thunder watched Tanzey. Not sure she would ride past his village and on to her parents' ranch, Rolling Thunder frowned over at Big Bow. "Follow her!" he growled. "See that she does not go farther than our village!"

Big Bow nodded, then took off after her.

Rolling Thunder gazed over at Brant Fire In The Sky. "Do you have more to say, or do you accept my decision about things?" he said, his voice weary.

"I wish to have no hard feelings with you," Brant Fire In The Sky said. "But I have to say, Rolling

Thunder, that my sister can be pushed just so far. Do you think it is wise to continue forbidding her so much? Do you not fear losing her love?''

"She loves too deeply ever to turn her back on me," Rolling Thunder said, slowly nodding.

He reached a hand to Brant Fire In The Sky's shoulder. He clasped his fingers onto it. "And you?" he said, searching Brant Fire In The Sky's eyes. "And how do you feel about not being given your total freedom just yet? Is resentment against me and my people building inside your heart? Or do you see that my decisions are wise?''

"I understand that you know my deep love for Feather Moon and know that it could abruptly end if my being with the Comanche is misinterpreted by the soldiers at Fort Phantom Hill," Brant Fire In The Sky said. "But I do not like being held back, as though I am still a captive. I would like to be given back my ability to choose what *I* see is right and wrong for myself and my wife." He swallowed hard. "I do not ask for anything for my sister, for I know that it is no longer my place to do so. She is yours. I accept that."

Again he swallowed hard. "But I feel less than a man by saying that, and by not fighting for my sister's rights *and* freedom," he said guardedly.

"Never think of yourself as weak only because you do what is right for all concerned," Rolling Thunder said, then rode away from him in a hard gallop toward the village, his warriors following his lead.

Tanzey grumbled beneath her breath and gave Big Bow a sour look as she rode up in front of Rolling Thunder's lodge.

She wheeled her horse to a trembling halt, ignored the stares of the Comanche people as they waited by the outdoor fire for the hunters to return, and stamped on inside Rolling Thunder's lodge.

Her cheeks burning with anger, her heart pounding, Tanzey paced back and forth as she waited for Rolling Thunder to return.

She had a few choice words to say to him.

She was through with being mealymouthed with him.

She was through bowing down to him!

If he loved her, he would understand her frustrations better!

He would understand why she had to go and check on her parents!

"Or at *least* he can promise to check on them *for* me," she whispered harshly to herself.

Then she flailed her hands into the air, realizing that she had just again thought to compromise with him by thinking to *ask* him to do what *she* wanted to do, her*self*.

"No, I won't be pushed around any longer," she whispered, growing angrier by the minute.

She stopped and stared at the entrance flap when she heard the thundering of hooves arriving at the village. Her heart thudded wildly within her chest as she waited for Rolling Thunder to enter the lodge. She folded her arms across her chest and tapped one toe nervously as she continued to wait.

Where was he?

Why didn't he come into the lodge?

Surely he wasn't going to just ride out again so soon, and go on to the fort?

Her lips parted and her eyes widened when she heard the loud whoops and war cries of the warriors, followed by the loud thundering of the horses' hooves as they left the village.

Then everything was quiet.

Tanzey crept from the tepee.

She gazed around her.

Things seemed normal enough.

The women were going about their chores.

The children were playing.

The elderly men were sitting beneath the shade of cottonwood trees, whittling on sticks, smoking pipes or cigarettes, or gossiping.

Then her gaze fell on the two warriors who had killed the one brown bear. They were hanging huge pieces of bear meat on racks to dry, the blood dripping red from them. Their wives were marveling over the pelt, smoothing their hands over its softness.

Tanzey's gaze shifted. She was taken aback by how her brother so casually sat outside his lodge with his wife as they both carved into the other brown bear's carcass, its pelt already hanging and drying on a huge rack beside their lodge.

"How can he be so casual about everything when ... when ... our parents' lives might be in danger?" Tanzey marveled to herself.

She ran over to him. She grabbed him by the wrist, the knife in his hand dripping with blood as he stared up at her.

"Brant, put the knife down," Tanzey said, her voice flat. "You've got to come with me. We're going to go and check on Mother and Father."

"Tanzey, let go of me," Brant Fire In The Sky said, pleading at her with his grass-green eyes.

"Brant, Rolling Thunder is gone," Tanzey pleaded. "We can ride out, go check on our parents, then return before Rolling Thunder gets back. He would never be the wiser."

Her thoughts went back to the previous evening, when she and Rolling Thunder were talking about "trust." She wouldn't think about it now, how she would disappoint him if he discovered that she had gone against his wishes. Her parents' welfare came now before her own. If anything happened to them, and she hadn't at least attempted to set things right for them, she would never forgive herself.

"Tanzey, Rolling Thunder, his warriors, and the soldiers from Fort Phantom Hill will be checking on our parents," Brant Fire In The Sky said. He stared at her hand that still gripped his wrist. "Sis, let go. You aren't proving anything by acting this way."

"Brant, I never thought I would ever call you a coward," Tanzey said, slowly dropping her hand away from him. "But how can I not when you sit there so nonchalant and uncaring?" She placed her hands on her hips and glared at him. "Just stay there with your pretty wife and carve your meat. I'm not sure if I will ever forgive you."

Brant Fire In The Sky dropped the knife to the ground. He rose quickly to his feet, grabbed Tanzey by a hand, and briskly walked her to the back of his lodge.

"Listen to me, Tanzey Nicole," he said, his eyes narrowed with anger. "I didn't ask to be brought here. I didn't ask to be taken captive! But I *was*. And it has not turned out as I had thought it would. I have found something here that I never had before. I'm in love with a beautiful woman. Tanzey, she's my *wife*. And I am soon to be a father! I will risk nothing that might cause me to lose my wife and child. And if you don't understand, Tanzey, to hell with you!"

Tanzey paled. She gasped. "But, Brant, our parents?" she said, her wrist burning where his fingers squeezed.

"Tanzey, stop and think about it," Brant Fire In The Sky said tightly. "What can you and I do that the soldiers and Rolling Thunder can't? That is why they are getting together on this mission . . . to check all of the ranches, which will include ours."

He inched his hand from her wrist, then placed both hands to her waist and drew her into his embrace. "Sis, please be patient," he said softly. "There is so much at stake here. Please go back to Rolling Thunder's lodge. Relax. Soon word will be brought to us that our parents are all right. Isn't that all that's important?"

Not wanting to think that her brother was a coward, loving him too much, and understanding how someone could love as fiercely as he loved, Tanzey nodded.

"All right," she murmured, yet she knew that she would sneak away from the lodge at her first opportunity. For the moment, Big Bow was standing guard. But he would slip up, somehow, and she would take advantage of that moment.

She gave her brother a soft hug, then went back to Rolling Thunder's tepee and waited.

She watched through the smoke hole overhead for the color of the sky to change. And when the gray light of night began pushing the blue sky from the heavens, Tanzey grabbed her rifle. She picked up a knife and went to the back of the tepee. No longer caring if Rolling Thunder discovered her gone, knowing that she was right to go and see about her parents, she carved into the buckskin fabric until she had a space large enough to step through.

She rushed from the lodge, and ran breathlessly to the corralled horses.

The sky was pitch-black when she rode away from the Comanche village, the moon thankfully hidden beneath a thick cover of clouds.

Tanzey gripped the reins tightly as she sent her steed into a hard gallop across the land.

She raised her eyes to the sky and said a soft prayer.

She prayed that she would find her parents alive and their ranch left untouched.

She prayed that she would return to Rolling Thunder's lodge before he discovered her breach of trust!

She only hoped that when she returned, it would not be with sorrow over having been too late for her parents.

Chapter Sixteen

Remorse is memory awake,
Her companies astir—
A presence of departed acts.

—EMILY DICKINSON

The closer Tanzey drew to her parents' ranch, the more tense she became.

That smell.

She sniffed the air.

What was that smell?

It was a mixture of many things, most unpleasant.

She drove her steed onward in a much harder gallop. She lay low, her knees clutching the sides of the horse, her fingers raw from grasping the reins too tightly.

Soon she found herself riding into a heavy, gray haze.

Smoke!

Charred wood!

Singed grass!

And ... and ... dead carcasses!

The moonlight revealed first one dead cow, and then another, their bodies hardly recognizable.

She gulped back the urge to vomit from the stench as she rode through the black ash of burned grass.

Flames stirred again as her horse's hooves rode through the grass. The flames lapped at the horse's legs, causing him to whinny and shake his heavy mane nervously.

Tanzey was overwhelmed with fear from the expectation of what she was soon to find. She bit her lower lip to keep herself from crying out in despair.

Death and destruction this close to her parents' property was not a good sign.

The soldiers . . . Rolling Thunder and his warriors . . . were not in time to save her parents from the attack.

Rolling Thunder had been right to keep her away for that reason.

But Rolling Thunder not allowing Tanzey to communicate with her parents ate away at her heart. They had died not knowing she and Brant were still alive. No one had been given the chance to even say good-bye!

"Rolling Thunder, I should hate you for that!" Tanzey cried to the heavens, no longer able to keep everything bottled inside herself.

But hate was the farthest thing from Tanzey's mind right now. She held a tiny ray of hope that her parents might have fled their ranch before the attack.

Perhaps the soldiers had gotten there with their warnings and had urged them to go to the neighboring fort for protection until the murdering villains had been found and stopped.

She hung her head and swallowed back a sob, knowing that her father would have never deserted his land, no matter who brought the warning.

Even if she had been there, he wouldn't have taken cover at the fort.

He was a proud man.

He would never flee from the face of danger.

He would stay and protect what was his.

Tears streamed from her eyes, knowing that her mother would not have gone without him. She would have stayed by his side, even though she didn't know how to fire a gun. She had refused to be taught. She had shivered visibly every time her husband had tried to place a pistol in her hand, warning her that there might come a time when she would need it to protect herself.

But now, as Tanzey finally caught sight of the smoking ash where the ranch had once stood, she knew that even her extra gun would not have stopped what had happened here.

The house.

The bunkhouses.

All of the outbuildings.

The corral.

Everything had been burned to the ground.

Dizzy, Tanzey drew a tight rein and for a moment closed her eyes.

She said the Lord's prayer to give her solace.

She saw flashes of her past, where she had been with her parents, laughing, playing, hugging, kissing.

How could she stand it another second?

The tears came from her eyes in a rush.

Sobbing hard, she leaned down against her horse and hugged him.

Then she slowly straightened her back.

She slid from the saddle.

She dropped the reins.

As she walked slowly toward the house, troubled questions tumbled through her brain.

Where would she find the remains of her parents? Or would she?

What if they had been burned to ashes?

What if she could never give them a Christian burial?

Was the rubble of the house going to be their grave?

Ash swam and spewed around her ankles as she walked through it. She peered through the dim moonlight. She was not sure how she could enter the remains of the house. Charred timbers lay everywhere. Remains of furniture could be seen here and there.

And, like ghosts, the chimneys of the two fireplaces loomed up from the ashes.

Slowly she began walking around the outside perimeters of the house, trying to find a place of entrance.

And then she stopped.

Her eyes widened and her throat became constricted when the moon revealed something to her at the back of the house.

"Mother!" she cried. "Father!"

She clasped a trembling hand over her mouth and held back a scream as she stared from one to the other.

They lay on their stomachs beside one another, her father's arm lying over her mother in an obvious attempt to try and save her.

The attackers had shot each of them in the back as they had tried to flee from their house.

"You heartless bastards!" Tanzey screamed as she pulled at her hair.

Then something came to her that gave her cause to be somewhat thankful.

Her parents had not died in the fire!

They had not suffered in that way!

At least their deaths had come swiftly.

With tears rolling down her cheeks, she fell to her knees beside her mother.

Then she gasped and turned her eyes away when she found her mother's green eyes staring at her in a death stare as her face rested on one cheek against the ground.

Tanzey's heart pounded.

Her throat was dry.

Knowing that she had to get control of herself, to do what was required of her, then get back to the village, where she could find safety again, Tanzey took a deep breath.

She brushed tears from her eyes.

She lifted her hair back from her shoulders.

Then she turned toward her mother again and lovingly closed her eyes. She took the time to comb her fingers through her mother's long red hair. She bent a soft kiss to her cheek.

Then she went to her father and closed his eyes, leaned over and hugged him, then rose quickly to her feet and looked guardedly around her.

She was still alone, mutely so.

Everything was ghostly quiet, whereas the usual sounds at night here on the ranch had been aplenty, from the sounds of the horses and cattle, the songs of the crickets, an occasional hoot of an owl, and the howling of a wolf.

She had always enjoyed closing her eyes and listening at night, knowing that she would carry those sounds of her childhood with her the rest of her life.

Now the sun was beginning to rise.

She gazed toward the rubble that once was the bunkhouse. She shuddered to realize how many men must have perished there. Her thoughts went to Terry McKee, her favorite of all those who had worked for her father. He must have also died during the ambush.

She gazed at the barn. The sheep, cows, chickens, had all been silenced.

She looked toward the remains of the corral. The horses that had not been caught in the fire had been stolen.

"A shovel," Tanzey whispered to herself. "I've got to find a shovel."

She wanted to mourn her parents properly, but she knew the dangers of staying here too long. Who was to say whether or not the renegades and outlaws might come back on their way to their hideout?

Tanzey broke into a run toward the barn. If she was in luck, she might find a shovel, or a pitchfork, that she could use to dig the graves. She could not take the time to dig a deep grave. She had to hurry. She had to get back to safety.

Oh, Lord, she had to tell Brant!

When she reached the barn, she kicked at the charred remains with her moccasined feet, finally unearthing a shovel, its handle only half burned away.

Breathless, she ran to the creek. She would find soft enough soil on the embankment, which would enable her to dig a quick grave. When all of this was over and the culprits were hung by the neck until they were dead, she would direct the soldiers at Fort Phantom Hill where they could find the graves. They could come and get her parents' remains. They could then have a decent burial in the small cemetery near the fort.

Feeling only half alive, her emptiness so deep over the deaths of her parents, Tanzey finally got the graves dug and her parents lovingly covered by several inches of dirt.

She took enough time to say verses from the Bible

that she had memorized as a child while attending Sunday school in Kansas, then rode off in the direction of the Comanche village.

She almost collapsed in her brother's arms after dismounting before his lodge.

He gathered her up into his arms and carried her inside, his gaze wild as he looked at the ash . . . and . . . blood on her clothes and hands.

"Tanzey, good Lord, what . . . ?" Brant Fire In The Sky gasped, but did not get the rest of the words out when Tanzey flung herself against him and clung, while telling him between deep sobs what she had found.

Stunned, Brant Fire In The Sky held Tanzey close. He closed his eyes as he envisioned all that she had described to him. He tried to block it from his consciousness, for the knowing was too painful.

Brant Fire In The Sky placed Tanzey on her feet, then ran from the tepee.

Tanzey wiped tears from her eyes as she gazed over at Feather Moon, who stood there, her hands resting on the tiny ball of her stomach, eyes wide.

Then Tanzey stepped aside as Feather Moon ran from the lodge.

Tanzey lowered her eyes and held her face in her hands as she listened to Feather Moon trying to console her husband, while Brant's deep sobs and cries of remorse tore at Tanzey's very being.

She left the tepee, stopped and gazed at her brother for a moment as he clung to Feather Moon, then walked lifelessly toward the river and dove in.

She swam and swam until her arms ached with the effort. She wanted to get rid of the stench of the blood, the dead, and the burned ash.

But no matter how much she was able to get off

herself and her clothes, the memory of her murdered parents would remain forever.

She realized it had not been God's plan for her to be with her parents. Therefore, she would not condemn herself or Rolling Thunder.

"Why, God?" she cried as she half crawled from the water, her knees weak. "Why did they have to die? Why did they have to die like *that*?"

Panting, Tanzey lay on the soft banks of the river for a while, then pulled herself up from the ground and went back to the tepee.

Only half aware of what she was doing, Tanzey took off her soiled clothes and tossed them outside.

Naked, her hair dripping, she went to the bed at the back of the lodge and eased onto it.

She relived everything that she had seen and done tonight until she was exhausted.

She closed her eyes and escaped into a deep sleep.

Then she felt something wonderful that drew her awake . . . Rolling Thunder's arms as he drew her up on his lap and cradled her close.

Sobbing, she cuddled. She pressed her cheek against his chest. "They are dead," she murmured. "Oh, Rolling Thunder, my parents are dead."

"*Huh*, yes, I know," he said solemnly. "We went there. We saw the destruction. We found the fresh graves."

"Then, you know . . . ?' ' she asked, leaning away from him, gazing into his eyes.

"*Huh*, I know that you were there and that you buried your parents," he uttered. "I have spoken with your brother. He told me everything."

"I had to go," Tanzey said, swallowing back a sob. "Can you understand?"

"*Huh*, I understand, but I cannot say that I am happy that you went against my wishes," he said, lifting her chin with a finger, their eyes locking. "What you did was foolish. You could have been killed."

"Rolling Thunder, I could hate you, you know, for keeping me from my parents these past several days," Tanzey said, her eyes searching his.

"But you do not hate me," he said. He framed her face between his hands and brought her lips close to his. "You see now that had I allowed you to go, you would possibly also be dead."

"Yes, I know," Tanzey said, sighing when he gave her a soft, comforting kiss.

Then he sat her down on the bed and handed her a thick bear robe. "Time will heal your hurt," he said softly. "I will help with the healing."

"I'll never be able to forget how they looked," Tanzey said, visibly shuddering. She snuggled into the robe. "I wish I could have helped them . . . I wish I could have said a final good-bye."

"The last time you were with them was a time of joy and happiness, was it not?" Rolling Thunder said. He took her hand and led her to the trunk of books.

"Yes, I was always happy with them," Tanzey said softly. She forked an eyebrow when he led her to the floor by the trunk and sat down beside her.

"Then, think of that last time with them as your time of last good-byes," Rolling Thunder said.

He slowly lifted the lid of the trunk. "Such a good-bye then would have been better than a good-bye while dying," he murmured.

He turned to her. "Do you not see the logic in that?" he said, his eyes searching hers. "Did you not have many happy good-byes with them while they were alive?"

"*Huh*, yes, many . . ."

"Then, when you think of your parents, think of those times instead of what you saw tonight."

"I never thought to think of it in that way," she said, marveling over the truth in what he said; over its logic. If she could block out tonight, the rest of her memories were wonderful and sweet.

She reached a hand to Rolling Thunder's cheek. "Thank you," she murmured. "I love you so much."

He took her hand and kissed the palm, then nodded toward the books that lay just inside the trunk. "I have heard by talking with white pony soldiers that some white men's books are written to make people's weariness fade," he said softly. "Do you see any of those books in this chest? Is there one among these that can help lift your burden?"

Tanzey's gaze fell on a Bible.

She lifted it, and her fingers trembled as she lay it on her lap and began thumbing through it. So many passages were familiar. Her mother had repeatedly read them while she was teaching the small children in her Sunday school class.

"That is a book of your liking?" Rolling Thunder asked, watching her turn the pages of the "talking leaves." That had been his first opinion of books, that the pages were leaves and that the words on the pages talked.

Tanzey clutched the book to her bosom. "Yes, this book can give me much comfort," she murmured. "It's a book filled with God's words and thoughts. Yes, it will help lift my burden."

Then she frowned at him. "You have never explained where this chest of books came from," she said softly. "I have often wondered." She swallowed hard. "You know how at first I thought you had stolen them. I know how angry that made you. I knew that I was wrong. I . . . I . . . knew that you would tell me in time exactly why they are in your possession."

"Colonel Franks has a full library of books. He had these to spare. He gave these to me as a gift," Rolling Thunder said. He lifted a book from the chest and opened it. He slowly turned the pages.

"Colonel Franks did not give the books to me because I could read," he said softly. "But because he saw how intrigued I am *with* books. I see their worth. I attach value to books. I cannot read, but I wish one day to be able to."

"Come and sit beside the fire with me," Tanzey said, taking his free hand. "I shall read verses from the Bible to you, for you see, Rolling Thunder, of all the books on the earth, this one is the most valuable."

Rolling Thunder lay the book he had been thumbing through aside. He went and sat by the fire with Tanzey. As she snuggled close to him, she began to read him the Psalms.

Slowly her pain, her heartache, began to wane.

Then she thought of a question she had not yet asked.

"Did you find the heathens who killed my parents?" she asked as she slowly closed the book. She gave Rolling Thunder a weary, sad look.

"Again they eluded us," Rolling Thunder said.

"I feared so," Tanzey said, lowering her eyes.

Chapter Seventeen

If only now I could recall that touch,
First touch of hand in hand—
Did one but know!

— Christine Georgina Rossetti

Several Comanche dawns had come and gone and Tanzey still could not shake her grief.

And knowing that those responsible for her loss were still out there somewhere, free to wreak more havoc on more innocent people, didn't make it easier for Tanzey.

The soldiers and Rolling Thunder's warriors had searched to the point of exhaustion, but no traces of the villains had been found.

"It is another Comanche dawn, and you still cannot place a smile on that pretty face?" Rolling Thunder said as he turned to Tanzey in their bed.

Tanzey fought back tears, as she had each day upon first awakening. Each dawn made her realize all over again that she had another day to get through.

She wiped tears from her eyes when Rolling Thunder placed his muscled arms around her and turned her to face him.

"Look up at the smoke hole," he said. "The soft pink of the sky as the sun rises promises another beautiful day. Before the sun is replaced by the moon today, I vow to you that you will place your sadness behind you."

"I so badly want to," Tanzey said, her eyes wavering into his.

The way he looked at her, his love and devotion for her in the depths of his eyes, caused Tanzey to tremble with an ecstasy she had denied herself these past days. She had felt shameful in that she desired her beloved war chief with every ounce of her being while her parents were lying in the ground, never to love again.

She was at least thankful for one thing. Her parents now lay in a cemetery close to Fort Phantom Hill. Tanzey had chosen the grave site . . . a shady spread of land where the wind sang through the towering cottonwoods all day.

That had given Tanzey some solace, to know that her parents were in their final resting place.

Also, upon Tanzey's request, her parents shared the same pine coffin, their bodies touching.

"Have I not seen to your comforts well enough during your time of mourning?" Rolling Thunder murmured, brushing thick locks of her hair back from her face. His gaze moved slowly over her nakedness, having fought back his desire while she had not wanted *that* sort of comforting.

But he felt that perhaps making love might be the only way to pull her from her self-imposed exile and her guilt.

"*Huh*, yes, how sweet you have been to me," Tanzey murmured. She scooted closer to him, their bodies sensually touching each other. "You have been so sweet and gentle, caring for me both day and night.

You have made sure that I have not wanted for a thing."

"Except peace of mind," Rolling Thunder said. He placed his hands to her cheeks and drew her face closer to his. "I could not give you something that you would not let yourself accept."

He brushed a soft kiss across her lips. "It is time, my sweet Tanzey Nicole, to place your sadness behind you. Accept what fate has handed you. Do you know that it was written in the stars that your parents would die before you, even before you were a seed in your mother's womb? As it is written in the stars that I am going to make love to you this morning, and that you will return the loving, twofold."

Tanzey snuggled closer. "*Huh*, yes, twofold," she whispered, knowing that he was right, that it *was* time to start living again.

She now realized, from the sudden deaths of her parents, that life could be short. She did not want to waste another moment of her life by wallowing in self-pity.

There was so much more to life than that.

There was Rolling Thunder!

There was how he made her feel!

There was her beloved brother!

No, she would not deny herself these precious moments any longer. She had a man who loved her, who even cherished her. She would not chance losing that or *him*.

And she had some amending to make. Through the trauma of these past days, Feather Moon had tried to make friends with Tanzey, to help with her burden, as Feather Moon had helped lift the burden from her husband's shoulders.

Feather Moon had come and sat with Tanzey several times, trying to encourage Tanzey to participate in decorating bags with beadwork, explaining that how she chose to decorate them was called the "lazy stitch," and that she used porcupine quill embroidery more than beadwork.

Tanzey had ignored Feather Moon.

But now, somehow, Tanzey would make it up to her, not only because Feather Moon had come to her in friendship, but also because Tanzey felt that a wall was slowly forming between herself and her brother because of her feelings toward Feather Moon.

Yes, today she would make friends with Feather Moon, but only after she made things up to Rolling Thunder!

"*Toquet-mah-tao-yo-toquet*, close your eyes," Rolling Thunder said huskily, drawing Tanzey from her thoughts. "Let me love you."

"Let me love you first," Tanzey said, moving to her knees over him. "Let me show you just how much I *do* love you. These past few days I am sure you had moments of doubting that I do."

"Not once have I doubted your love for me, not even since our first encounter," Rolling Thunder said, lifting his hands to her breasts, cupping them.

Tanzey sucked in a breath of pleasure and held her head back as he rolled his thumbs over the nipples, causing them to harden against his flesh.

And then she felt his hands at her waist, lifting her, placing her on her back.

She gazed up at him as he knelt beside her, his eyes dark with a building passion.

"Close your mind to everything but us," Rolling Thunder said. "Yesterday is gone forever. Let it *be* gone. Let us think of only now; of only our future. There is so much to look forward to."

"Yes, so much," Tanzey said, lifting a gentle hand to his cheek, touching it.

He took her hand and lowered it to her side. "I will be the one doing the touching," he said. "I will awaken desire in you that you did not know existed. Your whole body will be aflame with it. Your mind will know nothing but intense pleasure."

"Make love to me," Tanzey whispered. "Please, my darling, make love to me now."

She moaned when he leaned over her and his mouth moved over first one nipple, and then her other, his hot, wet tongue flicking, his hands moving slowly and seductively over her body, causing ripples of pleasure to swim along her flesh.

She whimpered tiny cries when one of his hands found her woman's center. She strained herself upward against his hand as he began to stroke her in a wild, dizzying rhythm. She could feel the pleasure spreading. It was a lazy warmth that left her weak and wanting.

Her spasmodic gasps filled the morning air when Rolling Thunder knelt between her thighs and his tongue now flicked where his fingers had just been.

He placed his hands beneath her buttocks and lifted her closer to his mouth, his hot breath on her sensitive center causing Tanzey to toss her head from side to side.

But soon, feeling the pleasure peaking, Tanzey twined her fingers through his hair and urged him away from her. "Please ..." she whispered, her pulse racing.

Rolling Thunder rose above her and plunged into her pulsing cleft. Their bodies strained together, lifting and falling in rhythm with his strokes within her, their lips tremoring as they kissed, long and deep.

Rolling Thunder's hands ran down Tanzey's body, caressing her, making her shiver.

He stroked her slim white thighs, then found her throbbing center.

His fingers moved purposely slow on her, taunting her, teasing, stroking her fiery flesh, all the while not letting up on his rhythmic strokes within her.

And then he leaned away from her and rolled over onto his side. He gripped her shoulders and led her over him, where her knees were on each side of him. His body hardened and tightened as her mouth moved over his flesh until he groaned, her lips and mouth drugging him, his sensations searing.

His eyes dark and knowing, he reached for her and drew her up over him, so that her body blanketed his, her breasts crushing against his chest. He pulled her head down, and their lips met. He gripped her tightly as he shoved himself into her.

When he entered her in this way, Tanzey's blood quickened. She kissed him passionately as he plunged into her, over and over again.

Nestled close to him, she abandoned herself to the torrent of feelings that washed over her.

She could feel the excitement rising.

His hands cupped the rounded flesh of her buttocks.

He whispered fierce words of love to her between their fevered kisses.

She clung to him around his neck, breathless as the pleasure soared.

Rolling Thunder fought to delay the final throes of passion.

He fought to go more slowly.

He held her within his arms and rolled her beneath him.

Again he filled her with his thick, manly strength.

He kissed her hungrily, his hands kneading her breasts, her nipples sensitive against his flesh.

Tanzey moved her body sinuously against Rolling Thunder's.

She felt his breath catch and hold, her own breath coming in ragged gasps.

Then they both became still.

Rolling Thunder placed his hands to Tanzey's cheeks.

They gazed into one another's eyes, seeing the desire. His eyes held hers.

They smiled as the silence vibrated between them.

And then, overwhelmed by the sweet, painful longing, Rolling Thunder gave Tanzey a desperate, hungry kiss.

He kissed her with a mouth that was urgent and eager.

He enveloped her within his muscled arms, and he held her tightly against him.

There was one more moment of hesitation when neither hardly breathed.

And then came that moment of explosion when their bodies spasmed together.

Tanzey arched toward him.

She clung to him as they fed from each other's passion.

When they came down from that cloud of rapture and lay exhausted within one another's arms, Tanzey sighed.

"Is that sigh because you are happy, or because you are still sad?" Rolling Thunder asked as he leaned away from her to gaze at her.

"I sighed because I am so radiantly happy, *and* finally at peace with myself," Tanzey said, tracing the outline of his chin with her forefinger.

He took her hand and held it close to his heart. "Do you feel my heartbeat?" he asked. "Do you know that each of those beats are for you?"

"I'm not sure if I deserve that," Tanzey said, lowering her eyes, remembering how she had avoided him these past several days. A part of her had wanted to hate him because he had not allowed her to return home when she had wished to.

Another part of her forgave him.

Now she held no one responsible except for those marauding, murdering villains.

"Never blame yourself for feelings brought on by the actions of others," Rolling Thunder said.

He held her face between his hands and drew her lips to his.

He gave her a soft kiss, then held her close again as they watched the sky becoming blue overhead through the smoke hole.

"It's going to be a beautiful day," Tanzey murmured. "I . . . I . . . have something that needs to be done. I have apologies to make."

"I do not have to ask who you are speaking of," Rolling Thunder said, nodding.

"You seem to have the ability to read my mind," Tanzey said, giving him a quick glance.

"My *mah-ocu-ah*, woman, do you not know that I know you now, as though I have known you forever?" Rolling Thunder said, snuggling her closer. He burrowed his nose into the sweet scent of her hair. "I know that you have been feeling guilty for having ignored your sister-in-law. Today you will make amends, and even then *that* will be behind you."

"I do hope to begin anew today," Tanzey said, sighing. "There is so much more to life than . . . than . . . sadness."

"There is *you*," Rolling Thunder said, laughing softly.

Again he kissed her.

Soon Rolling Thunder's hands seemed to be everywhere along Tanzey's body at once.

She became delirious with sensations.

Again desire raged and washed over her.

Caught in Rolling Thunder's embrace, she felt her entire body responding to his every nuance of lovemaking.

All of her senses were yearning for the promise that he was offering her, their bodies rocking, swaying, lifting, falling, as he plunged into her.

She smiled and rode with him again on the road to paradise.

Chapter Eighteen

Where thoughts serenely sweet express,
How pure, how dear their dwelling place.

—LORD BYRON

Several more days had passed. Thanks to Rolling Thunder's patience and encouragement, Tanzey was finally feeling more like herself.

She was excited about today's horse race even though she was not allowed to participate—it was for men only.

The drums beat in unison from somewhere close by.

People crowded around.

The horses that would enter the race had been rubbed with grass so that they were shining and looked their very best.

All was joy in the camp.

Tanzey stood back with Daisy and watched as many visiting bands of Comanche arrived for the festivities.

Yesterday she had gone with Rolling Thunder as he had rounded up six of his best fleet horses. He had taken them to a secluded flat several miles distant from his village, and tested the speed of each horse.

In the end he chose the one that would represent him today . . . his very own steed, his beautiful white mustang. It had outrun all of the others.

Tanzey gazed at Rolling Thunder. She admired him as he mounted his horse with grace and began slowly pacing his steed back and forth before his lodge. He waited for the others to ready their mounts. The race would be held just outside the village, in the widest stretch of the valley.

Her heart beat soundly at the sight of Rolling Thunder. Fresh from a bath in the river and wearing only a breechclout and moccasins, his sleek and hairless copper skin shone beneath the rays of the sun.

His long and flowing midnight-black hair was ornamented with glass beads and silver gewgaws.

He wore bands of fur around both of his wrists and ankles.

He held his broad shoulders squared, his jaw tight.

Although Tanzey knew that he realized that her eyes were on him, he did not look her way. His full focus was on the race that lay ahead of him. He had told her that out of six previous races, he had won them all. As then, if he won today, he would take the competitors' horses.

Tanzey's gaze shifted to her brother. Brant Fire In The Sky sat tall in his own saddle, confidence in his eyes as he also slowly paced and tested the agility of his proud steed. Now that he was a part of the Comanche, as though he had been born of their blood, Brant had been given back his pinto that he had ridden since he was a lad of ten.

Until even this morning, his horse had been kept tied away from the others, where Brant could not see him. Brant had even thought that his pinto might have been killed or traded.

But today he and his horse had been reunited. Tanzey could see the same camaraderie between steed and master as she had that very first day of their bonding.

It was good to see that at least a part of their past remained intact after so much had been robbed from them.

Daisy grabbed Tanzey's hand. She yanked on it and drew Tanzey's attention her way.

Tanzey gazed at Daisy and smiled, then discovered an excitement in the depths of Daisy's eyes that she had never seen before as she stood watching Brant Fire In The Sky. It was obvious that Daisy was attracted to him.

Tanzey placed a gentle hand to Daisy's chin and directed her eyes into hers. "You are watching my brother?" she said softly.

Daisy blushed and nodded.

"But, Daisy, my brother is married," Tanzey said, seeing an instant hurt enter Daisy's eyes.

Daisy's smile faded, and she slowly nodded.

"I'm sorry, Daisy," Tanzey said, drawing the sweet and lovely lady within her arms.

She sympathized with Daisy for loving someone she could never have, for Daisy had already suffered enough.

But nothing could change the destiny that had led Brant Fire In The Sky and Feather Moon into one another's arms.

Nor did it seem that anything could ever happen that might bring Daisy's voice to life again.

Daisy stiffened and drew quickly away from Tanzey's arms.

Tanzey stepped back and silently questioned her with her eyes.

Daisy nodded toward an Indian from another band of Comanche. He was leading a horse by a rope behind the lodges, occasionally looking nervously over his shoulder to see if anyone was watching.

When his gaze moved toward Tanzey, she looked quickly away before he caught her staring at him.

Again Tanzey gazed into Daisy's eyes, where she saw anger and defiance, which had to mean that Daisy knew that this warrior was up to no good.

"Should I follow him?" Tanzey asked. "Do you wish to go with me?"

Daisy's eyes lit up. Her lips flickered into a cunning smile. She nodded, then took Tanzey's hands.

Tanzey and Daisy moved through the crowd of Comanche men, women, and children. Up until now the atmosphere had been a cheerful one, where there had been a pipe dance, a dance of love and friendship shared by the bands of Comanche today.

Before the day had begun, Rolling Thunder had told her that until trouble began and there were raids upon the white community as well as Comanche land, his village had been known to have frequent visitors who were hospitably entertained by himself and his people.

But now those times of fun and laughter were few and far between.

Yet when they did entertain, it was done with much zest and laughter. For at the moment the evilness of the world was forgotten.

Except for what lurked now at the back of the lodges, Tanzey thought to herself.

She and Daisy peeked around the corner of a tepee and watched the warrior. Out of the eye range of everyone else, he chewed up some unidentified medicine, which he spit in the horse's mouth and ears.

Tanzey questioned Daisy with her eyes. She watched Daisy's lips form words, as Daisy managed, in her own way, to relay to Tanzey that this medicine placed in the racer's mouth and ears was power in the Comanche view. She also told her that no woman was to go near the racer when it had had medicine made for it.

"Is this practiced often?" Tanzey whispered.

Daisy frowned and nodded viciously.

"But surely not by Rolling Thunder," Tanzey whispered. "We should go and warn him."

Daisy grabbed Tanzey by the hands. She shook her head back and forth, her eyes wide. She told Tanzey that Rolling Thunder also practiced such doctoring of horses. Early this morning he had spit the medicine into his own steed's mouth and ears. Did she not even now see the brightness of Rolling Thunder's horse's eyes? Its feistiness? The way it pawed nervously at the ground? The way it snorted, time and again?

Tanzey was stunned speechless. Just as she had begun to accept some of the Comanche customs, she was abhorred by how they doctored their horses before the races.

Daisy smiled smugly and told Tanzey that just wait and see—this elderly Comanche had placed too much medicine in his horse's mouth and ears! Rolling Thunder's horse would win.

Tanzey looked back in the direction of the conniving warrior and was startled to find him gone. She looked guardedly from side to side, then stepped back from the tepee and into the open just as all of the racers were being led from the village.

Feather Moon ran over to Tanzey. She smiled at

her, took her hand, then went with Tanzey and Daisy to stand among the other spectators.

Tanzey's pulse raced as the horses were lined up, their riders all looking confident. Tanzey looked from Brant Fire In The Sky, to Rolling Thunder, and back again to each of them. She could not help but be disappointed in Rolling Thunder. If he *did* win the race, he would not have won it fairly and squarely.

She smiled to herself. Rolling Thunder had never raced against her *brother. She* had. *Many* times. She knew her brother's skills with horses, especially his prized steed! It would do Rolling Thunder good to be beaten by her brother's pinto!

Then her confident, smug smile faded. There was no way she could expect Brant's horse to win. Rolling Thunder's had been doctored! *Sure* he would win.

In a sense, Rolling Thunder had tricked her brother! His shrewd scheming to win horses from the other bands of Indians made Tanzey resent Rolling Thunder.

Tanzey narrowed her eyes and pursed her lips tightly together as she gazed angrily at Rolling Thunder. He patted his steed, calming him as all of the other horses lined up on each side of him. A warrior was standing at one side, a long lance tied on the end with a white flag.

The crowd was silent as they waited anxiously for the race to begin. The race would end at the river. The one who reached it first would plunge his horse into the water.

Now Tanzey understood why this was an inevitable part of the race. Surely it was to wash the effects of the medicine off the horse so that it would not suffer any longer than was necessary by the dreaded potion.

Once the winner was declared, she expected the

river to become filled with many horses and warriors, for surely they all had tainted their steeds!

When the warrior gave the lance a heaving pitch, sending it and the white flag soaring through the air, the horses leapt out from the line and began the short run toward the river.

Tanzey soon discovered that in the matter of horsemanship, she doubted whether there was a race on the face of the whole earth that equaled the Comanche's. They not only raced, but put on colorful demonstrations. Some warriors lay along the sides of their horses while under full speed, while others even stood on their horses, hollering and waving a hand in the air.

But Tanzey felt too serious about the race to be charmed by any of those antics. She doubled her hands into tight fists at her sides. "Come on, Brant," she whispered to herself. "Beat the son of a gun war chief. He was wrong to trick you!"

Her heart pounded as she watched Brant Fire In The Sky and Rolling Thunder race ahead of the others, their horses now neck and neck toward the finish line.

"Come on, Rolling Thunder," Tanzey whispered as she watched him lie low over his horse, his reins flicking.

She blushed when she realized for whom she had rooted!

Rolling Thunder!

But of course, why wouldn't she?

She had thought of nothing else the whole night through.

After having made love with him, he had talked of nothing but the race, his excitement riding high with the hopes of winning another one for his people.

Although she did not think his methods were fair,

there was still a large part of her that wanted him to win—but only because she knew it meant so much to him.

Feather Moon screamed and hollered as Brant Fire In The Sky's horse drew ahead of Rolling Thunder's by a full head's length.

Tanzey glanced over at Feather Moon, who seemed to have momentarily forgotten that she was with child, for she was jumping up and down, her eyes wide with excitement.

And then Feather Moon's excitement faded, and she sighed with disappointment when Rolling Thunder's horse gained on Brant Fire In The Sky's and passed him.

Tanzey was now torn about who she wanted to win. For both men it would be a victory that could enhance them in the eyes of the Comanche people.

Brant Fire In The Sky would be even more solidly interwoven with the lives of the Comanche.

· And Rolling Thunder seemed always to be looking for ways to reassure his standing with his people. Someone was always waiting on the sidelines to take his place as war chief. She knew that he would be humiliated if that happened. She wanted nothing but the best for the man she loved, even if he achieved it . . . by . . . somewhat cheating.

Tanzey covered a shriek of excitement behind her hands as once again Brant Fire In The Sky's and Rolling Thunder's horses were neck and neck.

Their horses' nostrils were flaring in loud snorts.

Their chests were heaving with exertion.

Sweat pearled their sleek manes.

And then Brant Fire In The Sky plunged his horse into the water before Rolling Thunder. He was still in the saddle as horse and master popped to the surface.

Brant Fire In the Sky shouted and hollered, his eyes wild with the wonders of his win.

Rolling Thunder and the other horsemen came to shuddering halts at the river's edge.

Tanzey scarcely breathed as she watched Rolling Thunder's reaction to losing. She studied his face, seeing nothing akin to disappointment or anger. Instead she saw a keen admiration as he smiled down at her brother.

"Congratulations! The victory, my *hait-sma*, close friend Fire In The Sky, *ein-mah-heepicut*, it is yours!" Rolling Thunder shouted at Brant Fire In The Sky. "Savor the win, for the next race will be *mine*."

Laughter filled the air.

Suddenly all of the riders and their horses were in the river, bathing, splashing, dunking.

Tanzey was stunned by the outcome of the race, not so much by Brant Fire In The Sky having won it, but because of the reaction of the others who had not. By the way they were behaving, everyone so happy and full of laughter, it seemed a victory equally won.

And after the warriors and horses were out of the water and Brant Fire In The Sky had been awarded his several horses—even Rolling Thunder's proud steed—all of the visitors left, leaving the village still and calm.

Tanzey waited in Rolling Thunder's lodge for him.

Day had turned to night.

Crickets chirped and frogs croaked down by the river.

Tanzey had changed from her dress to a soft, flowing cotton gown.

Her hair had been brushed until it lay in a soft heap over her shoulders.

Her face shone from a fresh scrubbing.

And she was comfortably full, for the long day

through she had been given platters of food by one or another. For courtesy's sake alone, she had eaten what had been offered her, discovering different tastes and foods from anything she had ever eaten before.

She heard Rolling Thunder outside the lodge shouting a good-bye to some visiting Comanche who had lingered longer than the others.

Anxious to be alone with him, Tanzey watched Rolling Thunder come inside the tepee. He had removed his hair ornaments and the bands of fur around his wrists and ankles.

He had even discarded his moccasins somewhere else, perhaps to dry outside the entranceway of the tepee.

All that he had on was the scanty breechclout. Seeing the outline of his manhood pressed against the wet buckskin fabric as he knelt down on his haunches before Tanzey made her heart skip a beat.

"And how was your day spent away from me?" Rolling Thunder asked as he placed his gentle hands to her cheeks. "Did you miss your war chief?"

"I did . . . until . . . I had cause to wonder about you," Tanzey found herself saying.

Rolling Thunder's eyes widened. "What did I do to make you question anything about me?" he asked, forking an eyebrow.

"Don't you know?" Tanzey said. She placed her hands on his and guided them from her cheeks. She watched him drop his arms to his sides.

"If I did, would I be questioning you?" Rolling Thunder said, his eyes searching hers.

"Rolling Thunder, you *should* have lost the race," Tanzey blurted out. "If you had won, it would have not been done fairly."

When that drew silence from him instead of a response, Tanzey decided to continue. "How could you, Rolling Thunder?" she said.

She looked away from him, into the slow-rolling flames of the fire. "If you were caught cheating at a crap table in a saloon or gambling hall in the white man's world, you would have been shot. What you did today surely deserved no less punishment."

Rolling Thunder placed his hands to her waist and guided her to her feet, facing him. "You are speaking of the medicine I gave my horse?" he asked.

"*Huh*, yes, I am," she murmured. "Tell me I am wrong. That you didn't doctor your horse for the race."

"I cannot say that to you because it would be a lie," he said, sliding his hands up to her shoulders. "It is practiced among my people. But this is something done in private. It is each warrior's own private thing before a race."

"But it seems so cruel," Tanzey softly complained.

"The medicine has no lasting effect on the horses," Rolling Thunder answered matter-of-factly. "You must understand that horse racing is profitable. Today, for your brother having come out of the race the victor, those who came from other villages paid Brant Fire In The Sky well in pelts, other valuables, and horses. But, as I do when I win, your brother did not selfishly profit from the race. He shared everything with the people of our village, as a whole."

Tanzey's eyes widened. "He *did*?" she asked softly.

"He did this after you came to the privacy of our lodge," Rolling Thunder said, taking her hand, leading her down onto the pelts by the fire. He drew her next to him and held her close. "So you see? Nothing bad comes from winning, *or* doctoring horses *for* the win."

"But, Rolling Thunder, my brother won without doctoring *his* horse," Tanzey said, gazing up at him.

Rolling Thunder's lips quavered into a slow smile. "Are you certain of that?" he said, chuckling.

"No!" Tanzey gasped, paling. "Please tell me he didn't."

"Is he not Comanche now?" Rolling Thunder said, pride in his eyes at the thought of how much Brant Fire In The Sky pleased him by his acceptance of his Comanche people and their customs.

"In part," Tanzey said softly.

"Then, that part of him that is total Comanche does as Comanche do, even before racing his horse," Rolling Thunder stated. "He, too, learned the art of doctoring. He did it well, did he not? His horse beat mine. My horse is now *his*."

Before Tanzey had the chance to say anything else, or voice another complaint, Rolling Thunder silenced her words with a rushed kiss. His hands sliding up inside her gown caused slow fires to ignite along her flesh.

"In time, you . . . too . . . will think and do everything Comanche," Rolling Thunder whispered against her lips. "But for now, my pretty Tanzey Nicole, it is enough that you know how to *please* a Comanche! Love me in your special way, Tanzey Nicole. Let me love you."

"Yes, yes," she whispered breathlessly as he lifted her gown over her head, revealing her full nudity to the heat of his passion-filled eyes. As he gazed at her, the warmth of desire spreading through him, he removed his breechcloth and tossed it aside.

He drank in the sight of her as though she were some fine wine; then he blanketed her with his body.

Slipping his arms around her, he lifted her close to him, reveling in the touch of her breasts against his chest. "You have such a pretty and delicate mouth," he whispered against her lips. His entire being throbbed with a quickening desire as he crushed his lips to hers.

Tanzey lifted her legs over him as she felt his manhood delving into her rose-red slippery heat.

She became alive inside like a fire was spreading, igniting her sensations throughout her, startling her in its intensity.

Rolling Thunder slipped his hands from beneath her. He wove one between their bodies and cupped the soft, creamy flesh of a breast, his thumb rolling and kneading her nipple.

His free hand slid on down her body and covered her mound of pleasure. With one finger he began stroking her swollen nub, while he moved rhythmically within her with his aching shaft.

Tanzey's body pliant in Rolling Thunder's arms, he stroked her until she sobbed with pleasure against his hot lips.

He caressed her softly, soothingly, meditatingly, smiling when she gyrated her hips, to draw him more deeply inside her.

Tanzey became alive with the raw awareness of him, his quick, eager fingers driving her wantonly wild.

Then his hands moved over her flesh, discovering anew the slimness of her body below her breasts, the supple broadening of her hips, and her long, smooth thighs.

There was not one ounce of her that did not delight him.

To touch her, to hold her, to caress her, to plunge his manhood into her, was paradise.

He slid his lips from her mouth and left a wet trail

along the slender column of her neck as he moved his lips slowly toward her breasts.

When they got there, he sucked a nipple, causing Tanzey to draw in her breath sharply.

She gave a little cry when his teeth nipped the nipple; then his tongue flicked wetly over it.

Finding himself close to that brink of pleasure when he would be momentarily rendered mindless, Rolling Thunder lay his cheek against Tanzey's.

Breathing erratically, he closed his eyes. He placed his hands beneath her hips and lifted her close so that he could sink himself more deeply inside her as his strokes speeded up.

Tanzey clung around his neck, the pleasure spreading like wildfire inside her.

She was so close.

So .. very . . . close.

Together they found the ultimate of release.

Their bodies shook and quaked together.

They kissed passionately.

Their hands twined together over their heads.

After they came down from their plateau of pleasure, Rolling Thunder rolled away from Tanzey.

Panting, he spread his legs and arms out and closed his eyes.

"Was the excitement with me better than that felt during the horse race?" Tanzey teased, kneeling beside him, her hands moving slowly over his damp body.

"Much better," Rolling Thunder said. Smiling, he opened his eyes. He gazed up at her. "Yet, I do not know if that is quite true."

"What?" Tanzey said, gasping softly.

"Do you not see that part of my excitement of the race was because I knew that once it was over I would be with you, making love?" Rolling Thunder

said, placing his hands to her wrists, bringing her
down beside him. "My beautiful Tanzey Nicole. No
matter what I do, or where I am, I find myself hur-
rying to get back to my lodge, and only because you
are here, waiting. Will you always wait for me? Will
you always be mine?"

"Always," Tanzey whispered, cuddling close.

For the moment she was not concerned about tam-
pering with the horses before the race. Yet she feared
there might be something else about his customs that
she would find hard to accept—that, in the white
man's world, could get a man hung!

Chapter Nineteen

And on that cheek and o'er that brow
So soft, so calm, yet eloquent.

—LORD BYRON

Early the next morning, Rolling Thunder and Tanzey woke coughing. Smoke filled the tepee instead of rising and escaping through the smoke hole.

"Has something clogged up the smoke hole?" she asked as Rolling Thunder rolled from the bed and hurried into a pair of fringed breeches.

"No, I fear it is something worse," he said. "I will go outside and inspect."

"What do you think is happening, or is *about* to happen?" Tanzey asked. She hurried from the bed and into a buckskin skirt and blouse, and then her moccasins.

"*Kee-mah*, come with me," Rolling Thunder said, flipping his long hair back from his shoulders.

Tanzey scampered from the lodge with him. She stood at his side as he peered toward the heavens. She followed his gaze and saw nothing but blue skies and an occasional drifting white, cumulus cloud.

"The sky lies," Rolling Thunder grumbled.

He made a quick turn, and Tanzey went with him

behind the tepee and walked through knee-high grass toward the river.

"Do you see over there how the spiderwebs are narrow and hanging just above the grass line?" Rolling Thunder said, pointing toward a spiderweb that glistened with dew's moisture in the early morning light.

"*Huh*, yes, I see," Tanzey said. "But what can you tell by that?"

"Normally, if the weather is going to be clear and dry, the spiderwebs would be long and thin and spun high off the ground," Rolling Thunder said. He took a quick glance toward the sky. "The spiderweb, as does the smoke curling down instead of rising, foretells a dangerous storm."

"A dangerous storm?" Tanzey said, in awe of how he knew this. Since her childhood in Kansas, she had been terrified of storms. She would never forget how quickly tornadoes could develop during the long, hot sweltering summer months.

She would never forget how things sounded while she waited, terrified, in the storm cellar built deep into the earth behind her house, as the winds whipped around her house and through the trees.

She could close her eyes even now and recall in detail the one time their house had been pitched and tossed around as though it weighed no more than a box of toothpicks. Everything had been destroyed above the closed door of the cellar.

"I have lived in Texas for some years now, and I have not yet experienced a tornado," Tanzey blurted out. "Do tornadoes come in this area?"

Rolling Thunder turned a frown her way and nodded. "I have seen only one monster wind in my lifetime and that was enough for my parents to search for a protective shelter for our people. I was but three winters of age," he said. "I even now make sure that shelter is ready at all times for my people. I do not wish for my people to ever be at the mercy of the black, swirling winds of a tornado."

"Do you expect a tornado today?" Tanzey asked, an involuntary shiver racing across her flesh. Without even hearing his answer, she knew that he *was* anticipating one.

At least in Kansas there was shelter in the storm cellar. She had seen no such shelters in the Comanche village.

"*Huh*, yes, that is what I fear," he said, stopping at the riverbank.

Tanzey watched him as he fell to his knees and began inspecting something down on the ground.

"What are you looking at?" she asked, forking an eyebrow.

He motioned for her to come down beside him.

She knelt and gazed at a huge anthill and many ants scampering into the anthill in single file.

"See how the ants rush to their home in the ground?" Rolling Thunder said, his eyes never leaving the tiny black creatures.

"Yes, I see," Tanzey said, wondering what ants had to do with anything. If Rolling Thunder truly suspected a storm was near, she did not see why he was wasting time observing ants! She hated ants, even more than spiders! They gave her a creeping, crawling sensation up and down her spine.

"The ants walking in a straight line as they hasten into their lodge, instead of running around in scattered masses outside, is an omen also of threatening weather," Rolling Thunder said, rising quickly to his feet.

It was then that they heard their first rumble of thunder.

Tanzey rushed to her feet and turned in the direction of the sound. The trees were too thick to see the sky, to see how quickly the fast-developing storm was approaching.

"The warnings I have seen today, as well as the sound of distant thunder, are too many omens to ignore," Rolling Thunder said. He gave Tanzey a frown. "Come with me. Help me to warn my people. We must get everyone to the cave. And we must take what horses we can with us. Who is to say what devastation will be wreaked across our land today?"

Tanzey ran with Rolling Thunder back to the village. Fear could be seen in the people's eyes as they scurried around to best secure their lodges, then left with their arms filled with what meager possessions they could take with them.

Tanzey walked beside Daisy, who carried her wailing child wrapped in a blanket close to her bosom.

Several warriors were on their steeds, leading a large herd of horses on ahead of the people.

Tanzey had lost sight of Rolling Thunder a long time ago, as well as her brother.

She gazed over at Feather Moon as she breathlessly followed alongside Tanzey, her hands on the round mound of her tummy.

Tanzey could not help but be concerned about Feather Moon and the child she carried within her womb. Each step seemed to be a great effort for her, yet she had not wanted to chance riding a horse in her condition.

When Brant Fire In The Sky had suggested that she travel on a travois, she had refused. She had not wanted to look weak in the eyes of not only her husband, but also the people. She was their princess. She wanted to prove to everyone that she was not a child carrying a child!

Until recently Tanzey had always seen Feather Moon as spoiled, stubborn, and self-centered. She had changed her feelings somewhat, yet today the young and pretty pregnant woman was showing her stubborn side again—and perhaps at the wrong time. The child's welfare was at stake; especially if the hill they were trudging up became any more steep than it already was.

Even Tanzey was finding it difficult to climb it!

Thankfully the wide-open spaces of a cave came into view at the top of the hill. It led back into a mountain. Tanzey felt some relief to know that their shelter here was as safe, even more so, as the storm cellar back in Kansas.

When Feather Moon let out a soft moan, Tanzey turned to her just in time to see her fall to the ground.

"Oh, Lord, no," Tanzey cried.

As Daisy watched, her arms too filled with her child to go to Feather Moon's assistance, Tanzey knelt down beside Feather Moon and lifted her head so that it rested gently on her lap.

Feather Moon sobbed as she clutched her stomach. "I have pain," she cried. She looked desperately up at Tanzey. "The walk has been too much for the child." She reached a hand to Tanzey's arm and clutched it. "Help me, Tanzey. Help me."

Before Tanzey could do anything, Brant Fire In The Sky was there, leaping from his horse. He reached down and lifted his wife into his arms.

"My husband, I was not wise today," Feather Moon whispered, tears flooding her eyes as she gazed up at him. "I . . . should . . have chosen a travois over walking."

"You are going to be all right," Brant Fire In The Sky said, his voice breaking. "I shall carry you the rest of the way. I will get you comfortably beside a fire. I shall hold you and rock you. Both you and the child will be safe. You both will be all right.''

Tanzey stood beside Daisy as Brant Fire In The Sky carried his wife up the final steep crest of the hill.

Daisy reached a hand to Tanzey, drawing her eyes to her.

Tanzey read Daisy's lips as she formed words of concern on them, letting Tanzey know that she was worried about Feather Moon. She let Tanzey know that although she loved Brant Fire In The Sky with all of her heart, she did not want anything to happen to his wife!

Tanzey embraced both Daisy and the child, letting Daisy know that she understood.

They leapt apart, eyes wide, when a great flash of lightning lit the sky all around them, a great burst of thunder soon ensuing.

The sky was dark and threatening overhead.

Lurid streaks of lightning flashed over and over again across the heavens.

"We must hurry onward," Tanzey told Daisy as people scrambled around them in an effort to get to the cave before the rain began to fall.

For certain, a fierce storm was soon to come, but it was not going to be a tornado. The sky did not have the same appearance as she had seen in Kansas prior to a tornado.

No, this was not going to be a tornado, but it was going to be fierce. She could see the great, rolling white clouds that were racing toward them overhead. If they were lucky, perhaps one lodge or two might be spared during the ravaging windstorm!

Just as everyone got safely inside the cave and the many horses were corralled in the canyon at the one side of the cave, the rain began falling in torrents.

Tanzey helped build a fire, then led Daisy and her child over close to it, where she had spread a blanket for them.

Tanzey searched the faces for Rolling Thunder, relieved to find him kneeling beside Brant Fire In The Sky, both gazing down at Feather Moon, who lay snuggled between blankets, her face flushed as the pains continued in their intensity.

Tanzey gazed down at Daisy, who was now nursing her child, a blanket covering her breast.

Then, her eyes on Feather Moon, she went and knelt down beside Rolling Thunder. "Is Feather Moon going to lose the child?" she murmured, never having been around anyone who was in labor.

"If her pains continue, the child might be lost to her and Brant Fire In The Sky," Rolling Thunder said, placing a gentle hand to his cousin's cheek, which was damp with cold sweat.

"I'm so sorry," Tanzey said, swallowing hard as Feather Moon's eyes moved to her.

When Feather Moon managed a soft smile, Tanzey smiled back and reached over, taking one of Feather Moon's hands.

Outside, the winds were strong.

The lightning continued to split the heavens.

The thunder growled and rolled and echoed through the cave.

"She is so afraid of storms," Brant Fire In The Sky mumbled as he sat down and drew Feather Moon onto his lap. He snuggled her close as Tanzey slipped a blanket up around her.

And then Tanzey followed Rolling Thunder to the cave entrance. She hugged herself with her arms as she watched the angry display of the heavens, and how the force of the wind was bending the thrashing trees double to the ground.

Her gaze moved quickly to Rolling Thunder when he looked upward and held his hands toward the sky and began to pray.

"Oh, Wise One Above, our Sure Enough Father, cease the storm!" he cried. "Spare us. Spare our homes! Spare Feather Moon her pain!"

As though a magic wand were waved over the land, the rain stopped falling, the lightning ceased to flash, and the winds stopped.

Everything became quiet as the menacing clouds floated away.

Amazed at how the storm had stopped so suddenly, and *why*, because Rolling Thunder had prayed that it would, Tanzey stared at him. She realized she knew so little about him. She became more in awe of him as each day passed. He was special in so many ways.

"See in the heavens?" Rolling Thunder said, making a wide sweep with a hand as he followed the curve of a rainbow with it.

Tanzey looked quickly up at the sky. She sighed, for never had she seen such a beautiful rainbow and blue sky! "It is so beautiful!" she said softly.

She squeezed closer to Rolling Thunder as his people rushed to the entrance of the cave and peered up into the heavens. She could hear soft chants of thank you to their father in the sky.

Some grabbed at Rolling Thunder, thanking him for his prayers that had been answered.

Rolling Thunder turned to his people. "It is time to return home," he said. "For those of you whose homes are gone, those of you who did not suffer the same tragedy will lend their muscle in building new lodges!"

There was a scramble to get out of the cave.

Tanzey stood aside and waited until everyone was

gone; then she went to her brother, who had his wife up in his arms, ready to carry her to the village.

"Are your pains better?" Tanzey asked as she smoothed a damp lock of hair back from Feather Moon's brow.

Tears flooded Feather Moon's eyes as she slowly shook her head back and forth. "I fear I am losing my child," she said, her voice breaking. She gave her husband a sad, long look. "Husband, please take me home."

Brant Fire In The Sky nodded, gave Tanzey a downcast look, then walked away, carrying his wife.

Daisy came to Tanzey. She slowly rocked her child back and forth in her arms.

"It does not look good for Feather Moon," Tanzey murmured. "I'm so afraid for her *and* the child."

Daisy held her child closer and nodded.

Rolling Thunder came to them. He reached a hand to Tanzey and smiled at Daisy. "Let us go now," he said softly.

When they arrived at the village, they discovered that not much had been swept away by the storm. Only two lodges had been destroyed. Tanzey was quick to offer her help.

She soon discovered the intricacies of raising a tepee. One lodge had twenty-two poles made out of pine. They had to be straight and slender. Four poles were used as a foundation. To set it up, these four poles were first tied near the top and set upright. The butt ends of the poles were then pulled out and evenly spaced in a circle. Ten to seventeen hides of buffalo were used to make the covering.

The lodge she helped to erect was of an average size, twelve to fifteen feet in diameter across the floor. The tepee was tilted slightly backward, a smoke hole left at the top.

The door faced east.

A narrow ditch around the outside kept the floor dry.

Surprising to Tanzey, all in all it took only fifteen minutes to raise the tepee.

By sundown, the village was back in good enough shape for everyone to bathe, eat, and look forward to a full night of rest.

And just as they were ready to retire for the night, another band of Comanche came into Rolling Thunder's village, on foot, their horses having scattered during the fierceness of the storm.

Tanzey watched, touched deeply, when Rolling Thunder said that the meat of his people was free to those who came.

He gave them food and clothes, and said they could stay and be a part of the lives of his people as long as they wished.

Tanzey had learned long ago that, to the Comanche, generosity was so highly valued, that he who had need of something had only to indicate his desire and he would receive it as a gift.

A piercing scream drew Tanzey's head around. She looked wild-eyed at her brother's lodge. "Feather Moon," she whispered, then ran to the tepee and hurried on inside.

"She's bleeding!" Brant Fire In The Sky cried, frantic in his fear of what was happening to his wife.

Tanzey's heart went out to her brother and his wife. She turned on a heel when she heard footsteps behind her.

She paled when a large, tall man came into the lodge. He was dressed in a flowing robe. His black hair dragged to the floor.

She recognized him.

He was Tohobt Nabituh, Blue Eyes, the village medicine man.

Blue Eyes turned to Tanzey, his eyes as blue as the sea. He pointed toward the entrance flap. "*Mea*, go!" he said in plain enough English.

Pale, Tanzey took an unsteady step away from him.

Chapter Twenty

If thou must love me, let it be for naught,
Except for love's sake only.
— ELIZABETH BARRETT BROWNING

Mookwarruh, Spirit Walker, the village medicine woman, followed closely behind Blue Eyes.

She stopped and gave Tanzey an uneasy gaze, then placed a gentle hand on Tanzey's arm. "You must *gea*, go," she murmured.

She glanced over at Brant Fire In The Sky and spoke to him. "Even you, white husband to our princess, must go," she said softly. "No one but Blue Eyes and Spirit Walker are allowed in the lodge of the ailing. We must be free of interferences to perform our services for our princess."

Tanzey watched the incredulous look on her brother's face turn to anger. Although most saw him as gentle and cooperative, under these circumstances he was not understanding.

"I can't leave," he said. He scooted closer to Feather Moon on the bed and hovered protectively over her. "This is my wife. She needs me. And what of my child? I must do everything I can to help save my child!"

Spirit Walker went to Brant Fire In The Sky. She knelt down beside the bed and gazed softly into his eyes. "I understand how you feel, and I admire you for it," she murmured. "But as you know, the Comanche have their ways of doing things. You, who once lived in the white world, have *yours.* You must abide by Comanche law while living with the Comanche. That law states that no one but the medicine man and medicine woman can be with your wife during her time of trouble."

Brant Fire In The Sky's eyes wavered as he glanced up at Tanzey.

Tanzey swallowed hard.

And although she knew how badly her brother wished to stay with his wife, he had no choice but to leave.

She smiled at him and nodded.

Understanding Tanzey's meaning, Brant Fire In The Sky gazed at her a moment longer, then turned to Feather Moon. He slid a hand beneath her head, gently lifted her lips close to his, then kissed her.

Feather Moon weakly twined an arm around his neck and returned his kiss, then whispered to him. "My beloved, I will fight hard to save our child. *Nei-com-mar-pe-ein,* I love you for always."

"As I love you," Brant Fire In The Sky whispered back to her. He gave her a last kiss, then gazed into her eyes. "I shall be just outside the entranceway."

"I know," Feather Moon said, then winced when a sharp pain shot through her abdomen. She panted as she tried to get her breath. She closed her eyes as tears soared across her cheeks.

"Brant . . ." Tanzey said, reminding him that he must leave as the medicine man and medicine woman moved on each side of the bed.

Brant Fire In The Sky stumbled to his feet.

He wiped tears from his cheeks as his eyes lingered on his wife.

Then he turned and left the tepee with Tanzey.

Daisy was waiting outside. When she saw how distraught Brant Fire In The Sky was, she went to him and took one of his hands.

"I know how you must feel, unable to be with your wife," she mouthed with her silent words.

She went further and relayed that things were already not as the medicine woman and medicine man wished them to be. Under normal conditions, when someone was ill, preparations were made for a separate lodge. This time Feather Moon's condition did not give them time for such a lodge.

"I know the customs are made for a reason," Brant Fire In The Sky said, having made out most of what Daisy mouthed. Every day he was finding it easier to read her lips as she became a closer friend to him, someone he sorely admired and cared for.

He turned and stared at his tepee, then turned back to Daisy. "I hope the medicine man and medicine woman are not hindered from helping my wife," he said, his voice breaking.

Daisy spoke again in her silent way. She told him that if he wished, she would do what *she* could to help Feather Moon.

Tanzey was touched deeply by Daisy's unselfish affection toward her brother.

As each moment passed, Tanzey saw just how special this woman was. She hoped that her voice would return. She cursed the man who did this to her, hoping that somehow he had paid for his transgressions!

"What can you do?" Brant Fire In The Sky asked, searching Daisy's face, drawn to her sweetness as never before.

From afar he had watched and admired her, for

even though she was burdened with a past that had left her speechless, she was still the epitome of warmth, beauty, and understanding.

Had he met her before he had met his wife, he would have taken her under his wing and protected her like a mother bird protects its young.

No, he did not feel the same sort of love for Daisy that he felt for his wife, but it was something special that had grown with knowing her.

She explained, as best she could, about the "Dancing With The Wheel" healing ritual, which she had learned by watching others during her stay with the Comanche. She had not performed it yet herself, but knew it well enough to do it.

Rolling Thunder came to stand beside Tanzey. He had stood outside his lodge watching the three.

"And how is your wife?" Rolling Thunder asked Brant Fire In The Sky.

Brant's eyes wavered. "I am almost certain now that she is going to have the child before its time," he said. "I . . . might . . . lose them both."

Daisy went to Rolling Thunder and gazed intensely up at him. In her special way, she asked him if she could perform the "Dancing With The Wheel" healing ritual for Feather Moon.

Always touched by this woman's gentleness, while so much had been robbed from her, Rolling Thunder slipped his arms around Daisy's shoulders and drew her into his embrace. He held her tightly, then eased her from his arms.

"*Huh*, yes, you can perform the special healing ritual," he said, smiling down at her. "Feather Moon is fortunate to have such a friend as you."

Daisy gave Rolling Thunder a wide smile, a big hug, and then she turned to Tanzey and explained what was needed for the ritual.

Tanzey and Daisy left the village and picked arm-loads of wildflowers, then returned.

Tanzey held the flowers in the crook of an arm while Daisy spread a blanket in front of Feather Moon and Brant Fire In The Sky's lodge.

Daisy then centered herself on the blanket.

Standing, she lifted her hands toward the heavens and began to silently pray for Feather Moon's recovery and for the safety of the child, calling in the healing energies from the sky, sun, and wind.

She offered her prayer to the six directions, then held her hands out for some of the flowers.

Tanzey was in awe of how beautiful the performance was, and by how sweetly Daisy performed it. Smiling, she gently handed her the flowers.

Daisy plucked the petals from the flowers and let them fall through the air onto the blanket. She knew that this would draw in the powers of the colors she was using, and of the plant kingdom. The flowers would act as aromatherapy.

Daisy lowered herself onto the blanket and gently rolled around in the petals. She raised them in her hands and let them fall lovingly on her body, making a thin blanket of them over herself.

She continued to focus on the color healing that she wanted from the flowers, and how each of the different colors could heal Feather Moon.

She thought about how the petals looked floating down to the earth, as though they were sunbeams dripping from the sun.

She acknowledged the plants that were with her, helping, healing, and giving to Feather Moon.

She could feel their energy, allowing it to waft on into Feather Moon's lodge and into her being.

She could feel the nurturing power of the earth

underneath her, knowing that the same was beneath Feather Moon.

Daisy continued with this ritual for thirty minutes, then slowly raised herself up.

She made a prayer of thanks and honor to the spirits and elements that helped Feather Moon.

Tanzey had felt something during the ceremony, as though she had been brought into the process of healing herself.

She only hoped that one day she, too, would be able to perform such rituals, to prove to Rolling Thunder that she was worthy of being among the Comanche, as one with them.

A crowd had assembled to watch the performance. There was total silence as Daisy looked around her. While performing the healing ritual, she had felt as though she were in a trance.

Now her cheeks flushed hot at the sight of so many admirers.

She stepped timidly off the blanket.

Rolling Thunder was there to embrace her, and then Brant Fire In The Sky.

Tanzey watched the embrace of her brother and Daisy. She knew something was there between them, yet she also knew that it was something to be left unspoken. Brant Fire In The Sky loved his wife endearingly. His heart was aching and his eyes were tormented.

Daisy went to Tanzey. They embraced.

"It was so beautiful," Tanzey whispered. "Daisy, *you* are so beautiful."

She felt Daisy's embrace tighten.

Then they both jerked apart when a sudden continuation of shrieks came from inside Brant Fire In The Sky's lodge, followed by a strange sort of silence.

Brant Fire In The Sky's eyes were wide as he watched the entranceway.

Rolling Thunder held him back from going inside.

And then something else filled the morning air. The soft, sweet sound of a newborn baby's first cries.

"Did you hear that?" Brant Fire In The Sky shouted, his eyes wide. "My child! It is born! It is alive!"

The medicine man and woman came from the lodge. They nodded toward Brant Fire In The Sky.

He rushed inside the lodge and knelt down beside the bed.

Everything within him mellowed when he saw the tiny baby lying in the arms of his wife.

Tears filled his eyes as Feather Moon smiled over at him.

"A son is born to us today," she said, her words so weak Brant Fire In The Sky could scarcely understand her.

That was when Brant's euphoria waned. He not only heard the weakness of his wife's voice, he saw it in her eyes and by the way she was breathing.

As he lifted his son into his arms, so taken by him, he realized that the child was too small; so small, in fact, he fit into the palm of his hand.

The child was so fragile, Brant Fire In The Sky was afraid to touch his tiny toes, fingers, arms, and legs.

"Do not let him die," Feather Moon whispered harshly. "He is so small. His lungs, I fear, are not developed enough! I should have carried him two more months!"

Almost afraid to move the child from his hand, but knowing that the child must have nourishment soon, Brant Fire In The Sky leaned low over Feather Moon and gently placed the child to her breast.

As the child tried to suckle a breast that seemed

lacking in milk, Brant Fire In The Sky's insides froze. He tried to focus on the positive, on how the child looked so much like his mother, with skin so beautifully copper in color, with eyes as dark as midnight.

He saw something, though, that the chid had taken from his side of the family—a magnificent shock of red hair on its tiny head!

Brant Fire In The Sky's thoughts were interrupted when the medicine woman and man came back into the tepee.

Spirit Walker knelt down beside the bed. She smoothed damp locks of hair back from Feather Moon's brow. She glanced nervously down at the baby, who still had not been able to draw milk from the limp, tiny breast.

Blue Eyes came and stood over the bed. He frowned. "The baby is unhealthy," he said. "It is too small. It is sickly. You know, princess, that it is best to cast aside sickly children."

Feather Moon's eyes widened with fright.

Her heart pounded with fear.

She tried to lean up on an elbow, but was too weak.

"No," she cried. "Do not let my child die. Please!"

Brant Fire In The Sky was too stunned to speak. Then he glared at the medicine man. "My son will not be allowed to die!" he shouted. "Get out of here! You are heartless!"

Feather Moon reached a desperate hand out for her husband. "Do not speak to Blue Eyes in such a way," she gasped. "He is a revered medicine man."

She turned pleading eyes up at Blue Eyes. "Please forgive him," she asked. "Please change your mind about our *child*."

Blue Eyes folded his arms stubbornly across his chest. His jaw tightened.

Spirit Walker gazed with pity down at Feather Moon, then left the lodge, her eyes downcast.

Tanzey ran up to Spirit Walker. She grabbed her by an arm and drew her eyes to her. "I heard my brother shouting," she said in a rush of words. "What's happened? What has made him so angry?"

"Too much sadness is in your brother's lodge," Spirit Walker murmured. "The child is too small to be healthy. Feather Moon is too weak to live for much longer. And Feather Moon's milk is not enough for the child." She shook her head slowly back and forth. "It is too much for me to watch. I go to my lodge."

Shocked, Tanzey could only stand there and stare at her brother's lodge.

Then her gaze turned to Daisy, who gripped her arm.

With her free hand she pointed toward her breasts.

She gestured to Tanzey that she could feed the child. She had enough milk for two babies.

She asked Tanzey to go and tell the medicine man that she offered her breasts to the child!

Tanzey gave Daisy a grateful hug, then entered the lodge, even though she got a sour look from Blue Eyes. She gazed down at Feather Moon. She was stunned by how pale she looked and how weak her breathing was.

She then shifted her gaze to the child. She could see it fighting to get milk from a breast that was obviously empty. She stifled a sob behind her hand to see just how tiny the child was.

Brant Fire In The Sky turned and saw her there. He rushed to his feet. "Blue Eyes says it might be best to let my son die!" he cried. "And . . . and . . . I don't believe that Feather Moon is going to live." He lunged into Tanzey's arms. "Sis, oh, sis."

"There, there," Tanzey murmured, caressing her brother's back.

"My son is hungry, yet there is no milk," Brant Fire In The Sky cried.

"Yes, there *is*," Tanzey said. She placed her hands at his waist and gently eased him away from her. She looked into his eyes. "Daisy says your child can suckle from her breast. Let's get the child now, Brant, and take him to her."

Blue Eyes overheard the conversation. "The child will not feed from anyone's breast," he said sullenly. "Not until I decide its fate, whether it lives, or dies."

Tanzey had to hold Brant back as he doubled his hands into two tight fists at his sides and started for the medicine man.

"No, Brant," Tanzey said, guardedly watching the large medicine man. "Let's give this time. I'm ... sure ... we can work something out."

"Let me go and talk to Rolling Thunder about this," Tanzey said, her voice drawn. Tanzey moved between Brant and Blue Eyes. "Brant, please?" she whispered.

Brant Fire In The Sky panted hard, his anger eating away at his insides. His eyes locked in silent battle with Blue Eyes.

"Be quick, Tanzey," Brant Fire In The Sky ordered. He gave his wife and child a quick, worried glance.

Tanzey followed his gaze. Her eyes wavered when she saw how lifeless the baby lay in Feather Moon's arms.

Tanzey rushed from the tepee. She went to Rolling Thunder and grabbed his hands. "You've got to do something," she cried. "Blue Eyes won't let the child get nourishment. Daisy has offered to feed the child since Feather Moon *can't*. But Blue Eyes refuses to allow it. Do something, darling. Please?"

Rolling Thunder's eyes wavered into hers. He took her hands and walked her away from the gawking crowd, where silence lay like a cloud over everyone as they waited to hear of their princess's welfare, and also her child's.

When Tanzey and Rolling Thunder were away from his people, Rolling Thunder held Tanzey's hands and gave her a look of apology. Yet everything he said inflamed her anger and worries even more.

"The matter of the child and my cousin are out of my hands," he stated. "The medicine man's word is law when it comes to decisions about newborn children. Please understand, my pretty Tanzey Nicole, that infants are normally welcomed in the Comanche village, as a valuable addition to the tribe. Girls are accepted, but boys are preferred. If a child is a boy, the father paints a black spot on the door of the tepee to inform the tribe that it has been strengthened. But not this time. The boy is too frail!"

"Then you are saying that you can do nothing to help save the child?" Tanzey said, her voice breaking, abhorring the practice of the Comanche.

"I am saying to you that my duties as war chief do not give me powers over the Comanche medicine man and woman," he said, his jaw tight. "Now we must wait and trust that Blue Eyes makes a decision that will be in the favor of the child and its mother. Do you know that everyone anxiously waits to see if the child is allowed to live? No one wants the first child born of their princess to be cast aside to die."

When the weak cries of the baby wafted through the air, Tanzey's heart ached.

She had never felt as helpless as now.

Chapter Twenty-one

O, the heart that has truly loved never forgets,
But as truly loves on to the close.

—Thomas Moore

Several hours had passed. Tanzey and Daisy were sitting outside Feather Moon's lodge, awaiting the medicine man's decision about the newborn child and praying for Feather Moon's recovery.

Tanzey glanced toward the tepee. The child had cried from hunger until it was exhausted.

Now everything within the lodge was silent except for Blue Eyes' chants and the rattle he shook incessantly as he performed his magic over Feather Moon.

Rolling Thunder had told Tanzey about the medicine bag that Blue Eyes had taken into the lodge with him. In the bag were objects that the Guardian Spirit identified its powers with. It contained sweet grass, herbs, feathers, gristle of a bear snout, and beaver oil.

Rolling Thunder had also explained to her that the Comanche had two special places to go for medicine. One special place was Medicine Mounds. It was a line of rounded hills in Texas, between the Pease and Red Rivers. He said that it was not hard to locate the mounds. They were conspicuous, the cones rising three hundred fifty feet above the surrounding plain. It was believed that it was a dwelling place of a powerful and benevolent spirit.

While the moon was dark and full, Blue Eyes had gone there and prepared his cures from the gypsum waters of a spring at the base of the mounds.

Suddenly the child began to cry again. Tanzey's heart ached to hear just how weak the cries now were. She was afraid that Blue Eyes had chosen to let the child die, for it did not seem as though the child could go on much longer without nourishment.

Her heart went out to Feather Moon, hearing her child's cries as she lay dying herself. Surely the crying was tearing her apart! It took all of Tanzey's will-power to keep from going inside the tepee and demanding the child, to bring to Daisy's breasts!

But looking over at Rolling Thunder, who sat with many of his warriors around the evening fire, made her think twice of doing anything that he forbid.

As she watched him, she was torn with feelings.

Normally he was a man of good heart.

But now? As he let the child cry its lungs tired, the child possibly taking its last breaths, Tanzey was not sure how she should feel about him.

She shivered at the thought of having a child who was as premature and weak as Feather Moon's. Would Rolling Thunder stand aside and allow the medicine man decide to let his own child die?

Tanzey's troubled thoughts were brought to a halt when Daisy rose to her feet and began nervously pacing. Daisy began talking, her every word showing her deep concern for the baby.

Eyes wide, Tanzey rose slowly to her feet. She stared disbelievingly at Daisy. She was talking! For the first time since her rape . . . Daisy . . . was talking!

Daisy stopped and stared at Tanzey, only now aware herself that she had been talking!

So happy to have finally found her voice, she laughed softly, then broke into a loud ringing laugh.

Tanzey went to her and embraced her. She held her close. "Your voice is so beautiful," she murmured. "So very, very beautiful."

Tears flooding her eyes, Daisy eased from Tanzey's arms. "It was because of the child," she said, gazing over at the tepee, where there was a strained silence again, except for the medicine man and his rattle.

Tanzey gazed at the lodge. "The child has stopped crying," she said, her voice breaking. "I wonder if that means . . ."

"No, it can't," Daisy said, then broke away from Tanzey and ran into Brant Fire In The Sky and Feather Moon's tepee.

Tanzey was stunned that Daisy went into the lodge, and was aghast at what she had when she rushed out from the tepee: the small child held protectively within her arms.

"God, Daisy . . ." Tanzey said, paling.

Daisy gave her a half glance, then ran on to her own lodge.

Tanzey gaped openly at Daisy's lodge, fearing for her having taken the child, then ran to the tepee and hurried inside.

She stopped and covered her mouth with a hand as she stared down at Daisy and the child. Daisy was sitting on a soft cushion beside her lodge fire, the child suckling hungrily at her proffered breast.

Daisy smiled up at Tanzey. "Don't you see that I had to do it?" she murmured. She gazed down at the child. Her free hand caressed one of its tiny legs, then an arm. "He would have died. How could I have allowed that when I have so much milk?"

"Yes, how could you?" Tanzey said, touched deeply by the sight of the child and this sweet woman who defied everything and everyone by caring so much. She watched the child's fingers contentedly kneading Daisy's breasts and knew that was where he belonged.

Tanzey knelt down beside Daisy. She kissed her cheek, then rose quickly to her feet when a flurry at the entranceway drew her attention.

Her insides grew cold when Blue Eyes entered, his eyes filled with fire as he stared down at the nursing child.

When Blue Eyes took a step toward Daisy, Tanzey placed herself quickly in Daisy's path. What Daisy had done was right. It was wrong of the medicine man to come here and interfere.

"Please go away," Tanzey murmured. "Let the child have nourishment. Let the child *live*."

His glower was so fierce, it made Tanzey shiver with fear.

Yet she still did not move.

Her gaze shifted and moved past Blue Eyes when Rolling Thunder hurried into the tepee. Her eyes pleaded with him after he assessed the situation.

"Rolling Thunder, make Blue Eyes realize the wrong in what he wants to do," Tanzey begged. "Look at the child. See how he suckles? If he has this nourishment, surely he will live. Why would anyone want him to *die*? Just because he is tiny now, does not mean that he will be weak as he grows up. I can see him as one day being a powerful warrior, can't you?"

Frowning, Rolling Thunder went to Tanzey. He placed his hands at her waist and gently lifted her and set her aside.

He stood over Daisy, staring at her and the child.

"Rolling Thunder, I am ever so grateful for everything that you have done for me," Daisy said softly. "Please do nothing now to make my respect and love for you turn to hate."

Rolling Thunder took an unsteady step away from her. "You ... can ... speak ...?" he said, his voice showing his shock.

"The concern for the child has given me back my voice," Daisy said softly. "Now do you see the importance of this child to me? Because of him, I have regained my ability to speak. Please let me repay him by offering him my milk, not only now, but for*ever*."

Tanzey went to Rolling Thunder.

She stood at his side.

She took his hand.

He gazed down at her.

Their eyes locked.

Then he once again gazed at Daisy, touched by her words, her ability to *speak*, and by how the child was so content as it still fed from Daisy's breast.

Blue Eyes came to Rolling Thunder and shoved him aside. As he knelt down to take the child, Rolling Thunder clasped a tight hand on his shoulder.

"Do not touch the child," Rolling Thunder said flatly. "Your only concern now should be Feather Moon. Go to her. Do what you can to make her well."

Blue Eyes rose slowly to his full height. He glared at Rolling Thunder, shook his shoulder free of Rolling Thunder's tight grip, then left the lodge in a huff.

Tanzey turned to Rolling Thunder. She flung herself into his arms. "Thank you," she murmured. "Oh, Lord, thank you."

Tears rushing from her eyes, Daisy looked up at Rolling Thunder. "I knew that you would do what was right for the child," she said, her voice breaking.

"Your heart is too good not to care whether or not the child lives."

"It is good to be able to truly talk with you," Rolling Thunder said. He bent to a knee and gently touched her cheek. "I am glad that things now will be better for you."

"It's all because of you," Daisy said softly. She paused, then said, "And, Rolling Thunder, I think it's time you know my true name . . . a name not easily said silently."

"It is?" Rolling Thunder asked.

"Samantha Kay Bishop," she murmured. "I am called Sami by some."

"A beautiful name for a beautiful lady," Rolling Thunder said. "Do you wish now to be called Sami or Daisy?"

Daisy got a troubled look in her eyes. "It is best that I am called Daisy," she said. "My rapist doesn't know me by that name. If he is looking for me, he will be looking . . . for . . . a . . . Sami."

"Daisy it will be, then, while you live among my people," Rolling Thunder said tightly, not wanting to remember the rape.

Rolling Thunder brushed a soft kiss across her lips, then left the lodge with Tanzey.

Tanzey stopped when she saw a lot of activity around Feather Moon and her brother's lodge. "Oh, no, surely she has died," she said, a sob lodging in her throat.

"*Ka*, no, she has not died," Rolling Thunder said, drawing her into his embrace. "Blue Eyes is trying something more to save her. Two tepees will be joined together with an opening between them. A hole will be dug in each tent, about two feet deep. In one of them a fire will be built, while on the other side, a lump of mud, as large as a man's head, will be placed. All around the hole, as well as the lump of mud, the ground will be stuck with willow sprouts. Feather Moon will be placed in one of the lodges. Musicians will play their instruments all night and all day tomorrow, if needed."

"I would like to go and be with Feather Moon, but Blue Eyes won't allow it," Tanzey said, turning to watch the two tepees being brought together.

"No, and that is not something I can change," Rolling Thunder uttered. "It is enough that I have defied the medicine man once. I shall not try it a second time."

"I understand," Tanzey said, watching her brother follow the medicine man as he carried Feather Moon into one of the two, joined tepees.

"No one can pass close enough to the two lodges to allow their shadow to fall on the tents, or the sick one in the lodge will surely die," Rolling Thunder explained. "If all is done right, Feather Moon will live. If she dies, then it will be said that something went wrong in the ceremony."

"I am suddenly so tired," Tanzey said, leaning against Rolling Thunder.

"Let us go to our lodge," Rolling Thunder said, already leading her there, an arm gently around her waist. "There is not much else we can do now but wait. The child will be all right now that it is with Daisy. I will say soft prayers to the heavens throughout the night for our sweet princess Feather Moon."

"Yes, and so will I," Tanzey said, entering the tepee with him.

Soon a soft fire glittered its shadows along the inside walls of the lodge.

A good meal had been eaten.

Baths had been taken.

Tanzey was now cuddled next to Rolling Thunder in their bed.

He held her until she fell asleep.

But sleep would not come to him. He kept thinking of Feather Moon. He did not expect her to live, and he knew that it would be hard to accept such a loss. She meant so much to everyone. She had been their princess since she had been ten winters of age.

He smiled when he recalled her feistiness as a child and her stubbornness as an adult. Even those faults did not take away her loveliness, nor the fact that everyone adored her.

If she should die, she would be sorely missed.

He was thankful for, at least, the child. He had no doubt now that he would live. Thanks to Daisy, he ... would ... live.

A sound, something like the loud swishing of wings outside his lodge, made Rolling Thunder's heart skip a beat.

"An .. owl ... ?" he whispered harshly, shuddering at the thought of what its meaning would be, if it were.

Death!

Chapter Twenty-two

While summer flowers with moonlight dews were wet,
And winds sighed soft around the mountain's brow,
And all was rapture then which is but memory now!
—CHARLES SWAIN

The Comanche village was in a state of shock over the death of their beloved Princess Feather Moon.

The drums beat incessantly.

Mourners lifted their voices to the heavens from morning until night.

Tanzey stood back with Daisy and gazed at Brant Fire In The Sky, who stood at the opening of a small cave that he had chosen for the burial of his wife.

She then looked at Rolling Thunder, who stood on the opposite side of the opening from her brother. Never had she seen him so solemn, so torn with sadness. Her heart went out to him. She wanted to go to him and be with him. But it was her place to just observe, not participate.

The burial place for Feather Moon had to be located west of the lodge in which she had died. Rolling Thunder had led him to this small cave that sat not that far from their village, a place where Rolling Thunder and Feather Moon had played as children.

Earlier in the day, before the burial rites had begun, Rolling Thunder had shared some memories with Tanzey. He had told her how Feather Moon had loved this small and special cave, and how, as a child, she had pretended that it was her very own lodge.

With tears shining in his eyes, Rolling Thunder had told Tanzey how Feather Moon, with her long and flowing hair and laughing eyes, had giggled as she had served Rolling Thunder "pretend" food and "pretend" drink in the cave.

It had been her playhouse then, her resting place now.

Tanzey had helped the women prepare Feather Moon's body for the burial. It had been hard to help shape Feather Moon's body for her grave. As was Comanche custom, her knees were bent to her chest, and her head was bent forward, to the knees. A rope bound her body in this position.

But before having done this, Tanzey had lovingly bathed Feather Moon's body, then stood back as some of the Comanche women had overlaid Feather Moon's face with vermilion, and sealed her eyes with red clay.

Facing the rising sun, Feather Moon's body was now inside the cave.

As the drums beat out their steady drone in the distance, Brant Fire In The Sky took Feather Moon her personal belongings.

Tanzey watched her brother take in Feather Moon's favorite calico gown, cooking kettle, her tools for dressing skins, and so many other things that had been of personal value to his wife.

When Feather Moon's favorite horse, her proud sorrel, the very horse Feather Moon had been riding on the day of Brant's capture, was brought by a

young brave to the cave entrance, Tanzey paled and
sucked in a deep breath.

The horse's mane glistened from having been
brushed for this occasion.

On his back was Feather Moon's favorite saddle.

At the horse's right side was Feather Moon's rifle
in a gun boot.

At its left side hung her sheathed knife and her
buckskin bag, which carried her "medicine."

Knowing what was to happen now, Tanzey
grabbed for Daisy's hand and clutched tightly to it.

Tanzey's heart pounded as she watched Big Bow,
Feather Moon's favored warrior, come with a rifle
and stand back only a few feet from the beautiful
sorrel.

Not able to bear to watch the horse's life being
snuffed away, Tanzey turned her eyes and closed
them. She only wished that she could close her ears
to the sound of the gunfire, but was only able to
wince when the single shot rang through the air.

She flinched as though shot herself when she heard
the thud of the horse fall to the ground.

Not wanting to see the dead horse, Tanzey continued to look away from the cave entrance.

When she thought that the horse might be tucked
inside the cave with Feather Moon's body, only then
did she turn her head slowly around and again
watch the burial rites.

Several warriors were at the cave entrance, sealing
it off with huge boulders, sticks, and dirt.

And when this was done, Brant Fire In The Sky
stood beside Rolling Thunder as he alone sang the
death song.

Willing herself not to cry anymore, Tanzey listened
to Rolling Thunder chant. She listened to the words,
touched by them. . . .

"Wise One Above, you are making Feather Moon a spirit," Rolling Thunder sang. "Where is she now? You are making Feather Moon a spirit. There is danger where Feather Moon walks. Even the eagle dies. Where Feather Moon walks, there is death. And Feather Moon shall walk no more."

Rolling Thunder turned and faced his Comanche people. He could feel Tanzey's eyes on him as he began to speak his thoughts about the departed.

"Although I bear only the humble title of war chief, I have been chosen today to speak in behalf of my cousin, your beloved princess, whose name I can speak no more, for to do so would be a mark of disrespect."

The female friends and relatives of Feather Moon began showing their grief by again wailing.

But Rolling Thunder spoke above them, for he still had more to say about his cousin. "My beloved cousin was buried facing the west so that at the resurrection she will arise and march eastward, again to take possession of all the country the white man has taken from the Comanche."

Rolling Thunder turned and gestured with his hands toward the cave. "The spirit of my beloved cousin even now mounts the spirit of her slain steed and rides straight to the sun and the pastures of the Happy Hunting Ground, where she will remain an extended time."

He turned and faced his people again. He reached his hands toward the heavens. He lifted his eyes heavenward, then closed them. "My beloved cousin rides her steed even now in a valley longer than our own groves, streams, and meadows," he cried. "Where she rides, there is no rain or wind. The climate is always mild. The water is always cool. There is no darkness there because the Wise One Above is

everywhere. There are buffalo, deer, elk, and antelope in abundance.''

Smiling, Rolling Thunder opened his eyes and
gazed from person to person. ''Where our princess
rides today, pounded corn is forever at hand,'' he
said, his voice filled with peace. ''Horses there are
faster than the wind. Beautiful birds are in the tree-
tops. There is no suffering or sorrow there. Death
and resurrection are not uncommon.''

Rolling Thunder's smile faded, and he swallowed
hard as he gazed over at Brant Fire In The Sky. ''Husband of the departed, do not despair. Your wife, who
died from childbirth, will receive special treatment in
the afterworld beyond the sun,'' he said solemnly.
''Her suffering is past and she now only rides in
sunshine, her smile as radiant as the stars. The Comanche afterworld is beyond the sun where it sets in
the west. All things there are perfect.''

Brant Fire In The Sky lowered his head in his
hands. His sobs filled the air, silencing the mourning
cries and wails all around him.

Rolling Thunder still gazed at Brant Fire In The
Sky. He went to him and lifted a comforting hand to
his shoulder. ''Eventually, after an excursion in the
celestial pastures, my beloved cousin's spirit must be
reborn of the Earth Mother and returned to keep up
the population and power of the tribe,'' he informed him.

Brant Fire In The Sky's eyes opened widely. He
gazed up at Rolling Thunder.

Rolling Thunder nodded. ''Not in our time will we
know she is among her people again,'' he said. ''But
she *will* be as filled with spirit and laughter as
before.''

Brant Fire In The Sky swallowed hard. Again he

buried his face in his hands, hardly able to contain his sorrow.

Rolling Thunder patted Brant Fire In The Sky's shoulder, then turned to his people again. "Let us all return to our village," he said softly. "Carry your mourning with you, but remember that my cousin was a strong-willed person when alive, so is she now, in spirit. She would not want you to be saddened by her death. She would want you to think of her at peace, and overwhelmed with a wonderful love that she has found in the great beyond with the ancestors of her long-ago past."

Everyone filed by and hugged Rolling Thunder and Brant Fire In The Sky, then walked somberly back toward their village.

Tanzey ran up to Brant Fire In The Sky and hugged him. "Things will be all right," she murmured. "You ... have .. a son. Live for your son."

"It is because of a son that I lost a *wife*," Brant Fire In The Sky said, his voice drawn with bitterness.

Tanzey gasped when she saw the anger in his eyes. "Brant, no, that is not the way to think," she murmured. She placed a gentle hand to his cheek. "Brant, please? For the baby's sake?"

He reached up and removed her hand.

"I have lost everything today," Brant Fire In The Sky said, his voice breaking. "Do you hear? Everything! So say no more to me about the child, about what is best for me, or about *any*thing. I'm leaving, Tanzey."

"No, Brant, please ..." Tanzey pleaded, taking his hands. She held them tightly when he tried to jerk them away. "Give it time, Brant. Please? For me, if not for the child? I'm not sure I could live without you. You are a part of me. You ... are ... my twin!"

She could see a quick haunted expression fill his

eyes. She fought back the urge to cry, as she had to be strong now for her brother.

Brant Fire In The Sky gazed at her for a moment, then nodded. "All right, sis," he said. "I'll try. But don't push the baby on me, do you hear? As far as I'm concerned, Daisy can have him."

Tanzey paled. She eased her hands from his and stared at him as he walked away, his head hung.

"That is not your brother saying those things," Rolling Thunder said as he came and placed a gentle, comforting arm around Tanzey's waist. "It is his mourning that speaks for him. He will see past that mourning soon and want his son, for in his son is a part of his *wife* that he will never want to part from."

Tanzey's gaze shifted from her brother to Daisy, who was walking just behind Brant, her own head hung. Both her child and Brant's had been left behind in the village under the care of a Comanche woman whose breasts were filled with milk from the recent birth of her own child.

Daisy had confided in Tanzey only yesterday that she was becoming too attached to Brant's son. If Brant did eventually take the child away, Daisy said that she would feel as though a part of her heart would be stolen.

And Brant's child still bore no name. Every time it was mentioned to Brant to give the child a name, he just looked away, as though no one had spoken to him, as though the child did not *exist.*

"The normal time for a husband's mourning is three to fifteen sunsets," Rolling Thunder said, leading Tanzey on away from the cave. "When that time is over, I will speak once again to your brother about the way life should be for him and his son. I hope that I will not be forced to use words and tactics that might turn your brother into my enemy while drawing him back to his normal self."

"Surely in time he will get past this," Tanzey said softly.

"His love for my cousin was as high as the sky," Rolling Thunder said, gesturing toward the heavens with a hand. "So I do not expect him to get past this easily."

"I'm sure you will know what to say and when to say it," Tanzey said, snuggling closer to his side.

Tears silvered her eyes at the thought of Feather Moon being left behind in the cave, never to see her again. She could not help but feel despair herself, yet knew that it was nothing compared with how Brant felt at this moment. She shuddered to think of how she would feel if anything ever happened to Rolling Thunder.

She gave Rolling Thunder a trembling smile. "Please stay safe," she murmured.

Rolling Thunder stopped and drew her into his arms. "My beautiful Tanzey Nicole," he said, smiling down at her. "I am with you today, tomorrow, and for always."

He wove his fingers through her long red hair and drew her lips to his. But as he kissed her, she could not be all that comforted by his words.

She knew how quickly death could take him away from her!

She kissed Rolling Thunder as though it was their last moments together!

Chapter Twenty-three

Love? I will tell thee what it is to love!
It is to build with human thoughts a shrine,
Where Hope sits brooding like a beauteous dove;
Where time seems young, and Life a thing divine.
                                        —CHARLES SWAIN

Another Comanche dawn showed its beautiful pink-ish hue through the smoke hole overhead, casting streams of light over Rolling Thunder's back as he lay above Tanzey, blanketing her with his body.

Tanzey drew a ragged breath as Rolling Thunder's lips touched her mouth, his tongue surging through her lips, touching hers, tip to tip.

She clung to his rock hardness as he plunged his manhood into her, withdrew, and plunged again.

She sighed as one of his hands enfolded one of her breasts.

As he kneaded the breast and kissed her, soft moans repeatedly surfaced from inside Tanzey.

Wanting to delay the moment of euphoric bliss, Rolling Thunder moved more slowly within her, then faster, with quicker, surer movements. His raging hunger became more fueled by her kiss, and by how she wrapped her legs around him, bringing her closer to his heat.

Cradling her close, his lean, sinewy buttocks moved rhythmically, his hands now beneath her, taking in the roundness of her hips.

He groaned in whispers against her lips as the flood of emotions leapt within him in ecstatic waves. "I have never loved like this before, nor ever shall again," he whispered huskily.

Tanzey was a tempest of emotions. Never had she felt as loved or as needed.

A tremor went through her body when Rolling Thunder bent his head to one of her breasts. His mouth closed over the nipple, his tongue flicking.

Tanzey sucked in a breath of rapture when he then rolled her nipple with his tongue.

As Rolling Thunder breathed in the sweet scent of her body, his mouth searing her flesh, his tongue tasting her, his hands clasped Tanzey's buttocks and molded her slender, sweet body snugly against his.

Firing his passion, he plunged more deeply within her, moving rhythmically.

He took her mouth savagely in his, their kisses now more fevered and eager.

Their bodies tangled in a torrid embrace.

Rolling Thunder reached for Tanzey's hands and held them above her head, their fingers intertwined, their tongues touching.

A madness seemed to engulf them both. Tanzey's passionate response seemed *dangerous*.

Perhaps this was because she and Rolling Thunder had not made love for many days and nights.

Not since Feather Moon's passing.

The whole village had been in mourning for fifteen days and nights.

But at midnight last night it was declared through

the village that the mourning should be left behind them. They all felt that their beloved princess was in the afterworld with her ancestors.

Feather Moon was happy.

She was at peace.

Today those whom she left behind on this earth would resume their normal daily activities.

Brant, Tanzey worried to herself. What ... of ... Brant? He had not yet come from his lodge since the passing of his wife. Listless, sad, and distant, he mourned her deeply.

And he still wouldn't look at his child, much less give him a name. He still blamed his son for Feather Moon's death.

"You are not altogether here with me," Rolling Thunder said as his body stilled against Tanzey's. He gently brushed a soft kiss across her lips. "Come back to me. I hunger for you. Do you not feel the same? Where has your mind taken you?"

"I'm sorry," Tanzey murmured. She gave Rolling Thunder a long-lashed, apologetic look. "I didn't know that you could tell that my mind had wandered from ... from ..."

"Shh," Rolling Thunder whispered. He slid a finger over her lips, silencing her apology. "I know you are filled with concern over your brother. I, too, fear for him, for his *sanity*. His mourning has taken too much from him. Today I shall go to him. I shall see that the mourning ends *today*."

Tanzey slid his hand aside. "I don't think it will be that easy," she said. "But, darling, please, *please*, do try."

She was calmed by his kiss and strong hug.

She twined her arms around his neck and felt a tremor when he began his rhythmic strokes again, filling her, lifting her.

Tanzey sighed against his lips as she felt that wonderful euphoria building inside her.

She clung to Rolling Thunder as his body plunged over and over again into hers, his seed filling her with its warmth.

And then they lay quietly together.

Their breaths mingled as Rolling Thunder whispered how much he loved her over and over again against her parted lips.

"You make me so happy," she whispered back. "You make me feel so ... so ... feminine."

"You are all *mah-ocu-ah*, woman," Rolling Thunder said, chuckling beneath his breath. He rolled to his side and turned to her, his hands roaming slowly over her creamy skin. "So white. So soft. So delicate."

He smiled at her. "*Huh*, yes, you are all woman, and you are *mine*," he declared.

"I would feel better if we were married," Tanzey said, lowering her eyes almost bashfully.

"The Wise One Above has already blessed our union," Rolling Thunder said softly.

"I'm not that certain that *my* God has been as eager to accept what you and I have done together," Tanzey said, sighing.

She looked toward the Bible that she had left lying on top of the trunk, then turned her eyes slowly back to Rolling Thunder. "There is much in the Bible about adultery and how it is condemned by the Almighty," she said, her voice breaking. "We cannot be condemned for adultery. But I wonder ..."

He twined his fingers through her hair and drew her mouth to his, silencing her worries. He kissed her with a lazy warmth, then held her close to the contours of his body.

"Do not condemn your*self* with such worries," he said. "Accept what is and rejoice over it. How many can say they love as deeply as you and I? How many have ever found *such* a love as ours? There can be no wrong in such a bond . . . in such devotion."

"But vows have not been spoken," Tanzey pursued guiltily.

"They will come when the time is appropriate, when there is nothing to take away from the moment," Rolling Thunder said. He caressed her back with slow sweeps of his hand. "And rest assured that by Comanche standards, we are already considered married."

"What?" Tanzey said. She leaned up on an elbow and looked incredulously into his eyes. "How . . . can . . . that be?"

"My beautiful Tanzey Nicole with eyes of grass and hair of flame, if a couple sleeps together all night, they are considered married," he said, smiling. "Does that not mean that we have been married since our first time together, sexually?"

"Truly that is how it is done by the Comanche? There is no ceremony?" Tanzey said, eyes wide. "All along, in the eyes of your Wise One Above, and perhaps even my God, we have been married from our first night of making love?"

"No, that is not entirely so," Rolling Thunder said. He placed a gentle hand to her cheek. "There will be a marriage ceremony, a ritual that must be played out between us. *Then* we can truly call ourselves man and wife."

"What ritual . . . ?" Tanzey asked, but stopped suddenly and looked toward the entrance flap when Brant Fire In The Sky's voice spoke up from outside.

"Tanzey? Rolling Thunder? I have come to say good-bye before I leave the village," Brant Fire In The Sky said, causing Tanzey to gasp and rise to her feet.

Rolling Thunder leapt to his feet and jerked on his fringed breeches while Tanzey yanked a buckskin dress quickly over her head.

They left the tepee together.

In the dim light of morning, Tanzey saw that Brant Fire In The Sky had his horse ready for travel and a buckskin bag heavy with his belongings. He had clipped his hair shorter, and he wore his cowboy boots instead of moccasins.

He also wore his wide-brimmed hat . . . everything to deny his Comanche life.

"Brant, no," Tanzey whispered harshly, paling.

"Sis, don't say anything," Brant Fire In The Sky said, his voice drawn. "I'm doing what I must. Don't you see? I can't stay here. The memories are all around me. I miss her so much I can hardly stand it."

"But, Brant, don't *you* see?" Tanzey said, fighting back tears of frustration. "Leaving isn't the answer. You can't leave your sorrow behind. It's imbedded deeply within your soul. Without loved ones around you, to help you, you will be overwhelmed by loneliness."

Rolling Thunder placed a hand between Brant Fire In The Sky and Tanzey. He gazed from one to the other, then nodded to Tanzey. "Let me speak my thoughts to your brother," he said hoarsely. "Then, when I am finished, if he still wishes to leave, *say* nothing else to him. He is a man who must search his own heart for his own answers."

Tanzey swallowed hard. She glanced quickly over at her brother, then nodded at Rolling Thunder. "All right," she murmured. "But *please* say the right things. *Please* encourage him to stay."

Rolling Thunder's eyes locked with Tanzey's for a moment; then he gave Brant Fire In The Sky a steady, unnerving gaze. "Leaving is cowardly," he said flatly. "You must look forward to life, not backward. You must go today on a mustang venture with the Comanche warriors of my village. Soon will be the time to go on the yearly trek to Mexico and also to Fort Worth, to make trade. Many horses ... many good *trade*."

Brant Fire In The Sky shuffled his feet nervously as Rolling Thunder continued to give him a steady stare.

"It is your place to make trade so that you can bring home to your *tua*, son, that which makes his life more comfortable," Rolling Thunder said tightly. "It is *your* place to appoint someone of distinction to *name* your child. It is shameful that you have gone this long without seeing that this was done. It is shameful that you have not held your son since your wife's passing. If you ride away from this village without having as much as considered what you are doing to your child by abandoning him in such a way, the Wise One Above will not ride with you. You will be a man without a *soul*. That is worse than being a man without a country."

Brant Fire In The Sky lowered his eyes.

His shoulders slumped.

He sighed heavily.

"I wish to also remind you that there has not yet been a celebration for you that was promised after saving this war chief's life," Rolling Thunder said. He placed a firm hand on Brant Fire In The Sky's shoulder. "Things come in order. There will be the horse roundup, then the celebration. Somewhere between those two things planned, you *will* go to your son and take over the duties of a father."

Brant Fire In The Sky slowly lifted his eyes. He gazed at Rolling Thunder. "I do wish to stay," he said, gulping hard. He shifted his gaze to Tanzey.

"And I'm sorry I have caused you such pain. I . . . I . . . just felt as though I had lost everything. I was wrong. I have you. I will always have you. As twins, our bond has always been so strong. I could not have gotten far, sis, without returning to you."

Tanzey rushed into her brother's arms. She hugged him tightly as her tears bled into the soft buckskin fabric of his fringed shirt. "I love you so, Brant," she sobbed. "Had you left, I would have felt as though a piece of me was missing. When I thought you were dead, I felt so empty. . . . We must never part, Brant. Never. Thank you for staying."

Brant Fire In The Sky burrowed his nose into the depths of her hair and released a few of his own tears.

Then he gripped her shoulders and held her away from him. Their eyes locked. "I'm staying, but I . . . I . . . still cannot bring myself to see my son," he said, his voice breaking. "It's still too soon. Perhaps if I wait somewhat longer, when I gaze at my son I won't see his mother and hate him for him having caused her to die. I want to love him, sis, not hate him."

"And you will," she said. She placed a gentle hand to his cheek. "How could you not? He's such a beautiful child, so innocent of any wrongdoing. To blame him is to blame your wife for having him. You don't want to feel that way, do you? Don't you know that if she were alive, she would cherish the child? She would adore him? Please, Brant, don't wait too long. The child needs to know your arms and recognize your voice. A child needs these things from a parent, to be able to grow up into someone that is stable of mind. A child . . . needs . . . a father . . . a *name*."

Brant Fire In The Sky dropped his hands to his sides. "What you say is true," he said. "I'll go on the mustang roundup. When I return"—he looked away—"I promise I will make things right with my son."

He gazed over at Rolling Thunder. "You said something about me appointing someone of distinction to name him," he uttered. "Is that the way it is done by the Comanche? The father, himself, does not name the child?"

"Someone of your choice will do the naming," Rolling Thunder said. "That *is* the way of the *Nermer-nuh*, Comanche."

"Then, when I am ready, will you do me the honor of naming my son, Rolling Thunder?" Brant Fire In The Sky said, his voice again breaking.

Rolling Thunder smiled. "It is good to know that you *will* see that the child is named without being asked again," he said. "And, *huh*, yes, it will be my pleasure to name him."

"I look forward to going on the mustang roundup," Brant Fire In The Sky said, lifting his heavy bag from the back of his horse. "I'm certain that's what I need. Several hard days in the saddle. That ought to make me think of something besides my loss."

"*Huh*, yes, getting my rump sore as hell in the saddle is the best thing I can think of to get my head on straight," Brant Fire In the Sky joked, laughing softly as he winked at Tanzey. "Don't you think so, sis?"

"Yes, I do believe so," she said, her eyes twinkling into his.

Then she turned anxiously toward Rolling Thunder. "Can I go with you on the roundup?" she said in a rush of words. "I know as much as any man about mustanging."

Recalling the day she caught the mustang in the same manner he knew so well, and knowing how well she rode a horse, Rolling Thunder's lips lifted into a smile.

"Yes, you can ride with us while mustanging," he said. He chuckled when he saw the pure joy his words had brought into her eyes.

Tanzey let out a loud "whoopee."

Laughing, she grabbed her brother's hat from his head and tossed it into the air.

She had not known until now how much she had missed those sorts of adventures. After coming to the Comanche village, her breeches had been taken away, and she had worn nothing but women's clothes since.

She sobered when she saw no amusement in Rolling Thunder's eyes. She knew that he wanted her to be a lady and someday a *mother*.

She went to him and twined her arms around his neck. "Please don't change your mind about my going," she murmured. "I promise that when we return, I'll be a lady again. But while on the trail, please don't expect me to behave delicately. I love being part of the *men*. It will be the last time I will ask to go with you. I . . . promise . . ."

"The last time," Rolling Thunder growled. "The *very* last time."

She nodded anxiously, then smiled coyly up at him, for the moment becoming the woman that he wished her to be. She leaned up and whispered into his ear. "I believe we were interrupted awhile ago, weren't we?" she said. "Can the mustanging be postponed just a few more hours, my love? I've things I want to say to you. I've things I want to *do*."

She could hear Brant Fire In The Sky chuckle beneath his breath.

She could hear him leading his horse away.

Her shoulders swayed in anticipation when Rolling

Thunder swept her up into his arms, and carried her back inside his lodge.

When he placed her on the bed, she gazed into his lustful eyes.

She reached her arms out for him. "*Kee-mah*, come to me," she whispered. "It seems that I still have much to prove to you."

Chapter Twenty-four

Wild nights! Wild nights!
Were I with thee,
Wild nights should be
Our luxury!

—EMILY DICKINSON

As Tanzey rode straight-backed in her saddle, her legs encased in fringed buckskin, her hair flowing in the breeze behind her, she glanced over at her brother, who rode to her side. She remembered their horseback outings together in Kansas, free and wild as the wind.

The excitement of being on horseback today, on her way to catch wild mustangs, was just as exciting as the roundups in Kansas.

In fact, it was more exciting, more challenging, because Brant's future with the Comanche depended on it. If he continued to mourn his wife after the hard-fought-for roundup, then his future with the Comanche would be bleak. He would no longer be looked to as someone special, the man who saved their war chief from a certain death.

More than likely he would be scorned and banished from the tribe, as useless.

Tanzey swallowed hard, hoping that the latter would not ever become a reality. She loved her brother and did not want to ever say a final good-bye to him. She wanted him to be a Comanche like herself.

Her gaze shifted and her insides did a slow melting when she gazed at Rolling Thunder, who sat so kingly tall in his fancy Comanche saddle. He was not aware of being watched, for his eyes were elsewhere, constantly on the search for the first signs of the herd of wild mustangs.

Today his thick black hair lay in two long braids down his muscled back. He wore only a breechclout and moccasins, the attire worn by all of the other warriors, as well as her brother.

His bronze skin was sheened in brilliant sunshine, highlighting the muscles that rippled across his shoulders, down his arms, and even lower, where his thighs were pressed against the sides of his horse.

She gazed at length at his high cheekbones, his classic nose, his tight jaw, his lips, and his hands!

A tremor coursed through her as she recalled the magic those lips and hands created along the curves and hidden, secret crevices of her body.

Oh, how alive he brought her with the mere touch of a hand, or his lips, or . . . his . . . tongue.

To think of their moments together this past night made her feel hot with passion.

It was hard to get those times with him off her mind, even though she knew that she must be as alert today as the others while searching for mustangs.

But with Rolling Thunder at her side, with the power of his presence so very near, she found it hard to concentrate on much else, but him.

Suddenly Rolling Thunder raised a hand, a silent gesture for his men to stop.

Tanzey drew a tight rein.

Her horse shuddered to a quick halt.

Tanzey followed the trail of Rolling Thunder's steady gaze and saw that the hoofprints left in the dirt were not those of unshod horses. They were made from horses that had been tamed and ridden by white men—and perhaps renegade Comanche.

She knew now that the Comanche horses were not ordinarily shod, but a man's favorite horse, if tenderfooted, could be fitted with a rawhide boot soaked in water and tied over the sore hoofs.

Some of the other riding horses had their hooves toughened by walking them slowly back and forth near the heat and smoke of a fire.

Tanzey stiffened when Rolling Thunder's gaze slowly lifted and he stared across a straight stretch of land that was divided by a high, smooth ridge, its summit accessible from both sides by an easy, gradual ascent. A canyon reached away from one end of the ridge. The many hoofprints led there, where someone could easily make a hideout, if hiding is what was on their minds.

Tanzey knew that it was also a perfect place to hide stolen horses!

Tanzey watched Brant Fire In The Sky ride over next to Rolling Thunder. She listened as they discussed the hoofprints and the canyon.

Big Bow came and joined the conversation.

"Those responsible for burning and plundering ranches have not been found," Big Bow said, his eyes lit with fire. "Perhaps the search ends here?"

"If so, I imagine we will find those who are responsible for my parents' deaths among them," Brant Fire In The Sky scowled, causing Tanzey to flinch with the thought of possibly being this close to the murderers.

"Let us go into the canyon," Rolling Thunder said, yanking his rifle from the gun boot at the side of his horse. "Let us see just whose horses *did* make these prints."

He gazed past Brant Fire In The Sky to Tanzey. His eyes wavered. He feared now that he had brought her into danger. Yet he could not chance sending her back, for he would not let her out of his sight while renegades and murdering white men were on the loose.

He had no choice but to take her with him. While she was at his side, he could protect her.

"*Kee-mah*, come," he said softly. "Ride at my side again. If there is an outburst of gunfire, stay close." His jaw tightened. "And do nothing foolish. This is no time to prove anything to anyone. I want you to come out of this alive."

Tanzey swallowed hard. She nodded.

Then she grabbed her own rifle from the gun boot. She glanced over at her brother, who was armed for a possible attack.

"Be careful, Brant," she said, her voice drawn. "Lord, Brant, please . . . be . . . careful."

"You shouldn't be here, sis," Brant Fire In The Sky said. "Lord, I wish you were back at the village, safe."

"Brant, no one is safe anywhere as long as the renegades and outlaws ride together, caring not who they kill, or who they steal from," Tanzey said, her fingers tightening around the rifle. "I am as safe here as anywhere." Again she swallowed hard. "And if those murdering scalawags who killed our parents are hiding out here, I want to have a part in capturing them. I would even be glad to put a bullet in each of their hearts."

"Sis, don't take any chances," Brant Fire In The Sky said, his eyes wavering into hers. "Do as Rolling Thunder says. Stay close."

He paused, gave her an uneasy gaze, then said, "Let the men do the killing, if killing needs to be done, Tanzey."

"I can't promise anything," Tanzey said softly. "Just please watch your back, Brant. Those responsible for our parents' deaths are not only heartless, they are damned cowards."

Rolling Thunder looked over his shoulder at his warriors. "Let us go forward!" he said, waving his rifle in the air.

Tanzey rode between her brother and the man she loved toward the canyon.

When they moved into the shadows of the high, smooth ridge, they rode slowly, their eyes examining every clump of trees and every fallen boulder.

They rode onward, then all hell seemed to break loose. There was an ambush from both sides. The white outlaws and Comanche renegades seemed to come out of the cracks on the walls of the canyon on their horses.

The air was rent with the noise of the war whoop and gunfire.

There was a scurry of horses.

There were screams of the wounded, and thuds of bodies as they fell from their horses, dead.

Tanzey became disoriented by the clash of men and horses and gunfire. The dust stirred up by the horse's hooves blinded her. She felt the sting of rocks graze against her flesh as they fell from the walls of the canyon.

And then she felt someone's arm slip around her waist.

She was dragged roughly from her horse and thrown across the lap of a rider.

Tanzey's screams could not be heard above the noise of the fighting.

And she found it impossible to move.

She was being held on the man's lap with force.

She flung her arms and feet in the air, yet she still could not work herself free.

She gazed sidewise and could not see the face of the assailant. The dust and the smoke from the steady gunfire was too thick.

But she did know that she was being carried away from the fight, for the sounds became more distant by the minute.

And with the distance, came the clear, fresh air, giving her finally the ability to see who her captor was.

She gasped when she saw the face of a white man, a livid white scar crisscrossing his brow.

"Howdy, ma'am," Lieutenant Dan Adams said, chuckling as he gazed into Tanzey's wondering eyes. "Nice to make your acquaintance."

"Who the hell are you?" Tanzey screamed, still struggling to get free.

She reached around and dug her fingernails into his hand. Even that didn't cause him to loosen his grip.

"Lieutenant Dan Adams at your service, ma'am," he said, chuckling. "I've gone and done you a service, wouldn't you say? By stealing you away from those murdering, thieving Comanche?"

"You!" Tanzey gasped. "You're the man Colonel Franks told me about. You were dishonorably discharged. He suspected you were the one who led the

outlaw gang and who rode with Comanche renegades. Lord . . . he . . . he was *right*. You are probably
even the one responsible for my parents' deaths."

"And who might your parents have been?" Dan
asked, forking an eyebrow.

Tanzey told him their names, and the location of
their ranch.

"Yep, I recall that ranch and how I had to shoot
the man and woman," he said matter-of-factly. "I just
couldn't let them get away, now could I? They had
seen my face. They could have fingered me to the
colonel. My life wouldn't have been worth spit, then,
now would it?"

His confession, so proudly spoken, made Tanzey
grow numb inside.

And then her feelings turned to rage. "How can
you sit there and so calmly confess to my parents'
murders?" she screamed, struggling unsuccessfully,
even harder to get free. "Turn me loose! Let me at
you! You'll wish you'd never known me *or* my
parents."

"Tsk, tsk," he said, laughing sarcastically. "Just listen to you now. You aren't talkin' like a lady." His
eyes went over her and her attire. "Yet *look* at you.
You don't even dress like a lady. I think that means
you've not met a man who was man enough to turn
you into a lady . . . until now. I'm goin' to teach you
things you never dreamed a man and woman could
do together. Even that damn Comanche war chief
wouldn't know the likes of lovin' that I know."

"You filthy, murdering bastard," Tanzey hissed.
"You'll never get the chance. Once you let me loose,
you're the same as dead."

"Now, I'd watch makin' threats," Dan said, winc-
ing when a sharp pain shot through his wounded
arm.

Tanzey turned her head and saw blood seeping through his shirtsleeve on his other arm. This gave Tanzey the confidence that she had almost lost. The arm holding her down was free of wounds. The one holding the reins seemed to be weakening by the second.

"You're not only a bastard, you're stupid," Tanzey said, laughing into the wind. "While messing with me, you're going to bleed to death."

"I've been shot before," Dan growled. "It ain't killed me yet."

Tanzey grew quiet as he continued riding at a hard gallop, then wound his way through a thick stand of cottonwoods toward the shine of a creek in the distance.

She smiled to herself. She knew that he could not last long with the amount of blood that he was losing. She *would* have the last word, *and* she would take much delight in shooting him! She would fill him full of lead, and even that would not be enough to avenge her parents' deaths.

But it would be a start, she thought wryly to herself.

Panic filled Rolling Thunder when he saw that Tanzey was nowhere in sight. Through the scramble of the horses during the worst of the fight, he had lost track of her.

As he wheeled his horse around to search for her, he winced, dropped his rifle, and grabbed at his left arm. A bullet grazed his flesh just above the left elbow.

He gritted his teeth to bear the pain.

He closed his eyes, waiting for the final blow.

But the firing suddenly ceased all around him.

The dust settled.

He saw that some of his warriors were wounded. Several white men were dead.

However, the leader, the infamous Lieutenant Dan Adams, had escaped.

Then Rolling Thunder spotted Tanzey's horse, the saddle empty.

"Tanzey!" he cried, his voice filled with anguish.

Brant Fire In The Sky rode up next to Rolling Thunder. He gasped when he saw his sister's saddle empty. Then he saw the wound on Rolling Thunder's left arm.

"Forget the wound!" Rolling Thunder said, bending low in his saddle to retrieve his rifle from the ground. "We must find Tanzey! Lieutenant Adams has surely taken her captive!" He gazed at those warriors who were still on their horses. "Ride with me!"

Tormented, Rolling Thunder bitterly turned to those who were tending the wounded on the ground, then wheeled his horse around and rode away.

Brant Fire In The Sky rode at Rolling Thunder's right side, Big Bow at his left.

"Killing will not be good enough for that man!" Rolling Thunder shouted, ignoring the pain in his arm as the blood trickled in bright rivulets from the wound. He held the reins with the hand of his wounded arm, the rifle in his other.

"Pity the man if he harms my sister!" Brant Fire In The Sky shouted, his eyes narrowed with intense hate. "I shall tear him apart, limb by limb."

Rolling Thunder glared over at Brant. "He is mine," he grumbled through clenched teeth.

Brant Fire In The Sky's eyes locked with Rolling Thunder's in silent battle.

Chapter Twenty-five

*Learn to win a lady's faith
Nobly, as the thing is high,
Bravely, as for life and death,
With a loyal gravity.*

—ELIZABETH BARRETT BROWNING

Dan drew a tight rein beside the creek. "You want to be released?" he chuckled, as he gazed down at Tanzey with amusement. "I make it a habit to please ladies."

Laughing throatily, he released his hold on her and gave her a hard shove from his lap.

Tanzey screamed as she fell to the ground, her behind landing against the hard-packed earth with a loud thump.

Aching, and feeling awkward, Tanzey watched Dan dismount, his aim on her steady as he took a solid footing on the ground and stood threateningly over her.

"You son of a bitch," Tanzey hissed. As she slowly rose from the ground, she caught him glancing at the pool of blue water under the hanging cottonwood branches.

He took a quick look at his arm, where the blood

still steadily seeped from the wound, then at the water again. His tongue moved thirstily along his bottom lip.

She could almost read his mind. He wanted a drink of that water so bad he could almost taste it.

He wanted to bathe his wound and bind it.

But to do those things, he would have to take his eyes off his captive.

And he knew that if he was caught off guard for even that one minute, Tanzey would make her move.

"Go ahead," Tanzey taunted, nodding toward the water. "Take a drink. Bathe your wound." She laughed throatily. "I promise I'll behave."

"Like hell you would," Dan spat back. Sweat pearled his brow as the pain deepened and spread along his arm. "And I'd watch your tongue if I were you. If you tempt me too often, I'll just kill you and be done with it."

"Go ahead and *fire* your rifle," Tanzey said, placing her hands on her hips. Her eyes gleamed mischievously. "Let's see just how long it would take for Rolling Thunder and my brother to find you and kill you."

"Yeah, I know that," Dan grumbled. "Do you think I was born yesterday?"

His gaze swept over her, pausing at the curves of her breasts, which were pronounced through the sweat-soaked buckskin fabric of her shirt, and then lower, at the tininess of her waist.

With a puzzled look on his face, he gazed into Tanzey's eyes again. "I've been watching the Comanche camp from a bluff, and I've seen you there," he stated. "I've seen you go into the war chief's lodge and stay the night. Does that mean what I think it means?"

"That means that I love him and will soon marry

him," Tanzey said, lifting her chin proudly. "Even your abduction of me won't stop that wedding, for, *sir*, Rolling Thunder will hunt you down. Pity you then, the low-down, murdering scoundrel that you are. And my brother? He might be the first to take a shot at you. You shouldn't have killed our parents. Somehow, someday, one of us will see you dead."

"Your brother doesn't even know that I'm responsible," Dan scoffed. "I was damned crazy for bragging to *you*. It was bad enough to have you mad at me for taking you hostage. Now, for damn sure, I have to keep an eye on your every move. I'm almost tempted to turn you loose and go on my way. The odds of coming out of this fracas alive would be better. It seems that most of my men were slaughtered back there in the canyon. I've got to go it alone, at least until I get another gang rounded up."

"Oh, you poor thing," Tanzey taunted. "And who ambushed who back there? I believe you and your men took that first shot."

"Yeah, and where did it get us?" Dan said, his eyes narrowing. "Now all of our bounty will surely go to waste, for I, sure as hell, won't go back for it at our hideout. And all of those horses we stole? Damn it all to hell, I hate losing them worse than those gold watches, diamonds, and other valuables I stole from the ranches."

Tanzey paled. Her shoulders swayed as she became dizzy from knowing just how evil this man *was*.

She quickly turned and placed her back to him, the urge to vomit strong at the depths of her throat.

She swallowed, over and over again, until the bitterness was gone.

Then out of the corner of her eye she saw that by her having turned her back on Dan, he had taken this opportunity to sink to his knees beside the creek to get a drink.

Her heart pounding, she eyed the rifle that lay on the ground at his side, and then him.

Could she move quickly enough?

Or was he listening for her to try it?

Would he shoot her dead?

Wanting to chance anything to get away from this vile man, who surely would soon kill her, Tanzey decided that, yes, she must try and get the gun. She saw it best to die while at least trying to save her life.

Her pulse racing, Tanzey leapt forward, bent low to reach for the gun, then fell to one side and gasped with fright when Dan was quicker, grabbed up the gun, and aimed it at her.

"I thought I'd test you," he said, sneering as he took a slow step toward her. "Seems you failed. I know now I can't chance keeping you with me any longer. And I don't have to shoot you to kill you."

He grabbed the rifle by the barrel and raised it high over Tanzey's head, causing her to pale and glance quickly up at it. "I'll just kill you silent like with the butt of my rifle," he scorned. "The cracking sound of your skull breaking won't be loud enough to bring that damn Comanche war chief in this direction."

He laughed. "When he *does* find you," he scoffed, "there won't be much left of you after the buzzards feed on your carcass."

Tanzey flinched and raised her arms over her head in a protective gesture. She closed her eyes and waited for the impact the would down her.

Her life strangely flashed before her eyes in that brief second .. and then gunfire broke out.

Her eyes widened, and she looked quickly down at her body.

He had decided to shoot her after all!

But where was the blood?

Where was the pain?

She had heard two gunshots.

Dan cried out in pain, drawing Tanzey's eyes to him.

She took an unsteady step away from him and gasped when she saw him drop his rifle, then crumple to the ground, stopping to rest on his knees while blood spurted from two fresh wounds, one on each of his arms just above his elbows.

His yowling made Tanzey's hair stand on end at the nape of her neck.

She shivered when she saw the pain he was in, his eyes wide with disbelief as his arms hung limply at his sides and blood seeped into the ground beneath his fingers.

Tanzey was too stunned to move.

Then she heard something else.

Horses approaching!

She turned with a start, relieved as she saw her brother and Rolling Thunder riding toward her, both of their rifles smoking from having just been fired.

Rolling Thunder wheeled his horse to a quick stop and slid from the saddle. He dropped his rifle and ran to Tanzey. He gathered her into his arms. "I was in time. If he had . . ."

"I'm all right," Tanzey purred, clinging.

Then she became aware of something wet and warm trickling down onto her hand, from Rolling Thunder's wound.

Paling, she eased from his arms. Her knees weakened when she saw the wound on his left arm, and the blood that had dried around it.

"You've been shot!" she cried. She looked desperately up into his eyes. "Oh, Rolling Thunder, darling, you've been shot."

"It is only a flesh wound," he uttered. "The bullet only grazed it."

Brant knelt down beside Dan. He chuckled as he looked from arm to arm, then into the man's pain-filled eyes. "Seems both our aims were accurate, Rolling Thunder," he said. "A bullet for each arm. Too bad we didn't aim lower. I'd have enjoyed shooting something off this son of a bitch."

"He's not going to be in any condition to use it, so why shoot it off?" Rolling Thunder said, chuckling as he gazed down at Dan.

His smile faded.

He stepped away from Tanzey and moved to his haunches directly in front of Dan.

He coiled his fingers through Dan's thick hair and gave it a yank. "I have never taken a scalp," he said in a low, measured hiss. "Brant Fire In The Sky, do you think I should take this scalp and wave it on my scalp pole for all to see?"

"If you don't, I will," Brant Fire In The Sky said venomously. He leaned closer to Dan's face.

Dan no longer cried with pain. His eyes were wide as he looked from man to man. "Be merciful," he said, his voice breaking. "Go ahead and kill me."

He looked past them, at Tanzey. "Tell them to get it over with, do you hear?" he begged. "I don't want to be taken back to an Indian village. I've heard tales of what happens to their captives. I'd rather die now, than after being degraded in front of a pack of savages!"

The word "savage," and how the white man used it to define Rolling Thunder's people, made Rolling Thunder see red. He raised a hand and brought it across Dan's face in a hard, jarring slap.

"Confess your sins," Brant Fire In The Sky hissed as he watched blood trickle from Dan's nose and from the corner of his mouth. "Are you responsible for the raids on the ranches?"

Dan refused to answer.

Tanzey went down onto her knees between Brant and Rolling Thunder. "He confessed to having killed Mother and Father," she said, swallowing back a sob. "He bragged to me about it."

She flinched when Brant Fire In The Sky slapped Dan, not only once, but many times.

"Enough," Rolling Thunder said, grabbing Brant Fire In The Sky's wrist, stopping him. "Let us take him back to our village. We will let our people decide his fate, for today he and his men killed many of our beloved warriors."

"He told me about his hideout, and about the stolen material that he has taken there," Tanzey murmured as she rose slowly to her feet while Brant and Rolling Thunder yanked Dan to his feet. "It's in the canyon. I'm sure if you send some men in there to find his hideout, you will find many valuables, as well as captured horses."

"Do something about my wounds!" Dan cried, tears rolling down his cheeks. "I'm going to bleed to death."

"Moments ago you begged for death, and now you ask to be spared?" Rolling Thunder taunted. He glared into Dan's eyes. "Which is it, white man who disgraced the name of 'soldier'? Death or life? How do you wish even to die?"

"For Christ's sake, quit playing these word games with me," Dan begged. "Place tourniquets on my arms. Stop the blood flow. Lord in Heaven, the pain! It's unbearable!"

Rolling Thunder shoved Dan back to the ground.

He ripped shreds of cloth from Dan's shirt and wrapped his wounds tightly, the blood soon ceasing to flow from them.

Then Rolling Thunder grabbed Dan back to his feet and shoved him toward his horse. He followed him there, then gave him another shove as Dan groaned and tried to get into his saddle.

With Dan finally in the saddle, his arms hanging loosely at his sides, Rolling Thunder mounted behind him.

"Tanzey, ride my steed," Rolling Thunder said, nodding toward it.

"Rolling Thunder, *your* wound," she said, pleading up at him with her eyes. "You've seen to this murderer's wounds, yet have not seen to your *own*. Come and sit by the water. Please let me at least bathe the blood from your arm."

"Later," Rolling Thunder grumbled. "I have other things on my mind."

Knowing that his mind was set, Tanzey mounted Rolling Thunder's horse.

She rode proudly between her brother and the man she loved, relieved they were all right.

But her joy was short-lived when they arrived back at the sight of the ambush. She looked past the dead white men, to those Comanche warriors who lay dead on the ground, the survivors having already prepared travois for their return to their village.

She now knew just how lucky she was to still have Rolling Thunder and Brant.

She even knew how lucky *she* was to be alive!

Too many had died today.

Their deaths had been useless!

For an innocent horse roundup to change so quickly was a tragedy.

She dreaded returning to the village, for she knew

how many hearts would be broken. Mourning would start again just when it had ended.

Could Rolling Thunder's people bear any more sadness?

Tanzey's thoughts changed when Rolling Thunder shouted at his warriors to go and find the hideout and bring back the plunder.

It now belonged to the Comanche!

Whatever they found would pay for winter supplies.

Several warriors and Brant Fire In The Sky rode away.

Tanzey helped wrap the dead in blankets, then tied them securely onto the travois.

Soon Brant Fire In The Sky and the warriors returned. Tied to their horses were piles of buffalo skins, Mexican blankets, rifles and revolvers, culinary utensils, and bags of jewelry.

Also in tow were at least thirty horses, some tamed mustangs, others beautiful steeds having been stolen from white settlers.

Several mules had also been retrieved.

"It seems we have a horse roundup after all," Rolling Thunder said sarcastically. He waved a hand toward his warriors. "Take them to our village! They are now ours!"

While all of this had been going on, Dan had been held back by two warriors. He had watched, his eyes wide, his throat dry, as the dead Comanche had been prepared for traveling, while the dead outlaws and renegades that had been his companions had been covered by rocks.

Then Rolling Thunder went to him. He gazed over at his friend Big Bow. "Unclothe the white man," he hissed from between his pursed lips. "You know what to do next to him."

Watching and wondering what Rolling Thunder had in mind next for Dan Adams, Tanzey placed a hand over her mouth and silently watched.

Dan struggled and cried as his clothes were removed and tossed aside. He tried to fight with his lifeless arms as a dressed deerskin was thrown over his head and drawn down over his face.

"I'm going to suffocate!" he cried. "Is this how I am to die? You humiliate me in such a way, then snuff the breath away from me? I always knew the Comanche were heartless! You are the most heartless of them all, Rolling Thunder!"

One of the Comanche warriors came up to Dan and knocked him in the ribs with the butt end of his rifle.

Dan doubled over, yowling.

Then he became silent when a string was wrapped around his neck, securing the deerskin in place.

Tanzey held her breath as Big Bow grabbed a sharp knife from his sheath at his right side and skillfully cut two holes in the skin for Dan's eyes, then cut a hole under the nose and in front of the mouth, sufficiently to admit air that was necessary for respiration.

Tanzey watched Dan take several deep breaths, the fabric of the skin sucking in strangely around his mouth and nose with each breath taken.

"Now, bring us one of the mules you found at the hideout!" Rolling Thunder shouted at his warriors.

Tanzey still stood back and silently watched.

When the mule was brought to Rolling Thunder, she got much delight in seeing Lieutenant Dan Adams humiliated even more by how he was being placed on the mule for transportation back to the Comanche village.

Nude, his face covered, he was roughly placed on

the bare back of the mule, where flies and gnats buzzed all along the mangy flesh of the animal.

Tanzey did not flinch one iota when Dan yowled with pain as his wounded arms were yanked around, and his hands were tied behind him at his wrists by stout thongs of buffalo hide.

His feet were then brought as near together as possible under the body of the mule and firmly lashed.

In this position, it was possible for him to roll sidewise, but impossible to extricate himself from the beast.

Unable to see, Lieutenant Dan Adams would be in perpetual suspense of what might happen to him next.

Tanzey paled when her gaze swept quickly elsewhere. She stared at the warriors, who were using their knives to shave the tails of their steeds.

Then they lit a fire with twigs and used the burned ash to cover their faces.

One by one they mounted their steeds, so many of them having a travois with a body of a fallen comrade attached to their horses behind them.

Tanzey did not question any of this, for she had to believe that it was all a part of the mourning that had just begun for their friends.

She watched Rolling Thunder cover his own face with ash. She gasped behind a hand when Brant Fire In The Sky covered his, yet she knew that she should not have been all that surprised, for he was now more Comanche than white, and practiced their rituals, as though he had never known any other life but this.

Rolling Thunder went to Tanzey. As their eyes locked in silent understanding, he placed gentle hands to her face and slowly smoothed some ash into her flesh.

She swallowed hard and fought back tears as he led her to his horse. With a keen gentleness he placed his hands at her waist and lifted her into the saddle.

Still without saying anything to her, he gave her a soft smile, then went to Dan Adams's horse and mounted it.

Big Bow handed Rolling Thunder the rope that had been placed around the mule's neck.

Rolling Thunder nodded a silent thank you and glanced back at Dan, who was lying motionless and quiet across the mule. He smiled, then sank his heels into the flanks of the horse and rode off in a slow lope.

Tanzey rode beside Rolling Thunder. She felt a deep sadness as she glanced over her shoulder and watched the slow procession behind her.

A puffy white cloud slid over the sun, giving some momentary reprieve from the heat, yet Tanzey shivered. She felt death all around her and dreaded returning to the Comanche village, where everyone would soon be forced to share her feelings. She could already hear the wails, the cries of despair, and the hopelessness that would shroud the village.

The clouds crept away overhead.

The sun emerged again with its bright, shimmering heat.

Tanzey became aware of dark shadows moving on the ground.

She looked quickly upward and cringed when she discovered the beady eyes and wide-spread wings of many buzzards as they dipped lower and lower from the sky. They, too, smelled the undeniable, rancid, ugly stench of death.

Chapter Twenty-six

I have no life but this,
To lead it here;
Nor any death, but lest
Dispelled from there.

—EMILY DICKINSON

Rolling Thunder and Tanzey in the lead, the procession of Comanche moved slowly into the village, wailing. If only one or two had died, they would have entered quietly.

As the survivors of the slain fell on their knees beside their loved ones, only those remaining on their feet noticed the bound captive.

Not even being told who he was or what his crime was, one by one the Comanche people took a turn at spitting on him. He was obviously responsible for their dead comrades.

Tanzey slid out of the saddle. She flicked tears from her eyes as the dead were removed from the travois.

She watched grieving wives snip off handfuls of their hair, while others slashed at their skin with either fingernails or knives.

Tanzey then walked over and stood beside her

brother as Rolling Thunder tried to comfort the mourners, hugging them, promising them gifts of their choosing.

One family might choose a horse, another a year's ration of food, another clothes for their children.

No matter what their choices were, Tanzey saw Rolling Thunder prove once again how giving he was. Perhaps never in her life had she known anyone as generous.

"Get me off this thing!" Dan Adams cursed in a raspy wail. "You damn savages, stop . . . spitting . . . on me!"

The word "savage" being spoken again by the captive drew Rolling Thunder's quick attention.

He turned and glared at the condemned man, then stamped over to the mule and cut the ropes, shoving Dan to the ground.

Rolling Thunder returned the cold, piercing stare of Dan's eyes through the small slits of the deerskin sack. He smiled wryly as he placed a moccasined foot squarely on Dan's abdomen and dug his heels into the man's flesh.

Dan yowled and tried to wriggle free, but Rolling Thunder's hold on him was relentless.

Rolling Thunder looked over at Big Bow. "Drive the posts in the ground!" he commanded, his voice flat and void of feeling.

There was a scurry of activity as several warriors helped Big Bow pound two posts into the ground, three feet apart, and close to the center of the village.

Rolling Thunder slid his foot away from Dan. He planted his fists on his hips and glowered down at him. "Stand!" he hissed.

Dan's eyes wavered into Rolling Thunder's. "How can I?" he said, his voice drawn and shallow. "My ankles are still tied. So are my wrists."

"That is so," Rolling Thunder said, chuckling. He straightened his back and smiled smugly down at Dan. "Stand or be shot on the spot."

Tanzey smiled softly at Rolling Thunder, then gazed down at Dan. She shuddered when she saw the extent of his wounds, and how the flesh was puckering and becoming inflamed around each of them. If he didn't die at the hands of the Comanche, he would more than likely die from infection. Gnats and flies were even now feeding on the blood that had dried on the wounds.

Moaning, Dan tried to rise, but his tied ankles did not permit it.

In a flash Rolling Thunder was on his haunches cutting the ropes at not only Dan's ankles, but wrists, as well.

"I am tired of wasting time on you," Rolling Thunder said, sliding his knife back inside its sheath. He grabbed Dan by a wrist and yanked him to his feet. "You either walk to the posts, or be dragged."

Unsteady on his feet, Dan turned and eyed the high posts, then gulped hard and turned back to Rolling Thunder. "You aren't going to . . ." he began, but was stopped when Rolling Thunder gave him a hard shove that sent him sprawling to the ground once again.

"Do not ask questions!" Rolling Thunder shouted. "Get on your feet again and go to the posts!"

Tanzey had never seen Rolling Thunder this angry, or this cold-natured.

But witnessing this change in personality did not sway her feelings for him. This dishonorable lieutenant, this soldier turned outlaw, deserved everything he had gotten, and whatever was now planned for him. He had admitted to murdering her parents with no remorse.

Perhaps some of her parents' belongings had been recovered from the hideout. She was not about to go and see if she was right. If her mother's wedding band was among those stolen properties, Tanzey was not sure if she could stand it. Her stepfather's dried blood was in the gold inscription on the underside, an inscription of undying love for her mother.

It would be, to her, like losing her mother all over again!

Yes, it was best left alone.

Dan screeched and howled as he was made to stand between the posts, his arms drawn up as far as they could reach and tied to a stake.

His legs spread apart, his feet were tied to the posts near the ground.

Tanzey hoped that he was suffering terribly!

Daisy appeared beside her and stared wild-eyed at the staked man. Daisy recognized the man's voice! It was the voice of her rapist!

"Daisy, what is it?" Tanzey asked, reaching to take one of Daisy's hands, but never getting to. She collapsed to the ground in a dead faint.

"Rolling Thunder! Something is wrong with Daisy!" Tanzey screamed, dropping to her knees beside her special friend.

Brant Fire In The Sky knelt down on Daisy's other side. "What happened?" he asked.

Tanzey glared at Dan, then gazed at Daisy again as Rolling Thunder came and lifted her into his arms. "It has something to do with Dan Adams," she murmured. She reached a hand to Daisy's brow and smoothed her hair back from her face. "When Daisy looked at him, it was as though she was looking at a ghost . . . or . . . a *demon*."

"I'll take her to her lodge," Rolling Thunder said, turning to walk away.

But Dan's loud taunting laughter made him stop, his feet seeming to be frozen to the packed earth beneath them.

"Sami, Sami," Dan taunted in a shrill voice. "I wondered what happened to my Samantha after I screwed her! I should've known the Indian would take her to his lodge." Delirious and wrathful, he carried on. "How could he not have wanted such a pretty woman to warm his blankets at night? She's quite a screw, isn't she, Rolling Thunder?"

Dan looked slowly over at Tanzey. "How is it an Injun could have two pretty white women to screw?" he shouted. "What magic do you possess, savage, to get two white squaws to share your bed at night with you?"

Rolling Thunder's heart pounded so hard inside his chest from disgust and hate, he felt dizzied by it.

Glaring, his pulse on fire with rage, he turned slowly and looked at the tiny slits on the deerskin, where he saw mocking eyes staring back at him.

"Brant Fire In The Sky, come and take Daisy," Rolling Thunder mumbled, relinquishing her to Brant Fire In The Sky.

Stealthily, as everyone quietly watched, Rolling Thunder moved toward the white man, who still talked mockingly to him.

Tanzey rushed to her brother's side.

Daisy slowly opened her eyes, then wider when she again heard that scornful voice.

She motioned to Brant Fire In The Sky to place her to her feet, then stood stiffly between Tanzey and Brant as Dan continued his mocking tirade.

"Sami!" Dan shouted when he saw her standing again, quietly watching him. "Remember me, Sami? Remember having sex with me? Sure, I raped you, but you can't tell me you didn't enjoy it. If that sav-

age there hadn't stopped me, I would've taken you
with me to my hideout. You would've learned how
it felt to be a captive of a *white* man instead of a
savage redskin. This redskin savage only came to
your rescue while I was having some fun with you
so that he could take you to his lodge and have fun
with you himself. You being here at the Comanche
camp is damn proof of that!"

Rolling Thunder stopped in mid-step, stunned to
know that this perverted man was Daisy's rapist!
Rolling Thunder had not recognized him, for he had
not been close enough to see the face of the man who
had wrestled Daisy to the ground.

When he heard a choking sob behind him, Rolling
Thunder turned quickly and gazed with pity down
at Daisy. He knew what she was recalling ... the
viciousness of her rape!

Daisy burst into tears.

Tanzey tried to comfort her, but words failed to
reach her.

Rolling Thunder went to Daisy and drew her into
his arms, feeling the fierceness in the way she clung
to him. "Are you going to be all right?" he asked
softly.

Daisy eased from his arms and looked up at him
with desperation in her eyes. And when she tried to
speak, no words were there, only a strained, muted
silence.

The trauma was too much.

Rolling Thunder vowed that Lieutenant Dan
Adams would die a slow, agonizing, unmerciful
death. Not only would his voice be taken away from
him forever. But also his life!

Daisy broke away from Rolling Thunder and ran
to her lodge.

Tanzey ran after her. She entered Daisy's lodge right behind Rolling Thunder.

Her body racked with harsh sobs, Daisy lay across her bed, facedown.

Tanzey rushed to the bed and sat down beside Daisy. She drew her into a gentle embrace. "Daisy, please say something," she murmured. "Oh, sweet Daisy, please do not fold into yourself again and not talk. Please don't let that evil man cause you any more pain. He isn't worth one more minute of your suffering. *He* is suffering now. *He's* finally paying for his *crimes!*"

Daisy still didn't respond.

She kept her eyes pressed tightly closed.

She clung desperately to Tanzey.

The commotion had awakened both infants. Tanzey gazed toward both cradles. Crow feathers were tied to them to keep away evil spirits. Stuffed bats were tied to the end of the cradles, which were used to watch protectively over the children.

Daisy's son, Patrick, seemed content enough as he waved his arms playfully, his eyes innocently wide as he stared up at everyone.

But Brant Fire In The Sky's son was not as content.

He began fussing, then burst into loud yowls, his fists waving, his legs kicking.

Tanzey gazed first at the child, then at Daisy, who was not responding to the cries.

Brant Fire In The Sky had followed her to the tepee, but had not come inside. He was still stubbornly refusing to see his son.

But now it was time for Brant to act like a father!

Tanzey eased from Daisy's embrace. She gently lowered her to the bed and slipped a blanket over her. She gave Rolling Thunder a soft smile, then hurried from the lodge.

She took Brant Fire In The Sky's hand.

"Your son is crying," she said softly. "Daisy isn't well. She can't care for the child. Brant, the child needs you. Please go to him. It's time, Brant. It's time."

The child's cries became loud and demanding.

Brant Fire In The Sky turned and stared at the closed entrance flap, tormented by his son's cries.

"Daisy needs you," Tanzey prodded.

Tears came to Brant Fire In The Sky's eyes.

He swallowed hard, then grabbed Tanzey into his arms.

He held her close. "Thank you, sis," he said, his voice breaking. "Thank you for bringing me to my senses."

"I love you so, Brant," Tanzey whispered, lovingly caressing his back. "Now, go. Your child needs you. *Daisy* needs you. Don't you see? Time is wasting."

Brant Fire In The Sky broke away from her and went inside the tepee.

Everything was quiet.

His child no longer cried.

Brant Fire In The Sky still could not look toward his son's crib.

Instead he knelt down beside Daisy's bed.

He took her hands. "Daisy, look at me," he said, his free hand at her chin, forcing her eyes up to meet his. "Daisy, please be all right. Please speak again. I want to hear you tell me all about my son. Oh, Daisy, sweet Daisy, how can I ever find enough words to thank you for caring for my son? Never have I known anyone as generous, or as sweet, as you."

Daisy's eyes fluttered open. She gazed at Brant Fire In The Sky, yet still she did not speak.

When Brant Fire In The Sky's son began to cry

again, she gestured with a hand toward the crib. With her eyes she pleaded with Brant.

He understood the plea.

He swallowed hard and turned toward the crib.

Tanzey covered her mouth with her hands when Brant went to the crib and stood over it.

Remembrances of Feather Moon's loveliness ran through Brant Fire In The Sky's mind as he stared at the child's copper flesh and coal-black eyes. Except for his son's shock of red hair, he was Indian in all respects, the picture image of his beautiful mother, the Comanche princess.

How ... could ... he not love this child? he thought to himself, ashamed over how long it had taken him to finally realize the goodness his wife had left him!

When he drew the child into his embrace, and began rocking him slowly back and forth in his arms, he was taken by his son.

Daisy held her arms out for the child.

Brant Fire In The Sky went to her and placed his son in her arms, touched as he watched the child suckle at one of her breasts.

"Although I knew it was not my place to, I have named the child," Daisy murmured, giving Brant a sweet smile. "I named him partly after you. I call him Little Fire."

Eyes wide and jubilant, Tanzey rushed to the bed. She stood over it beside her brother. "Daisy, you spoke!" she reveled, gazing down at her.

"Thanks to Brant Fire In The Sky," Daisy murmured, reaching her free hand out for him, glad when he twined his fingers through hers. "Oh, Brant Fire In The Sky, don't you know that you don't need, ever, to thank me for caring for your son? It has been pure bliss to have him, to feed him, to coddle him."

Daisy looked past him, at Rolling Thunder. "You heard me call the child by a name that I gave him," she said softly. "I know that it is the custom for the father to appoint an important person to name his child. I am certain you would be the one chosen by Brant Fire In The Sky. Can the child keep the name I gave him? Or do you choose to change it?"

"The name is beautiful," Rolling Thunder said, sliding an arm around Tanzey's waist. "The child can keep the name Little Fire until his vision quest."

"Thank you," Daisy murmured. "I do so love the name."

She turned wistful eyes up at Brant Fire In The Sky. "Do you approve of the name?" she asked softly.

"It's beautiful," Brant Fire In The Sky said, reaching a hand to his son's face, running his fingers gently over its soft contours.

"Brant, he needs you," Daisy murmured. "Now that you have again held your son, please don't ever turn your back on him again. He needs to hear your masculine voice. He needs to be held by you, his *father*."

"I am here for him, always," Brant Fire In The Sky declared. "And, also for you."

Touched by how her brother and Daisy were drawn to one another, and wanting to give them privacy, Tanzey gave Rolling Thunder's hand a soft yank.

When he gazed down at her, she nodded toward the entranceway.

He understood her meaning and went with her outside.

Tanzey's jubilance was short-lived when Dan Adams shouted some obscenities at her and Rolling

Thunder. "He must be silenced soon," Rolling Thunder grumbled.

The sound of Dan's voice caused Daisy to panic. She reached a trembling hand to Brant Fire In The Sky. She desperately clutched at his arm. "That man must never know about the child," she said quickly. "In my eyes, he *isn't* my child's father."

"He will never know," Brant Fire In The Sky reassured. He gave Daisy a soft smile. "Believe me, he . . . will . . . never know."

Chapter Twenty-seven

I love you because you have done
More than any creed could have done,
To make me happy.

—ANONYMOUS

In the shadows of glowing bonfires blazing throughout the Comanche village, a war dance was performed before Lieutenant Dan Adams would be put to death.

Tanzey sat amid the crowd on a blanket. Daisy was at her side. They were both still as they watched the warriors perform their various frenzied, wild dances.

Tanzey glanced upward. The moon was a full, bright circle in the sky. The splash of stars twinkled like diamonds against the backdrop of black. If not for the sounds of the scrotum rattles and beating of drums, the night would be a perfect setting for lovers.

Instead it was a night filled with sorrow, anger, and a hunger for vengeance.

Earlier in the day, Rolling Thunder had told her that under no circumstances could the Comanche war dance occur during the daylight hours. That was bad medicine.

In addition, he told her the war dance was also called the "vengeance" dance, which he preferred to call it tonight. Dan Adams's death, before daylight tomorrow, was the vengeance they all hungered for!

Tanzey shifted her gaze and watched Rolling Thunder dance among his friends and relations around a great, roaring fire. Like the other warriors, her beloved was blanketed and painted, the great daubs of red paint above and below his eyes the most prominent.

She looked from warrior to warrior. They were highly bedecked with feathers, beads, and multicolored ornaments. Their tomahawks and scalping knives were in their uplifted hands as they circled in a spasmodic trot, uttering their hoarse guttural songs.

As they proceeded, their pace accelerated and their songs grew louder, rising gradually from a monotonous grunt into an indescribably long howl.

Occasionally a warrior would break away from the others and rush over to Dan Adams, where he was still tied.

While Dan screamed from fright, the warrior would seize great clumps of his hair and go through the pantomime of scalping him. Then he would join the other warriors and continue to dance.

Such a sight sent chills through Tanzey. She shuddered at the thought of just how vicious his death might be, for she knew the depths of hate in the hearts of these Comanche people. Too many burials had taken place these past few days, and all because of this one evil man whose heart had surely never known goodness.

In an attempt to cast off the thought of what lay

ahead, Tanzey thought of this morning when she had
first awakened in bed with her Comanche war chief.

They had made enduring love.

They had lain there for so long, just holding one
another, just whispering sweet things in each other's ears.

They had made love a second time, their bodies
straining together, their lips tasting, their hands
feeling.

And then they had to return to what the day had
in store for everyone, as well as . . . the night.

Rolling Thunder had told her what to expect from
the moment he left the lodge this morning until later
tonight, when they would join one another in bed.

After they had left their lodge, the day's ritual soon
began. Tanzey was instructed how to help construct
a large arbor that would be used for that night's ceremony. The arbor was constructed with poles and
brush. The dimensions were eighty to one hundred
feet square.

Young braves dug a deep trench in the ground,
where a huge fire had burned from the noon hour
until now.

For most of the afternoon, after the arbor was finished and the prisoner had been staked to the ground
close to the open fire, the warriors who were to participate in the vengeance dance had paraded around
the village on their horses in single file, singing
war songs.

When the time came for the dance to begin later
in the evening, after the moon had replaced the sun
in the sky, the warriors had dismounted their horses
and had gone into the arbor, where they had sat
snugly around the huge fire.

The sacred pipe had been filled.

It had been lit and offered to the Spiritual Powers,

a supplication to the Wise One Above, to give them more courage and power.

The pipe had then been passed to each warrior.

When that had been completed, the people of the village had filed into the arbor and taken their positions in a wide circle back from the fire.

And once the dancing began, it went on incessantly for hours.

As now, they circled in a half-crouching attitude, keeping time with their feet to the beating of the drum and buffalo scrotum rattles.

They emitted unearthly yelps that sounded more like coyote and the wail of the panther than men.

It was a distinctive, ferocious sound, made purposely to give one cold shivers.

To Tanzey, nothing could be more strange than this chilling war dance. But she sat with her back straight and her chin lifted, showing pride for the man with whom she would soon speak vows, as he hopped and skipped along with the other dancers, his eyes occasionally sliding her way, his lips momentarily lifting into a smile.

And then he would become solemn again.

His eyes looked straight ahead.

His heart throbbed from the excitement of the occasion.

It had been many moons since his warriors had performed the war dance while a mortified prisoner watched.

Without even looking at Dan Adams, Rolling Thunder knew that the evil man's fear was mounting by the minute, knowing his doom was growing close.

Dan had to know that the dancers were getting exhausted. They had performed the vengeance dance for many hours without stopping.

They had even refused offers of food and drink.

Their prime objective was to reach that moment when the prisoner would know how his end would come.

Even only a few of Rolling Thunder's people knew what was planned for the evil, murdering white man!

And those were the ones whose arrows had been readied for the kill.

Rolling Thunder did not wish to think of the glory of the kill. Finally one less murderer would ride the range. Yes, the man deserved to die. His sins were many!

But Rolling Thunder had always managed to settle things with white eyes in a peaceful way!

He had only killed when cornered, or when shot at.

He had never gone out for the sole purpose of searching and killing!

So tonight, when he shot his arrow along with the others into the white man's body, it would not be with pride.

Nor with joy.

But he did wish to get it over with.

Once behind him, he and his people could move forward with their lives.

And, he feared Tanzey's reaction to such a kill! Yes, she had good cause to hate the man.

But to sit there and witness dozens of arrows flying into a white man's flesh might be too traumatic for her.

If she abhorred such a practice, might . . . she . . . in the end, even abhor the man who ordered it done?

Yes, Rolling Thunder feared the outcome, yet knew that his people's choice of death for this man had been made, and Rolling Thunder would not alter the decision. Never would he look cowardly in the eyes of his people!

He was their war chief.

He must continue to deserve the title, if not by warring on a field of glory, at least while protecting his people from a man such as Lieutenant Dan Adams!

Tanzey frowned as she studied Rolling Thunder's expressions. He seemed suddenly detached from the dancing. Even though he still moved in unison with his comrades, he no longer chanted. He was silent.

Tanzey glanced over at Dan. She could see the shine of his eyes as he peered fearfully through the slits of the deerskin. She could tell by his stiffness that he was filled with fear and concern for himself.

And he should be, she thought to herself. Surely the dancing would soon cease, and everyone would know the final fate of this evil man.

She was tired of wondering about it herself.

All she wanted now was to get this man out of her life and get back to the good things in life.

She had waited a lifetime, it seemed, to begin her life with Rolling Thunder, as his wife.

She was getting so attached to Daisy and Brant's children, she secretly pined for a child of her own.

She smiled at the thought of holding her child, her breast being suckled while Rolling Thunder looked on, proud of their son or daughter.

Although she one day wanted a child that was the perfect image of Rolling Thunder, she secretly wished first for a daughter. She would take delight in brushing her long flowing hair, braiding it and tying it in beautiful ribbons. And dressing her in lacy dresses.

Lace? she thought suddenly, an eyebrow arching. She smiled as she remembered where she was and how the daughter would be raised . . . with the Comanche, whose clothes were not frilly and lacy, but made instead of buckskin.

Well, she then decided, if not lace and frills and ribbons, she would make sure her daughter's dresses were made of the softest, whitest doeskin, embellished prettily with colorful beads.

She was jarred back to the present when the music suddenly ceased and a hush swept over everyone as the warriors stepped away from the dance circle.

"Everyone move back from the fire and the prisoner," Rolling Thunder shouted, accepting his bow and quiver of arrows as a young brave brought them to him.

There was a scramble of scurrying feet as everyone did as they were told.

Tanzey and Daisy held hands and moved with the others, then stood together, their eyes wide. The warriors who had been dancing lined up in front of the prisoner, arrows notched in each of their bows.

Their aim was the same—their arrowheads pointing directly at the prisoner.

Tanzey gasped and grew pale when Dan Adams cried out for mercy, straining against the ropes that held him to the posts.

"No!" he screamed. "Please! Please don't kill me with arrows! Oh, God, have mercy on my . . ."

There was a quick swish of arrows.

Dan's last words died on his lips as twenty or more arrows sank into the flesh of his body.

Tanzey stared at him, numbed by the sight, yet unable to stop herself from thinking how uncannily his body looked like a pincushion.

Silence lay heavy throughout the crowd as all eyes stayed glued to the dead man, whose head had lowered, his chin resting strangely on one of the arrows that had entered just below his Adam's apple.

Then Rolling Thunder lifted his voice in great whoops, his eyes gleaming as he turned to his people.

He then lowered his bow to his side, his face somber. "*Suvate*, it is finished," he said solemnly. "Now we begin life anew without interruptions."

While he spoke, behind him the body was being removed from the posts. Tanzey half watched Dan's body being carried away toward the forest while Rolling Thunder still spoke softly to his people about today's activities, and then tomorrow's.

Tanzey's eyes went solely to Rolling Thunder when he mentioned Brant Fire In The Sky's name, pride thick in how he spoke of him. "Tomorrow we will do what has been delayed for too long because of circumstances beyond my, or your, control," he said.

He reached a hand out for Brant Fire In The Sky, who went to him, smiling.

Rolling Thunder handed his bow and arrows to a young brave, then placed his hands on Brant's shoulders. "You have fought, you have hunted, and you have danced the vengeance dance with the Comanche," he said, his voice steady. "Not so long ago you risked your life to save this war chief. The delivery of our horses to the railhead at Fort Worth, and to Mexico, will be delayed. Tomorrow you will have *your* day. Tomorrow, my brother, you will receive your war honors!"

Tanzey let out a joyful sob as she watched her brother and Rolling Thunder embrace so tightly. She knew that nothing could ever take away their devotion to one another.

Theirs was a bond of all bonds!

Daisy leaned closer to Tanzey. "I am so happy for

Brant Fire In The Sky," she whispered. "Rolling Thunder looks to him truly as a brother."

"And how are things between you and my brother?" Tanzey whispered back to her, her eyes twinkling into Daisy's.

"In time I believe he will love me as I love him," Daisy said, sighing as she still stared at Brant. "Right now, his heart is still whispering Feather Moon's name when he stares up at the stars in the heavens. But I think the whispers grow fainter the closer he allows himself to get to me."

"Things will work out," Tanzey said, slipping an arm around Daisy's waist. She glanced over at Daisy's tepee, then at Daisy. She smiled mischievously. "I've noticed Brant in your lodge later and later each night. Perhaps one of these nights he will *stay*."

"I am praying for the night he will fasten the ties at the entrance flap while he is still inside instead of out," Daisy said, flushing.

Tanzey smiled knowingly, then stepped aside as Brant Fire In The Sky came and led Daisy to her tepee.

Rolling Thunder came and drew Tanzey within his arms. "Did my way of taking the white man's life change your feelings for this war chief?" he asked.

"Do you truly think you could ever do anything that could make me love you less?" Tanzey murmured, blanking out the memory of Dan's torturous death.

Rolling Thunder eased her from his arms. He took her hands and smiled down at her. "Let us go home, then," he said, his eyes dancing into hers.

"Yes, home," Tanzey said, proudly walking at his side toward his lodge.

"I shall leave you there for only a while," Rolling Thunder said softly.

Tanzey looked quickly over at him. "You're leaving?" she said, her keen disappointment showing.

"For only as long as it will take for me to wash today's dust, paint, and death from my skin and hair," he said, frowning. "I want to come to you fresh and new, like all our tomorrows."

Tanzey stopped him and faced him. "I shall go with you and bathe with you," she said, her cheeks blushing at the thought of what they might share in the river. It would be more than mere bathing.

A quick need leapt into Rolling Thunder's eyes. He reached down and swept Tanzey into his arms and carried her toward the river.

He carried her far upstream where there would be no intrusions.

There were only the moon and the stars, and an owl that was perched overhead in a tree as they undressed.

A loon quavered its eerie sound across the water as Rolling Thunder carried Tanzey into the river.

When he was waist-high and Tanzey clung to his neck, he showered her face with passionate kisses.

Tanzey's voice quavered as she whispered her love for him while Rolling Thunder's tongue flicked one of her nipples, then licked it.

In the curling shadows of night, Tanzey's hands swept down Rolling Thunder's body. Her fingers tremored as she circled them around his rock-hard shaft. She could hear him gasping with pleasure as she moved her hand on him in long up-and-down sweeping movements.

Then he lifted her by the waist so that her legs were wrapped around his hips.

With his hands cupping the rounded, soft flesh of her buttocks, he held her in place.

As she clung and rocked with him, and they kissed, he impaled her with his velvet-tight sheath.

Their groans mingled as he plunged into her rhythmically, their kiss long and sweet.

Rolling Thunder's tongue plunged inside Tanzey's mouth and flicked, her tongue touching his, her head spinning with the building euphoria.

They soon took flight together, soaring into the heavens with their joined pleasure, their bliss like warm, sweet sunshine blending their flesh, as though they were one.

When they pulled apart and the moon was a soft sheen across Tanzey's face, with her eyes she questioned Rolling Thunder why he was looking so amusedly at her, softly laughing.

"What is so amusing about my face?" she finally asked as he gently ran a finger across her chin.

"My war paint is now yours," Rolling Thunder said, chuckling. "My paint rubbed off on your face."

Tanzey giggled, then laughed throatily.

Her laughter was stilled by Rolling Thunder's lips as he once again kissed her.

"Life is like an eagle's feather to me at this moment," he whispered against her lips. "So soft, so good."

"It is the same for me, my love," Tanzey murmured, resting her cheek against the muscled flesh of his chest. "Surely nothing else can happen to spoil what we have found together."

"There are always white men who wait for the moment to ruffle the feathers of peace that I am feeling at this moment," Rolling Thunder said, his voice drawn.

He sighed deeply. "But let them come," he said.

"I shall deal with them, one by one, and hope that one day in the future the white race will realize that the red man was here long before they were, and deserve the respect that is due them."

Tanzey swallowed hard, for too many white men saw all Indians as savages, whereas, in truth, it was the white man who turned savage when faced with the red man.

Tanzey could find no words of encouragement, when she knew that whatever she said might prove to be a lie.

Instead she clung to him and whispered, "I shall always love you."

Chapter Twenty-eight

The heavens reward
Thee manifold I pray.

—ANNE BRADSTREET

The celebration for Brant Fire In The Sky to receive his war honors had begun at daybreak and continued into dusk. There had not been the usual dancing and laughter usually shared by the Comanche on special occasions. It was too soon after the burial of their many loved ones.

But there had been an abundance of food shared among them. Nothing could be served until Rolling Thunder had cut off a morsel of boiled meat and offered it to the Wise One Above, holding it first toward the sky and then burying it.

Sitting on a raised platform beside Daisy at the forefront of the crowd of Comanche people, Tanzey held her nephew on her lap. She gazed down at Little Fire, whose eyes peered up at her through the blankets in which he was wrapped.

She then laid him in her lap facing toward her and slowly rocked him back and forth. She laughed softly as she watched his eyes grow heavier with sleep, then closed them.

"He's so sweet," Tanzey murmured, once again aching to have a child of her own, which was something very mysterious and new for her to think about. While she had behaved so tomboyishly throughout the teen years of her life, she had never given children a thought.

In fact, when her parents' friends had come to call with their children, she had seen them only as a nuisance, scoffing to herself that never would *she* be burdened with children. Surely children stifled one's freedom, and never did she want to give up riding horses, going fishing, or challenging her brother in all sorts of games meant only for boys.

But now she wanted a child of her own.

She glanced quickly up at Rolling Thunder, where he stood among his friends, Brant their central focus as they talked and laughed. Whenever she thought of having a child, she envisioned Rolling Thunder holding the child, *their* child.

Their world would then be complete.

They would be a family.

"Tanzey, you look as though you are in another world," Daisy murmured, drawing Tanzey's eyes quickly around. "What are you thinking about?"

"Children *and* Rolling Thunder," Tanzey said, her eyes sparkling. "I want to have Rolling Thunder's child."

Daisy slid her son into the crook of her left arm, made sure his blanket was securely wrapped, then reached a gentle hand to Tanzey's arm. "As I want to have Brant Fire In The Sky's," she said softly. Blushing, she lowered her eyes, then slowly lifted them again and smiled at Tanzey. "Tonight, Tanzey! Tonight he has promised to stay with me! I don't think I've ever been so excited about anything."

"I'm so happy for you," Tanzey murmured. She

searched Daisy's eyes and found no fear of being with a man in them. Daisy had been with only one man, and that was by force.

Surely when Daisy thought of being with Brant sexually, her mind strayed to the brutal force in which she had been taken.

Yet all that Tanzey saw in Daisy's eyes was an anxiousness, felt only when thinking of the man you loved.

Daisy's eyes shifted to Brant Fire In The Sky. "Isn't he so handsome?" she said, sighing. "I truly never thought I had a chance with him. Ever since he arrived, my heart has not behaved normally. But I saw how instant his love was for Feather Moon. I forced myself not to think of him, not . . . to . . . want him."

"Don't expect too much from him, at least not yet," Tanzey said softly. She, too, had witnessed Brant's love for Feather Moon. His *total* commitment to her had been proven by how he turned his back on his family and white man life since he had been taken captive by the Comanche princess.

He had not even fought the captivity because of his sincere feelings for Feather Moon.

Daisy turned her eyes to Tanzey again. "I know," she said, swallowing hard. "I doubt that Brant Fire In The Sky will ever love me as much as he loved Feather Moon. But whatever love he gives me, no matter how small, or large, it will be enough, for you see, I have enough love for the both of us."

Although they had eaten often during the day, it was time to eat again. And after the platters were removed this last time, the serious ceremony for Brant Fire In The Sky would begin.

Tanzey gazed at Brant as he sat down among the warriors, Rolling Thunder close at his side. As he began eating, she could tell how anxious he was by

the way he barely touched his food and by the way
his left cheek twitched.

A middle-aged woman leaned low and stretched
out her arms to Tanzey.

Tanzey understood what she wanted. She was
there to take Little Fire to his cradle, as another
woman was there to take Patrick. The nights in early
autumn were damp and chilly. The warm fire of a
lodge was where a child should be.

Smiling, Tanzey relinquished the child to the
woman as Daisy gave over her own.

Then heaping platters of food were given to them.

"I don't see how I could be hungry, but I *am*,"
Tanzey said, laughing softly.

"That's what happiness does for you," Daisy said.
"Anyhow, that's how it affects me. I am ravenous."
She took a bite of one of the Comanche's truly favorite sweet dishes. It was a mush made of buffalo mar-
row, mixed with honey and crushed mesquite beans.
Honey added flavor to the Comanche diet. It was
bagged in skin containers and could be kept
indefinitely.

Tanzey nodded and took a bite of the mush. She
had learned a lot about the Comanche eating habits.
She knew that they were very fond of hard, parched
corn, and broiled venison. Every day, throughout the
camp, the aroma of meat broiling or sizzling over an
open pit fire could be smelled.

She knew also some of their superstitions. They
would not broil or boil the meat over the same
flames. It was a sign of defeat and evil.

And no one could pass near where meat was cooking. Not even a shadow was allowed to fall across
the cooking meat.

Tanzey shifted her gaze and watched some of the
warriors step up to a large slab of venison that hung

on a spit over the flames of the fire. They each cut off a piece of the meat, then held it between the fingers of one hand, while with the fingers of the other they scooped up some kiln-dried corn that had been boiled and mashed and served in a large dish made of bark. They filled their mouths alternately with flesh and vegetables.

Tanzey was told that sometimes food became scarce around February and March, the season designated *ateum*, meaning, "When the babies cry for food."

Rolling Thunder had told Tanzey that when food was scarce, a Comanche ate almost anything, even the food that was usually taboo to them—fish and fowl, as well as frogs.

She had been told that coyote was also taboo. The coyote was the *"trickster"* of Comanche mythology—a *demigod*. Rolling Thunder had told her that the coyote had medicine. If the Comanche harmed one, it would get back at them in some way.

She had watched the Comanche men come from the river some evenings with sacks filled with turtles. She had stood back, quiet and somewhat mortified by how they threw the turtles alive into a crackling fire, then later raked them from the fire, their shells broken open, the contents eaten with a horn spoon.

But there was one of their practices that made Tanzey shudder even now, and almost lose her appetite while thinking about it. When a cow, deer, antelope, or elk was killed, it was not uncommon to open their veins and drink their warm blood.

Also, the fresh warm liver covered with the contents of the gall bladder was considered one of the finest delicacies. Children crowded around the ones who were butchering and begged for it.

Another practice that had made Tanzey wince the

first time she had witnessed it being done was how
the Comanche would cut into the udder of an animal
and suck the warm mixture of milk and blood with
the greatest of pleasure.

They didn't eat the heart, because it was a ceremonial gesture to propitiate the Animal Spirit.

To finish off Tanzey's meal, and forgetting that
which she might never get accustomed to, she sucked
on a wild plum, gathering the juice onto her tongue,
swallowing it.

The platters were cleared away by several women
scurrying about.

All remaining food was carried away.

Tanzey scooted closer to Daisy.

They held hands when the warriors all rose and
Brant Fire In The Sky stood before them, his shoulders squared, his jaw tight, his eyes anxious. He was
dressed in a brief breechclout and was barefoot. His
fiery red hair had grown long again and was drawn
back into two braids that fell down to his waist behind him.

A warrior approached Brant Fire In The Sky and
rubbed oil of a beaver across his chest, down his
muscled arms and legs, and then on his back, as
though he was being prepared for war; the oil was
regarded as absolute protection from the rifle bullet
of an enemy.

After the oil was spread completely over Brant Fire
In The Sky's flesh, the firelight sheening it, Rolling
Thunder stepped up to him.

Total silence fell across the crowd as they watched
the ceremony.

Tanzey's heart thudded as she looked from Brant
to Rolling Thunder, the two most beloved men in
her life.

"Brant Fire In The Sky," Rolling Thunder began,

placing a gentle hand on Brant's shoulder. "Today you will enter into a solemn league and covenant with me and my people," he said. "You will become a *true*, *free* member of this tribe . . . a respected *warrior*. You have proven time and again that you are worthy of this title. Do you promise to perform all duties of a Comanche warrior? Do you promise to help provide for, protect, and obey the laws of the Comanche people? Do you vow to obey this war chief in all things, in both peace and war?"

"I do," Brant Fire In The Sky said, nobly lifting his chin. "And I proudly carry with me at all times my Comanche name Fire In The Sky."

Rolling Thunder smiled at him. "A name given to you by our departed, beloved princess," he said, nodding. "She was wise to make you more Comanche, than white. She was wise to take you as her husband."

"With pride I carry the memory of your beloved princess inside my heart," Brant Fire In The Sky said, nostalgia thick in his words. "I will never shame her memory by being less than Comanche in the eyes of her people!"

"That is good and I believe you," Rolling Thunder said. He nodded to a young brave who held within his hands a sharpened stick of wood eleven inches long and two inches square.

The young brave handed Rolling Thunder the stick, then stepped back and again became a part of the crowd of observers.

Rolling Thunder gazed down at the stick. On its different sides there were carved numerous figures representing skeletons, scalps, tomahawks, and various other like devices.

He then gazed into Brant Fire In The Sky's eyes. "Earlier you were instructed what to do with this ceremonial device," he said, holding the stick out for him. "It is now time."

Without hesitation, Brant Fire In The Sky took the stick.

Hardly a breath could be heard through the crowd of Comanche when Brant Fire In The Sky used the sharp end of the stick to open a vein on the back of his hand, then carefully bathed the carved characters on the stick with his blood.

When this was done and the blood flow ceased, he gave the stick back to Rolling Thunder.

"Your blood now mingles with the *Ner-mer-nuh*, Comanche," Rolling Thunder said, relinquishing the stick again to the same young brave, to be carried away and stored in a holy place. "You are now, in every way, one of us. Now you will enjoy *all* freedoms of the Comanche. You now have the right to come and go as you please from our village. Our village is yours. Our hunting grounds are yours. Everything that is the Comanche's is equally yours because you have earned the total trust *of* the *Ner-mer-nuh*, Comanche."

Rolling Thunder drew Brant Fire In The Sky into his arms and gave him a tight hug.

"Welcome, brother, into my world," Rolling Thunder said. He fondly patted Brant on the back. "In you, I see many long-gone warriors reincarnated!"

"I am filled with such pride," Brant Fire In The Sky said, his voice breaking.

One by one the Comanche people filed past Brant Fire In The Sky and gave him hugs and smiles of acceptance.

After the last person came to Brant Fire In The Sky, he went to Daisy. He held his hands out for her. She took them and slowly rose to her feet.

Together they went to her lodge.

Everyone watched as the entrance flap was closed.

The fire within the lodge revealed Brant Fire In The Sky's shadow as he tied the strings inside the flap, securing it for the night.

"Let us go home and tie our own flap closed," Rolling Thunder said, sliding an arm around Tanzey's waist.

Inside the lodge Tanzey slipped out of her dress as she watched Rolling Thunder place another log across the fire.

When he turned toward her, she offered herself to him, the fire's glow dancing across her pink, naked flesh.

"I want a child," she murmured. "Tonight, my love, let's make a child. Everything else seems so perfect. Why not add to our happiness?"

She watched Rolling Thunder disrobe.

When he was standing totally nude before her, she went to him and ran her hands over his muscled body.

He sucked in his breath when she enfolded his shaft within her fingers and began moving them on him. He closed his eyes and held his head back, stiffening when the pleasure spread in hot leaps throughout his body.

He gasped and shivered when he felt something new and wonderful on his manhood. He gritted his teeth to keep himself from crying out when Tanzey's tongue and lips pleasured him.

With hazed-over eyes, he wove his fingers through her hair and drew her lips closer.

His hips moved quietly backward and forward, helping her find that certain rhythm that he was seeking. The pleasure so great, he clenched his hands into tight fists at his sides. His mouth was dry with the building euphoria.

Except for Rolling Thunder's soft gasps, silence vibrated around him and Tanzey.

And when he felt he was near that peak, which would send him into spiraling splashes of ecstasy, he opened his eyes and placed gentle hands to Tanzey's shoulders.

Feeling his eyes and hands on her, Tanzey gazed up at him and found him looking down at her. His eyes held hers.

Suddenly he swept her up into his arms.

With a groan he pulled her against him.

He kissed her with a mouth that was urgent and eager.

After carrying her to his bed, her eyes filled with unspoken passion, Rolling Thunder knelt down over her. His mouth, tongue, and hands were suddenly everywhere.

When he knelt lower, and his lips and tongue worshiped her woman's center, her hips responded and she thrust her pelvis toward him.

Only vaguely aware of making whimpering, mewing sounds of contentment, Tanzey tossed her head back and forth. His tongue was driving her delirious with pleasure, his hands caressing.

And when he moved over her and one of his knees parted her thighs, her breath caught as she waited for him to enter her with his magnificent thrusts.

Tremors cascaded down her back as he flicked his tongue over first one nipple, and then the other.

His fingers teased circles around her breasts, then lower, around her belly, then lower still, until he pinched and rubbed and kneaded her throbbing woman's center.

Then he kissed her with a fierce longing.

Her body lifted somewhat from the bed when he shoved himself into her warm, tight valley.

Over and over again he thrust into her, each time reaching more deeply, each time awakening and arousing sensations that were new to her.

Rolling Thunder slid his hands beneath her and eased her legs around his hips, which gave him an even easier access to her wet, warm center.

Surges of warmth flooded his senses.

He groaned.

He sucked in great gulps of air, then lay his cheek against hers and closed his eyes as the wondrous feelings of release overwhelmed him.

His body quaked violently into hers.

As Tanzey tumbled over the edge into ecstasy, she clung to him.

Moaning with pleasure, she met each of his thrusts with an upward, thrusting movement of her hips.

"I'm there," she cried, closing her eyes, breathing hard. "Fill me, darling! Fill me!"

Rolling Thunder moved his lips across the curve of her throat. He pressed his face between her breasts. He breathed in the sweet scent of her as his final thrust sent the great spurts of his seed deeply into her.

And then they lay quietly together, their fingers intertwined.

Tanzey was the first to speak. "I love making babies," she said, giggling.

"Perhaps we should try for a hundred?" Rolling Thunder teased back, his eyes dancing into hers.

"Or perhaps a thousand," she said, laughing softly.

Then she leaned up on an elbow and gave him a somber look. "Do you think we did make a baby tonight?" she asked softly.

"Perhaps not," Rolling Thunder said, watching her expression turn to dismay.

"Why ... not ...?" she asked, disappointed.

He leaned low and brushed a soft kiss across her abdomen. "Because, my beautiful Tanzey Nicole, perhaps there is already a baby growing inside you," he said, then caught her smile of relief and drew her into his embrace again.

"I was wrong to tease you like that," he apologized. "I never want to fill your mind with doubts, even for one moment. I will not ever do that again."

"Either way, it's a fun thing to talk about," she said, sighing. "I do so badly want to be a mother."

"And so you shall," Rolling Thunder promised her. "And ... so ... you shall."

"Gentle Sky," Tanzey whispered against his cheek.

"What did you say?" he asked, forking an eyebrow as he gazed into her eyes.

"I just gave our daughter a name," Tanzey said, smiling up at him. "Gentle Sky. Do you think that's pretty?"

"It is pretty, but what if the name should be a *tua's*, son's, name?" Rolling Thunder asked. Cherishing the feel of her breasts pressed against his chest, he drew her closer.

Tanzey eased away from him and sat up. She gazed down at him with wavering eyes. "Do you mind so terribly much if I concentrate on having a daughter first, a *tua*, son second?" she asked. She scarcely breathed as she waited for his response. She knew that men prided themselves in having a son.

But was it necessary to have a son first, she wondered, hoping that for Rolling Thunder it wasn't that important.

"Your wish is also mine," Rolling Thunder said. He swept his arms around her, laid her back, and rose over her again.

This time they made love slowly.

Chapter Twenty-nine

Set me as a seal upon thine heart.

—KING SOLOMON

The journey to Mexico and Fort Worth to sell horses and make trade was behind them. The day was crisp and cool. The whipping, howling wind caused the entrance flap to shudder and shimmy, breaking the silence in Rolling Thunder's lodge.

Tanzey brushed her hair, wanting it to glisten on this special day.

"After today my bond with Rolling Thunder will be official. It will be complete," she whispered to herself, thrilling at the thought of finally being able to call him her husband.

Rolling Thunder had told her how the ritual must be played out. Some of what must be done seemed innocent enough, even welcomed, while other aspects of it caused her smile to fade.

She sat down on a thick cushion beside the warmth of the fire and laid her brush aside.

As she watched the flames rolling smoothly across the logs, she thought of how guardedly Rolling Thunder instructed her on the final steps of their marriage bonding today; the sacrifice they would share.

No matter how strange it all seemed to her, she was prepared to finalize their marriage bonding.

She placed a tender hand over her abdomen. Her monthly flow had not arrived when it was due. There was no doubt in her mind that she was pregnant!

Rolling Thunder had not noticed anything different about her, not even how her breasts were slowly changing.

She could tell the difference. They felt heavier already. They seemed firmer!

But that was only what a woman could feel.

The change was not yet a visible one.

"I shall tell him tonight," Tanzey whispered. "It will be my own special gift to him for a wedding present."

She gazed down at her dress, made of delicate white doeskin. It was Daisy's wedding gift to Tanzey, made by Daisy's own fingers. Each bead that had been sewn on the dress had been done with love. The beads, all colors of the rainbow, had been sewn into designs of flowers across the bodice and down the entire front of the floor-length dress.

It was apparent that Daisy had taken special efforts with how she fringed the ends of the sleeves and hem of the dress. When Tanzey walked, the thick fringes made a soft, swishing sound around her ankles.

Tanzey had never had such a close friend as Daisy

And Tanzey was so happy for Daisy. Brant Fire In The Sky not only gave her his love, but also married her. Their ceremony had been private, as was the Comanche tradition.

There was to be no fanfare among Rolling Thunder's people as Tanzey and Rolling Thunder spoke their vows of marriage. How Tanzey and Rolling Thunder would become man and wife was between only themselves, and ... and ... Brant Fire In The Sky.

Her brother was to be the recipient of her suitor's gift, normally received by a father. However, her brother was her only remaining male relative, so he would be offered Rolling Thunder's special gift of a horse. The gift to Brant Fire In The Sky had to be one of Rolling Thunder's most prized possessions.

Tanzey reached for the moccasins and slipped them on, her eyes on the entrance flap. Rolling Thunder had been gone for some time now, perhaps two hours. She wondered if he had yet taken the horse to Brant.

When Rolling Thunder had shown Tanzey which horse he was offering to her brother, she was surprised to see it was the beautiful black mustang she had downed but not captured. Rolling Thunder had come up on her that day right after she had fired the shot that had confused the beautiful mustang!

Rolling Thunder had awakened earlier than Tanzey many mornings in a row. He had searched and searched until he had finally found, captured, and tamed the mustang. She had not known that he had given it a name long ago after seeing it among the other wild horses.

Lightning.

Brant was soon to own Lightning!

And even though the horse would belong to her brother, she knew that she would have the opportunity to ride it whenever she wished.

"Yes, I shall ride him often," she whispered to herself.

She slid a hand across her abdomen and smiled.

"Well, perhaps not as often as I would if I was not carrying a child within my womb," she said, smiling.

No more waiting, the day had arrived when they would make that final commitment. Finally Rolling Thunder would be her husband!

Yet there was one thing threatening to spoil the day—a custom that seemed inhumane, callous, cold-hearted, and *cruel*. Rolling Thunder was to sacrifice a wild mustang.

Even when Rolling Thunder explained to her that he would choose only the weakest horse, she found it hard to accept. The weakest mustangs were often killed by stronger mustangs. The life of the wild mustang was challenging. They did not chance being slowed down by those that were not able-bodied enough to keep up their daily flights of searching for food and water holes, as well as fleeing the clutches of man—be they red or white-skinned.

She had recently witnessed a mustang being killed by one of its own kind. There had been no mercy as the weak, thin mustang had been downed and unable to fight off the pounding hooves, or the nips and bites to its hide.

Tanzey and Rolling Thunder witnessed the killing while horseback riding only a few days ago. She had wanted to aid the defeated mustang, but Rolling Thunder had stopped her. He had wanted her to see how wild mustangs thinned their herds and how nature takes its course.

There was another reason he had encouraged her to watch. When he hung the heart of a mustang outside the entranceway today, she would not be as abhorred by the sight of it, as she would have been had she not seen the slain mustang. Rolling Thunder would sacrifice the weakest mustang of the herd.

"Still I dread the moment I must see it," Tanzey

whispered to herself. "And to think that I even have to touch it, and .."

She turned with a start when she heard a sound behind her. Daisy entered bringing ... three pairs of beautiful earrings made of long, thin shells—the earrings Tanzey had admired on Daisy.

"I have brought you just one more gift," Daisy said, holding the earrings out for Tanzey. "It would please me so much if you would wear them."

"But to wear them, I'd have to have my ears pierced," Tanzey said guardedly.

"Yes, and I have come to do this for you," Daisy said, pressing the earrings into Tanzey's hands. "If you do not wear these, you will be the only woman in this village who doesn't wear earrings. Wear them. See how it pleases your husband."

"I so badly want to, but . . ." Tanzey murmured.

"No buts," Daisy said. She left the lodge for a brief moment, then returned with a small buckskin bag. "Go and sit by the fire. I will be gentle."

Tanzey hesitated, then went and sat down on a cushion. "I do want to be like the other Comanche women in every way," she said softly. "Please do it quickly, though, or I might change my mind."

Daisy laughed softly as she lay her paraphernalia on a mat beside her. She placed a sharp cactus spine into the outer flames of the lodge fire. After it was hot enough, to be sure that it was sterile, she held it close to Tanzey. "Hold back your hair. I will be quick. The pain will be brief and then you will be even more beautiful for your husband."

Tanzey closed her eyes, stiffened, and grimaced as Daisy burned three holes along the helix of each ear.

She swallowed hard when Daisy then ran a greased straw back and forth through the holes, took it out, re-greased it, and ran it through the holes again.

Then she hung the earrings in place.

Tanzey was relieved that it was over. She had truly suffered only a mild discomfort.

Daisy held out a small mirror for Tanzey. "Did I not say that the earrings would enhance your loveliness?" she murmured.

Tanzey stared at the earrings—*never* had she looked as feminine.

She hugged Daisy. "Thank you," she said. "I love them."

"And so will your husband," Daisy said, stepping away from Tanzey when she heard the sound of an approaching horse just outside the lodge. She gathered up her paraphernalia. "I really must go now." She brushed a soft kiss across Tanzey's cheek. "Be happy, Tanzey."

"I've never been happier," Tanzey said, then slowly stood up as Daisy fled from the lodge.

Tanzey waited to see if the horse approaching outside stopped. If so, she would wait a few more moments before stepping outside. She had to give Rolling Thunder enough time to tie the special riding horse to a post. That was a part of their ritual today, and what she would do with the horse once she stepped outside and saw it.

When the horse stopped just outside the lodge, Tanzey knew that Rolling Thunder was there. He also would have already offered his wedding gift to Brant Fire In The Sky. A horse was the most acceptable gift to a Comanche.

Today the midnight-black stallion would surely thrill her brother. He would have no hesitation taking it. That would mean Rolling Thunder was accepted by Tanzey's family.

"My dear brother, no horse was needed, was it?"
Tanzey whispered to herself. She knew that her
brother was so fond of Rolling Thunder, he almost
worshiped the ground he walked on. He would cherish this special gift, as none other ever given to him.

The horse just outside the entrance flap whinnied.

Her knees weak from the building excitement
within her, she moved slowly toward the door.

And when she lifted the flap and gazed into the
dark eyes of the beautiful brown-spotted steed, she
stepped outside and stroked its soft mane.

Smiling, she looked from side to side, knowing it
was the custom for the suitor to wait out of sight, to
see if the woman allowed the horse to stay there or
if she chose to turn it loose.

If she turned the horse loose, it meant no, that she
did not want the man as her husband.

If she drove the horse into the man's herd, it meant
that she wished for her and her beloved to be together for eternity.

Proudly, and with a lifted chin, Tanzey untied the
horse's reins from the post and began leading it
through the village. All of Rolling Thunder's people
knew what was happening today, that their war chief
was finalizing his marriage to the flaming-haired
white woman.

Showing their respect, they were all inside their
lodges.

Even their dogs were inside with them, making
sure they did not interfere in the rituals being acted
out between the lovers.

It was late afternoon. The sun had begun its descent behind the distant mountains. The wind had
died down to only a breeze, yet sliced across the
flesh of Tanzey's flesh like someone brushing her face
with feathered ice.

But she paid no heed to the chill of the day as she continued to lead the horse away from Rolling Thunder's lodge, soon to be legally hers. She walked toward Rolling Thunder's corral, the horse dutifully following behind her.

She smiled to know that somewhere in hiding her beloved watched her.

She lifted the pole that kept Rolling Thunder's horses inside the corral, where the best of his horses had been herded late last night.

She led the brown-spotted mustang inside with the others.

She untied the rope from around the horse's neck with trembling, anxious fingers.

She tossed the rope aside and watched the steed mix with the others.

Then she turned and began her journey back to Rolling Thunder's lodge.

After she was inside the tepee again, she began another wait, pacing and making nervous glances toward the entrance flap.

The sound of Rolling Thunder's footsteps stopping just outside the entrance flap made Tanzey stop and turn quickly.

Her pulse raced.

Her throat went dry.

Yet she walked determinedly to the entrance flap and lifted it.

She forced herself not to think about what it was that she took from the small rope that dangled from the pole beside the entrance flap.

She did not let herself think of how warm it was and why.

She would not think of this heart having only moments ago been inside a living, breathing thing!

She would concentrate only on getting through this ordeal.

This final step must be taken to seal her bond with Rolling Thunder or she would be shunned by him forever!

She would not hesitate another moment before finishing it.

As she knelt down beside the fire and gently put the horse's heart in the frying pan, she felt a presence behind her. She turned a soft smile over at Rolling Thunder as he knelt down beside her.

"See? I told you I could do it," Tanzey said, her voice weak as she shoved the pan into the hotter coals, where the flames lapped around it. "Soon we shall eat this meat. The ceremony will then be completed. You will be mine, my darling. Forever and ever."

"*Huh*, yes, forever," Rolling Thunder said, aching to hold her, to kiss her, to make love to her.

Their union was almost finalized in the eyes of both of their gods.

They both waited anxiously for the meat to cook.

And when it was finally done, Tanzey plucked it from the pan with a sharp stick and laid it in a wooden platter.

Rolling Thunder slid his knife from the buckskin sheath at his right side. "I will divide the meat into equal parts," he instructed. "We shall share it, equally."

Again dread filled Tanzey. Although she knew that some bands of Comanche made it a habit to eat horseflesh on a regular basis, this band didn't—and hopefully never would.

When Rolling Thunder offered her a platter of meat, she hesitated, trying hard not to envision a lovely horse, then hurriedly shoved a piece of the meat into her mouth.

Again she tried to keep her mind blank of what she was eating.

Again she took another piece until her plate was empty.

Too anxious to empty her plate, she had not even noticed Rolling Thunder eat his portion of meat.

But now, as she stared at his plate, she saw that it was empty.

Rolling Thunder took her plate, stacked it on his, then set them aside.

With a thumb, he gently smoothed any signs of grease from Tanzey's lips, then leaned over and brushed a soft kiss across her mouth.

"My wife, my own," he whispered.

Tanzey closed her eyes, her breath stolen by the sweetness of his kiss and how he so tenderly kneaded her breasts through the soft material of her dress.

In what seemed a soft haze of bliss, Rolling Thunder carried her to their bed. Slowly he removed her clothes, then stopped and gazed at her earrings. "And so you allowed Daisy to pierce your ears I see," he said, his eyes twinkling into hers.

"You knew that she planned to?" Tanzey asked, forking an eyebrow.

"*Huh*, yes, we discussed it," Rolling Thunder said, touching an earring. "She asked my advice about approaching you with the earrings. I urged her to."

"I'm glad," Tanzey said, twining an arm around his neck. "Don't I look extra feminine tonight, my darling?"

"The most beautiful of all women I have ever known," he said huskily. "So very, *very* feminine."

He lay down over Tanzey and blanketed her body

with his. His hands swept beneath her hips and lifted that soft, sweet place closer to his throbbing heat, then entered her in one deep thrust.

Tanzey sighed from the wild, sensuous pleasure. She rocked with him as he drove in swiftly and surely, his hands now on her breasts, kneading. His fingers pressed urgently into her flesh, his thumbs circling her nipples.

His whole insides on fire with passion, his mouth sought hers, and when he kissed her, his tongue surged through her lips, seeking, searching, probing.

Tanzey trembled as she became further alive beneath his caresses, the fingers of one hand stroking her woman's center as he still plunged over and over inside of her.

They were matching passion with passion.

There was not a part of Tanzey's body that did not feel the rapture, the wondrous bliss that came with being with her husband in this way.

Husband, she marveled to herself, the word, the meaning behind it, making her entire being throb with happiness and a quickening desire.

Their bodies strained together hungrily, and then they slowed their pace, their gaze shifting toward the entranceway, to something they both heard.

The chill wind whistled around the tepee outside.

The fire in the fire pit popped and crackled.

In the distance someone played a haunting refrain on a flute.

Then someone's voice joined the music, soft and lilting, so sweet it seemed to flutter like a bird's wings.

"The flute is being played by Big Bow in honor of our marriage vows," Rolling Thunder said. "The voice is Playful Turtle's, the young woman who will soon be appointed our village princess, to take the place of one too soon lost to us."

"I don't remember seeing her here at the village," Tanzey murmured, touched by the sweetness of the voice.

"She has not been here with her people," Rolling Thunder said softly, now gazing into Tanzey's eyes. "She has been with an ailing aunt in another village. Recently her aunt died. Playful Turtle has returned to us now to do her duty to her people, as her duty to her aunt is completed."

"I hope one day to see a daughter of ours reign as a princess of your people," Tanzey said, reaching a hand to his jaw, softly tracing it with her forefinger.

"Gentle Sky," Rolling Thunder said, repeating the name Tanzey had already picked for the daughter they both wished for. "Yes, someday Gentle Sky will be our people's princess."

He chuckled and brushed a kiss across her brow. "But first we must have a daughter to give the name Gentle Sky *to*," he said, once more shoving his throbbing manhood inside her velvet, tight sheath. "Then we will teach her all ways of princesses."

He gave Tanzey a fierce, fevered kiss. With a quick eagerness his fingers were in her hair. He drew her lips more tightly against his.

Her body pliant in his arms, his free hand slid beneath her and lifted her closer, so that her breasts crushed against his chest.

Tanzey's head reeled as the pleasure mounted. She drew in a ragged breath, then moaned against his lips when she finally reached that plateau that she sought with her beloved.

They clung.

They rocked.

They groaned.

Breathless, his eyes closed, Rolling Thunder rolled away from Tanzey.

She turned to her side and snuggled against him. "Darling, I think now is a good time to give you a wedding gift," she murmured, clinging to him.

"A gift?" Rolling Thunder said, forking an eyebrow as he looked down at her. "It is not the place for a woman to give a man a gift on the day of their total commitment."

"May I change the customs just a tiny bit?" Tanzey asked, smiling softly at him.

"You can do anything you wish on this, your special day," Rolling Thunder said, snaking an arm around her, lifting her up so that she lay above him.

Her hair tumbled down, across her shoulders, and spread across his chest. "I think we may be able to give that name to our daughter in less than, let's say, eight months?" she said, holding her breath as she watched for his reaction.

His eyes wide, he stared up at her. "Are you saying . . .?" he began, but she interrupted him.

"Yes, I am saying that I am pregnant," she murmured. "Are .. you . . . happy?"

He wove his fingers through her hair and brought her mouth down to his. The way he kissed her, so filled with fire, so filled with emotion, was his answer.

She was so glad that his jubilance matched her own.

Chapter Thirty

O! Stay, —O! stay, ————
When did morning ever break
And find such beaming eyes awake
As those that sparkle here!

—THOMAS MOORE

Tanzey awoke feeling lazy and more content than she had ever felt in her life. She gazed over at Rolling Thunder, who was still asleep. He was curled up on his side, facing her, looking more like a small, innocent boy than a powerful Comanche war chief and husband.

She trembled with ecstasy as she recalled their night of lovemaking, and from knowing that she was now truly married to Rolling Thunder. They were going to begin their lives today, as though it was the first day of their lives. All troubles, woes, and sadness would be left behind them.

They were going to forge ahead with only good thoughts.

Nothing or no one was going to spoil their happiness.

Nothing would change that special bond that linked them together as though they were one.

Tanzey turned to Rolling Thunder and softly traced his facial features. He had such a noble nose.

And how soft his lips were. They sent her spiraling when he kissed her in all her secret places.

Tanzey did not see Rolling Thunder stir. Nor was she aware of his change in breathing or the movement of his eyes behind his closed lids.

But her gentle touches had awakened him.

He scarcely breathed as her fingers continued tracing his lips, reveling in even her slightest touch.

But he felt a playful urge he could not deny himself. He opened his lips and quickly sucked her finger inside his mouth, causing her to gasp, then laugh.

"You wicked man," Tanzey said as he opened his eyes and she saw the quiet amusement in their depths. Her insides tremored as his tongue flicked around her finger. "Rolling Thunder, you'd better stop, or . . ."

He reached for her hand and slid her finger from his mouth. He swept his arms around her and drew her atop him. "Or what, my beautiful wife?" he said huskily, feeling the heat rising in his loins at the touch of her soft mound of hair at the juncture of her thighs pressing down against his manhood. He felt his manhood growing, soon tight against her soft flesh.

He shifted his body somewhat, spread his legs so that she lay comfortably between them, then reached a hand down and caressed her soft center.

"Or I won't allow you to leave this bed until you have finished what I innocently started," Tanzey said, her breath catching in her throat when she felt him shove his magnificently thick hardness within her.

She threw her head back as he began his rhythmic

thrusts upward and within her, his fingers still kneading her swollen nub.

Bucking up into her, the pleasure spreading through him, Rolling Thunder slid his hands upward, across her belly, then filled them with her breasts and kneaded them.

A voice outside the lodge stopped their love play.

The panic, the demand in the voice, caused them to draw apart and leave the bed.

After they were dressed, Tanzey went with Rolling Thunder to the entranceway. She waited anxiously as he untied the ties, then lifted the flap and gazed out at Brant Fire In The Sky.

"Several of our horses were mangled in the night by boars," Brant Fire In The Sky said, raking his fingers through his long red hair, to get it back from his face. "I was awakened only moments ago. Lightning is one of the casualties."

"Boars?" Rolling Thunder said, stepping on outside. "Lightning . . . is . . . dead?"

Tanzey stood beside him. She shivered at the thought of the vicious, sharp-tusked animals. She could hardly stand the thought of the lovely horse being killed in such a vicious way.

"The attack has the earmarkings of the boar I was hunting on the day I was brought to your village," Brant Fire In The Sky said. "It's a sow. She's the herd's leader."

"Boars are a dreaded animal of the Comanche," Rolling Thunder grumbled. "For years, I have been after the same killer boar. Recently it has been elsewhere wreaking its havoc. This is the first time in many sunrises that the boar has made an appearance on Comanche soil."

"Let's go together today, Rolling Thunder, and kill it," Brant Fire In The Sky prodded. "It would be my pleasure to skin it and watch it cook slow over an evening fire."

"We shall set a trap," Rolling Thunder said. "We will need plenty of corn. The corn will attract the boars."

Brant Fire In The Sky said, eyes wide with excitement to go on the hunt again, "We will spread the corn out and draw them into the center of it, then kill the sonofabitches."

Tanzey smiled at Brant's way of talking, his anger bringing out the usual slang used by the cowhands at their ranch when they were out on the hunt or roundup.

She could tell, though, that Rolling Thunder did not appreciate such language, for the Comanche never spoke in such a way.

Tanzey liked seeing that side of her brother surface again. It made her feel the same old camaraderie they had together with the rest of the men on their horses.

They were happy now, but in a different way. And she knew that after the boar was finally killed, he would again become the new Brant, who lived the Comanche way instead of the white way.

"I want to go," Tanzey blurted out. "I'd like to go after that boar myself. It's been a thorn in our family's side for as long as I can remember. And now it has brought its meanness to this village, as though it knows that Brant and I live here."

"Why would you think it is singling you out?" Rolling Thunder said, shifting his gaze back and forth between Tanzey and Brant.

"Because I killed the sow's babies," Brant Fire In The Sky said, his voice drawn. "There was a stampede. I was chasing our cattle. The boars were in a pack. They got in the way. My horse trampled the babies before I even knew they were there. The sow's eyes narrowed on me. As though it had human feelings, it seems hell-bent on seeking vengeance for the death of her piglets."

"Then, it is time to stop the vengeance," Rolling Thunder said. He turned to Tanzey. He placed a gentle hand to her cheek. "You must not go. It is too dangerous. There is a child inside your womb. At all cost, you must protect it."

"This would be the last time I would ride a horse," Tanzey pleaded. "Surely this one last time won't hurt anything. I am only barely pregnant."

"I have witnessed women losing babies very early in their pregnancy," Rolling Thunder countered. "The first three months of a woman's pregnancy is a vulnerable time for the child."

Daisy came from her lodge and gazed from Tanzey to Rolling Thunder. She then went to Tanzey. "You can spend the day with me," she murmured. "I've invited Playful Turtle for tea. You could come. We could all become acquainted. I think it would be good for you, Tanzey, just to sit demurely by the fire, instead of in a saddle."

"I don't know," Tanzey said, sighing.

When she caught both Rolling Thunder's and Brant's determined looks as they stared at her without smiling, she knew the seriousness of how they felt about her not going with them.

"Oh, all right, Daisy, I shall visit with you while the boars are being hunted," she said, frustrated.

"Come soon," Daisy said, leaning to brush a kiss across Tanzey's cheek.

"I shall go and bathe and then be there," Tanzey said, lifting her skirt.

She stopped long enough to give her brother and husband a heavy-lashed look, but they were now too involved in making plans for the hunt to even notice how much she suddenly felt left out of their lives.

They were comparing their sacred bundles. In both were placed a hat made from the skin and hair of a buffalo cow, and four arrows—two painted for hunting and two for battle.

There were several other smaller venerated objects.

Tanzey turned and started to go on inside when a warm hand grabbing her gently by a wrist stopped her.

She turned and gazed into the warm, gentle eyes of her husband.

He leaned his lips next to her ear. "Promise to warm the blankets for my return?" he whispered. "And do not ever think you take second to anything else in my life. You *are* my life."

Suddenly it was no longer important that Tanzey wasn't a part of the men. Her husband and his love for her made her remember how wonderful it was to be a woman. She would never ever again forget.

"Yes, I promise," she whispered back.

She pressed her body against his as his mouth slid around and claimed her lips in a hungry, hot kiss.

Then he stepped away from her and walked with Brant Fire In The Sky through the village, stopping at each lodge, alerting the warriors about the hunt.

Smiling, and still tasting her husband's kiss on her lips, Tanzey hurried inside the lodge and grabbed a towel, a change of clothes, and a bar of soap.

Humming, she walked in the early morning's light toward the river.

The corn spread beneath a huge live oak tree, Rolling Thunder and Brant sat on their horses with the other warriors awaiting the arrival of the boars. They had searched until they had found where the wild animals had left the earth upturned from having dug roots and tubers for an early-morning feast. Acorn shells lay empty also along the ground only a short distance away.

The hungry boars had also found a nest of rabbits, leaving many bones and spots of fur lying along the ground.

"The damn pests seem to have eaten a lot already today," Brant Fire In The Sky grumbled to Rolling Thunder. "Maybe we didn't get here soon enough with the corn."

"If not today, tomorrow," Rolling Thunder reassured. "If need be, we will camp here and catch them early tomorrow as they come to feast on the corn."

"Tanzey's impatient, Rolling Thunder," Brant Fire In The Sky said, resting a hand on the rifle in his gun boot. "She might come looking for us."

"No, I do not think so," Rolling Thunder said, his eyes gleaming. "She made me a promise. She is not likely to break it."

"A promise?" Brant Fire In The Sky said, forking an eyebrow. "I didn't hear her actually *promise* that she wouldn't get on a horse and follow you."

"The promise had to do with something left unfinished this morning," Rolling Thunder said and looked away.

Brant Fire In The Sky stared at Rolling Thunder for a moment longer, then smiled slyly. "I see," he said, nodding. "My sister, the wife. I wonder how long it will take for me to get used to her change in personality from being a tomboy, to a lady."

Rolling Thunder frowned at Brant Fire In The Sky. "Even though she wore clothes of a man before she met me, never forget that even then she was a lady," he said flatly.

"Touché," Brant Fire In The Sky said, chuckling.

Brant started to explain but was stopped when he heard the sound of the boars approaching a short distance away. It was a sound that he would never forget ... the shuffling of their hooves, their squealing and grunting that filled him with hate.

Recalling the one near disaster with the boar all those many years ago, Brant Fire In The Sky wiped sweat from the palms of his hands onto his fringed breeches. After the sow's piglets had been stomped to death, the sow had not only stared at Brant Fire In The Sky with an intense hatred, she had taken off after him, her tusks tucked ready for the kill.

Brant Fire In The Sky's horse had bucked, throwing him to the ground.

Twice he was nearly gored and narrowly escaped the sow's anger by climbing a tree.

But he had soon lost his footing. He fell to the ground, stunned.

When he had regained his composure and started to push himself up, he found the sow pawing the ground, its dark, evil eyes on him, ready for the kill.

But Tanzey had come just in time, firing her rifle, sending the sow in the opposite direction, soon hidden from sight among the thick brush.

Because of Tanzey, he was still alive.

His heart pounded as he slowly removed the rifle from his gun boot.

"There they come," Rolling Thunder said, removing his own firearm. As the boars came into sight, he saw that the band was traveling at a trot, then slowed to a walk as they approached the trick feeding station.

In the dim light of early morning, the boars were quick to find the bright yellow corn scattered over the ground under the live oak tree.

The boars, all fifteen of them, ranged in color from

a solid black or brown, to various spotted patterns. Except for a few younger boars, they were huge, perhaps weighing three hundred fifty pounds. Both sexes had tusks three to nine inches long that were a formidable weapon for them.

A female watched as three of her young scrambled after the delightful discover of corn. Their grunts of content filled the air as they ate.

The female then entered, grunting and squealing her dominance, followed then by the other boars that crowded in around her.

When one of the males, who occupied the lowest position in the herd's social structure, feasted too much on the corn, crowding others away, one of the females reminded him of his place by slashing a gash in his shoulder with her tusks.

"Something is wrong here," Brant Fire In The Sky said, his eyes anxiously sorting through the animals. "The sow that we're after? She isn't here."

"Are you sure this is the herd she rides with?" Rolling Thunder asked, himself sorting through the hungry, snorting animals.

"I'm certain," Brant Fire In The Sky grumbled, suddenly going cold inside at the thought of where she might be. Surely she still carried her grudge. And if she had watched Brant and Tanzey from the forest, she would now be aware of where each of them was.

The last time he saw Tanzey, she was headed toward the river, so innocent, so happy, so alone, so . . . weaponless . . .!

Pale, panic filling him, Brant Fire In The Sky wheeled his horse around and rode away in a hard gallop.

Confused, Rolling Thunder stared after him.

Rolling Thunder then followed Brant Fire In The Sky and edged his horse over close to his. "Why do

you ride like a man possessed toward our village?"
he shouted.

When Brant Fire In The Sky gazed over at him, he
said Tanzey's name. Rolling Thunder went cold.

His jaw tight, his reins coiled so tightly around his
fingers they ached, he sank his heels into the flanks
of his horse and rode onward.

The boar!

His *Tanzey!*

He prayed to the Wise One Above.

He now saw the wrong in having left her alone!

He hoped that a boar did not have the capacity to
hate so much!

Chapter Thirty-one

Fly not yet 'tis just the hour
When pleasure, like the midnight flower,
That scorns the eye of vulgar light,
Begins to bloom for sons of night,
And maids who love the moon!

—THOMAS MOORE

Wanting to be out of the river before the others started arriving for their morning baths, Tanzey stepped onto dry ground.

Shivering, she reached for her towel and quickly wrapped it around her.

She began briskly drying herself while staring at the water, wondering how on earth she would be able to bathe in the river all winter. The water was already too cold.

Since she had not yet spent a winter with the Comanche, she did not know how they bathed.

And with the child growing inside her womb, she feared the shock of the water might bring on an early delivery.

She would never forget how quickly Feather Moon's life had been snuffed away from delivering a child too soon.

Tanzey did not want to meet the same fate.

Nor did she want her husband to be left to raise the child alone.

But as virile and handsome as he was, she knew that he would not be alone for long. The thought of someone else sharing his bed, and hers and Rolling Thunder's child, made a keen jealousy sweep through her.

Tanzey had to make sure that did not happen.

She must protect this child inside her.

Dropping the towel, she grabbed her dress and slipped it over her head. She welcomed the warmth of the clinging buckskin material against her trembling flesh.

Then she bent over, her brilliant red hair almost touching the ground as she briskly rubbed her hair with the towel.

A sound behind her made her stop with a start. It was no normal sound. It was most certainly not made from footsteps approaching her from behind.

It was a grunting, and then a loud squeal.

Having seen, then frightened off the boar that day it had Brant cornered in a tree, was enough for Tanzey to recognize the sound of a wild boar.

Her heart sank when she realized that she had foolishly come to the river without a weapon. Rolling Thunder had warned her to have a weapon with her at all times, be it a knife, or a rifle . . . just in case.

He warned her time and again that many an outlaw roamed this land whose arms and bedroll had been empty for way too long.

But rape wasn't what she feared at this moment.

Being gored was her prime concern.

Slowly she slipped the towel down from her head.

Slowly she straightened her back.

Slowly and scarcely breathing, her throat dry with

fear, she turned to see where the boar might be and what its intentions were.

Just as she had thought, she found herself being stalked by the very sow that had plagued her family.

In its gleaming eyes she saw an intense hatred.

In its grunts and squeals she could hear its threat.

Its curved tusks were at least nine inches long.

Tanzey watched the tusks as the sow slowly swayed its head from side to side, its one hoof pawing the ground, as though it was readying itself for that final plunge. One piercing from those tusks in the right place would make for a swift death.

Instinct drew Tanzey's hands to her abdomen, the child again on her thoughts.

Would fate be this unfair?

Tanzey had always thought that the boar had a mind of its own, and that its tusks would find its way either to Brant's heart or hers. The day the boar's piglets were killed was surely etched on the sow's brain.

Tanzey saw it even now, how the piglets were stamped to death by the stampeding horses, and of how the boar's screams of despair had filled the air . . . It had glared at Tanzey and Brant before running off with its herd.

The same as it was glaring now.

Yes, its intent was to kill Tanzey.

Panic filling her, Tanzey looked toward the river Could she find safety there?

She then looked past the boar, toward the village. Surely someone would come soon for their bath and find her cornered.

Then Tanzey stared at the boar once again. The boar was inching closer. Foam was dripping from the corners of its mouth. Its eyes were narrowed, the rising sun reflecting in them, red.

Her heart pounding, her knees weak, Tanzey turned and dove into the river.

Without looking back over her shoulder, to see if the boar was following her, she swam for deeper water. She had never seen boars in water. In mud, yes. But never actually swimming in the river. Hopefully, this sow would prefer land this time.

But the boar could swim and ran to the water. Carefully it edged into river and followed Tanzey.

Growing more tired by the minute, her dress twisting around her ankles, threatening to pull her under, Tanzey worried once again about her child.

Just how much longer could she last in the water?

Just how much farther would she have to swim to be safe?

A sudden gunfire filled the air behind her.

Tanzey turned and stared when she discovered Daisy standing there, smoke spiraling from the end of a pistol.

Treading water, Tanzey stared at the dead boar just before it sank in the water only a short distance from her. It had followed her in the water! It was going to gore her to death in the water!

The realization made Tanzey grow weak in the stomach. She had come this close to dying. If not for Daisy, she would probably even now be dead.

Then Tanzey looked past Daisy. Tears filled her eyes as she watched Brant Fire In The Sky and Rolling Thunder arrive on horseback, their rifles drawn, their eyes wild with fear.

After wheeling their steeds to a quivering halt, Rolling Thunder spotted Tanzey, dropped his rifle, and dove into the river. He swam toward Tanzey, where the current was strong and swift.

When he reached her, breathing hard, his chest heaving, Tanzey crumpled into his arms.

"Thank God," she murmured, clinging to Rolling Thunder as he made his way back with her toward shore. "I truly thought I was going to die, Rolling Thunder. First the boar, and then the water. I . . . doubt . . . that I could have made it back to shore. My energy is gone. Totally gone."

"You were lucky the current did not suck you down and send you beneath the water downriver," Rolling Thunder said, swimming past the pool of blood made by the death of the boar.

"The current was not as much of a threat as the boar," Tanzey wheezed out, her lungs aching. "If not for Daisy . . ."

"I did not know she even knew how to fire a gun," Rolling Thunder said, planting his feet on the rocky bottom of the river. He whisked Tanzey into his arms and carried her onto dry land.

Daisy and Brant Fire In The Sky came to them.

Daisy reached a hand to Tanzey's brow and gently shoved her wet hair back from her eyes. "Tanzey, are you all right?" she asked softly. "Oh, Tanzey, after I got the children fed and asleep and came to the river for a bath, I saw the boar jump into the river. I don't know how I got the courage, for I was numb with panic when I realized the boar was after you. I could only think of one thing—getting you to safety. Something helped me with my aim, because it took only one bullet to down the boar."

"The Wise One Above was your guide," Rolling Thunder said, smiling down at Daisy. "Thank you for saving my wife. We both shall always and forever be in your debt."

"You owe me nothing," Daisy said. "You have already given me so much, it is I who may never be able to repay you."

"The child," Tanzey said, gazing down at her abdomen. With her eyes she pleaded up at Rolling Thunder. "Do you think what happened today endangered the safety of our child?"

"You are strong, so will the child inside you be strong," Rolling Thunder stated. He saw how purple her lips were, and how the wet dress clung to her skin. "The swim and the trauma may have not harmed you. But your exposure *to* the cold for such a long time might. I will take you home now. We must make you warm again."

Arm in arm, Brant Fire In The Sky and Daisy watched Rolling Thunder carry Tanzey in a soft trot toward the village.

Then Brant Fire In The Sky turned Daisy to face him. Gently he eased the pistol from her hand, placed it on the ground, then drew her into his arms and gazed lovingly down at her. "My but aren't *you* full of surprises," he said, chuckling. "My little pistol-packin' momma. I love it."

He lowered his mouth to her lips and kissed her passionately.

Rolling Thunder carried Tanzey into their lodge. He placed her to her feet and hurriedly drew her wet dress over her head.

Tanzey was so cold, her teeth were chattering. She welcomed the warmth of a thick bear robe around her shoulders. She snuggled into it as Rolling Thunder dried her hair with a towel.

"You are lucky to be alive," he said in a stiff, scolding fashion. He placed a finger to her chin and lifted her eyes to hold his. "Why did you not take a firearm with you to the river? Have I not warned you over and over again about the dangers of not being protected at all times? Do you promise not to be that foolish again?"

"Yes, I promise," Tanzey said, her lower lip curling into a pout.

Sobbing, the robe fell away from her as she eased into his arms. "I've never been as afraid," she cried. "I thought I was going to die."

Rolling Thunder held her tightly in his embrace, stunned to see her this deeply affected by the incident. Only one other time before had he witnessed this more delicate side of her personality—after he had driven her almost unmercifully for days, making her labor hard, to prove a point to her. She had folded up like a wounded puppy that day and cried.

Today there was more humbleness, more fear. And he had to believe it was because of the changes in her body . . . her pregnancy.

Not wanting her to feel this threatened by anything, ever, he whispered reassurances while his hands caressed her back. "You are safe with me," he said. "You *and* the child are safe with me. Cry it out, my beautiful Tanzey Nicole, my wife. Get the hurt, the anger, the fear, out of your heart. Let the tears wash it all away."

Feeling like a child of three, whose feelings were as delicate as a hummingbird's tiny transparent wings, Tanzey cried until she began to slowly feel the burden lift from inside her.

Her tears faded into soft sobs.

Her sobs faded into a feeling of peace, of joy, of happiness.

She flicked tears from her thick lashes, then turned her gaze up to her husband.

"Over and over again you prove to me just how gentle and understanding you are," she murmured. "I cannot help but think, darling, at times like this, of those foolish white people who call Indians savages, and sometimes even worse. If only those misguided people could know *you* as *I* know you, surely things would be different for you and your people."

She placed a gentle hand to his cheek. "You are of such a kind and caring heart," she said. "If the white people could be like you, there would be no more sadness and hardships among your people. You would live equal with the whites. You would not have to worry about possible starvation during the long winter months. You would not have to worry about more of your land being stolen, or of being accosted by whites who take delight in seeing Indians suffer."

She eased into his arms again and clung to him. "I wish I could make it so," she murmured. "But I am only one person, only one voice, and I am a female. Women have no voice in this country."

"You have a voice in Comanche country," Rolling Thunder grumbled. "You speak your mind whenever you need to. Your voice will always be welcomed among my people."

"Thank you," Tanzey said, then once again shifted her thoughts to her child. "Rolling Thunder, what of our child? Do you think it is all right?" She eased from his arms and gazed up at him. "Rolling Thunder, today I . . . I . . . forced myself to swim much farther than my body wanted to. Do you think the child felt the strain? Do you think we might lose it?"

"Worrying is more a threat to our child than any physical labor you performed today," Rolling Thunder said, trying to force a lightheartedness into their talk.

Although he was afraid himself for the welfare of their child, he must not allow her to feel his alarm.

He must turn Tanzey's thoughts away from it.

He must comfort her.

At this moment, with Tanzey warm and sweet in his arms, she was all that mattered.

"Are you calling me a worrywart?" Tanzey teased back, herself knowing that she must put her bothersome fears behind her. As long as the child still seemed all right, it was Rolling Thunder whom she wanted to reassure. At this moment, with him so warm and wonderful in her arms, he was all that mattered.

"A worrywart?" Rolling Thunder said, forking an eyebrow. "A wart knows how to worry?"

Tanzey laughed softly and cuddled against him again. "Darling, my robe has fallen to the floor," she whispered. "I am quite naked."

"Yes, you are," Rolling Thunder said, sliding his hands down her back. He cupped the soft, round curves of her buttocks within his hands. "Should I place the robe around you again, or would you rather have your husband blanket you with his body?"

"Your body is much warmer," Tanzey murmured, her pulse racing as he swept her up into his arms and carried her toward their bed. "Please cover me, my darling, with your warm flesh. Please hold me. Kiss me."

Rolling Thunder gently eased her back onto the bed. And as she watched, he undressed, then crawled onto the bed with her. He straddled her with his knees, then gently pressed her down with his weight.

His lips came to hers in a frenzied kiss. She came alive inside with a slow fire licking through her body, burning where his fingers touched as he petted and caressed her vulnerable, sensitive spots. When he shoved himself into her throbbing center, magnificently filling her, his hips thrusting hard, Tanzey's breath caught in her throat.

Tremors cascaded down her back when he began his rhythmic strokes, his fingers tracing circles around her breasts, just missing the nipples each time so that they would strain with added anticipation.

She thrust her pelvis toward him, taking him inside her even more deeply.

She rocked and swayed with him.

She writhed with pleasure and moaned as she felt the pleasure spreading.

His mouth was hot on her lips as he kissed her with passioned fire. His tongue flicked. Hers answered, touching his, flicking his.

Then his lips lowered. They closed over a nipple. He sucked. His teeth nipped.

She moaned. She tossed her head back and forth, her sodden hair thrashing and flailing.

Lost in passion's reverie, spasmodic gasps filled the air as they again found the ultimate of pleasure in one another's arms.

Afterward Tanzey lay cuddled in Rolling Thunder's arms. "My darling husband, no one knows better than you how to warm a woman's body," she said, laughing softly. "Now I feel as though *I* am the flame."

"So light my fire again, my wife," Rolling Thunder whispered huskily.

She complied.

Chapter Thirty-two

April dawning in her eyes
Reflects the wonder of the skies.

—EDWARD O'BRIEN

Twenty Years Later
Canada

"Wife, stop your pacing," Rolling Thunder said, grabbing one of Tanzey's hands to stop her. He gently drew her into his embrace, his gaze taking in her loveliness.

Even at her age of forty, and soon to be a grandmother, she still was beautiful. The slight trails of wrinkles along her brow, and at the corners of her eyes and mouth, were something she wore proudly. She had given birth to five healthy children. She had given of herself to each of them equally so that none of them felt slighted.

Yet she had always made time for her husband, their nights alone still filled with passionate lovemaking.

"But I should be with Gentle Sky," Tanzey said, her eyes wavering into Rolling Thunder's. "Our daughter is soon to give birth to our first grandchild.

A mother's place should be with her daughter at such a time as this."

"A mother's worries would crowd the lodge where those who have been assigned to assist Gentle Sky are there, seeing to her every need, helping her through the pain, making her understand it," Rolling Thunder said softly.

He reached a hand to Tanzey's hair. It had lost some of its luster where gray strands wove through the red, yet it was so beautiful and unusual from that of the Comanche women, it still caused Rolling Thunder's breath to catch.

And their two daughters, Gentle Sky, who was their firstborn and now their village princess, and Moon Flower, their second, had hair as flaming red in color, their skin more like their father's, in its copper sheen.

Their three sons were the exact image of their father, Comanche in every way. Little Thunder was their youngest and was six winters of age.

"Yes, I know you are right," Tanzey said, sighing. "I should feel blessed enough that Proud Fox brought our daughter to *our* village here in Canada, to have the child. Now we can hold the infant in our arms when it is only seconds old. If they stayed at the reservation in Oklahoma, we would never see our grandchild."

"It has been good to have them with us these past four months," Rolling Thunder said as they both studied each other, seeing how age had changed them.

She was seeing his wrinkles, as he had seen hers. He hoped that she still saw him as handsome, a word that he had grown used to through the years.

He had always scoffed at the word, yet had secretly enjoyed having a wife to think of him as special.

He was proud that they had clung to their happiness as they had aged together, even though their lives had been touched sourly by the white man's interference.

It had not only been their lives, but his entire band of Comanche, that had been in danger of being destroyed by the whites.

During their twenty years of marriage, they had seen much sadness and many hardships placed upon the Comanche due to the white man's greed for land.

Rolling Thunder felt blessed, though, that it was not his people who had been ravaged by the white pony soldiers. Black Kettle's Cheyenne people had been heartlessly massacred when their village on Sand Creek had been attacked in 1867.

Another Cheyenne village, on the Washita River, had been attacked by the golden-haired man named Custer, leaving most Cheyenne and Comanche afraid to fight back.

And the United States government had been unable to keep whites off the land promised the Comanche.

For the most part, the white pony soldiers were intent on either killing Rolling Thunder's people, or making sure they were on land that was useless to the whites—on land they called reservations.

Not wanting to see his people imprisoned on useless land and not wanting his people wiped out, Rolling Thunder had swallowed his pride and had led his band to the safety of Canada, where they had finally found a semblance of peace.

It was sad for Rolling Thunder to know that his firstborn lived on a reservation, her husband having chosen that over what he called the "foreign" land of Canada.

"It is good that, for now, our other children are at Brant Fire In The Sky and Daisy's village," Tanzey said, easing out of Rolling Thunder's arms, to sit by the fire. He followed her and sat beside her. "I fear they would feel my neglect as I anxiously wait for Gentle Sky to give birth."

"They have never felt neglected," Rolling Thunder said, lifting a log on the fire. "But, *huh*, yes, it is good that Daisy and Brant Fire In the Sky came and asked them to spend a few days with them. Their village is only a half day's ride from here. As soon as Gentle Sky gives birth, we shall send word."

Proud Fox's voice outside the lodge drew them quickly to their feet. They rushed outside, silently questioning Proud Fox with their anxious eyes.

"No, the child is not yet born," Proud Fox said, placing a gentle hand on Tanzey's shoulder. "Spirit Walker, who is still your band's medicine woman, has informed me that it will be perhaps another full night."

Recalling Feather Moon's fate after having trouble with giving birth to her child, Tanzey paled. Panic filled her. "What's wrong?" she cried, her heart skipping a beat.

"There is nothing wrong," Proud Fox said, taking Tanzey's hands, softly squeezing them reassuredly. "She does not even have pains now. She rests. The child rests. I have been told that the child has yet to drop into its birthing position. So, Tanzey, I suggest you also rest. There is much weariness and tiredness in your eyes."

"You are certain that Gentle Sky is all right?" Tanzey asked, her throat dry. "That the child is all right?"

"If I was not certain, do you think that I would be standing here with a steady voice and calm hands?" Proud Fox said, laughing softly.

"I want to go to her," Tanzey said, looking past him at the lodge in which her daughter lay.

"You nor I can enter the lodge," Proud Fox stated.

"It is taboo. We must wait until the child is born. *Then* we shall marvel together over the child *and* its mother."

Tanzey slipped her hands free from Proud Fox's. She turned to Rolling Thunder. "I have been a part of the Comanche's lives for twenty years now and I still cannot accept all of their customs," she murmured. "This one, especially."

"It is no different now than when I could not come to you during your time of having our children," Rolling Thunder said, slipping an arm around Tanzey's waist. He gave Proud Fox a silent nod of goodbye as he led Tanzey toward the entranceway. "*Keemah*, come, my wife. Your place is with me. Not our daughter."

Tanzey smiled weakly over at him as they entered the warm, quiet place of their lodge.

Then recalling what she had collected in the forest earlier in the day, to use after their first grandchild was born, as a special way to celebrate, she turned to Rolling Thunder and stopped him.

She looked mischievously into his eyes.

She saw that now was much better than later to give him the surprise. It would be a way to pass the time more expediently than lying in bed, restless as she waited for the first cries of her grandchild to fill the Comanche village.

"Darling, would you do me a favor?" she asked softly, her eyes dancing into his.

"If you are going to ask me to use my persuasion as civil chief to get inside our daughter's birth lodge, I will have to use my persuasion on you, asking you not to ask this favor of me," Rolling Thunder muttered. "Although my title of civil chief holds more clout than when I was war chief, it is frowned upon by my people to single out favors because I am civil chief."

"It's nothing like that," Tanzey said, understanding his position, one that she had never taken advantage of.

"Then, what is it that you ask of me?" Rolling Thunder said, forking an eyebrow.

A smile slowly played along his lips as he recognized the mischievous glint in his wife's eyes.

And before she had a chance to explain away her sudden, mischievous behavior, normally sexual in nature, he placed a hand gently over her mouth.

"Do not explain," he said huskily. "Just tell me what you want me to do. I shall do it."

"Sit by the fire and keep your back turned to me," Tanzey said, slowly turning him around to face away from her. "I shall tell you when to turn around again."

Rolling Thunder chuckled.

He sat down on a thick cushion beside the fire pit.

His eyes on the dancing flames of the fire, he stretched his legs out comfortably before him and crossed them at their ankles.

He could hear her scurrying around behind him.

Soon a fragrance of roses came to him, making him fork an eyebrow in wonder of what they had to do with she had planned for them.

And to smell them so distinctly, there had to be many of them.

His mind became scrambled with questions.

Where had Tanzey kept the roses hidden?

Why had she?

What was she going to do with them?

Then a thought came to him that made his heart sing.

She had surprised him one other time with the "Red Rose Passion Ceremony." After the birth of their child, when enough time had passed that they could be together sexually again!

It was a woman's way of telling her man how much she loved him—a celebration *of* love.

Rolling Thunder smiled to himself. His wife had planned to use the ceremony to celebrate their first grandchild.

But now possibly having to wait another full night for the child to be born, and not wanting to spend it worrying, she had decided to celebrate early.

"You can turn around now," Tanzey murmured.

Rolling Thunder rose to his feet.

With a thumping heart, he turned slowly around.

His breath caught in his throat when he saw her standing there so shapely, so delicately beautiful in her nudity, the fire dancing in a soft glow along her body.

This was all enhanced by the backdrop of rose petals, which she had scattered all across their bed and around it on the floor.

Standing among the petals, it was as though she had been born of them, a flower herself in her loveliness.

"Come to me, my darling," Tanzey murmured, beckoning toward him with her outstretched arms and hands. "Lie with me amid the roses. Breathe in their scent with me. Let me massage your body with their soft petals. Let us, you and I, become a part of them. Let us become consumed by red rose passion."

So taken by the sight, his hunger for his wife having never waned through the years, Rolling Thunder's shoulders swayed in his passion.

His eyes flaring with hungry intent, he hurriedly undressed.

Then, broad-shouldered and muscled, he went to her and swept her against him, his mouth on fire as he kissed her.

Cradling her in one arm, Rolling Thunder led Tanzey down onto the rose-covered bed.

He leaned over her.

He showered heated kisses over her taut-tipped breasts.

His hands moved seductively over her, gathering her breasts within them, rolling their nipples, then moved them lower.

Feeling her wetness where her heart's desire was centered at the juncture of her thighs, he rubbed her woman's center with the palm of his one hand, while the other hand went back to a breast, kneading.

Tanzey's body was growing feverish.

Currents of heat swept through her, firing her passion, her needs, her desires.

She moved her trembling hands over Rolling Thunder until she found his rock-hard readiness, the velvet tightness, the heat of his manhood twitching sensitively as she ran her fingers over it.

Gasping, the pleasure spreading through him like wildfire, Rolling Thunder rolled away from Tanzey and lay on his back, his eyes closed.

His pulse raced, his face grew hot with ecstasy, when he felt her tongue flicking along his stiff shaft.

When her lips began nibbling at him, he felt the threat of reaching the ultimate of pleasure too soon.

He wanted to wait.

He wanted to postpone the bliss.

He wanted to savor her each and every touch.

He wanted to experience the red rose passion ceremony to the fullest.

And she had just begun.

Placing his hands to Tanzey's waist, he lifted her away from him.

His eyes were passion-glazed as he smiled up at her. "Did you promise a massage?" he said huskily.

"Yes, I did," Tanzey said, giggling. "I guess I got too carried away too early."

She knelt over him and picked up a handful of rose petals. "Darling, you just lie there," she said silkily. "Enjoy. Feel the sexual energy of the rose petals. Feel the passion."

"They are red," he said huskily. "Red draws in the powers of passion and sexuality. You found these in the forest, did you not? I knew they were there. I knew you would find them. The Wise One Above planted them for us. They were given to us to share . . . to enjoy."

She bent low and brushed a kiss across his lips. "Yes. Enjoy, my love," she whispered. "I so enjoy *giving* pleasure."

He reached his arms out on each side of him, and then spread his legs.

When she began massaging his body with the rose petals, slowly moving from place to place, lingering where he was the most sensitive, he closed his eyes and groaned sensually.

"Feel the passion?" Tanzey whispered, rubbing his stomach with the rose petals. "Open up to all of your senses, my love. Feel the softness of the petals."

When she began massaging his manhood with the roses, the pleasure was so intense, Rolling Thunder bit his lower lip to keep from crying out.

"I am sending the rose passion through your love shaft," Tanzey murmured, her face blushed with her own rising rapture. "Do you feel it? Do you smell it? Do . . . you . . . taste it?"

"Yes, yes. . . ." Rolling Thunder said huskily, now writhing.

"No, darling, you must lie still amid the petals," Tanzey said, placing a gentle hand on his stomach, urging him to lie more quietly. "Breathe long, slow, deep breaths. Be thankful for the blessed sexual energy your Great Spirit has given you."

Rolling Thunder lay quietly awhile longer, then unable to hold himself back, wanting to share the ultimate of pleasure with her, he suddenly reached up for Tanzey and rolled her beneath him.

"The passion is wholly felt," he said, filling her with his heat. His steel arms enfolded her. He kissed her hungrily.

Tanzey felt his hunger in the hard, seeking pressure of his lips. She answered his kiss with her own hunger. The pleasure rose up inside her, spreading, swelling. She inhaled the sweet fragrance of the roses, herself having been blessed with the ceremony, herself overcome with the feverish heat of the moment. She was frantic with need of him.

Her body soon turned to liquid fire as they reached the ultimate of rapture together.

Rolling Thunder knelt down beside her. He reached for a handful of the rose petals. "Let me now massage you," he said.

Her heart throbbing, never getting enough of him once they began their lovemaking, Tanzey closed her eyes and reveled in the touch of the roses, so soft, they felt as though she was being bathed in some wonderful French perfume.

Again they made love, then fell asleep in one another's arms, the roses clinging.

Something awakened them.

They both sat up with a start.

They looked upward, through the smoke hole.

It was pitch-black outside.

They had slept many hours.

They scarcely breathed as they listened for the sound again.

"Did we hear a . . . ?" Tanzey murmured, her heart throbbing.

And when the soft cries of a baby wafted through the fabric of their buckskin lodge, they both looked at one another, eyes wide.

"We weren't imagining things!" Tanzey cried, bolting from the bed. "We *were* awakened by a child's soft cries! It is surely our grandchild! Gentle Sky has surely given birth to our grandchild!"

Her fingers trembling anxiously, Tanzey grabbed a dress and slid it quickly over her head as Rolling Thunder slipped quickly into a pair of fringed breeches.

They almost collided as they turned to rush to the entrance flap.

Laughing softly, Rolling Thunder reached for Tanzey and steadied her, then took her hand.

Together they left the lodge.

Proud Fox ran toward them, waving his hands. "I have a son!" he cried. "You have a grandson!"

Tears of joy flowed from Tanzey's eyes. She gave Rolling Thunder a soft smile, then together they went to their daughter's bedside.

"I am so proud," Gentle Sky murmured, holding the naked child to her breast, where he hungrily fed from it. "Mama, Papa, a *tua*, son. I have given birth to a son! Your grandson!"

They gazed upon this tiny thing whose body was copper, and whose shock of hair was a scarlet red. "He is such a part of us all," Tanzey said, reaching over to softly touch his arm. "Thank you, Gentle Sky. He is such a beautiful baby."

"Thank *you*, Mama," Gentle Sky said, smiling up at Tanzey.

Then she turned soft, dark eyes up at her father. "Thank you, Papa. You have both made this moment possible. You gave me such a wonderful life. You are such wonderful parents."

"Gentle Sky, your mother and I have been so proud of you as a daughter, as we are doubly blessed now that we have a grandson by you," Rolling Thunder said, his voice thick with emotion. "I, the grandfather, will teach my grandson how to ride, shoot, and make bows and arrows. I will teach my grandson secrets of the hunt and trail, tribal history, traditions, legends, and other things he needs to know. He will be a powerful, revered Comanche warrior."

So happy, tears spilled from Tanzey's eyes. With her fingers, she flicked them away. "Sweet Gentle Sky, how could anyone ask for more from a child, than that which you have just given us," she murmured. "First a grandchild, and then such wonderful compliments. Again, thank you, Gentle Sky. You are a very special child to your parents."

Another Comanche dawn began creeping along the horizon in its golden light as Tanzey and Rolling Thunder embraced in their happiness.

"Thank *you*, my love, for making life so special for me," Tanzey whispered, stroking her fingers through his thick, dark hair.

"You would not mind being taken captive twice by this Comanche chief?" Rolling Thunder said, holding her away from him at arm's length, his eyes dancing into hers.

"A captive?" Tanzey murmured, looking adoringly into his eyes. "My darling, do you not know who the true captive was? It was *you*, for the moment I saw you I knew that you were mine. You were a captive of my heart, forever and ever."

"Just look at you two," Gentle Sky said, laughing softly. "You are as much in love now, as you surely were the first day you met."

"Not as much," Tanzey said, smiling into her husband's eyes. "But *more*. Much, much more."

Gentle Sky's nose twitched. "I smell roses," she said, looking from her mother to her father, then giggling when she saw a rose petal in her mother's hair. "So you two have been playing in the roses again, have you? Just how many times have you shared the Red Rose Passion Ceremony?"

"Not enough," Tanzey said, giving her daughter a playful smile.

Proud Fox sat down on the edge of his wife's bed. He took her hand and held it. "I hope that we are still sharing the rose ceremony when we have just turned grandparents," he said, gazing down at his wife.

"I promise you that we will," Gentle Sky said, looking from her husband to their child, smiling.

"I think we should leave the two lovebirds alone, don't you, darling?" Tanzey said, tugging on Rolling Thunder's hand as she walked toward the entranceway.

Rolling Thunder went outside with her. They stood together as the sun rose in its splendor, casting a glorious crimson light along the horizon.

Rolling Thunder turned to Tanzey and drew her into his arms.

"*Nei-com-mar-pe-ein*, I love you," he said, then lowered his mouth to her lips and kissed her.

Passionately, she twined her arms around his neck and returned the kiss.

She smiled to herself, thinking that here she was a grandmother, yet she still felt so young while in the arms of her husband!

She wondered if she would ever feel old.

She doubted that she would, not as long as she had Rolling Thunder to keep her as young and vibrant as a new bride!

LETTER TO THE READER

Dear Readers:

Rolling Thunder is the first book of an exciting new Native American series that I am writing. I hope you enjoyed reading it!

The next book in the series is *White Fire*. This book will be in the stores six months from the release date of *Rolling Thunder*. *White Fire* will be filled with much adventure and excitement, and is perhaps my most passionate book to date!

For those of you who are collecting my Topaz books and want to read about my backlist and future books, please send a legal-size, self-addressed, stamped envelope for my latest newsletter to the following address:

> Cassie Edwards
> R#3 Box 60
> Mattoon, IL 61938

I personally respond to all of my mail.

> Always,
> Cassie Edwards

WE NEED YOUR HELP
To continue to bring you quality romance
that meets your personal expectations,
we at TOPAZ books want to hear from you.
Help us by filling out this questionnaire, and in exchange
we will give you a **free gift** as a token of our gratitude.

- Is this the first TOPAZ book you've purchased? (circle one)
  YES   (NO)
  The title and author of this book is: *Cassie Edwards*

- If this was not the first TOPAZ book you've purchased, how many have
  you bought in the past year?
  a: 0 - 5   b 6 - 10   c: more than 10   (d:) more than 20

- How many romances in total did you buy in the past year?
  a: 0 - 5   b: 6 - 10   c: more than 10   (d:) more than 20 ___

- How would you rate your overall satisfaction with this book?
  (a: Excellent)   b: Good   c: Fair   d: Poor

- What was the main reason you bought this book?
  a: It is a TOPAZ novel, and I know that TOPAZ stands
     for quality romance fiction
  b: I liked the cover
  c: The story-line intrigued me
  d: I love this author
  e: I really liked the setting
  f: I love the cover models
  (g: Other: *I like The Indian Romance Books*)

- Where did you buy this TOPAZ novel?
  (a: Bookstore)   b: Airport   c: Warehouse Club
  d: Department Store   e: Supermarket   f: Drugstore
  g: Other: _____

- Did you pay the full cover price for this TOPAZ novel? (circle one)
  (YES)   NO
  If you did not, what price did you pay? _____

- Who are your favorite TOPAZ authors? (Please list) *Cassie Edward Fern Micheals*

- How did you first hear about TOPAZ books?
  (a: I saw the books in a bookstore)
  b: I saw the TOPAZ Man on TV or at a signing
  c: A friend told me about TOPAZ
  d: I saw an advertisement in_____magazine
  e: Other: _____

- What type of romance do you generally prefer?
  a: Historical   b: Contemporary
  c: Romantic Suspense   d: Paranormal (time travel,
     futuristic, vampires, ghosts, warlocks, etc.)
  d: Regency   (e: Other: *Indians*)

- What historical settings do you prefer?
  a: England   b: Regency England   c: Scotland
  e: Ireland   f: America   (g: Western Americana)
  (h: American Indian)   i: Other: _____

- What type of story do you prefer?
  - a: Very sexy ✓
  - b: Sweet, less explicit ✓
  - c: Light and humorous
  - d: More emotionally intense
  - e: Dealing with darker issues
  - f: Other

- What kind of covers do you prefer?
  - a: Illustrating both hero and heroine ✓
  - b: Hero alone
  - c: No people (art only)
  - d: Other_____

- What other genres do you like to read (circle all that apply)

Mystery	Medical Thrillers	Science Fiction
Suspense	Fantasy	Self-help
Classics	General Fiction	Legal Thrillers
Historical Fiction		

  American Indian. or Westerns

- Who is your favorite author, and why? *I Like ALL The Author's Who Write American Indian or Westerns*

- What magazines do you like to read? (circle all that apply)
  - a: People ✓
  - b: Time/Newsweek
  - c: Entertainment Weekly ✓
  - d: Romantic Times ✓
  - e: Star ✓
  - f: National Enquirer
  - g: Cosmopolitan ✓
  - h: Woman's Day
  - i: Ladies' Home Journal
  - j: Redbook
  - k: Other:_____

- In which region of the United States do you reside?
  - a: Northeast
  - b: Midatlantic
  - c: South
  - d: Midwest
  - e: Mountain
  - f: Southwest
  - g: Pacific Coast

- What is your age group/sex?
  - a: Female ✓
  - b: Male
  - a: under 18
  - b: 19-25
  - c: 26-30
  - d: 31-35
  - e: 36-40
  - f: 41-45
  - g: 46-50
  - h: 51-55 ✓
  - i: 56-60
  - j: Over 60

- What is your marital status?
  - a: Married
  - b: Single
  - c: No longer married ✓

- What is your current level of education?
  - a: High school ✓
  - b: College Degree
  - c: Graduate Degree
  - d: Other:_____

- Do you receive the TOPAZ *Romantic Liaisons* newsletter, a quarterly newsletter with the latest information on Topaz books and authors?

  YES   NO ✓

  If not, would you like to? YES ✓   NO

Fill in the address where you would like your free gift to be sent:

Name: *Betty Villarreal*

Address: *1519 MC.Hool Ave*

City: *Streamwood, IL*   Zip Code: *60107*

You should receive your free gift in 6 to 8 weeks.
Please send the completed survey to:

Penguin USA•Mass Market
Dept. TS
375 Hudson St.
New York, NY 10014